Going too Far

CATHERINE ALLIOTT

PENGUIN BOOKS

PENGUIN BOOKS

Published by the Penguin Group
Penguin Books Ltd, 80 Strand, London WC2R ORL, England
Penguin Group (USA) Inc., 375 Hudson Street, New York, New York 10014, USA
Penguin Group (Canada), 90 Eglinton Avenue East, Suite 700, Toronto, Ontario, Canada M4P 2Y3
(a division of Pearson Penguin Canada Inc.)
Penguin Ireland, 25 St Stephen's Green, Dublin 2, Ireland (a division of Penguin Books Ltd)
Penguin Group (Australia), 250 Camberwell Road,
Camberwell, Victoria 3124, Australia (a division of Pearson Australia Group Pty Ltd)
Penguin Books India Pvt Ltd, 11 Community Centre,
Panchsheel Park, New Delhi – 110 017, India
Penguin Group (NZ), 67 Apollo Drive, Rosedale, Auckland 0632, New Zealand
(a division of Pearson New Zealand Ltd)
Penguin Books (South Africa) (Pty) Ltd, Block D, Rosebank Office Park,
181 Jan Smuts Avenue, Parktown North, Gauteng 2193, South Africa

Penguin Books Ltd, Registered Offices: 80 Strand, London WC2R ORL, England

www.penguin.com

First published by Headline Publishing Group 1994
Published in Penguin Books 2012

001

Set in 12.5/14.75 pt Garamond MT
Typeset by Jouve (UK), Milton Keynes
Printed in England by Clays Ltd, St Ives plc

ISBN: 978-0-241-95829-2

Export edition ISBN: 978-0-241-96127-8

Chapter One

'. . . so if everyone would just keep their seats for a moment,' boomed the voice over the loudspeaker, 'Mrs Penhalligan will present the prizes for the best-turned-out pony and rider.'

There was a faint ripple of applause and Nick nudged me hard in the ribs. 'Go on,' he whispered, 'you're on!'

'Eh? What?' I looked around. People seemed to be nodding and smiling at me encouragingly. Oh Lord, was this it, was this me? I'd been miles away, actually, at a different, rather grander horse show. The Horse of the Year Show, in fact. Yes, there I'd been in the middle of the great Wembley Arena, pinning a red rosette on to Harvey Smith's mount, smiling graciously as I presented him with a huge silver cup, the applause of the vast stadium ringing in my ears, when all of a sudden here I was being hauled out of my reverie and on to my feet by my husband.

'Go on!' he urged.

'B-but, where do I go?' I blustered. 'Where's my hat?'

'You're sitting on it!'

'Oh no!' I retrieved the flower-strewn concoction from under my bottom and punched out the crown, feeling flustered and confused. The applause from the tiny Helston Gymkhana crowd was beginning to sound a little tired.

'For God's sake, get going,' hissed Nick, propelling me

towards the white tape of the collecting ring. 'Everyone's waiting!'

'But which one do I give the cup to?' I hissed back, desperately scrambling around to find my shoes, which I'd kicked off in the heat and which now seemed to be under everyone else's seat but my own.

'The bay gelding on the end, you idiot,' he muttered. 'It's already been judged – all you have to do is present the prizes!'

He yanked up the white tape and shoved me under. Still cramming my hot, swollen feet into shoes I'd bought a size too small on the grounds that they might make my feet look petite, I shot underneath it, losing my hat again on the way. I grabbed it, rammed it down hard on my head and turned back.

'Yes, but what the hell is a bay gelding when it's at –'

'Ah, Mrs Penhalligan,' purred an extremely agitated voice in my ear as my arm was seized in a vicelike grip. 'Come along, my dear, we've been looking everywhere for you!'

The grip on my arm tightened as I was frogmarched away by a very determined gentleman who'd materialized at my left elbow. He was dressed from head to toe in Harris tweed and came complete with white whiskers, a brown felt hat and a large red 'official' badge on his left lapel. We appeared to be heading towards a line of horses in the middle of the ring.

'Just give out the rosettes, my dear. The riders will pin them on to the bridles themselves,' he murmured, hastily thrusting four rosettes and a cup into my hands. 'Start at one end of the line and move slowly along to the other. Off you go now!'

'Er, yes, but which end of the line do I –'

'Marvellous,' he muttered, 'marvellous result for Clarissa!' and with that he burst into noisy applause and scurried back into the crowd.

I clutched the rosettes. Clarissa? Who the devil was Clarissa? I peered at the fiercely intimidating quartet of fourteen-year-old pigtailed girls astride their fat little ponies. They looked like something out of a St Trinian's film and could all quite easily be Clarissas. I took a tentative step in their general direction and smiled nervously, peering intently at their grim little faces. Totally impassive, except – hang on, suddenly I noticed that something akin to a reaction was flickering on the face of the one at the far end. Surely she was – yes, she was nodding and smiling at me in an encouraging sort of way. That must be Clarissa!

I took a deep breath and marched smartly over. Well, I thought as I got closer and noticed her bright-green eye shadow, at least this one didn't look like her horse for a change, and she was really rather nicely turned out, which, after all, was the whole point of the competition, wasn't it? Instead of having one of those boring black jackets with the velvet collars, she had on a natty tweed affair. Admittedly it was a bit on the big side and had patches on the elbows, but she'd rolled the sleeves up for a touch of trendiness, rather like I do when I borrow Nick's.

I gave her a dazzling smile and handed over the red rosette, even going so far as to pat her beast's neck. I instantly wished I hadn't, as it was disgustingly hot and sweaty.

'Well done,' I beamed, wiping my wet hand on my skirt, 'jolly *jolly* well done.' I was pretty sure that 'jolly' was a word that was bandied about with abandon in horsy circles. 'Frightfully well turned out!'

'Ta!'

She seized the red rosette in a twinkling and her eyes lit up with delight.

I frowned. Ta! Clarissa? Surely not. Within another twinkling she'd rammed the rosette on to her pony's bridle and whisked the cup out of my hands, and before you could say 'congratulations' she was standing up in her stirrups, waving both arms delightedly to her family in the crowd. At least, I thought, turning to look, I *assumed* it was her family. There certainly seemed to be an awful lot of them, and they seemed equally ecstatic, standing up in their seats and doing an extravagant kind of Mexican wave in response.

Ah well, I thought, smiling benignly at Clarissa, much as I'd done to Harvey, what it is to make people happy. I wafted gracefully along the line to present the second prize to a girl who looked equally chuffed.

'I say, *frightfully* well done,' I brayed, well into my horsy stride now. 'Terribly well turned out and what a *delightful* pony you've –' Suddenly I stopped in mid-bray as an anguished wail broke out from the other end of the line.

'That's not fair!' bawled a blonde with heavy braces on her teeth, astride a fat brown pony. 'She's given it to Kimberly and they said I was the best! Why did Kimberly get the cup, Mummy? It's not fair!' and she promptly burst into floods of very noisy tears.

'Well, it's too late now, innit?' snapped back the girl at my end who I now saw was clearly very much a Kimberly and not a Clarissa. 'I've got it now cos the judge gave it to me, didn't you?' she demanded, giving me a defiant stare and clinging like billyo to the cup. Oh crikey.

'Er, oh dear,' I muttered, feeling myself flushing deep puce. 'I'm most awfully sorry, I seem to have made a bit of a –'

'You give that cup back right now, Kimberly Masters!' boomed a dragon's voice behind me, making me jump out of my skin. 'Give it straight back to my Clarissa! She won that cup and you know it, now hand it over!'

I turned to see an enormous tweedy woman, purple in the face with fury and with a matching purple hat squashed on to her Grecian 2000 curls, emerging from the crowd. She reached us in a matter of giant strides and bore down on the quite undaunted Kimberly, quivering with rage and shaking her fist in her face.

'Go on, hand it over right now!'

'Shan't,' pouted Kimberly, hugging the silver.

'You jolly well will, my girl, you see if I don't come and make you! And as for you,' she stormed, suddenly rounding on me, 'my Clarissa was far and away the best-turned-out gel here, any fool can see that, you ought to be sacked! Handing out cups to all and sundry – just look at the state of this one!' she cried, indicating the petulant Kimberly. 'Her jacket's a disgrace, a hand-me-down if ever I saw one, and she hacked six miles to get here from the council estate so her pony's up to his hocks in mud and sweating like a pig *and* she hasn't even plaited his mane. Best turned out? She couldn't win a fancy-dress prize at a cattle market! You give that cup back right now, Kimberly Masters, or I'll damn well come and take it from you!'

'You'll do nothing of the bleedin' kind, Daphne 'Eggerty!' roared another, equally furious, but decidedly less fruity female voice. 'My Kimberly won that fair and square and the judge's decision is final, in't that right?' demanded an angry peroxide-blonde woman in a lime-green shell suit who had joined the happy gathering. I recognized her as one of the enthusiastic Mexican wavers.

'Er, yes, you're quite right,' I quavered nervously. 'Usually the judge's decision *is* final, but, you see, I'm not actually here in, um, a judgemental capacity. I'm just sort of presenting the prizes.' I inched nervously away from these warring mothers. 'But you're right,' I added, nodding enthusiastically as the tweedy woman's face darkened, 'there certainly seems to have been some sort of a mix-up here, all my fault, I'm sure. Er, maybe if I took all the rosettes back and started again, we could –'

'No bleedin' way!' screeched Lime-green Shell Suit, waving a bright-pink fingernail in my face. 'No way! My Kimberly won that cup and we're gonna get her name put on it and 'ave it on the sideboard in the lounge and that's that!'

'Oh! Oh well, yes, of course, I'm sure it would look lovely but – oh look! Here's one of the judges! We'll let him sort it out, shall we?'

It was with intense relief that I caught sight of the official who was bustling furiously over. About time too, I thought, beginning to feel decidedly damp under the arms.

'Now now, ladies,' he soothed, as he eased his way between the irate mothers and stroked his moustache nervously, 'no need to get excited. I'm quite certain we can sort this out. I think perhaps Mrs Penhalligan got just a *teeny* bit confused, so perhaps if we started again, and maybe if I were to present the prizes we could –'

'Oh, what an absolutely marvellous idea,' I breathed, hastily thrusting the remaining rosettes into his hands, 'yes, terrific! If you would be so kind as to take over,' I was already scuttling backwards, 'that would be marvellous, because you see, apart from anything else,' I clutched my head dramatically, 'I've got the most appalling migraine coming on. Must be the heat.' I fanned my face energetically. 'Bye then, and so sorry about the mix-up, all my fault I'm sure, thanks ever so!'

With that I rammed my hat firmly down over my by now puce face, put my head down and hastened towards the edge of the ring and the gawping crowd beyond. I ducked underneath the white tape and without looking left or right, but aware that a million eyes were upon me, scurried through the murmuring masses which parted for me like the Red Sea. Scarlet with shame, I didn't even have the nerve to look around for Nick, but just headed doggedly for the exit gate. What a nightmare, what a complete and utter nightmare, just get me out of here!

I flew through the gate, rounded the corner and was just scampering off down the lane in the direction of home and sanctuary when I heard footsteps pounding along behind me. I dared not look round – please God, don't let it be one of the mothers, please God! A moment later Nick drew level with me and grabbed me by the arm.

'Hey, slow down, will you,' he panted between bouts of convulsive laughter. 'Oh God, Polly, you've no idea the mayhem you've caused back there – you really are unbelievable!' He clutched his stomach, doubled up with laughter. I shook him off and marched on down the lane.

'Oh yes, go ahead, laugh,' I snapped, feeling a bit of eye

7

water coming on, 'very funny, I'm sure, but it's not you that's going to be the laughing stock of the village for the next six months, is it?'

'Oh, don't be silly, no one's going to laugh at you,' he said, trotting to keep up with me and trying hard to keep a straight face. 'It was just a simple mistake, that's all. I mean, let's face it, anyone could have thought that Kimberly Masters, up to her eyeballs in mud and mascara and in an old tweed jacket that clearly belonged to her father, was the best-turned-out pony and rider, anyone, Polly!' More helpless mirth followed this unkind observation.

'Well, she obviously came fourth, didn't she?' I snapped. 'I mean, she can't have been that bad!'

'There were only four riders in the competition, Poll,' he spluttered. 'She came last, actually.'

'Well, how was I supposed to know who to give the blasted cup to? I mean, I *asked* you, didn't I? Fat lot of good you were.'

'I said the bay gelding, remember? The bay gelding, not the black mare!'

'And just what exactly is a bay gelding? Eh? I mean, why didn't you say the blonde girl on the end with a mouth full of wire?'

'Bay is brown and gelding means it's had its balls off – you must know that by now!'

'No, I don't, actually,' I gulped, grabbing my beastly hat as it flew off towards a ditch, 'and, anyway, what was I supposed to do, crawl around on all fours checking out its genital arrangement or something? What a ridiculous way to describe an animal! You wouldn't describe a man as having brown hair and being circumcised, would you?'

'Not quite the same thing, Poll,' chortled Nick, who was clearly finding this whole affair highly amusing. 'It's a bit more drastic than being circumcised – hey, slow down, will you, and stop sulking. It doesn't matter; everyone thought it was hysterically funny. We haven't had a good row in the county for ages. Those two families will be at each other's throats for the next ten years now – it livens things up no end!'

I sighed gloomily but slowed down a bit. 'And trust me to be the one to liven things up,' I said, kicking a pebble viciously. 'Good old Polly, you can always rely on her to cock things up and give everyone a good laugh. Why can't I ever get anything right in this blasted village?'

Nick grinned, and put his arm round me as we walked along. 'Getting the Helston Gymkhana prizes muddled up is not exactly the end of the world, you know.' He gave my shoulder a squeeze.

'I know,' I said ruefully, 'but, all the same, I wish I was a bit more . . .' I bit my lip and gazed wistfully over the hedge to the field beyond us.

'What?'

'Well, you know, a bit more, sort of . . . county. And capable. I mean, don't you ever wish that you'd married someone with a name like Lucinda Raffetty-Bagshot or – or Camilla Ponsonby-Bunkup? Someone who knew her hocks from her elbows and could ride to hounds with one hand, milk a cow with the other and build a dry-stone wall with her eyes shut?'

Nick pulled me abruptly to a halt in the middle of the road.

'What d'you mean?'

'Well, you know, I'm not exactly country-house material,

am I? Don't you ever think you'd have been better off with one of Daphne Heggerty's girls, for instance?'

'What, you think perhaps the oldest one might have suited me, do you? Henrietta with the buck teeth who sprays you with water every time she opens her mouth? Or perhaps the next one down, Matilda, isn't it, whose voice has been known to smash glasses at dinner parties? God, I'd run a mile from girls like that, you know I would; they frighten the pants off me. You're all I've ever wanted, Poll, and don't pretend you don't know it.'

I gazed up at him and gulped. Yes, I thought, as I looked into his serious dark-brown eyes, yes I *did* know it, but by God it was nice to be reminded now and again, especially by this most taciturn and undemonstrative of husbands. Talk about an uncharacteristic display of affection. My eyes watered briefly, but this time it was nothing to do with cocking up the prizegiving. I gave him a watery smile.

'You're all I've ever wanted too, you know,' I whispered.

'You're so unoriginal, aren't you?' he muttered as he bent down to kiss me. 'Can't you even think of your own sweet nothings? D'you have to nick mine all the time?'

I giggled. 'What d'you mean, "all the time"? They only occur about once in a blue moon or when England win a Test match, which is even less.'

'Well, I don't want to overdo it, got to be economical with my pleasantries, you know. It wouldn't do to let you get a big head, got to keep you on your toes!'

Suddenly a speeding car turned the corner and came hurtling towards us, nearly knocking us flying as we stood laughing and hugging in the middle of the lane.

'Look out!' yelled Nick, as he pulled me on to the grass verge.

'OUT OF THE WAY!' roared an irate Daphne Heggerty as she thundered towards us in her open-topped Range Rover, grey curls blowing in the wind and a horse box rattling around behind her. 'Stop bloody snogging and get out of the road!'

We flattened ourselves into the hedge as she roared past, leaning heavily on her horn. She was still purple with fury and a boot-faced Clarissa was sitting beside her, totally devoid of a red rosette or a silver cup, I noticed. So Lime-green Shell Suit had won the day after all.

'Try brushing up on your prizegiving rather than your sexual prowess!' was her parting shot to us as she flew over the brow of the hill and out of sight. The horse box nearly took off as it bounced around behind her, a surprised-looking pony nodding out of the back. We watched her go and giggled.

'She just can't believe Clarissa hasn't won the cup for the fourth year running, can she?' said Nick with a grin. 'Still, she's given me a marvellous idea. Come on!'

He seized my hand and pulled me towards the stile in the hedge. We climbed over into the field and he hurried me along, down towards the copse that marked the very edge of our land by the Helford River.

'Where are we going?' I panted, hobbling in my heels and rather unused to so much exertion.

'For a walk, and then perhaps a rest. It is, after all, a very hot afternoon, isn't it? Don't you think a little relaxation is in order? And then, as Daphne said, there's our prowess to brush up on, what d'you think?' He grinned and squeezed my hand.

I laughed, suddenly feeling decidedly happy. As I hobbled along I marvelled at how quickly and dramatically my moods could change. Odd, wasn't it, how one minute I could quite cheerfully slit my throat and the next I could skip happily through a meadow with my husband, on my way to an alfresco assignation?

We made our way through the long spring grass, already lush and sprinkled with cow parsley, across to the valley on the opposite side of the field, and beyond that to the gravel path that led to the river. We wound our way down, hand in hand, and reached the little copse that edged the bank. It was cool and secluded and we lay down on the mossy grass together with a sigh.

'A siesta?' I muttered, as Nick's arm curled around me.

'Absolutely,' agreed Nick, 'or rather,' he added with a smile, as he removed my crushed hat from my head and tossed it into the river, 'what I like to call a siesta *complet*.'

Chapter Two

The next morning I opened my eyes and lay in bed, listening to the birds singing outside my window and watching as a shaft of sunlight fell in a small bright square on my duvet cover. I stretched out a hand to check if Nick was beside me. He wasn't, of course, been up for hours no doubt, but I always liked to check.

I languished there for a while, thinking back to the events of the previous day. I smiled. So I'd mucked up the prizegiving, so what? What did a piffling little thing like a prizegiving matter when I had the most unpredictably sexy husband in the world? When was the last time Daphne Heggerty was seduced by her old man in a secluded copse down by the river bank, eh?

I swung my legs over the side of the bed and grinned to myself as I wandered down to the kitchen in search of calories. The sunlight was streaming in through the kitchen windows. I pushed open the back door, stuck my head out and was immediately ambushed by the sweet Cornish air. I inhaled deeply, held it a moment, then let it out with a contented sigh. Ahhh . . . pure nectar. You don't get air like that in London, you know, not much carbon monoxide in that little lungful. Someone really ought to bottle it and send it up to the poor old townies to waft over their cornflakes. I stuck my chest out and took another bracing snort, but it was a snort too far; my twenty-a-day lungs objected wildly to this sudden on-slaught of purity and I had a major coughing fit. Gasping and wheezing, I reached hastily for my cigarettes on the Welsh dresser, desperate for my more usual morning fix.

With fumbling fingers I lit the first of many over the gas ring and predictably singed my fringe at the same time. When I'd pulled all the burned bits out and sworn suffi-ciently, I tugged my T-shirt-cum-nightie down over my bottom and settled down on the back doorstep, deter-mined to enrich at least one of my senses. It wasn't difficult. I might have comprehensively fouled up the smell of the morning air with burnt hair and low-to-middle-tar tobacco, but nothing could foul up the perfect pastoral scene that greeted my eyes. As I rested my chin on my knees and gazed out at the patchwork of fields and woods in the distance, I blew smoke rings in the hazy blue air and counted my seemingly endless blessings.

You're a lucky girl, Polly Penhalligan, I told myself sternly, a very lucky girl indeed, and don't you forget it – just look at this place! The sweeping, majestic lawn, the meadow beyond dotted with sheep and spring lambs, and even further away – I squinted my rather myopic eyes – the glassy Helford River shimmering in the distance. Magic. And here you sit, on this well-worn manor-house step, mistress of all you survey. I frowned and tapped some ash on to the grass. Well, no, all right, perhaps not the river, perhaps I wasn't mistress of that – I had a feel-ing, English laws being what they were, that that probably belonged to everyone – but, certainly, this particular *view* of it was mine, wasn't it?

I leaned back on the door frame happily, then frowned

again. Try not to be too smug, Polly; it's not very attractive. But then again, I mused, plucking at a daisy, it was so terribly hard *not* to be smug. And it wasn't as if I didn't appreciate it all – God no, on the contrary, it still made my eyes boggle just to think about it. I let them boggle quietly for a moment as I sat and quietly savoured the joys of being Mrs Nicholas Penhalligan.

I smiled. It had, let's face it, been pretty convenient of me to fall in love with a man who owned quite a sizeable chunk of Cornwall, hadn't it? Not that I'd have minded if he'd been a pauper or anything, an estate agent even – Lord no, I'd have had him anyway; he was my idea of heaven with or without the lucrative trappings, but it did somewhat *cushion* life, didn't it? It was, shall we say, a nice little bonus, to get not only a handsome (very), intelligent (screamingly), sensitive (sometimes), loving (at unpredictable moments like yesterday) husband, but also Trewarren House and a thousand acres of Cornish countryside thrown into the matrimonial contract just for good measure.

Ah yes, the countryside. I sighed and stretched my legs out into the dewy grass, aware that there was no holding back the smugness now. It really was such bliss. How could I ever have been happy in London? God, the noise, the traffic, the pollution, the crime! Whereas down here, well, none of that, and all the good things were just so – well, so *abundant*, weren't they? Look at that grass, for instance – I tugged at a clump with my toes – have you ever seen such luxuriant growth? My eye snagged suddenly on my bare legs, and I frowned and tucked them up beneath me. Well, yes, OK, there was some pretty luxuriant growth on those too, and perhaps they were a trifle fatter than they'd

15

been in the past, but what did it matter? I wasn't about to pour them into ten-denier tights and excruciatingly uncomfortable four-inch heels and totter off to work for my living, was I? No, I was simply going to squeeze them into my oldest jeans and take a leisurely stroll around the farm. When I felt up to it, of course, in an hour or so perhaps. No rush.

I rested my head lazily against the door frame, feeling the sun on my face. Yes, in an hour or so I'd probably amble off and check out the cow sheds, pass the time of day with the farm hands, chew on a straw, lean on a gate, that kind of thing – nothing too taxing for a Monday. Then I might pick a few flowers for the house and ask Mrs Bradshaw, my daily, to arrange them attractively in a crystal vase, and then when Pippa arrived I'd pretend I'd done them myself and – Christ! I sat bolt upright with a jolt. Pippa! I'd almost forgotten she was coming – what time had she said? Mid-morning? I turned round and craned my neck to see the kitchen clock. Ten thirty. Phew, relax, Polly, bags of time. Mid-morning was about one o'clock in ad-man speak; she wouldn't be here for ages.

I shook my head and sighed. Poor Pippa, it would be lovely to see her again, but what a shame it wasn't a purely social call, what a shame she was down here on business. Couldn't stop long, she'd said, too much to do. Looking for a location, she'd said, to film yet another grotty commercial, no doubt. I plucked a dandelion and frowned, twirling it in my fingers like a parasol. Yes, poor old Pippa, still stuck in the ad racket. When I'd bailed out two years ago to marry Nick, the Penhalligan part of Penhalligan and Waters, Pippa had wrung her hands in dismay, claiming the typing pool would never be quite the same without the other half of the dastardly secretarial duo. She'd stuck it out solo for a bit, but when Nick finally sold his half of the agency to Waters and we decamped down here to his farm on a permanent basis, Pippa had decided that that was definitely the moment to throw in the Tipp-Ex and go.

And off she'd gone, surprisingly – considering her secretarial background of answering the telephone only on the twentieth ring, reading *Harpers & Queen* whilst typing memos and only taking a letter when severely bullied into it – to become really quite something of a high-flier in a film-production company.

She raved about it of course, but then she would. It sounded like bloody hard work to me. Whenever I rang her for a two-hour long-distance gossip she always seemed to be dashing off to a shoot or a meeting or some such other ghastly corporate event. It made her tetchy too – why, I remember once I'd had to drag her out of a meeting to ask her something absolutely crucial – like whether I should pick out the pink or the green in the drawing-room curtains when I recovered the cushions – and she'd been absolutely livid.

'Polly, have you seriously dragged me out of that presentation to ask me about your sodding cushions?' she'd hissed down the phone. Most huffy, and quite unlike her usual do-the-bare-minimum-and-piss-off-on-the-dot-of-five-thirty self.

I bit my lip thoughtfully as I twiddled my toes in the long grass. I did hope she wasn't turning into a career girl or something dreadful. Work really was so terribly over-rated. What she needed, of course, was a husband, preferably a rich one. I'd tackle her about it when she arrived, find out more about this chap she'd been seeing, Josh, or something. She'd gone awfully coy about her love life recently and I suspected it was going downhill fast.

Still, I mused, as I reached up to the shelf by the back door and flicked the biscuit tin down in a practised manner, I really ought to get dressed before she arrived or she'd be under the mistaken impression that all I did as a married woman was sit around in my nightie eating biscuits when nothing, actually, could be further from the truth.

I prized the lid open eagerly and my hand hovered nervously as I braced myself for the biggest decision of the day. I dithered. Hobnob or WI flapjack? I mustn't be greedy, and to have both would be just that. In the end I plumped for one of the larger flapjacks and wondered, as I masticated idly, just how long it actually took to get to one's hips. Were we talking hours? Days? Weeks? Or was it, in fact, almost instantaneous? I glanced down thoughtfully, but not too censoriously, at my increasingly generous hip, bottom and thigh lines. Something really had to be done about all that. Tomorrow. Yes, tomorrow I'd start a new regime. I'd go into Helston and buy some bigger clothes. I sighed. I did what I could with leggings and baggy jumpers of course, I'm nothing if not imaginative, but there was no denying the fact that two years of doing little more than reaching for the biscuit tin was beginning to take its toll on my sartorial style.

Yes, it was two years now since Nick and I had finally, and blissfully, tied the knot in that heavenly little church in Manaccan. Clutching my posy of orange blossom and white lilies I'd floated up the aisle in a sea of raw silk, followed by a flurry of darling little bridesmaids whom I'd never seen in my life before. In a state of pre-match nerves I'd sobbed to Mummy that I simply must have some tiddly attendants and why the hell didn't I have any handy nephews and nieces we could wheel out like everyone else did, so that finally in desperation I think she'd resorted to Central Casting, or an agency or something. Anyway, they'd all looked divine and the whole thing had gone off tremendously smoothly and everyone said it hadn't mattered a bit that I'd passed out cold on the wedding cake just as Nick and I had been about to cut it. I'd obviously slightly misjudged the amount of champagne needed to steady my nerves and numbed them instead, but, as I said, it hadn't mattered, and Nick had just been thankful he hadn't cut my head off with the bogus regimental sword Mummy had also rustled up for the occasion. The cake had been surreptitiously scraped off the floor straight on to plates, my dress had sponged beautifully and I'd come round in an alcoholic haze, headdress askew, just in time to articulate my goodbyes to a few remaining guests before being whisked away to the most romantic honeymoon imaginable in Antigua.

I helped myself to a Hobnob and settled down to bask in the memory of that idyllic little hotel on the sun-drenched beach, where the only minor inconveniences had been the wrong socket for my hair dryer and the Spanish honeymooners in the next room who'd insisted on shouting '*Arriva! Arriva!*' – rather competitively we thought – through the thin rush-matting walls.

I smiled and crunched my way nostalgically through a few more calories, but as I did so I heard a crunch of an altogether different kind coming from the other side of the house. My mouth froze in mid flapjack. I listened. Christ! That sounded suspiciously like tyres on gravel. Pippa couldn't be here already, could she?

I jumped up in alarm, ran through the house to the large sash window in the hall at the front and peered out. Sure enough, a very sexy little red Alfa Romeo was cruising to a halt in my front drive. Groovy car, I marvelled enviously, could that really be Pippa's? What on earth were they paying her these days? I watched as the car door swung open and one long, slim, sheerly stockinged leg appeared, followed by another. They straightened to reveal the rest of Pippa's most elegant self, immaculately clad in the most prohibitively expensive-looking drop-dead Chanel suit I've ever seen.

'Pippa!' I squeaked, bursting forth through the open window in a flurry of excitement and chocolate-stained T-shirt. 'You're early! Hang on, I'll come to the front door.'

She waved back, but looked rather dubiously at the craters in the drive that she was apparently required to cross in order to gain access to the house. I shut the window and ran to the door. When I flung it open she was still poised nervously by the car, clutching her quilted handbag and surveying the puddles, a vision in pale pink with black trimming, her shiny blond hair blowing out behind her like a silk fan.

'What's happened to your drive?' she wailed. 'It's like a bloody assault course!'

'We ran out of money,' I shouted. 'Had to put a new roof on the cow shed instead!'

'Well, I'm glad the cows are all right, but what about my heels?'

'Oh, come on, Pippa,' I grinned, rather enjoying her townie predicament. 'Just get a move on and stop making such a fuss!'

'Oh, all right,' she grumbled, nervously picking her way through the mud. 'Come on, Bruce,' she threw back over her shoulder. 'Wake up, for God's sake, we're here!'

A blond head suddenly popped into view above the dashboard in the passenger seat and a pair of bleary blue eyes were rubbed sleepily. Bruce? Who the hell was Bruce? She'd brought a man with her and I wasn't even dressed? I pulled my T-shirt down over my bottom and hid behind the door.

'You didn't say you were bringing anyone!' I hissed, as Pippa finally made it across the threshold.

'Oh, it's only Bruce,' she said airily, hugging me enthusiastically and thrusting a bunch of tulips up my nose. 'He's the location-finder, had to come with me to check out the venues, you see. Gosh, it's good to see you, Polly – come *on*, Bruce!' she yelled back at the car.

Bruce opened his door but appeared to be equally put out by the drive.

'Couldn't you have got a bit closer?' he wailed plaintively. 'I've got my Gucci loafers on!'

'Oh, stop being such a pansy and hurry up. I want you to meet Polly.'

'You're cruel, darling,' muttered the gorgeous, suntanned blond creature who stepped gingerly from the car, 'very cruel. But luckily, Brucey Boy's used to it.'

I instinctively pulled in my tummy muscles and sucked in my cheeks as he tiptoed across clutching a little black bag, but I couldn't help thinking I'd never seen such a fuss over a little bit of mud, especially from a man. Of course, as he reached us, it took less than a nanosecond to realize that Bruce was not your average man, at least, not one of the red-blooded heterosexual variety I'm so fond of.

'Bruce, this is Polly; Polly, Bruce,' announced Pippa as he climbed shakily up the front steps, looking back over his shoulder like someone who's just scaled the north face of the Eiger.

'Terrible drive,' he muttered, taking my hand, 'terrible. But none the less, enchanted, my dear, positively dazzled, by both the house and your good self, and dying to take a peek inside.'

Hoping fervently that he was referring to the house and not my good self I ushered them in.

'Bruce is a professional nosy parker,' explained Pippa as I led them through the vast hall smothered in ancestral portraits. 'He gets away with it by calling himself a location-finder but it's really just an excuse to poke around other people's houses.'

'Oh, but this is divine!' squeaked Bruce, clasping his tiny hands together with joy and twirling round the hall. 'Oh please, no further! Let me linger a moment and savour!'

We lingered and he savoured, prowling excitedly around the portraits, touching frames, peering at signatures.

'Oh yes!' he breathed. 'Yes! Utter magic, utter, utter magic!'

He tore himself away from the pictures and stood back to survey the whole hall, taking in the ancient banisters, the flagstone floor and the huge chandelier hanging from the heavily corniced ceiling.

'Absolutely sublime,' he pronounced, 'especially, my dear, after the simply hideous places we've seen today.'

He gave a quick shudder of revulsion and raised a plucked eyebrow in my direction.

'I mean, wouldn't you think a picturesque period farmhouse with attractive grounds would be an easy enough brief in rural Cornwall? Wouldn't you?' he enquired urgently.

'Er, yes, I suppose I would.'

'Of course you would! But you'd be wrong. Shall I tell you why?'

I opened my mouth to invite him to do just that, but before I'd drawn breath he'd rushed on indignantly.

'Because just when you think you've found the perfect *grande maison*, the perfect country pile, you look a little closer and discover' – he gasped and clutched his mouth dramatically – '*quelle horreur*! It's got a pylon in the front garden, or there is an assortment of satellite dishes hanging from the roof, or they've got a circular washing line twirling around in the back garden set in rock-solid concrete, I mean, imagine! Imagine the *taste* someone's got to have to *do* that to their house!'

He gazed at me in horror, feigned a swoon, then quickly seized my arm. 'You haven't got a twirly washing line or a satellite dish, have you?' he asked anxiously.

I assured him we hadn't and he recovered enough composure to raise an immaculately manicured finger to his temple and massage it gently. I swear his bottom lip wobbled.

'I'm delighted to hear it, my dear, but of course it doesn't help me in my quest for a suitable house for the Doggy Chocs commercial. I tell you frankly, I'm distressed, most distressed,' he murmured. 'What on earth am I to tell Sam?'

'Who's Sam?' I asked, suppressing a giggle. I'd forgotten people like Bruce existed.

'The director,' explained Pippa.

'Too divine,' purred Bruce, eyes shining. 'Married, of course,' he added petulantly.

He sighed and turned away, resuming his survey of the portraits. Suddenly he gasped and clapped his hands.

'Heavens! What an unbelievably noble nose! Who's that?' He peered at one of the more imposing males in the collection.

'One of my husband's ancestors,' I explained. 'I'm not sure who it is but Nick comes from a long line of big-nosed bigots. You'll meet him later and, er, probably see what I mean.'

I couldn't quite imagine Nick instantly taking Bruce to his heart, so I thought it only fair to warn him of impending rejection.

'Can't wait,' breathed Bruce, 'I *adore* bigots.'

'Big mistake,' muttered Pippa, taking my arm as we went through into the kitchen. 'You should have said he was a sensitive little flower. Bruce is very into macho men, the butcher the better, in fact.'

'Christ. Nick will run a mile,' I murmured.

I filled the kettle while Bruce minced joyfully around the kitchen, exclaiming at all he saw.

'Oh, the beams, the *beams*, and – oh God, is that a range? Is it real?'

I assured him it was.

'And the floor! Proper flagstones, none of your imitation Battersea lark, ooh, aren't you clever to have a house like this and a bigoted husband to go with it?'

I grinned, thinking they'd been my exact same thoughts not a few moments ago.

'Where is the husband, by the way?' asked Pippa, sinking elegantly into the wheel-backed chair by the range and crossing her incredibly slim legs. I tried not to feel envious.

'With the sheep as usual. He knows you're coming, though, so he'll be in soon. It's ages since he set eyes on anyone in a skirt; he'll be delighted to see you but it'll play havoc with his blood pressure.'

I absent-mindedly flicked the biscuit tin down again as I spooned out the Nescafé, and, without thinking, helped myself to a flapjack. Pippa jumped up and was beside me in an instant. She grabbed my arm in a vicelike grip, eyes shining.

'I knew it!' she squealed. 'I just knew it! Didn't I say so in the car, Bruce? She is! You are, aren't you?' she asked urgently. 'Look at you – you can't keep your hands off the biscuit tin, and look at the size of you already! You old dog, why didn't you tell me? How many months are you?'

I stared at her in bewilderment. 'What? What are you talking about?'

'Pregnant! I knew it! Why didn't you tell me on the phone? How many months are you – four? Five? Funny how it shows on the face and neck, isn't it?' she observed, surveying me critically with narrowed eyes. 'And the legs, of course, but everyone always piles it on there. Can I be godmother?'

'Shut up, Pippa,' I said crossly, snapping the biscuit tin shut. 'What on earth are you banging on about? Of course I'm not pregnant. I'd have told you if I was.'

'You're not?' Pippa stepped back in amazement. 'I could have sworn – are you sure?'

'Of course I'm sure – don't be ridiculous. Don't you think I'd know?'

'But how come you look so – how come your face is all . . .' Pippa trailed off in confusion.

'Fat?'

'Well . . . yes.'

'Oh, thanks very much,' I said tartly. 'You always did have a sublime sense of tact, Pippa, but this is ridiculous!'

'Well, you said it!'

'Because you so obviously meant it!'

'But you must admit, Polly, you have put on quite a bit of weight and you are wearing that baggy maternity thing, and I knew you wanted to get pregnant so I naturally assumed –'

'Well, you assumed wrong,' I snapped, 'and this is a T-shirt, actually. Don't they sell them in London any more?'

'But you've been trying for ages, haven't you?' she persisted. 'Surely you should be – you know, sort of – pregnant by now?'

'Pippa, could we talk about this some other time?' I hissed, jerking my head meaningfully in the direction of Bruce, who was leaning against the dresser inspecting his nails with studied indifference.

'Oh, don't worry about Bruce,' said Pippa, dismissing him airily. 'He likes girl talk.'

'No, don't mind me,' said Bruce, as if it were *his* feelings I was concerned about. 'Treat me as an honorary girlie. I love all the chat, although I must say I could probably skip the pregnancy debate, not having a vested interest, if you know what I mean. Mind if I take a look around the rest of the house?'

'Please do,' I said, relieved to be shot of him. 'Here, take your coffee.' I handed him a mug.

'Thanks. And take no notice of this anorexic stick insect. I think you look lovely, very Rubenesque. Ta-ra!'

He wiggled off in the direction of the dining room, pert little bottom tucked well in, hand stuck out to one side holding an imaginary cigarette. I watched him go, gnashing my teeth at his covetable bottom.

'Rubenesque,' I muttered darkly, splashing milk into mugs, 'marvellous, isn't it? My best friend tells me I'm so fat I could be pregnant and a perfect stranger tells me I look like an overblown tart in a picture. Anything else you'd like to get off your chest while you're down here?' I banged the empty kettle down viciously on the hob.

'Oh, don't be like that, Polly,' said Pippa soothingly. 'I wasn't trying to upset you or anything, I was just excited for you because I knew you wanted to be pregnant.'

'Well, I'm not,' I said shortly. 'So that's that.'

I curled up on the old chintz sofa in the corner, usually occupied by Badger, our black lab, and sulked into my coffee. Pippa slunk furtively over, kicked off her shoes and curled up beside me.

'But . . . there's nothing wrong, is there?' she asked anxiously. 'I mean, you haven't got your tubes crossed or anything like that, have you?'

'No, of course not, it just takes time, that's all. These things don't happen overnight, you know, Pippa!'

'Don't they?' Pippa looked surprised. 'God, I always thought they did. I thought the moment you came off the pill, that was it – wallop, up the duff, in the club, off to the gorgeous gynae and before you knew where you were you had baby sick all down your jumper.'

'That's what I thought too, but it's simply not true. It's just a load of propaganda put about by our mothers who were clearly terrified we were going to get pregnant at the drop of a pair of trousers and flaunt the love child in front of the neighbours, but let me tell you, Pippa, it's much more complicated than that – there's a lot more to it than we've been led to believe.' I nodded sagely.

'Like what?' Pippa looked confused. 'I thought you just sort of . . . did it?'

I shook my head and smiled benignly at her. 'Oh, Pippa, you're woefully misinformed, very much behind the times. In the old days, yes, I'm sure they did just "do it", but these days, what with modern science and everything, well, it's much more technical, much more advanced.' I pursed my lips knowledgeably.

'It is? In what way?'

'Well, first you've got to read all the books, then you've got to take your temperature every morning, then you buy the egg-detecting kit and set up a sort of mini chemistry lab in your bathroom, complete with foaming test tubes and dipsticks and –'

'Egg-detecting kit?' Pippa's eyes were like dinner plates. 'What are you, a hen or something?'

'Pippa, one has to know when one's eggs are being dropped,' I explained patiently.

'Blimey, now you sound like a Wellington bomber. I had no idea it was so complicated.'

'Oh yes,' I went on airily, 'it's really quite intellectually demanding, and there's an awful lot of background reading to do too.' I sighed wearily. 'Terribly time-consuming.'

'Really?'

'Absolutely, it's essential. First you've got to raid the local library for all its infertility manuals just to convince yourself you've got knots in your tubes, fibroids in your whatsits or a husband who's firing blanks, then you've got to get hold of that *Horizon* video about the voyage of the sperm to the egg to realize there's actually only one milli-second a month when you can possibly conceive anyway and that unless you set the alarm clock for three in the morning and get bonking that very second you haven't a snowball's chance in hell of getting the timing right, then –'

'Christ! First the book, then the film –' Pippa's eyes gleamed dangerously. 'Well, at least you've got the T-shirt!' she guffawed noisily into her mug.

I viewed her icily. 'This is an extremely serious and sensitive subject, Pippa. It's no laughing matter, you know.'

'Sorry,' she said, composing herself with difficulty, 'but you know, if I were you, Polly, I'd throw all the books and paraphernalia away and just get down to it. It all sounds a bit ridiculous to me.'

'I can assure you,' I said primly, 'we "get down to it", as

you so charmingly put it, at the slightest opportunity, but, as I said, it's not quite as simple as that.'

'Doesn't it help if you stand on your head? I'm sure I've read that somewhere.'

I sighed. 'Believe me, I'd stand on my head and do cartwheels round the room if I thought it would do any good, but it doesn't.'

She frowned. 'But you're not worried, are you? I mean, you've only been married a couple of years and you're still jolly young.'

'No, I'm not bloody worried and I wouldn't have mentioned it at all if you hadn't brought it up in the first place!' I snapped.

'Sorry.'

'Still,' I mused, 'it would be nice. I must say, I'm looking forward to fridge magnets.'

'Can't you have those without children?'

'Not really. Looks a bit naff if you haven't got the finger paintings to go with them.'

'Oh. Right,' conceded Pippa, 'and, of course, it would give you an interest, give you something to do.'

'What d'you mean?' I said, bridling instantly. 'I've got plenty to do. God, I'm rushed off my feet down here!'

'Really?' Pippa looked surprised.

'Really? Really? Pippa, I never stop. I'm at it all day long!'

'At what?'

'Well,' I blustered, 'being bloody busy, that's what!'

'Yes, but what d'you do?'

'Well, you know, I – well, this house for instance!' I swung my arm round expansively to indicate its size. 'It's *incredibly* time-consuming!'

'But I thought you had a daily, a wench from the village or something?'

'Well, yes, I do, but even so –'

'Even so what?'

'Well, God, Pippa, I practically had to redecorate the whole place when we moved in, you know, it was in a terrible mess!'

'Really? Redecorate?' Pippa looked around at the rustic kitchen with its oak beams, flagstone floor and plain whitewashed walls. 'Looks as if it's been like this since the Middle Ages.'

'Oh, well, yes, the *kitchen* has, sure, but various other rooms had to be *completely* redesigned.'

'Which ones?'

God, she would go on, wouldn't she?

'Which ones?' I echoed, playing for time.

'Yes, come on, I want to see.' Pippa jumped up, seized my arm and pulled me to my feet. 'I want to see what you've done!'

'Well . . .' I faltered, dragging my feet literally and figuratively across the kitchen, 'the, um, the downstairs loo took forever, of course.'

'Really? Show me.'

I led her tentatively down the back passage and pushed open the door. She gasped, as well she might. For the walls of this very small room were painted the retina-searing yellow usually reserved for the tennis balls at Wimbledon or perhaps the armbands of midnight cyclists. On completing the job I'd realized of course that the colour chart had lied through its teeth and Morning Primrose was in fact more of a Morning Chuck-up, and in a panic I'd then tried to draw the eye away by madly stencilling fruit and flowers around the borders. Unfortunately the purple and green flora and fauna fought furiously with the acidic walls and the blue and red tiled floor. Busy was kind. Frantic was much more like it.

'Blimey,' said Pippa in awe. 'Not afraid to mix your colours, are you?'

'It didn't quite come off, actually,' I admitted. 'I think I was a mite ambitious.'

'Never mind,' said Pippa, blinking, as we turned and wandered back to the kitchen, 'it was worth a try. What else though? You said on the phone you were up to your eyes in decorating.'

'Oh, I was, it took ages to do that, you know.'

Pippa stared at me with wide eyes as she lowered herself into the sofa again. 'So that's it? The downstairs loo?'

'Yes, that's it,' I said tetchily, curling up at the other end. Christ, what did she expect? A reproduction of the ceiling of the Sistine Chapel? Sicilian murals all up the stairs? Franciscan angels winding their way down the banisters?

She frowned. 'But you work on the farm a lot, don't you?' she persisted. 'I mean, you help with the animals and that kind of thing?'

'Oh, not really,' I said airily. 'You see, Nick does most of it, and of course we have Larry and Mick and Jim.'

'So what do you do then?' She fixed me with a beady eye.

'Oh God, loads,' I said hastily, suddenly smelling danger and realizing what she was up to. 'There's – there's the garden, of course,' I said wildly.

'I thought you said on the phone you didn't know a

phlox from a fuchsia and you were going to get a man in to do it?'

'Ah, well – yes, OK, perhaps I did but – oh I know! Yes, of course, there's my cooking!'

'Cooking! You? Like what?'

'Well, like –'

'Yes?'

'God, don't be so aggressive, Pippa, I'm just trying to think what I do particularly well – oh yes, I know, my baking!' I finished happily.

Pippa eyed me suspiciously, as well she might. 'What, like cakes and things?'

'Er, yes, that's it.'

Not a lie at all, because in fact 'things' described my baking remarkably accurately. My particular 'things' were jam tarts. A circle of frozen pastry with a blob of jam in the middle. I had, of course, meant to master the oven and get down to some *serious* baking at some stage, and I'd even gone so far as to prop Delia up over the Aga and salivate greedily over her suggestions, but somehow, instead of my greed making me reach for the scales and the caster sugar, it seemed to lead inexorably to the biscuit tin again, so Delia was put back on the shelf to collect yet more dust and the rows of plump, golden scones and fluffy Victoria sponges continued to evade me. And Nick too, of course. Because, to be honest, he felt the deprivation much more keenly than me.

In the beginning he'd praised my efforts, keen to encourage me, but, let's face it, there are only so many tarts a man can take – so to speak – and when he came in starving hungry from the fields, having packed more physical exertion into one day than most men manage in a week, dying for a juicy fat slab of Dundee cake with his tea, I'd come to dread his weak pronouncement of simulated joy – 'Ah! Jam tarts again!' – as his eye lit nervously upon my sticky morsels cringing by the Aga. But of course, as I told myself regularly, there was still plenty of time, and one of these days I was going to get down to some *serious* baking.

'OK, baking,' conceded Pippa warily, only marginally placated. 'All right, but you can't do that all day, can you? And the thing is, Polly, I know it's beautiful down here, but I can't help thinking I'd go out of my mind with boredom after a while, either that or turn to drink. You're not drinking, are you?' Her eyes pinned me to the wall.

'No, of course I'm not drinking, and listen, Pippa, not everyone wants to run around being a high-powered executive, you know. Don't you ever feel the urge to rip off your tights and your Chanel suit and run around the fields barefoot?'

Pippa looked doubtfully at her immaculate pink concoction. 'Not really, and even if I did,' she regarded me penetratingly, 'I'd make damn sure I'd shaved my legs first.'

I flushed. 'Pippa!' I pulled my legs up sharply and sat on them.

'Well, it's true, look at you!' I tugged my T-shirt down desperately as she hoicked it up with a manicured nail. 'There are some things only your best friend can tell you, Polly, so I'm telling you. I suspected as much the last time I came down, but now I'm convinced. You've gone all fat and complacent because you've got your man, haven't you?'

'Pippa! I have not!' I was pink with indignation now – this was outrageous.

'Well, what's with the hairy legs then?' she persisted. 'And,' she added, peering with naked incredulity at the top of my head, 'bloody hell, look at this, what about these dark roots? You wouldn't have been seen dead walking around London like that in the good old days. Come on, Polly, it's not like you to take your eye off the ball – what's occurring?'

'Don't be silly,' I spluttered. 'I haven't taken my eye off the ball at all, it's just that, well, in the country, people don't worry about things like shaving their legs and touching up their roots. It's all sort of back-to-nature here.'

'Oh, so it's the country's fault, is it? You can't live in the country and shave your legs at the same time, is that it? What utter drivel. The two aren't mutually exclusive, you know, I'm sure the village shop would run to a razor, or even a tube of Immac, and what's all this back-to-nature rubbish? You always struck me as more of a back-to-the-wine-bar type.'

'Oh, OK, OK,' I said, caving in dramatically and reaching for a cigarette. 'So I haven't shaved my legs for a while, OK, Pippa, you win.'

I was getting bored with this lecture and my argumentative powers were flagging.

'No, it's *not* OK!' said Pippa sharply, suddenly thumping the arm of the sofa with her fist.

I jumped in surprise. She glared at me.

'If you must know, I'm really worried about you, Polly!'

My mouth gaped in amazement. She . . . was worried about me? Wasn't I supposed to be the one who was worried about –

'I know exactly what you're doing here,' she snapped, 'you're sitting around on your bum all day, doing bugger all except eating chocolate, watching telly and waiting to get pregnant, aren't you?'

'No, of course not,' I spluttered. 'I'm incredibly busy, and, anyway, since when have you been so keen on the puritanical work ethic?'

'I'm not puritanical, I'm just living my life, which is more than you're doing, and it's a crime. You're a beautiful girl, Polly, you've got it all and you're wasting it. You're piling on the pounds and going to ground down here, now why?'

'If you must know,' I snapped, 'I have to eat as many calories as I possibly can – it's part of my pre-conception diet. If I don't keep my weight up, I won't conceive; it's a well-known fact. Haven't you ever heard of child-bearing hips?' I added wildly.

'Balls,' scoffed Pippa. 'You're eating out of boredom and you know it. You've got nothing to do and no way of occupying your mind. You're bored out of your skull here.'

I felt my fists clenching. 'That's not true!'

'Of course it is, it's written all over you – I've got my man so I don't have to work and I don't care what I look like – it's as clear as day.'

I felt my face flame. We stared at each other.

'Well, if you think I'm so fat and boring, why don't you just go?' I snapped suddenly.

There was a terrible silence. She gazed at me. I watched her face grow pale. Then she got shakily to her feet, gathering up her handbag from the table.

'Right,' she whispered hoarsely, 'I will.'

Chapter Three

She walked unsteadily towards the door but didn't make it through it. I was up in an instant, pulling her back, hanging on to her arm.

'Oh God, Pippa, I'm so sorry, please don't go, I – I didn't mean it, really I didn't!' I cried.

She hesitated, but only for a second. In a twinkling we were hugging each other and sniffing and snorting into each other's hair.

'Sorry,' mumbled Pippa gruffly, 'didn't mean all that.'

'No, you're right, you're right!' I wailed. 'I'm a fat slob! I'm a failure!'

'No you're not.'

'I am!'

'Of course you're not a failure,' she said, not disputing, I noticed, the fat-slob element, 'but I'm so fond of you, Polly, and it upsets me to see you wasting yourself like this.'

'I know, I know!' I hiccuped into her sleek, recently highlighted hair. 'I'm a mess, a bag lady!'

'But it's all superficial,' she said, gently taking my shoulders and holding me away. 'It's all so easily rectified, just get yourself down to the hairdresser, have a few highlights, book an appointment at the leg-wax place and –'

'No,' I sniffed, shaking my head energetically, 'it's more than that – it's deeper. I'm rotten, rotten to the core!'

'Don't be silly.'

'I am!'

'No you're not.'

'Yes I am!'

And thus Bruce found us as he wandered in, clinging to each other, arguing, shrieking and crying simultaneously.

'Lordy-be,' he muttered, raising his eyebrows to heaven as he tiptoed past, 'I'm glad I'm a man sometimes.'

'Sorry,' I snuffled, grabbing a tissue from the dresser. 'Pippa was just telling me some basic home truths, had to be done.' I blew my nose hard. 'God, what's that?' I wiped my nose and stared with astonishment at the bundle of skin and bone under Bruce's arm, complete with red ribbon and mad, staring eyes.

'This is Munchkin,' announced Bruce proudly, stroking the pimple that passed as the chihuahua's head. 'I hope you don't mind me bringing her in but she was crying her little eyes out in the car.'

'I don't mind at all, she can join in the waterworks in here, but I can't vouch for Badger. He eats things that size for breakfast.'

Right on cuc, Badger miraculously appeared as if from nowhere, all thoughts of whiling away the morning rabbiting apparently quite forgotten. He stood to attention at Bruce's feet, nose twitching, tail erect, quivering with excitement and shooting beseeching glances in my direction. *Can I kill it?* his brown eyes seemed to say, *Can I kill it now?*

'Basket, Badge,' I ordered sternly. He dithered. 'Now!'

He slunk away to his corner, giving me a reproachful look, but still keeping a careful eye out lest Bruce should accidentally let the bundle slip, in which case he'd be only too pleased to retrieve it. It would be the work of a moment.

Bruce kept the terrified Munchkin clasped tightly to his chest and eyed Badger warily as he sat down at the kitchen table.

'Marvellous house,' he breathed, 'simply marvellous. Would make a fabulous location.' He eyed Pippa meaningfully.

'Don't even think about it,' said Pippa. 'Nick would never agree, would he, Polly?'

'Not in a million years,' I said, blowing my nose again noisily.

I could just see Nick's face if I so much as suggested a film crew run riot all over the house and garden; trampling the flowers, frightening the sheep and being all luvvie and artistic over his little patch of paradise.

'We'd pay you,' ventured Bruce hopefully. 'Quite well, actually, and we'd only need to use the outside of the house and perhaps a soupçon of the kitchen . . . ?'

I shook my head firmly. 'No way.'

Bruce sighed heavily. 'Shame. Great shame. The client would love this place; he'd go weak at the knees.'

'Yes, well, forget it, the farmer would go ballistic.'

'What would I go ballistic about?' enquired Nick, breezing in through the back door, grinning from ear to ear.

I swung round in delight. He looked divine as usual, his striking, angular face with its jutting chin and decidedly Roman nose already nut brown from the early sun, his straight dark hair slightly tousled and his brown eyes gleaming with health and the great outdoors. He was tall, broad and mine, I thought happily as he rumpled Pippa's perfect hair.

'Nick!' she squealed, jumping up and throwing her arms round his neck.

'Pippa, you're looking as delectable as ever,' he declared, kissing her mightily on the cheek. 'Hang on a minute, I'll just pop this in the oven.'

He untangled himself and stooped down to deposit a new-born lamb in the bottom oven of the Aga. He stood up and smiled.

'There!'

Pippa and Bruce stared at him in horror. Bruce clutched Munchkin to his chest, his eyes wide with fear; Pippa gulped and backed away.

'Jesus,' she murmured, 'that's a bit primitive even for you, isn't it? Aren't you going to kill it first?'

'Oh, I'm not cooking it,' said Nick, washing his hands at the sink, 'just warming it up. Don't panic, I'm not going to shut the door, but I've got to keep it warm. It's a sock lamb. Its mother died and it got a bit wet and cold in the field. When it's warmed up I'll give it a bottle.'

'Bit late in the year, isn't it?' I said, peering at the little thing shivering away in the oven.

'A bit, but these things happen. A late arrival.'

'And an orphan already!' Pippa looked stricken. 'What will happen to it?'

'Oh, it'll grow big and strong, lark around in the fields for a few months, and then I'll transfer it to the top oven and surround it with roast potatoes.' Nick grinned wickedly.

Pippa and Bruce did a collective gasp.

'The brute!' murmured Bruce with a touch of awe.

'Nick, how can you?' wailed Pippa.

'But you like roast lamb, don't you?'

'Yes, but –' Pippa looked seriously upset.

Nick took pity. 'OK, just for you, Pippa, I'll spare this one and let it skip in the fields indefinitely – Christ, what's that?' he said, spotting the mess under Bruce's arm and simultaneously holding out his hand to Bruce. 'Nick Penhalligan,' he muttered, keeping an incredulous eye on the dog.

'Oh, sorry, Nick,' I said quickly, 'this is Bruce. He works with Pippa – they're location-hunting – and this is Munchkin.'

'Is it indeed?' Nick looked at Munchkin as if he'd like nothing better than to pop her in the top oven right now and close the door firmly.

He smiled at Bruce, who was gazing at Nick with wide eyes, the power of speech having apparently completely deserted him.

'Been boring you with girl talk, have they? Polly's rather starved of female company down here so she's probably got verbal diarrhoea already. Anyone offered you a drink? Beer?' He opened the fridge door, pulled out a can of lager and waggled it in Bruce's direction.

Bruce, looking thoroughly bigot-struck now, simpered a negative response before backing away and draping himself decoratively over the Welsh dresser. There he posed, arms outstretched, head flung back and cocked to one side to display his profile, smouldering away at Nick through his lashes.

Nick looked momentarily alarmed, then recovered himself quickly. He'd been in advertising long enough to recognize the Bruces of this world, and also the devastating effect he seemed to have on them. He kept the beer for himself and backed hastily in the opposite direction, positioning himself firmly in the girls' camp next to Pippa, who was perching on the back of a chair.

'Let's have a look at you then!' he said, hauling her to her feet.

She grinned and gave a twirl.

'I must say, the world of film production seems to be suiting you down to the ground,' he said, marvelling. 'You look fantastic! Gosh, you're slim. Look at that for a figure, Polly!'

'I know,' I said enviously, 'you're going to have to let me in on the secret, Pippa.'

'Stress,' said Pippa proudly, smoothing her minuscule skirt down over her pencil-thin thighs. 'Having a proper job with real worries is the best diet in the world, you know. I had no idea it could be so effective.'

'Tell me about it,' groaned Nick, running his hands through his hair. 'I wondered why I was becoming a shadow of my former self. This place is obviously taking pounds off me, not to mention years.'

'But I thought it was going really well? I thought when you sold the agency you had bags of money to pour into this place?'

Nick sighed wearily and flopped down into a chair. 'I did, but unfortunately it got swallowed up by a series of disasters. Too much rain last year so we lost a lot of the hay, bad lambing the year before that, then there was that storm which took the roofs off most of the outbuildings – I tell you, I could do with a couple more advertising agencies to sell; I need miles of new fencing and every day some piece of badly made farm machinery seems to conk out on me.'

'It's not as bad as all that,' I said soothingly. 'Nick's exaggerating.'

Nick shook his head grimly. 'I wish I was, darling, but I tell you, unless something happens pretty damn quickly, next quarter's farm accounts aren't going to look too attractive.'

'You'll have to send your wife out to work again,' said Pippa with a mischievous grin.

'Ha! That'll be the day. I think Polly's retired for life, haven't you?' He leaned back in his chair and tugged teasingly at my T-shirt. 'I must say, you're looking particularly fetching today. Will we have the pleasure of seeing you in that little number for lunch as usual?'

'Oh, Nick, that's not true! You know jolly well I normally get dressed by lunch time!'

'Nip and tuck some days though, isn't it?' he said with a grin. 'Not that I mind, of course, I like to see you wafting round in that sexy négligé all ready for action – makes me feel like the milkman.'

I aimed a sharp cuff to his head and he caught my hand, laughing. 'Careful! Mind my curls! What's for lunch, by the way? I'm starving.'

God, Attila the Hungry was back in my kitchen being all forceful and demanding again. For better, for worse, but not for lunch, I decided grimly for the umpteenth time.

'Lunch?' I shrieked. 'What, now? Don't be silly, I've only just had breakfast!'

'Well, I had mine six hours ago and it's damn nearly twelve o'clock.'

'Is it?' I swung round in amazement and looked at the clock. 'Gosh, so it is.'

'What were you planning on giving Bruce and Pippa then?' went on my spouse, who was getting less adorable by the minute.

'Well, let me see . . .' I said, flinging open the fridge door and improvising wildly. 'There's some bread, and – and some cheese . . . at least I think it's cheese,' I said doubtfully, picking up a piece of extremely sweaty Cheddar. Damn. I'd planned to go into Helston before they arrived and pick up some cold meat. How on earth had it slipped my mind?

'Oh, we're not staying for lunch,' said Pippa quickly. 'We really must get back and report our findings to Sam. We spent the whole of yesterday down here and we said we'd be back by tea time today.'

'Don't want to get our botties spanked,' agreed Bruce, looking as if nothing would please him more.

'Oh, Pipps, I thought you were staying a while!' I wailed. 'Don't go yet, I want to hear all the news. I want to know what Lottie's been up to, who's been doing what to whom. Please stay. I'll rustle something up, really I will. I'm sure I could do something with this,' I ventured brightly, holding up the sad piece of Cheddar, 'make a pie or something. I'm quite big on pies.'

A stunned and disbelieving silence greeted this little announcement.

'Only porkie ones,' muttered Nick, rather disloyally I thought. I glared. At least Pippa had the grace to turn her incredulous guffaw into a massive coughing fit. I was beginning to feel more than a little inadequate here.

Pippa jumped up. 'Don't bother about food,' she said, slipping her arm through mine. 'Bruce and I had an enormous breakfast at the hotel this morning. Tell you what, let's just grab that bottle of wine I spotted in the fridge and take it out to the garden. We can leave the boys to man-talk in here.'

With a wicked glance at Nick, who looked horrified, she seized the wine and a couple of glasses, and with a wink at Bruce, who flushed with pleasure at the thought of being left alone with Nick, steered me outside.

We wandered arm in arm to a sunny spot in the middle of the lawn and sat down on the grass. I lit a cigarette.

'Still smoking then?' enquired Pippa with a wry smile.

'Pippa! You haven't given up . . . ?'

'You bet I have. It's too expensive now, and I'm damned if I'm going to kill myself. It's a vice, Polly.'

Somehow this piece of news shook me more than anything. Pippa and I had chain-smoked our way through the last seven years together. As we'd skipped our way through parties, jobs, love affairs and trouble, we'd always had our trusty packets of twenty by our sides. She was changing. For the better, of course, but it depressed the hell out of me.

'It may be a vice to you, but it's a hobby to me,' I said grimly, 'and you must admit it's got staying power. I've been doing it since I was sixteen. All my other hobbies turned out to be nine-day wonders – brass-rubbing, tapestry, they all ended in tears. Except sunbathing, of course, that's always stayed the course, but now the bloody sunbathing police are out to ruin that for me too. Why can't people just mind their own business? If I want to smoke and tan myself to death, I will. at least I'll look good in the coffin against all that white satin.'

I took a huge, defiant drag of nicotine, right down to my bootstraps. 'And anyway,' I said with an uncharacteristic glimmer of perception, 'I bet the only reason you've given up is because Josh doesn't like it.'

'Well, there is that,' admitted Pippa grudgingly. 'He's very anti.'

'You see! God, you must be smitten to give up for a man! It's never happened before, has it? Charles hated it and you wouldn't give up for him.'

Pippa said nothing. She pursed her lips and decapitated a daisy. I studied her closely.

'And when am I going to meet this boss of yours, eh? And how come you're not living with him yet? I thought you'd be well ensconced by now. How come you haven't got your bras hanging over his bath tub?'

Pippa shifted position and looked uncomfortable. 'Well, it's a bit tricky, actually,' she mumbled.

'In what way?'

'It just is.'

'Why? He's not married or anything, is he?'

Pippa flushed and bit her lip.

'He is! Bull's-eye! God, Pippa, you old dog, why didn't you tell me? You're having an affair with a married man, aren't you?'

Pippa squirmed.

'Come on, admit it!' I bullied. 'He's married, isn't he?'

'Only a little bit.'

'Only a little bit!' I shrieked. 'Married is married, Pippa. I'm shocked, shocked to the core.' I stared at her. 'What's it like?'

'What's what like?'

'Well, you know, doing it with a married man.'

'Exactly the same as doing it with a single man but with more logistic difficulties, and, anyway, it's not that shocking; it happens all the time.'

'Not to you, it doesn't,' I retorted. 'You've always been dead against that sort of thing. A dirty little slut is what you called Miranda Baxter when she went off with that bit of rough from Rumbelows – remember? You came over very high and mighty about all that!' I was enjoying myself immensely now. For the first time that day a little bit of moral superiority was creeping my way.

Pippa squirmed some more. 'That was different, Polly. That chap from Rumbelows had been married for years and had about ten children. Josh has only been married a year and he hasn't got any kids.'

'So why doesn't he leave his wife then?'

'Well, he feels so guilty. He knows it was a big mistake to marry her but he thinks that to walk out after only a year would be a bit rough. He feels he ought to give it a bit longer, and I can understand that.'

'You can? Crikey, you're more gullible than I thought! Get real, Pippa. He's having his cake and eating it and licking the bloody mixing bowl too!'

'What a distasteful analogy,' said Pippa, looking prim.

'Well, it's true – any fool can see that. He's got wifey at home cooking his dinner and ironing his shirts, and then he's got you at work running around in your Chanel suit being all sexy and provocative –'

'I am his assistant –'

'Doesn't mean you have to sleep with him!' I snorted. 'It's not part of your job description, is it? Come on, Pippa, he's got it made, but what's in it for you?'

'It's not as simple as that.'

'Course it is,' I scoffed, 'you're just a bit on the side as far as he's concerned.'

'How can you say that! You haven't even met him. He's mad about me, if you must know, and he's definitely going to leave his wife – it's just a question of time.'

Even as she said it I think she realized how empty and naïve the words sounded. Her eyes slithered past me and I detected a glimmer of a tear. She was smitten all right. I sighed, moral superiority forgotten.

'Oh dear. How unlike you to get yourself into this sort of mess.'

'I know,' she said miserably, pulling at the grass, 'and there's not a damn thing I can do about it.'

One or two practical suggestions along the lines of binning him occurred to me, but I decided not to voice them.

'Does everyone at work know?'

She shrugged. 'I'm not really sure. We keep it as quiet as possible but I've a feeling some people have guessed, Sam in particular.'

The back door clicked open behind us. We turned in unison and saw Nick and Bruce slowly making their way towards us across the lawn, their heads bowed, deep in conversation.

'Don't tell Nick,' muttered Pippa quickly. 'He'll be horrified. You know what he's like about that sort of thing.'

I nodded. 'I won't,' I promised, and meant it. Nick had some pretty uncompromising views about the sanctity of marriage and I didn't think he'd find Pippa's predicament very amusing.

Bruce's eyes were shining as he reached us.

'Nick's been showing me the antiques!' he beamed. 'Pippa, you should see some of the things he's got in there; the porcelain collection is out of this world, and the pictures – God, there's even a little Renoir drawing in the bathroom! You really must see it, Pippa. It's quite superb!'

'I have,' she smiled, 'but I'm afraid it's rather wasted on me. Makes a nice change to have an appreciative audience, eh, Nick?'

'It certainly does, and Bruce really knows his stuff. I've got one piece of porcelain, which is incredibly difficult to date. I'd eventually pinned it down to being mid-eighteenth century but Bruce here assures me it's late seventeenth.' He turned to Bruce. 'You must come and have a proper look around when there's more time. I know you've got to get back to London now but if you're ever in the area, drop by, there are some things in the safe I'd like you to cast your eye over.'

Bruce flushed with pleasure. 'I – I'd love to,' he stammered. 'I'd be absolutely delighted! My mother's in hospital in Truro so I come down here quite a lot, actually.'

'Oh, I'm sorry, anything –'

'Cancer, I'm afraid, and she's very old now too, so I come down about once a fortnight. I could easily pop in.'

'Great.' Nick smiled. 'Don't forget. Come and see us whenever you like.'

He held out his hand and Bruce pumped it up and down enthusiastically, his camp, mincing manners momentarily evaporated. 'I certainly will!'

Pippa got to her feet and brushed the grass off her bottom. 'Come on then, Bruce, let's hit the road and let these people get back to their muck-spreading.'

She gave me a hug. 'Ring me soon,' she whispered, 'we'll talk more.'

I hugged her back, sorry to see her go. She turned to Nick and took his arm as we wandered back to the house.

'You've made his day,' she murmured. 'Most people write him off as a big joke but you took him seriously.'

'Well, he knows what he's talking about,' said Nick. 'I was genuinely impressed. I wasn't flattering him.'

'I know, but thanks anyway.'

We walked back through the house and waved them off from the front steps. With the flick of a switch Pippa converted her covetable car into a sex machine and they roared off down the drive; Pippa's long blonde hair streaming out behind her, Bruce's hand fluttering back to us, Munchkin's red ribbon blowing in the breeze.

Nick put his arm round me as we watched them turn through the stone gateposts into the road and disappear around the corner.

'Good to see Pippa,' he murmured, 'but I couldn't live that sort of life any more, could you? The whole London scene, the social life, the ad-racket, thank God we were able to escape down here.'

'Mmmmm . . . thank God,' I murmured.

Nick gave my shoulder a squeeze. 'Must dash, I've got some fences to put up in the far field. I'll see you around tea time.' He strode off.

I turned and walked slowly back through the house. No, I mused, I certainly couldn't live like that any more – I'd gladly left it all behind me, and I'd gladly swapped it for this – but all the same . . . I made myself a cup of coffee and wandered upstairs. I paused on the landing and stared out of the window at the fields stretching far away into the distance. It was certainly beautiful, but . . . quiet. I frowned down into my coffee mug. What was this, Polly? What was the meaning of this sense of dissatisfaction that was slowly but surely seeping through me?

Chapter Four

I sat down and eyed my reflection in the dressing-table mirror. Damn, it was true; it was written all over my face, look – there, dissatisfaction – now why? Why, when only a couple of hours ago I'd been counting my blessings in the sunshine, secure in the knowledge that life couldn't possibly get any better? It was Pippa's fault of course. She'd come down and put the wind up me, jolted me out of my complacency with the earth-shattering revelation that I'd been living a boring life – me! The luckiest girl in the world!

I picked up my hairbrush and frowned, pulling some hair out of it. OK, granted, the last couple of years had been rather quiet, but never dull, never. Why, the gymkhana had only been yesterday and there was so much else to look forward to. The village fête for instance, that was only six weeks away, quite the social event of the county, and I'd been promoted to Tombola this year rather than Guess the Weight of the Cake like last year. I dragged my brush grimly through my hair as I recalled that fiasco. God, what a disaster. Some goon had forgotten to bring the cake along, so some other goon had suggested they guess the weight of me instead. I'd spent the whole after-noon with steam pouring out of my nostrils, roaring, 'What! Don't be so bloody ridiculous, I'm nowhere *near* eleven stone!'

Still, this year would be more fun, and of course there was the hunt ball to look forward to at Christmas – that was always an absolute riot. Yes, all right, eight months away. One village fête and one hunt ball. I put down my brush and gazed at my sorrowful reflection. Suddenly I scowled – oh, for goodness' sake, Polly, don't be ridiculous. You have a terrific time down here, you know you do! My eyes in the mirror looked shifty; they could spot a lie at twenty paces. I sighed.

It was true of course – country life was rather quiet. When I'd married Nick I'd willingly settled down to become a devoted, home-loving farmer's wife, determined to put my wild-child days of nightclubbing and partying behind me, but I couldn't help feeling slightly peeved that the opportunity to resist any form of social whirling had failed to even present itself. The closest I got to a night on the town was supper at the seafood restaurant in Helford, with Nick yawning into his prawns at nine o'clock because he had to get up and milk the cows at dawn.

Then there was the holiday question. The fact that farmers tended to summer where they wintered had come as quite a shock to me. Why, even as an impoverished secretary I'd managed two weeks horizontal and motionless in the sun, and I would even have been prepared to traipse around monasteries or peer at lumps of stone in the sweltering heat as men are wont to do, but no. Apparently we had to continue to traipse around the corn fields and peer at the sheep. Terrific.

My chin quivered momentarily in the mirror. I steadied it fiercely, horrified at my audacity. Bloody hell, Polly, don't be so wet! Don't sit here in your enormous pile of a house moaning about lack of entertainment, don't gaze out at your thousand acres complaining that life's a bitch – you're the luckiest girl in the world, remember? Get a grip!

I tried. I tried really hard. Then I thought of Pippa. Pippa, rushing back to London, swinging into her Soho office, laughing with the girls, flirting with the boys, rushing to the loo to touch up her make-up, bouncing into Josh's office to report her findings, sitting down opposite him and feeling the electric current surge between them – did I miss all that? A small, remote corner of my mind admitted that I did. Not the work, of course, but the fun, the excitement, the camaraderie.

I sighed, picked up my brush again and wondered idly if perhaps Pippa and her gang could pop in here for lunch, or a drink, when they came down to shoot their commercial, en route to whichever location they eventually chose. My brush froze in mid stroke and I gazed steadily at my reflection. Whichever . . . location . . . they eventually . . . chose. I watched my cheeks grow pink with excitement. My heart began to thump.

Why not? Why on earth not? It wasn't out of the question at all, why shouldn't they shoot it here? I'd dismissed it out of hand when Bruce had suggested it earlier, but if I could get round Nick – and I was sure I could – why ever not? It was perfect! Absolutely perfect!

I jumped off the stool and danced around the room, hugging myself gleefully. Oh, Polly, you clever girl, you clever, clever girl! It was a brilliant idea! I stopped twirling for a second and gazed out of the window. Imagine – a film crew in my house, shooting in my grounds!

I could see it all now, and I could see me in the thick of it – not this me of course, a different me, a pencil-thin, leg-waxed, highlighted me, clad in a succession of different outfits – Jasper Conran one day, Armani the next – smiling and laughing, dispensing tea to the crew, chilled white wine to the director, largesse to one and all. Oh, and the actors of course. I'd chat like mad to them – famous ones probably; they were all so hard up these days they practically all did commercials. God, it would be terrific fun!

My imagination went into furious overdrive as I saw us all having lunch together, out on the lawn probably. I'd cook a fabulous stew – well, buy some ham perhaps – and we'd sit at those long trestle tables like something out of *Far from the Madding Crowd*. I'd be at one end dispensing the stew – ham – and Nick would be at the other being all handsome and witty, and we'd have huge carafes of red wine and everyone would get incredibly merry and the really attractive actors would flirt like mad with me.

Then after lunch I'd wander over to watch the shoot and sit in one of those director's chairs with the canvas backs, looking elegant in something beige and tailored. No – no, I wouldn't, I'd wear black jeans and a waistcoat and look dead trendy and efficient with a pencil behind my ear and a clipboard to take notes, because of course as a local girl I'd become invaluable in some terribly technical kind of way, something to do with understanding the vagaries of the Cornish light, perhaps. Anyway, whatever it was, there I'd be, part of the crew practically, watching the shoot, which – yes – which would be going rather badly that day due to the fact that the leading lady kept forgetting her lines. The director would look a bit worried, he'd raise his eyebrows to heaven, then look over and give me a grim smile. I'd smile back, raising my eyebrows too – sympathetically of course, not bitchily – and then suddenly, that's right, *suddenly*, he'd stare at me in a more piercing, professional kind of way. He'd walk over slowly, scratch his chin thoughtfully and say something like, 'Tell me, Polly, have you ever done any acting?'

I gasped with excitement, threw myself on my bed in a fit of giggles and stuffed the duvet in my mouth.

Yes, yes, yes! This was it! This was the answer to all my problems! Not that I needed an answer, I thought hastily, and not that I had much of a problem, but having a film crew around would – well, it would certainly razz things up a bit, wouldn't it? Put something of a bomb under rural life?

I flipped over on to my back and stared at the ceiling. There was no doubt about it, it had to happen. But how? How would I ever get round Nick? How could I ever get him to agree?

Suddenly I sat bolt upright. Money. Of course, that was it. Hadn't he just said we were really strapped for cash, and hadn't Bruce also said we'd be generously reimbursed for our trouble? I'd make damn sure we were. I'd make sure Pippa got us such an unbelievably generous deal that Nick would find it impossible to refuse – we'd get hundreds, thousands, hundreds of thousands. I hadn't a clue how much actually, but we'd trouser a hell of a wedge, enough for a new tractor anyway, or – or a few miles of fencing. Nick would be delighted! But how to persuade him first of his impending delight?

I sucked the duvet and thought hard. This called for

tact and diplomacy. No good charging in feet first as usual and simply demanding it should happen. I had to be clever, subtle even, catch him at a good moment, when his defences were down, and if not his defences then certainly his . . . trousers.

I leaped off the bed, ran to my wardrobe and rifled feverishly through my clothes. Yes, of course, I'd seduce him. He liked nothing more than to feel I'd made an effort – these days that ran along the lines of washing under my arms and ironing a T-shirt – but this time I'd pull out all the stops, wear something low, something sexy, something outrageous, something – my hand froze on a hanger. I pulled it out and stared at the garment it suspended.

It was a basque. The one I'd worn under my wedding dress, in fact. It was white, lacy, boned for maximum figure hug and boob uplift and utterly beautiful and sexy. Sadly Nick had never seen it because of course after the wedding I'd taken off all my finery and changed into my going-away kit. Could this be his big chance? I fingered the lace. Why not? Naturally I'd wear my normal clothes on top so he wouldn't suspect a thing, but halfway through supper in the kitchen or – no, a candlelit dinner in the dining room – yes, halfway through that, just when he was feeling all relaxed and mellow and full of *boeuf en croute* and claret and was stroking my hand and murmuring, 'That was delicious, darling, what's for pudding?' Just at that moment, I'd whip off my T-shirt and say, 'I am!'

A trifle obvious? So what! He'd either find it hysterically funny or a massive turn-on, and either way we were bound to end up in a frantic heap on the floor, laughing like drains and tearing each other's clothes off. Then just as he was getting really carried away, just as he seriously couldn't control himself any longer and his breath was hurricaning into my ear, I'd hit him with the big plan. How could he refuse? Softened up by wine, good food, candle-light and tantalized beyond belief by my delectable, lace-encased body, he'd have no option but to pant, 'Yes, my darling, do whatever you want, of course your friends can shoot their commercial on my land, just let me get that bloody basque off you!'

I clutched the garment to my chest in delight, did a quick twirl of exultation around the room, and then abruptly stopped. I swung around to the mirror, holding the basque up against me. I peered more closely. It looked as if it might be a bit on the small side; I had been jolly slim on my wedding day. I frowned. Oh well, I'd just have to diet like crazy. Cut out all the biscuits. Simple.

Now! I threw the basque on the floor and set my hands decisively on my hips. The first thing I had to do was ring Pippa and arrange it all before she booked another location.

I raced downstairs and rang her at work. Her secretary answered – her *secretary*, for God's sake.

'Pippa Hamilton's office.'

'Oh, hello, I know Pippa's not there but could you ask her to call me, please?'

'Yes, of course. She's on her way back from Cornwall, but I'll get her to give you a ring later.'

'Thank you so much, the *moment* she comes through the door, please. My name's Polly Penhalligan. Please could you tell her it's very important, it's regarding the location of the forthcoming shoot,' I said importantly.

'I certainly will,' she replied respectfully.

I replaced the receiver and walked slowly upstairs again, chewing my thumbnail and smiling to myself. How uplifting it was to have something to look forward to, to have a plan. I was a great one for plans, but when the biggest and most ambitious one of my career had miraculously come off and I'd become Mrs Penhalligan I'd collapsed in a heap, flummoxed by my own success, all planned out, so to speak.

But not any longer. No, this plan was equally ambitious and far-sighted and would really put Trewarren on the map. Oh yes, this commercial was just the beginning. When it was over I'd register the house with loads of other film companies and they'd all be clamouring to use it. Remakes of *Pride and Prejudice*, *Rebecca*, *Wuthering Heights* – they'd all be made here. It would become a local tourist attraction; people would come from miles around to peer over the walls. I might even open it to the public, give guided tours, have a tea shop, sell souvenirs – a touch of the Raine Spencers – God, there'd be no end to the moneymaking schemes I'd dream up. I'd be an entrepreneur – more like Richard Branson than Raine Spencer, actually – it would give me a sense of purpose.

I sat down decisively at my dressing table and began to cleanse my face vigorously. I grinned at my reflection. Gosh, life was easy once you got a grip on it. I reached for a cigarette and wondered what else I could do to improve my lot. I dropped the cigarette. Yes. Absolutely. If Pippa could do it, so could I. I'd give up right now.

Pulling open my dressing-table drawer, I rooted around amongst the empty deodorant bottles and chewed-up lipsticks and found an ancient packet of Nicorette patches, bought on a whim with an excruciating hangover and an overwhelming desire never to smoke again. I'd obviously opened them because the instructions appeared to be missing, but I'd certainly never used them.

Now what did one do, I wondered – stick them on the arm? Like this? I slapped one on my wrist and waited. Nothing seemed to be happening. If anything, my need for a fag was increasing. I eyed the packet of Silk Cut and my hand twitched nervously. No, I mustn't. My hand twitched again. I shook more patches out and slapped one on the other arm – oh, and one on my cheek too, because perhaps it helped if it went near the mouth? I slapped one on the other cheek just for good measure. Well, that was four and I was still dying for a cigarette. In fact I seemed to have got hold of one, how odd. My other hand crept towards the lighter. Perhaps if I put a patch actually on my mouth it would have more of a chance to ward off the cigarette when it approached? It would certainly make it jolly hard to get it in. I was just plastering one over my lips with one hand and simultaneously trying to cram a cigarette in with the other, when I heard the door handle turn behind me.

I swung around to see Mrs Bradshaw, my daily, standing in the doorway. We stared at each other for a moment, then I ripped the patch off my lips.

'Oh! Er, Mrs Bradshaw, I didn't hear you arrive, I was just – just tidying up my drawers!'

Mrs Bradshaw cast a cold eye around the room, taking in the unmade bed, the still-drawn curtains, the piles of dirty washing on the floor, the clothes spilling out of the chest of drawers, and, in the midst of all this chaos, the lady of the house, in a chocolate-stained T-shirt and covered in patches. She folded her arms and pursed her lips.

I caught sight of my reflection. 'Oh! Oh, yes, these plasters, cut myself slicing the bread this morning, so silly. Now, wh-what exactly are you – we doing this morning?' I twittered nervously.

Mrs Bradshaw frightened the life out of me, but I'd inherited her with the house and had kept her on out of a sense of loyalty. Can't think why, she certainly didn't feel any loyalty to me. In fact, word had filtered back to me via the village that she'd fervently hoped Nick would marry his previous girlfriend, the glamorous actress Serena Montgomery, so she could swank that she worked for a film star. According to my sister-in-law Sarah, who lived on the adjacent farm, during Serena's brief occupation at Trewarren she and Mrs Bradshaw had been as thick as thieves, so it must have been a severe blow when he'd eventually plumped (an appropriate verb) for me instead. Not much kudos attached to charring for an erstwhile secretary with dyed roots, I imagined, a suspicion that was confirmed the day I overheard her on the telephone referring to me as 'that jumped-up fancy piece wot married my boss'.

Of course I should have fired her there and then, but I didn't. I had some crazy, misguided notion that I could charm her. I went for the egalitarian I-was-a-worker-too-once approach, but unfortunately overdid it to such an extent that sometimes I wondered who was working for whom. I was forever suggesting tea breaks lest I should be accused of overworking her, the result being that she took complete advantage of me and spent most of the morning sitting on her backside eating me out of chocolate biscuits and watching me with disdain as I made nervous small talk. Like now.

'Another beautiful day, Mrs Bradshaw!' I gabbled.

Mrs Bradshaw eyed me with a mixture of distrust and incredulity. 'If you like rain it is,' she growled eventually, in her deep Cornish brogue.

'Oh, er, has it been raining? Silly me, I hadn't noticed, only it was so beautiful earlier on, and of course I've got the curtains drawn so I can't see – not that I haven't opened them yet, I have, been up for hours, in fact. No, I was trying on some clothes, you see, didn't want anyone peeking in!'

I think it occurred to both of us to wonder who, apart from the sheep, might be lurking in the open country desperate for a peek at my untoned body, but we let it pass.

Mrs Bradshaw pursed her lips, waiting for her orders. What she probably would have liked to hear was, 'Right, Mrs B, clean the floors, do the windows, polish the silver and when you've finished all that I'll see what else there is,' to which she would have doubtless responded, 'Right you are, Mrs Penhalligan,' and scurried about her business, mop in hand.

Instead, I tended to fidget awkwardly, scratch my chin and say things like, 'Well, gosh, you probably know this place better than I do, why don't you just sort of see what needs doing and, um, have a quick flick round with a duster and maybe a Hoover if it's not too much trouble,' to which she'd sneer and move slowly towards the broom cupboard, before moving even more slowly into another room, probably to put her feet up. Mrs Bradshaw had a lot of sit-down-and-stop when it came to cleaning my house.

This morning, however, I'd had orders from above to get her to do something specific.

'Can't you get that bloody woman to clean the loos? Anyone would think it was beneath her,' Nick had stormed.

It was true. Someone was going to have to get to grips with some rather unattractive limescale and I was damned if it was going to be me. On the other hand I had the feeling she was damned if it was going to be her either. I braced myself, took a deep breath, and took the plunge, loowards, so to speak.

'Um, Mrs Bradshaw, there is actually something I'd like, or rather Nick and I' – I shamelessly dragged him into this for moral support – 'would like you to do this morning.'

I paused. Now most normal people would have taken advantage of this gap in the dialogue to say something like, 'Oh yes?' or 'Really?' but Mrs Bradshaw stayed silent. She just stared unblinkingly at me, like something out of a horror movie. I was rapidly losing my nerve.

'It's – it's the loos,' I managed.

The silence prevailed.

'Yes,' I went on courageously, 'I'd like you to clean them.'

There. It was out. I gulped, waiting. She eyed me contemptuously.

'There's nothing I can do about them toilets,' she growled. 'They're too old. You got limescale in them; they need replacin'. Them toilets have had too much use – that's their problem!'

I nodded vigorously. 'Ah, ah, right. Too much use, how right you are, we do use them an awful lot, too much probably, in fact, we're always using them, I am anyway, all the time!'

She regarded me more with pity than contempt now.

'Oh! Oh, no, not that I use them any more than the next person,' I gabbled, 'no more than is usual – I mean, I don't have, you know, a problem, or anything like that!'

Still the stony silence and the icy glare.

'But how clever of you!' I continued desperately. 'Yes, yes of course, new loos, that's what we need.'

She nodded briefly as if to illustrate that she'd won hands down, and turned to go, but not before she'd stooped to recover my basque from the floor, holding it between thumb and fingertip as if it were something revolting that Badger had brought in. She deposited it gingerly on a chair, gave me one last disdainful glare and left.

I sighed and slumped exhausted on the dressing table. Thank God she'd gone. I ripped my patches off and lit a shaky fag, taking it right down to my toenails. Then I pulled on my clothes and went out to find Nick.

He was in the cow shed, kneeling down, fixing one of the partitions between the stalls. I leaned over, resting my chin on the top.

'Mrs Bradshaw says we need new loos,' I reported gloomily. 'She says ours have had it.'

'Balls,' retorted Nick without even looking up. 'They just need a damn good clean. Tell her to pull her finger out.'

'Don't be silly, I couldn't possibly! I'm terrified of her!'

Nick paused. He wiped his mouth with the back of his

hand and looked up at me. 'Are you? Well, sack her then, for God's sake.'

I looked at him in horror. 'Oh, I couldn't do that either – it would be all round the village in minutes.' I had an idea. 'I know, you sack her!'

'Don't be silly, Polly, you'll have to do it, otherwise it'll be all round the village that you didn't have the nerve and you got your husband to do it.'

I sighed and wandered back to the house. He was right of course, so I was stuck with her. Too much of a woolly-minded liberal to tell her to buck her ideas up or I'd dock her wages, and too much of a lily-livered coward to send her packing. We'd just have to carry on as normal with her munching her way through my biscuit tin, despising me all the while, and me pussyfooting around trying to keep out of her way. I slunk down to the village for an hour or two with this very aim in mind, and when I came back through the front door was relieved to hear her slam simultaneously out of the back, bang on four o'clock and not a moment later.

Later that afternoon I rang Pippa. Finally, at six thirty, just when I thought she must have gone straight home, she answered.

'Pippa Hamilton.'

'Pippa, it's me, did you get my message?'

'Yes, I was going to ring you, but I've literally just sat down. I need to go through some papers, make a few calls, see my boss and generally sort myself –'

'Well, never mind about all that, this is important. Listen, I've decided to do it.'

'Do what?'

'The location thing. Lend you the house, the grounds, whatever you like.'

'Really? Are you sure? What did Nick say?'

'Oh, er, don't worry about Nick. I'll get round him later.'

'You mean you haven't asked him?'

'Well, not exactly, but I'll ask him soon. I know he'll agree.'

'Will he? I should have thought he'd hate the very idea.'

'Pippa,' I said a trifle crossly, 'believe me, I know my own husband. He'll be thrilled, absolutely thrilled. Especially when I tell him how much we're going to make from it.'

'Well, I'll have to talk to Bruce about that. I'm not sure what sort of figure he had in mind, but if you're sure, I'll put it forward at the next meeting as a suggestion.'

'A suggestion? You mean it's not definite? I thought you said this place was ideal?'

'It is, but I can't possibly just say yes over the phone. I'll have to talk to Sam and we'll have to show the client some pictures and that sort of thing.'

'OK, OK, I'll pop some photos in the post to you.'

'Fine, but I have to tell you we saw quite a good place in Devon on the way back, so don't get your hopes up too much.'

'What?' I was aghast. 'In Devon? But it wasn't as nice, surely?'

'Well, it was quite pretty, and closer to London of course.'

'Well – well, pretend you didn't see it!'

'What?'

'Pretend you didn't go there – they'll never know.'

'Polly, I can't do that!'

'Course you can! Pippa, think of all the fun we'll have – it'll be just like old times! You can stay here at the house and we'll stay up late drinking and smoking – well, drinking anyway, and we'll –'

'Polly, I can't possibly stay at the house. I have to stay with the crew.'

'Do you? Oh. Oh, but surely –'

'Listen, I've got to run, my other phone's going. I'll talk to Sam and Bruce and ring you back, OK? But don't bank on it – it's by no means certain. Bye.'

She hung up. I stared at the receiver incredulously. By no means certain? What on earth was she talking about? Surely she could wangle it? Didn't she know my happiness depended on it? What did it matter if the house in Devon was better? I shook my head in amazement. Goodness, what on earth had got into poor old Pippa? She was sounding so cross and businesslike these days.

I spent the next few days loitering by the telephone, willing it to ring. I was terrified Nick would get to it first to be casually informed that a film crew would be descending on him shortly, so I craftily unplugged the phone in the bedroom and set up camp by the one in the hall. I sat for hours on the really uncomfortable wooden chair at the bottom of the stairs pretending to do my tapestry. I'd started it when I first got married, thinking it was the sort of thing ladies who lived in large houses probably did, but I'd only managed about two square inches in as many years. It was predominantly a revolting shade of mauve and I loathed the very sight of it, but it was serving an awfully useful purpose now.

68

'Still doing that delightful cushion cover?' grinned Nick as he passed by for the fourth time that day. 'Why on earth d'you do it here? Surely the light's better in the drawing room?'

'I like it here. I think I shall cover this chair with it when I've finished, so it sort of puts me in the mood sitting here.'

Nick eyed me suspiciously. Unfortunately he knew me too well these days.

'You're up to something, Polly, I can tell.'

'Me?' I enquired, eyebrows raised innocently. 'Up to something? Don't be ridiculous, of course I'm not – I just like sitting here, that's all.'

'All right, have it your way, but I smell a rat.'

'Oh, Nick, just because I fancy a change of scene you automatically assume that – I'LL GET IT!' I screeched as the telephone rang.

I almost broke his fingers, wrenching it from his hand as he went to pick it up. Nick backed away in surprise.

'Yes? Hello?' I gasped. 'Pippa!'

I swung round to him, flushed and triumphant. 'It's for me! It's Pippa!'

'So I gathered,' he murmured, watching me in amazement. He didn't move.

I put my hand over the mouthpiece. 'See you later then,' I hissed, shooing him away with my other hand.

Nick shook his head incredulously, turned and walked out of the front door into the garden.

'Pippa!' I hissed, turning away and cupping my hand round the mouthpiece to muffle my voice. 'What's the news?'

'Well, it's all set. They liked the photos and they're planning to start shooting on the fifth.'

'Really? Seriously? You mean it's on? YIPPEE!' I leaped up and punched the air. Through the open front door Nick's head rotated in surprise, but he strode on.

'God, that's fantastic, Pippa, absolutely brilliant! The fifth of what?'

'May, of course.'

'May? But that's – that's only a couple of weeks away, isn't it?'

'About ten days. I know it's quite soon, but we're so behind schedule we've just got to get a move on. That will be all right, won't it?' Pippa sounded anxious. 'I've more or less said it's definite because you were so keen.'

'Oh yes, yes, fine.' Ten days. Christ!

'And Nick's OK about the whole thing?'

'Oh yes, delighted. Um, how much will we get for it, Pippa?'

'About seven hundred pounds, I should think, but I'll check with Bruce. D'you want to talk to him now?'

'Er, no, no, that's all right.'

Seven hundred pounds. I'd expected slightly more than that somehow. Still, it was better than nothing and it would certainly help our ailing finances.

'Oh, and, Polly, could you possibly send me a list of local hotels? I'll have to arrange for the crew to stay somewhere. Any ideas?'

'Sure, there are a few places in Helston. I'll give it some thought.'

'Great. Oh, and also a local kennel for the dogs.'

'Dogs?'

'Yes, they'll have to stay somewhere too.'

'What dogs?'

'The dogs in the commercial, you moron. I told you it was for Doggy Chocs Deluxe, didn't I?'

I sat down hard on the hall chair.

'Um, yes, at least . . . well, I probably forgot. Er, how many dogs?'

'Oh, not more than twenty, I shouldn't think.'

'*Twenty!*' I gripped the banisters.

'Well, I don't think it'll be more than that, but it all depends on how many Sam wants in the charging scene.'

The charging scene! I covered my eyes with my hand and groaned. Jesus Christ – the sheep! The cows! Twenty charging dogs! Nick!

'Polly? Polly, is this OK? I really hope so because it's all arranged now and I shall be in the deepest shit imaginable if it isn't.'

I gulped. 'Um, no, no, it's fine, Pippa, leave it to me,' I croaked. 'I'll – I'll get back to you about hotels and, um,' I gasped, 'kennels.'

'Great. Speak to you soon. Sorry I haven't got time to gas, but we'll have a long gossip when I come down – I've loads to tell you. See you in ten days!'

'Look forward to it,' I said weakly.

I replaced the receiver and walked, rather shakily, upstairs. I gazed out of my bedroom window at the pastoral scene below. All was quiet, all was tranquil. In the distance I could see Nick leaning against the tractor, talking to Larry, who was fixing a wheel. The field beyond them was dotted with sheep and young lambs, and the one beyond that with cows and their calves. In ten days' time they'd be dotted with lights, cameras, vans, trucks, a film crew, actors and twenty mad, rampaging dogs. My mouth felt inexplicably dry, my hands clammy. Blimey. What the hell had I done?

Chapter Five

Three days passed, four, five – still I hadn't told him. On the sixth day I took my courage into my trembling hands and decided tonight was the night.

I stole into Helston and bought the best fillet steak money could buy, a packet of the ubiquitous jam-tart pastry, and a tin of pâté. Originally, I'd imagined myself lovingly creating the last two components, but fear had got the better of my culinary skills and it was all I could do to slap the pâté on the fillet, cover it with frozen pastry and shove the whole lot in the oven before staggering to the wheel-back chair by the Aga and collapsing in a petrified heap.

Mrs Bradshaw, who was pretending to clean out a cupboard, was eyeing my preparations with amusement.

'Got a dinner party then, 'ave you?'

'Er, yes, something like that, Mrs Bradshaw,' I muttered, biting my nails.

'Pulling out all the stops for this one, ain't you?' she smirked. 'Made a pudding, 'ave you? Or is that frozen too?'

'What?' I was miles away – in the far field actually – wrestling with a rabid dog who'd got his jaws clasped tightly round a lamb's neck. 'A pudding? No, no that's . . . that's me!'

I leaped up. God, forget the dinner, there were some

serious preparations to do – I had to go and make myself alluring; we were talking a couple of hours here.

I fled upstairs and ran a hot bath, pouring as many smellies into it as I could lay my hands on. I wallowed for a long while, letting the extract of horse chestnut do its steamy business and eyeing my tummy and thighs nervously.

Luckily, the diet I'd chosen to follow over the last six days had been amazingly successful. It was called the too-bloody-terrified-to-eat diet. Every time I'd got a morsel of food near my mouth, I'd felt as sick as a dog, which had reminded me of the twenty or so soon to be marauding through our fields, which had reminded me in turn of Nick's unamused face, which had instantly made me drop whatever it was I'd been contemplating sending down the red lane.

Consequently, I'd lost about half a stone already, a hell of a lot, but was it enough, I wondered nervously, eyeing the basque hanging on the back of the bathroom door. I hadn't had the nerve to try it on yet, but time would tell. I stepped out of the bath, dried myself and stepped gingerly into the garment.

Time did tell. Half an hour later I was still wriggling around on my bedroom floor, squeezing bits of recalcitrant flesh into position as I tugged on the coat hanger that I'd slotted into the zip for extra leverage.

'Breathe in and – pull!' I muttered for the umpteenth time. 'Breathe in and – pull!' Jesus, the zip must be stuck or something, or the basque must have shrunk in the wash, because this was just ridiculous! There was no way I was this fat, no way!

I was working up a sensational sweat now, my hands were dripping wet and slipping off the coat hanger every time I tugged at it, my fringe was plastered nicely to my forehead and the rest of my hair was frizzing attractively in the heat. But I wasn't giving up, no way. I gritted my teeth and tried again, wrestling with the zip. No way, José, I was *not* giving up! I breathed in so hard my chest hit my chin, gave the zip one last superhuman wrench and – yes! It rocketed up to the top. I'd done it! It was up!

I lay there beaming with relief, albeit somewhat numbly. You see, I couldn't move, I was paralysed from chest to hips. I could move my neck, my shoulders and anything bottomwards, but anything pertaining to the torso was locked into the vicelike grip of this deceptively flimsy, lacy undergarment. My waist for instance. Impossible. I simply didn't have one any more, didn't bend in the middle; I had a poker for a backbone.

There was precious little scope for breathing either. One had to sort of – well, hyperventilate really. I gave it a go. Yes – short, chuggy breaths, that was the answer, going no further than the throat, and certainly not down to the lungs or tummy, a short circuit of nose, mouth and not much else. I practised for a bit and when I'd mastered it, decided it was time to try standing up.

I wriggled over to my bed and, with a little help from my bedside table, levered myself slowly upright. I swayed slightly as everything sorted itself out – blood, heart, lungs, kidneys, liver – they were all having to relinquish their old slots and jostle for new positions and the jostling was having an unfortunate effect on my equilibrium. I steadied myself on the wall and when I was sure at least a smidgen of oxygen had got to my brain, blinked hard and prepared for the acid test.

With my shoulders necessarily pushed up somewhere near my ears and my arms swinging around like an ape, I turned and addressed the mirror. I blinked. Gosh. Well, the top half didn't look too bad, I spilled riotously over in what could almost be called a voluptuous, alluring manner. Unfortunately I spilled out at the bottom too, just as voluptuously, but not quite so alluringly. I frowned at the rolling flesh which galloped so wantonly around my thighs. Where on earth had it all come from? Some of it was stuff I'd never even seen before.

I deliberately went a bit cross-eyed, thus blurring my vision as I went for The Whole Effect. Hmmm ... The Whole Effect was rather like a particularly porky sausage in the grip of a very determined bandage, but still, I consoled myself, it was really only the top half that mattered. By the time he'd got down to this stage the basque would be coming off anyway, wouldn't it?

Suddenly I froze. Heavy footsteps were coming down the corridor towards me. Christ, Nick! I just had time to throw on a dressing gown as he poked his head around the door.

'Everything all right?' he enquired.

'Yes, fine,' I twittered nervously. 'Why?'

'No reason, just haven't seen you for a while.' He stared. 'You look awfully pink, Polly, and what's happened to your hair?'

'Oh, er, it's just gone a bit frizzy, that's all – hot bath.'

'Just what I'm going to have, see you later.' He almost went, then popped his head back. 'Incidentally, something in the oven smelled a bit suspect. I turned it off but you might take a look.' He disappeared in the direction of the bathroom.

Christ, the beef! I quickly toned down my florid face with some talc, threw on jeans and a T-shirt, and with a little help from the banisters, lowered myself painfully downstairs to see what was cooking.

Burning was more like it. I pulled it from the oven and saw at a glance that the black pastry would have to go. I picked it off with a knife and was relieved to see that it had at least protected the fillet which, though cooked to distraction, still vaguely resembled a piece of meat. I threw some broccoli into one pan, some new potatoes into another and then, all cooked out, hobbled into the drawing room in search of something horizontal on which to prostrate myself.

Breathing in an upright position was becoming a real problem now; my insides were being crushed to smithereens and only a prone position seemed to give any sort of relief. I lowered myself painfully on to the sofa, thinking that what I really wanted to do was take this bloody thing off and have a telly supper and an early night. Never mind, it would all be over soon, and no pleasure without pain, et cetera, et cetera. I lay still, trying to sneak some air into my lungs. Damn, I'd forgotten to light the candles in the dining room. I struggled to get up. Sod the candles. I collapsed on my back and shut my eyes, experiencing a bit of head rush. Five minutes later, Nick strode into the room.

'Hello, darling, feeling tired?' He bent over and dropped a kiss on my recumbent form. 'Gosh, you're still pretty hot. Are you sure you're OK?'

'Fine, fine!' I bleated.

'The kitchen smells a bit more appetizing now. What are we having?'

'Oh, just a little *boeuf en cr* . . . *boeuf en* its own, and some seasonal vegetables straight from the garden, lovingly garnished with melted butter and freshly ground black pepper. Nothing very exciting.' I smiled weakly.

'Sounds great. I could just do with a bloody great steak. Shall I lay the table?'

'It's OK, I've done it.'

'Really? Not when I last looked.'

'Oh, not in the kitchen, I thought we'd eat in the dining room.'

'Oh? Who's coming?'

'No one, I just thought it would be nice for a change.'

Nick looked surprised. 'Oh! Oh, right, fine.' He rubbed his hands together and grinned. 'Well, let's go then, shall we? I'm starving.'

'Absolutely! Let's eat!' I grinned maniacally back. I simply couldn't move.

Nick started towards the door, then turned back. 'What's wrong?'

'Nothing, nothing really, it's just I twisted my ankle today and I can't seem to put much weight on it. You couldn't sort of help me, could you?'

'Sure.' Nick hauled me up, much the same way as one would haul up a drawbridge. Plank-like. He frowned.

'Does it hurt much?'

'Good Lord, no.' I shook my head vigorously. 'No, not much at all. You go on and I'll just go and put the finishing touches to supper.'

Walking like Arnie Schwarzenegger, all chest and pectorals, and breathing like an underwater diver, I disappeared off to the kitchen, where I immediately sensed that supper was not going to be the gastronomic delight I'd hoped for. The vegetables were not so much boiled as puréed, and the beef had a barbecued look about it. Still, there was plenty of it and Nick never really minded what he ate as long as it was abundant. I piled the plates high, tottered back into the dining room and, bending at the knees rather than the waist, lowered his plate in front of him.

'This looks great,' said Nick dubiously.

'Good.'

I tottered round and stood by my chair, eyeing it nervously. Would I be able to sit down? Let alone eat? Nick looked up at me.

'Well, come on, let's eat while it's still hot.'

'Sure.'

'Come on then, sit!' he said impatiently, grasping his knife and fork.

'I thought I might stand, actually.'

'Stand? What, to eat supper?'

'Well, it's just that my ankle —'

'Polly, your ankle will feel a damn sight better if you sit down and take your weight off it. Now come on, you're being really peculiar. What the hell's the matter?'

'Nothing, nothing.' I pulled out my chair, bent my knees, and keeping my torso ramrod straight, limbo-danced into it. Somehow I managed to slide into a semi-upright position with my buttocks perched right at the very front of the chair and my head resting on the back.

Nick regarded me over the table. He could just about

79

see my face over the mahogany. I smiled winningly. He sighed, shook his head wearily and began his meal.

'So, um, what sort of a day have you had, darling?' I began brightly, toying with a piece of broccoli that was just about level with my nose.

'Pretty good, actually, the lambs are all doing really well now. I'll probably wean them soon, put the ewes in the meadow by the wood and move the lambs into the back field. It'll give the grass a bit of a rest too.'

'Great, great,' I croaked.

I was beginning to feel most unpleasant. My circulation had clearly been completely cut off at the tummy and I was having violent rushes of blood facewards. It was on fire, absolutely flaming, and I could hardly feel my legs.

'It's good for the grass to have a rest, is it?' I gasped.

Christ, this was hopeless. I'd never get to the pudding stage; I was in too much pain. As soon as he'd finished what he was saying about the sheep, I'd whip my T-shirt off and get it over with. OK, so the seduction scene would come a little earlier than anticipated and he might not have finished his potatoes, but what the hell, anything would be better than this agony.

'Oh, without a doubt, you can't keep sheep grazing a field indefinitely. It strips the goodness out and . . .' And so he went on. And on and on.

More and more blood was rushing round my head now. I didn't know I had so much. Feeling sick and woozy, I concentrated like mad on Nick's face, on his voice, waiting for a gap in the dialogue, willing him to pause. Of course, it wouldn't do to undress when he was in the middle of explaining the grazing rotation, but the moment there was the briefest lull, I'd be in there. I clutched the bottom of my T-shirt, ready at a moment's notice to whip it over my head, but all of a sudden I had to transfer my hands to the table to steady myself. Nick's face was getting fuzzier and fuzzier, his voice fainter and fainter.

From my perspective everything went white, my head felt as if it was going to explode and in one spectacular close-up, the carpet zoomed up to meet me. From Nick's perspective I probably went an attractive shade of purple, foamed at the mouth and collapsed in a heap on the floor.

When I came to, I was lying on a sofa in the drawing room. I had a blanket over me and Nick was kneeling beside me, looking anxious.

'Polly? Polly, can you hear me, are you all right?' His sweet, much-loved voice was full of concern.

'Fine, fine,' I croaked. 'Much better, actually. Did I faint?'

'I'll say – you put the fear of God into me. One minute you were sitting opposite me and the next thing I knew you were flat on your back on the carpet!'

'Well, you know me,' I grinned weakly, 'any time, any place. The slightest opportunity, the least provocation.'

'Well, quite, and that's another thing, what's with the kinky underwear?'

I clutched my torso, I was naked under the blanket.

'My basque! Where is it?'

Nick held it up. 'I took it off – it was crushing the air out of you. No wonder you fainted; it left great weals on your body where those sticks had dug into you. I had no idea you were into bondage and all that sort of thing, Polly, why didn't you say?' He looked keen, if a little nervous.

I groaned. 'It's boned, that's all, to keep it up. It's not supposed to be masochistic, just sexy.'

'Really? It looks like an instrument of torture to me.'

'Well, I was a bit thinner when I last wore it, perhaps it was a bit ambitious.'

'A bit!' Nick guffawed loudly. 'I'll say! You must have used a shoe horn to get into it. I should try losing a couple of stone before you try this little number on again, Polly!'

A couple? I ground my teeth. That hurt. I sat up, clutching my blanket around me.

'Well, I'm sorry it looked so hideous,' I snapped. 'I only put it on for your benefit, you know. I don't enjoy having my insides crushed to a pulp.'

Nick looked puzzled. 'My benefit? Why?'

I bit my lip. 'Oh, it's a long story,' I muttered. Not now, Polly, this was definitely not the right time.

'Come on, darling, please tell me or I'll worry.'

Or was it? I looked at his face: anxious, concerned, loving. Yes, why not? When better, in fact? Here I was, stark naked under a blanket, having recently fainted. I was in an extremely delicate, vulnerable condition, wasn't I? He was hardly likely to ball me out, now was he?

I let the blanket fall down a bit to reveal some cleavage, gazed up at him through my eyelashes, and let my bottom lip wobble a bit.

'OK, but don't be cross, promise?' I whispered.

Big mistake. Nick regarded me grimly. 'Cut the crap, Polly, what's going on?'

Damn. I sighed. 'Well, you see, I wanted to get round you, to ask you something.'

'I gathered that, but is it so awful that you had to get dressed up like Miss Whiplash?'

'Well . . . the thing is,' I lied, 'Pippa asked me to do her an enormous favour, and in a very weak moment I agreed.'

'What?'

'Well,' I struggled on, feeling a bit sick, 'I promised her she could sort of use the house. Just for a bit.'

He frowned. 'The house? What for?'

I squirmed, curling my toes up tight. 'Well, for a shoot, actually, a commercial. As a kind of . . . location.'

His face turned to stone. 'You what?'

'Well, yes, I know I shouldn't have done, stupid of me really, but she was desperate, you see, Nick. She'd been to see all these different houses and none of them were any good and she said this would be ideal. She was looking so down about it all and not looking forward to telling her boss she'd had a wasted journey and' – I swallowed hard – 'well, I just sort of found myself saying yes.'

Nick stared at me. 'Well, you can just sort of find your-self saying no,' he said quietly, his eyes narrowing to two little pieces of flint.

I gasped, and clutched his arm. 'What! Oh no! No, Nick, I can't, you see, I promised.'

'Don't be silly,' he snapped, shaking my hand off. 'There is absolutely no way I'm having a commercial shot here – I'm amazed you even considered it. Did you really think I'd welcome a film crew traipsing all over my house, tramping through the garden, not to mention wrecking the crops and frightening the animals? No, I'm sorry,

Polly, it's out of the question and if you don't telephone Pippa right now and tell her so, I will.'

'Oh, but, Nick, I can't!' I wailed, wringing my hands. 'She'll have arranged everything by now – she'll kill me! Please think it over, we'd get paid really well, you know, you could put a new roof on the barn, maybe even buy some more livestock, it would be a new lease of life for the farm!'

'Rubbish, I didn't work in advertising all those years without knowing we'd get a few hundred quid and a great deal of damage. Now pick up that phone.'

'But, Nick, just think! It could be a going concern, this could be just the beginning, we could let big film companies use it, we'd get thousands, we'd – no! No, don't – all right, I'll do it!'

Nick had reached up to the shelf where the portable phone was, found Pippa's number in the address book, and was even now punching it out. I grabbed the receiver from him.

'Do it then, Polly,' he ordered.

'But –'

'*Now!*'

I gulped and slowly punched out the rest of the number. I bit the inside of my cheek, feeling truly sick. Pippa would never speak to me again, never, but it was either that or divorce. She answered.

'Hello, Pippa?' I quaked. 'It's me, Polly.'

'Hi! How's it going? Looking forward to the big day? I can't believe it's come round so soon! It's all going really smoothly this end, I got your list of hotels and kennels so I've booked all that, oh, and we've got a brilliant crew together, I can't wait to get going now! How are things with you?'

My mouth felt sticky, as if I'd been eating neat peanut butter for days. I dredged up some saliva from somewhere.

'W-e-ll, not so good, actually,' I quavered.

'Oh? Why's that?'

I snuck a look at my grim-faced husband. 'Er, well, you see, it's Nick.'

'Nick? What's wrong with him?'

For one crazy moment I nearly threw myself through this window of opportunity – yes, of course, Nick was ill, terminally ill, we couldn't possibly have a film crew traipsing round the house; he needed peace, quiet. I glanced up at the grim but healthy face beside me. The window slammed shut.

'Er, nothing,' I gulped, tightening my grip on the phone. 'He's not ill or anything but – well, the thing is, Pippa, he won't do it.'

'Do what?'

'The shoot. He won't hear of it.' I clenched my buttocks hard and shut my eyes. 'He won't even consider it. He says no, Pippa.'

There was a terrible silence.

'Pippa? Pippa?' I quavered eventually.

'I don't believe you,' she whispered. 'I thought you asked him ages ago; you said it was all agreed. You can't do this to me, Polly.'

'I know, I know,' I wailed. 'It's all my fault, but you see I kept putting it off and putting it off and actually – I've only just asked him. I'm so sorry, Pippa, really I am, but I'll make it up to you, I promise!'

'I'll lose my job,' she whispered.

'No, no, I'm sure you won't, say something awful's happened, say the cows have got foot-and-mouth, say we're riddled with ringworm, rampant with myxomatosis, say no one's allowed down here, say you'll have to go somewhere else, say –'

'Polly, you don't understand!' she shrieked. 'The crew is booked, the actors are booked, the client's coming down from Manchester and now you're telling me we don't have a location? We're talking about next week, Polly, *next week*! I won't be *able* to find a location, it's impossible!'

'But surely one of the other places you looked at would –'

'Not at a few days' notice – no, no way! And what's Josh going to say, have you thought of that?' Her voice cracked slightly. 'Have you thought about what sort of a position this puts me in? He's not just my boss, you know, he's my boyfriend and things are shaky enough as it is at the moment without me springing this on him – YOU JUST CAN'T DO THIS TO ME, POLLY!' she screamed.

I turned to Nick with eyes like saucers. I put my hand over the mouthpiece. 'I think she's going to cry,' I whispered.

I felt about two inches tall, smaller even. I felt slug-like, worm-like – I wanted to crawl away and die.

'Let me talk to her.' He took the phone, looking grim. 'Pippa, I realize this puts you in a tight spot, but this is quite literally the first I've heard of this little scheme. Polly sprang it on me a moment ago and I'm afraid there's just no way, not with spring lambs around and –' He listened. I watched his jaw drop, his eyes glaze over. 'Next week?' he said incredulously. 'Next week!' He turned to me furiously. 'Did you know it was scheduled for next week?' he hissed.

I nodded shamefacedly, unable to meet his eye. He licked his lips and addressed the receiver.

'Pippa, I had no idea . . . Yes, I can see that . . . Yes, terribly difficult . . . Oh God, yes, the client . . . No, of course not, but I still don't think . . . Oh, Pippa, look, please don't cry . . . No, don't cry, look, I'll – I'll see what I can do . . . Yes, yes, I will . . . all right, yes, I promise . . . It's all right, it's not your fault . . . Yes . . . Yes, yes all right, we'll work something out . . . Yes, I'll move the animals and . . . Dogs? What dogs?'

I stuffed my fist in my mouth, ducked quickly under the blanket and moaned softly.

'I see.' Even the muffling effect of the blanket couldn't disguise the steel in his voice. 'Yes, I see . . . Well, what can I say? I've given you my word now, but I'm not happy. I'm not happy about this at all. How many?'

I moaned again.

'Really.' His voice was dangerously quiet. 'Well, I'll ring you at work tomorrow and find out exactly what the arrangements are . . . Don't apologize, Pippa. It's not your fault . . . Goodbye.'

I stayed exactly where I was, staring into the darkness, biting hard on my knuckles, not daring to move. Two seconds later the protective blanket was whipped abruptly from my face.

'Did you know there were dogs involved?' he hissed into my nose.

'Yes,' I whispered.

'And you still said yes? When we have a farm full of

sheep and lambs? Cows due to calf at any minute? You still said yes?' He stared at me incredulously. I couldn't look at him.

'Christ!' he muttered eventually, shaking his head. 'It simply defies belief! What were you thinking of, Polly?'

'I don't know,' I whispered.

'You don't know. I see.'

There was a terrible silence.

'Sorry,' I whispered.

This was awful. I'd never seen him so furious, so white, so quietly livid.

'You put me in an invidious position, Polly,' he said between clenched teeth. 'They're due to start shooting next week. Pippa was distraught – she'd never have found another location. I had to say yes.'

I grabbed his hand. 'Oh thank you, oh thank you so much! You didn't have to, but you did, thank you!' I kissed his hand madly but he pulled sharply away.

'Don't, Polly.'

'I promise you everything will be all right,' I whispered miserably. 'It'll be really well organized and if a dog so much as sniffs a sheep's backside I'll kill it, I swear, I'll kill it with my own bare hands, but it won't, it won't happen, it'll all go like clockwork, you'll see!'

'It had better,' he said grimly, getting to his feet, 'because I'm warning you, Polly, if any of the animals are worried in any way, or if any of the crops are trampled, I swear to God I'll have them off my land before you can say Doggy Bloody Chocs Deluxe, do I make myself clear?'

'Absolutely,' I gulped.

'I hope so. And one more thing, Polly.' His eyes bored

into me. 'Don't ever try to manipulate me like that again. I'm doing this for Pippa's sake, not yours, please remember that.'

He turned on his heel, marched out of the room and thumped up the stairs.

I sat there quaking, listening to him stomping around upstairs. My God, he was mad. Truly mad. To the uninitiated he might seem tight-lipped, even a little cross, but to the cognoscenti like me he was hopping, steaming, irrevocably mad and I knew from experience that I had to keep right out of his way. Let him blow his top in private then wait for the dust to settle. Any sort of interference at an early stage could be fatal; my head could so easily roll.

I gulped and clutched my knees. Well, that had backfired a bit, hadn't it? And it had all seemed so harmless, just a bit of fun. I bit my lip miserably. I'd put Nick in an impossible position, I could see that now, and it was only his intrinsically kind heart and concern for Pippa that had stopped him from calling the whole thing off – God, I could have cost Pippa her job, how awful of me! Suddenly I flushed with shame. How dare I push people around like that? How dare I manipulate them? What on earth was the matter with me? Why did I get these little ideas into my head and let them snowball away out of control until they were great big scheming boulders? Did other people behave like this, I wondered, or was it just me? For once I felt truly ashamed.

I lay down and tucked myself into a foetal position, shivering miserably, hating myself. It was damned chilly without any clothes on, but there was no way I was going upstairs to get any, no way I was facing Nick. I made a little nest out of the blanket and hugged Badger, who'd quivered nervously up to me, sensing the wrath of Nick that was so often vented on him for chewing the furniture, and offering a wet nose, halitosis and moral support.

I suppose I must have drifted off to sleep because when I opened my eyes the fire had completely gone out and I was absolutely frozen. I wrapped the blanket around me and stole quietly upstairs. The curtains were drawn and the great hump in the duvet indicated that Nick was sound asleep. I slipped in beside him and hugged my knees, trying to get warm. A second later an arm wound round my waist.

'You're freezing,' he murmured.

'I thought you were asleep,' I whispered back, surprised he was even talking to me, let alone touching me.

'Too busy totting up the damage a pack of marauding dogs will cause.'

'I'm really sorry, Nick. I can't tell you how awful I feel.'

'You're a total dickhead, Polly,' he muttered, but not too unkindly.

'I know, but I've got great plans to remove the dick from my head,' I whispered, vastly encouraged.

'See that you do.' He leaned over and kissed me. 'Just see that you do.'

He leaned back on his pillow as if to go to sleep, but I wound my arms round his neck, full of relief and gratitude. I began to kiss him very thoroughly. 'Thank you, thank you . . .' I murmured, working hard on the stony facial muscles, 'thank you so much.' I kissed away.

'Polly, if you think you can get round me like this . . .' he muttered into my hair.

I worked harder.

'It takes more than a kiss and a cuddle, you know . . .' he grunted, 'more than that . . . yes, even more than that . . . that's a bit better . . . better still . . . keep going . . . you're getting there, Poll . . .'

Chapter Six

During the course of the next few days Nick and I made our respective preparations for the shoot. His took the form of moving his sheep out of harm's way and squeezing as much money as possible out of the production company, eventually bumping our fee up another five hundred pounds.

'Might as well take them for all we can get,' he said grimly, having clinched the deal on the phone with Bruce. 'It's not as if they won't leave us unscathed.'

He'd just about come down from boiling point but was still at a slow, rolling simmer and only managed to keep the lid on it if he wasn't provoked. I have a habit of being unwittingly provocative so I kept well out of his way as he and Larry moved hordes of sheep and cows into distant meadows, muttering dire curses under their breath.

My own preparations were of a slightly different nature. Having felt genuinely guilty and ashamed of myself, I bounced back surprisingly quickly, and on the day before the film crew was due to arrive I bustled excitedly off to Truro where I availed myself of every conceivable beauty treatment the town had to offer.

I was plucked, waxed, pummelled, manicured, pedicured, massaged, reflexologied and aromatherapied to within an inch of my life, before finally coming to rest at the most important venue of all, the cut, bleach and blow-dry establishment. As I settled back into my chair I bravely uttered the words every hairdresser longs to hear.

'I'd like to try something different, please,' I quavered.

On hearing these magic words my 'hair sculptor', as he was pleased to call himself, spat out his gum and flexed his wrists; his scissors flashed and he whirred into action. The result was a chunky shoulder-length bob, a wispy fringe, a head full of highlights, and not much change from £80, but it was worth it.

In fact, when I saw Nick's face as I sailed in through the back door of Trewarren armed with carrier bags, I decided it would have been cheap at twice the price. His jaw fell open and he almost dropped the current copy of *The Field* in the sink.

'Blimey,' he said slowly. 'What have you done?'

I grinned and dumped the bags on the kitchen table.

'I've done what I should have done months ago: I've taken myself in hand. D'you like it?'

Nick walked around me. 'It's great. You look like you did when I first met you.'

'Really?' I wasn't quite sure how to take this. 'But that was only three years ago – I haven't changed that much, surely?'

'Well, you were letting yourself go a bit, you know, Polly.'

'Was I?' I gasped. 'Why didn't you say so, for God's sake?'

'Oh, I don't mind, not much call for glamour-girl looks on a farm. What's in the bags?'

'Oh, just a few odds and ends.'

He grinned. 'Spent a fortune, have you? Well, it's about time you bought some new clothes, and I must say, the hair's a distinct improvement.' He grabbed an apple from the fruit bowl, took a bite out of it and made for the back door. 'See you at lunch time.' He strode out.

I beamed with delight. Talk about the right result! No more jeans and sweatshirts for me, from now on I'd swan around the farm like something out of *Vogue* – and I'd smell good too, I thought, reaching into a bag for my new Obsession spray. I squirted some on my neck. No more borrowing Nick's Right Guard deodorant and thinking that would do in the pong department – no, I'd absolutely reek of Ralph Lauren. I squirted some more on my neck, on my wrists, on the backs of my knees and up my skirt.

'Obsession,' I muttered, striking a dramatic pose, 'for the girl who's mysterious yet sexy, elusive yet sensual –'

'What's that terrible smell?'

I swung around. Sarah, my sister-in-law, had walked into my advert. She was wrinkling up her nose in disgust in the doorway.

'Oh, hi, Sarah, it's called perfume, not much call for it around here, I agree, but it's something women in civilized societies use to make themselves smell sexy and alluring. It's instead of the usual cow dung.'

'Oh, right, yes, rings a bell actually. I seem to remember in my far-off distant past squirting something like that behind my ears, when I lived in a town, of course, and wore shoes instead of clogs – gosh, I like the hair!' She circled me approvingly. 'Ooh, and what's in the bags, can I see?'

She delved in and pulled out a fuchsia pink skirt about eight inches long.

'Hey, look at this! God, how divine, but where are you going to go in it, the Young Farmers' bring-and-buy? The WI car-boot sale?' She giggled.

94

'Why not?' I said, grabbing it from her. 'Might shake them up a bit. From now on, Sarah, I'm changing my image. Just because I live on a farm, I don't have to look like one or smell like one – you won't recognise me. I'll be a new woman!'

Sarah sat down with a sigh. 'God, I wish I was a new woman, a completely different woman, in fact, not me at all.'

She ran her hands through her curly brown hair, her sweet, freckled face decidedly gloomy. I dumped the bags on the floor, hoping she hadn't seen the price tag on the skirt, put the kettle on for coffee and sat down opposite her.

Sarah was married to Nick's brother Tim and I was extremely fond of her. As far as female company went she'd saved my life when I'd moved down here, and not many days passed when we didn't partake of a tea bag or two in one or other kitchen. She worked her butt off in a riding stables for very little money whilst Tim tried to scrape a living from his terribly correct organic farm. They were very, very Green (in more ways than one, I thought privately) and full of high ideals and marvellous morals, but at the end of the day they were still exhausted and penniless, and, as I kept telling her, what was the good of having high ideals and marvellous morals if you didn't have any fun or any dosh?

'Trooble oop stables?' I said sympathetically, passing her a mug of coffee. 'Still shovelling shit out of some ungrateful stallion's stall? Tell them to get off their lazy hocks and do it themselves.'

She sighed. 'You know I wouldn't mind the hard work, Polly, if we just had a bit of fun now and again, but we

95

don't. Nothing ever seems to happen around here, does it? It's just work, eat, sleep, day after day, that's all I seem to do. For God's sake, I'm only twenty-three, and Tim and I never do anything any more; we don't go out to dinner, we don't even go to the cinema. I tell you, I'm fed up.'

'Sarah! I'm shocked. You know very well there's a Friends of the Earth rally in Truro next month!'

She ground her teeth. 'Terrific. Talk about life in the fast lane.'

I grinned. 'OK, I will.'

I leaned forward conspiratorially and told her about the shoot. She listened agog, suitably impressed by the fiendish way I'd arranged it all.

'Heavens, Polly, you're unreal. Isn't Nick furious?'

'Oh no,' I said airily, 'he's very relaxed. In fact, he's rather pleased now, quite proud of me, in fact. You see, we're getting a hell of a lot of money for the location fee and we'll be able to make all sorts of improvements to the farm. Who knows, we might even plant a few trees, do our bit for the rainforests, that kind of thing.'

Sarah looked incredulous. 'Rainforests are tropical, Polly!'

'Well, we could throw in a few cheeseplants, or yuccas perhaps – but the point I'm trying to make, Sarah, is that it's all very well having wonderful plans to save the world, and I'm the first one to say that ecology and all that environmental junk is terribly important, but if you don't have the money to implement those plans –'

'I THOUGHT YOU SAID THEY WERE COMING TOMORROW!' boomed an outraged voice in my left ear.

My coffee mug nearly leaped out of my fingers as I swung round in alarm.

'Wh-what?' I faltered.

'Tomorrow, you said, well they're bloody well here today!' Nick ground his teeth. 'And d'you know where they are? Eh? Go on, have a guess.'

'Er . . . where?'

'In my bloody barley field! Apparently they thought it was a marvellous place to park, terrifically handy, thought it was grass, you see, didn't have the nous to realize that some crops do vaguely resemble grass but aren't actually quite so robust and don't take kindly to having two-ton trucks parked on top of them! Of course, they didn't even stop to consider that it might be somebody's livelihood, oh no!'

'Oh my God,' I mumbled.

'Yes, oh my God,' he seethed, 'the nightmare's begun. I've got Larry redirecting them to the top field but if you could tear yourself away from your coffee morning for two minutes you might slip down and give him a hand. I've got work to do and I haven't got time to be a bloody traffic warden! Morning, Sarah.' He slammed out again.

Sarah raised her eyebrows. 'Doesn't seem too proud at the moment,' she murmured.

'Er, no, you may be right there,' I said, getting hurriedly to my feet. 'In fact I'd better get down there before the shit hits the fan.'

'You mean that wasn't it? Blimey, I'm getting out of here.'

She quickly drained her coffee and we went our separate ways.

I ran speedily to the barley field. God! A day early! Why hadn't Pippa let me know? I couldn't help feel inordinately excited, though, as I sped down the garden, across the first field and into the meadow beyond. They were here! They'd arrived! In fact I couldn't resist a couple of gazelle-like leaps as I bounded through the long grass. As I executed the second leap I caught sight of Nick wrestling with a ewe in the adjacent field. I instantly dropped the aerobics and adopted a slow, sober walk, head hung low, face suffused with guilt.

'Get a move on, Polly,' yelled Nick over the fence. 'Instead of prancing around you could get down there and help Larry!'

'Yes, sir,' I muttered meekly, doffing an imaginary cap.

Gosh, he was a bore. So they were a day early? So what? His unwavering misanthropy about the whole thing was beginning to annoy me.

In the distance I spotted a convoy of trucks and vans trundling out of the barley field, along the dirt track, and into the field immediately below me. Larry was waving his arms around, directing them in. I ran to join him at the gate and swung on it as the first of the lorries made its way towards us. I smiled cheerily as it trundled through and two young guys in the front smiled back, giving me a wave. As the six or seven vehicles rolled through I kept the smile glued to my face, despite the dust, whilst silently appraising the occupants. He's attractive . . . she's pretty . . . so is she . . . she's not – oh look, there's Pippa –

'Pippa!'

Pippa's Alfa Romeo bounced through the gate and stopped in the middle of the field. As she got out I felt slightly nervous. We hadn't spoken since that dreadful phone call.

'Hi!' I yelled.

She ran over and hugged me warmly.

'So glad it's worked out,' she muttered in my ear. 'It would have been awful to fall out over this.'

'We wouldn't have,' I promised, 'but I'm so thrilled you're here, albeit a day early. I thought you were coming tomorrow?'

'Didn't you get my message? I left a message with some yokel woman I couldn't understand, so perhaps she didn't understand me either.'

'Mrs Bradshaw? No, she didn't mention it.'

'Probably forgot.'

Or else, I thought, had deliberately kept quiet. It hadn't escaped my notice that Mrs Bradshaw was getting a vicarious thrill out of all the friction the shoot was causing between me and Nick.

I jumped suddenly as the passenger door of the Alfa Romeo slammed shut with an almighty bang.

'Josh! Come and meet Polly!' shouted Pippa. 'That's him,' she whispered in my ear.

A grim-faced middle-aged man strode towards us. He was wearing white jeans, a denim shirt and a black leather jacket, all of which were slightly too tight and looked faintly ridiculous on his rather portly body. He had a closely cropped black beard tinged with grey, and jet-black hair which was very thick at the front and sides but non-existent in the middle – a bit of a slap-head actually. His eyes were fierce and dark.

'Where the hell did you put my Filofax, Pippa?' he stormed as he approached.

'It's in your case,' replied Pippa soothingly. 'I didn't want you to forget it so I popped it in there first thing this morning.'

'In the office, you mean,' he said quickly, eyes like daggers.

'Y-yes, in the office, of course,' faltered Pippa, flushing. 'Where else?'

'Quite,' he seethed, shortly. 'Well, for future reference, don't touch my things without telling me. I nearly had a heart attack just then. I thought I'd forgotten it.'

'Right. Sorry.'

I looked down and kicked at a tuft of grass, feeling uncomfortable.

'Um, Polly, this is Josh,' said Pippa quickly, 'Josh Drysdale, Polly Penhalligan, my best friend and chatelaine of this vast estate!'

I held out my hand. So this was Josh. This was the married man who was causing Pippa so much pain and heartache. I couldn't see it myself, he looked at least forty and would have been no great shakes at thirty. What was someone as beautiful as Pippa doing with someone as ordinary – and bad-tempered – as this?

'Hi, Pippa's told me all about you,' I said with a smile.

Pippa looked horrified.

'I – mean, what you do, you know, at work, as a producer,' I gabbled quickly.

Josh gave a tight little smile. 'She's told me about you too,' he said grudgingly.

'Well, I hope she didn't tell you how I nearly cocked up

the whole bloody thing by not telling my husband you were com–'

'Um, Polly, can I show Josh around?' cut in Pippa with wide eyes and gritted teeth.

'Sure, come up to the house if you like, have a cup of –'

'Wait!' interrupted Josh, holding up his hand for quiet and cocking his ear to the car. We waited. 'Yes, I thought so,' he affirmed with a curt little nod, 'that's my phone.' He turned and ran back to the car.

Pippa rounded on me. 'Polly, *don't* tell him we nearly had a cock-up,' she hissed. 'I want him to think it's all going swimmingly!'

'Well, it is now, isn't it?'

'And *don't* act as if you know about us either!'

'Doesn't he know I know?'

'No! No one's supposed to know – it's all supposed to be incredibly secret!'

'But he's still leaving her for you, isn't he? I mean, he's not stringing you along or anything?'

'Of course not. I told you, he's mad about me, but just don't mention it, that's all!'

'OK, OK, calm down.'

'Right. So what d'you think?' she asked eagerly.

'Er . . . well. He looks very nice. I mean, it's so hard to tell when I've only just met him. How old is he?'

'Forty-three. Heavenly, isn't he? D'you know, I had no idea I was into older men until I met Josh, but I tell you, Polly, I'd never go out with anyone under forty again. There are so many advantages of being with an older man, it's incredible!'

'Really?' I said doubtfully. I could only think of the

disadvantages, like the baldness, the saggy tummy, the grey hair, the pathetic attempts at trendy clothes, but I wisely held my tongue. I turned to look at him as he leaned into Pippa's car, talking on the car phone. His jacket had ridden up at the back and through his tight white jeans I could see his Father Christmas boxer shorts. I shuddered. Heavens. Rather her than me.

A moment later he rejoined us, clutching his Filofax and accompanied by someone who provoked a knee-jerk reaction in me that I haven't experienced for some time. I gasped. Jesus. Now we really were talking heavenly.

This individual was about six inches taller than Josh, about eight years younger and about a hundred times more attractive. His nut-brown hair was streaked with gold and swept back off his face, curling slightly as it came to rest on the back of his collar. His face was tanned and his hazel eyes twinkled with gold flecks, rather like his hair. He had that enviable, expensive outdoor look you only get from swimming in hot seas, taking regular skiing trips and playing a spot of polo. We were talking fit and ready for action here. He held out a suntanned hand, flashed an immaculate set of pearly whites and dazzled me with his golden eyes. I nearly fell over.

'Hi, you must be Polly. I'm Sam Weston, the director of this motley crew. I'm so sorry, we obviously parked in completely the wrong field. Is your husband going to be livid?'

I went for his extended hand enthusiastically – so enthusiastically that I nearly missed and shot up his armpit – and flashed my very best smile in return.

'Oh no, not in the least, it really couldn't matter less!' I gushed.

'Well, that's a relief, I thought perhaps he was planning to sue us before we'd even started!'

'Ha ha! Good Lord no, don't be silly, he's delighted you're here, can't wait to meet you, in fact!'

'Really?'

'Yes, he used to be in the ad business himself, you see, so he's terrifically interested, can't wait to get – you know – involved again!'

'Great! Well, I'll tell you what, we need a few long shots of the house, so we'll probably stay down here for a bit, but once that's done I'll pop up and say hello, shall I? Explain what we're going to be doing?'

'Oh do, do – although, er, actually,' I said hastily, 'he's pretty busy with the sheep at the moment, but do pop up anyway. I'd love to hear your plans and, um, familiarize myself with your shooting schedule.'

I was rather pleased with this last little throwaway remark, remembered from my own days in the business.

I thought Sam looked suitably impressed, if a little surprised. 'Er, yes, of course, I'd be happy to run through the schedule with you if that's what you'd like.'

'Great! Two o'clock suit you?'

Sam looked a little taken aback. Steady, Polly, steady.

'Well, actually, we'll probably be right in the middle of shooting then, but when I get a moment I promise I'll come up.'

'Oh, yes, well, whenever,' I said quickly. 'I'm pretty busy myself, of course, got loads to do.' Stop it, Polly, you're behaving like some sort of frustrated housewife from the sticks; get a grip. I gave him an earnest, businesslike look. 'Now, is there anything I can get you? Tea? Coffee? Cold drinks for the crew?'

'Good Lord no, that's kind, but we bring our own catering service.'

'Oh really? Where?'

He turned and pointed. 'Big Winnibago in the far corner there, see?'

I turned and looked in the direction he was indicating but couldn't see anyone of that description, only a large sort of caravan affair.

'I see, well if Big Winnie wants any help you be sure to let me know, OK?' I smiled winningly.

Sam looked a bit confused 'Er . . . right, thanks.'

Josh tapped him on the arm 'Sam, a word . . .'

'The big Winnibago's a catering truck, you moron,' muttered Pippa in my ear, 'not a fat tea lady.'

'Oh!' I blushed.

Sam and Josh were deep in discussion now and looked as if they were about to wander off, when suddenly Sam turned back. He smiled.

'Oh, and listen, Polly, please don't worry. I promise everything will be left just exactly as we found it, no broken fences or open gates or anything like that. We're quite capable of keeping the country code. You won't even know we've been here; we'll be no trouble at all.'

He flashed his dazzling smile straight into my eyes and I felt a certain amount of knee tremble coming on. Gosh, he was attractive, and what easy self-assurance.

'Oh, I'm quite sure you won't be,' I said breathlessly, 'and don't worry – we're delighted to have you, really!'

'Thanks, and now if you'll excuse me I must get on. See you a bit later, I hope?'

By now I was absolutely charmed to the marrow. I opened my mouth to be equally charming back but was heavily out of practice and nothing came out, at least nothing coherent, just a sort of imbecilic squawk of pleasure. Luckily he'd already turned to Josh.

'Josh, a word about the light. I'm not convinced it's quite right yet so what I propose to do is this . . .' They wandered off deep in discussion.

'Wow,' I muttered when my voice had resurfaced.

'What?' said Pippa.

'Well, he's all right, isn't he?'

'Who, Sam?'

'Yes, Sam, I think he's divine. I'm surprised you're not after him, Pippa.'

'Oh no, he's married.'

'Well, so's Josh.'

'I know, but Sam's happily married, adores his wife. Anyway, what d'you mean? What's wrong with Josh?'

'Oh, nothing, nothing,' I said hastily. 'He's lovely, I just thought Sam was more sort of your type, that's all.'

'Why, because he's tall, darkish and handsome? I'm not that obvious, Polly. Josh may not be an oil painting but he's a jolly nice guy, and looks aren't everything, you know.'

'No, no, of course not,' I said hastily. I'd obviously offended her in a big way. 'Tell you what, Pippa, I know you're supposed to eat with the crew and everything, but why don't you and Josh have supper with us tonight?'

Pippa looked pleased. 'Oh, that would be brilliant! D'you know, in all the time we've been together I've never once been able to have supper with friends or do anything normal, it's so frustrating, but – oh God, wouldn't it look a bit obvious? A bit of a foursome? I'm sure Josh would think so.'

'Well, I'll ask Sam too if you like, that way he could fill Nick in on his plans.'

'Oh, OK, good idea.' She brightened considerably and took my arm as we wandered off. 'I know you're going to love Josh when you get to know him – Nick will too, he's just his type.'

'Er, yes, I'm sure.'

Actually I couldn't think of anyone less Nick's type, he was more the type he'd run a mile from, but I'd brief him to be tolerant for Pippa's sake.

'Got to go.' Pippa squeezed my arm. 'I'm supposed to be working, remember?'

She ran off to join the others.

I sat on the fence for a while and watched. Huge lights were being lifted out of vans and erected, people were moving props about and shouting to one other, make-up was being applied, hair was being coiffed, the whole place was buzzing with glamorous, frenetic activity. After a while my bottom began to feel numb, so I took one last lingering look, jumped off the fence and hurried back to the house, fizzing inwardly. As I galloped through the long grass I noticed how green and spring-like everything was and surprised myself by leaping the fence into the garden with uncharacteristic energy. I wondered, slightly nervously, if perhaps my sap was rising too, and if so why. Well, why not, I retorted. It wasn't often a dashing film director graced my dinner table, was it? This called for some serious glamour. I'd think big. So big that eight inches of extremely small pink skirt would undoubtedly make an appearance. I hurried excitedly into the house.

Chapter Seven

'You did what!' thundered Nick over the tomato salad half an hour later.

'I asked them to supper, that's all.'

'That's all! Christ, Polly, isn't it enough that I have these people making free with my property during the day? Do you really think I want to entertain them in the evening as well?'

'Oh, for goodness' sake, Nick,' I snapped, 'stop being so bloody pompous, you're behaving like an anally retentive Guards officer! OK, so you didn't want them here in the first place, but –'

'Too right!'

'– but now that they're here, why can't you just loosen up a bit and enjoy it? It makes a change to have something going on around here, to have some fun, for God's sake!'

'Polly, you may think it's fun to be mingling with these precious arty types – and my God, are they precious, I came into my own kitchen half an hour ago to find some middle-aged trendy called Josh maniacally sponging his white jeans and wailing about a little bit of mud – but excuse me if I don't share your enthusiasm! You haven't got to trail around behind them shutting gates, mending fences –'

'They promised they wouldn't do that. Sam – he's the director – he gave me his word there'd be no damage.'

'Well, bully for Sam, a media man's word is his bond, I'm sure. Tell him to take a look at the barley field before he makes any more rash promises.'

'Nick, what exactly is wrong with being a media man?' I snarled. 'We can't all make wholesome livings in the fresh air on our inherited farms, you know. Some people have to work in offices, and correct me if I'm wrong but I believe you were once a media man yourself, or have you forgotten?'

'No, I haven't forgotten, and I absolutely hated it, as you well know, which is precisely why I find it inconceivable that you actually *invited* these detestable people down here in the first place!'

I ground my teeth and leaned over the salad, slopping vinaigrette on my T-shirt. 'Nick,' I spat, 'these "detestable people", as you so charmingly put it, include, number one, my very best friend in the world, and number two, the man she intends to spend the rest of her life with. She's *extremely* keen to introduce us to Josh and I for one am keen to get to know him!'

Nick looked aghast. 'Josh? Pippa's going out with that creep in the white jeans?'

'Er – well, yes, but actually, Nick, you're not supposed to know, so forget I said that,' I said hastily.

'Why?'

'Well, because, because –'

'Because he's married, is that it?'

'Well, yes, I suppose he is a bit,' I said, falling into Pippa's trap.

'A bit? He's either married or he's not – Christ, what is Pippa up to?'

'Oh, for heaven's sake, Nick, don't be so high and mighty!' I stormed. 'You're so unbelievably smug, aren't you? You've no idea how difficult some people's lives are. Just because everything fell neatly into place for you, it doesn't mean –'

'Coo-ee!' A little blond head popped round the door. Bruce looked from me to Nick, registering our flushed, embattled faces.

'Oh dear, having a bit of a domestic, are we? Pardon *moi*, I'll come back a bit later,' he murmured, withdrawing.

'No, no, it's all right, Bruce, come in,' I said quickly. He might at least defuse the situation. 'Did you want me?'

The head popped back. 'Well, actually, no.'

The rest of Bruce sidled in and he perched his pert little bum on the edge of the table. He pursed his lips, clasped his hands together and gazed adoringly at Nick.

'I was after the man of the house,' he purred.

Nick pushed his chair back nervously. 'Er, yes, Bruce, what can I do for you?' he said as assertively as possible.

'A *petite* favour.' Bruce cocked his head prettily on one side. '*S'il vous plaît?*'

'Er, y-yes, fire away,' said Nick, much less assertively.

Bruce produced a book from behind his back with a dramatic flourish. It was *Miller's Antiques Price Guide*.

'Well, Sam doesn't need me for the moment,' he pouted, 'more's the pity, and since I brought dear old Mr Midler down, he and I were wondering if we might just take a wee peek-a-boo at your porcelain again. Would you mind?'

'Not at all, not at all, be my guest!' Nick looked relieved. 'I'm delighted you're so keen, help yourself. You know where the cabinet is. I'll just get you the key.' He stood up, took a jar down from the top of the dresser and fished it out. 'Here.'

Bruce clasped the key to his bosom. 'Too kind, too kind,' he murmured, 'and if I may be so bold, I'd like to take this opportunity to say how absolutely thrilled to bits we all are to be here and to be on the receiving end of your generous hospitality, which, I gather, knows no bounds. For, correct me if I'm wrong, but Brucey Boy heard on the grapevine that you're planning a little din-dins party for this evening! *Quel* fun!'

'Oh, well, yes, but –' I began.

'Oh yes, do come, Bruce,' cut in Nick wearily, sitting down again.

Bruce held up his hands in mock horror. 'Oh no, no, I couldn't possibly, I didn't mean –'

'No, do, you're absolutely right, our hospitality knows no bounds. In fact, it hasn't the faintest idea when to stop, it's like a bloody runaway train, and of course the more the merrier, eh, Polly? And the merrier we get the more fun we have, isn't that right?' He raised his eyebrows quizzically at me. I glared back, fuming silently.

'Well, if you're sure . . .' murmured Bruce, slipping down off the table. 'Meanwhile, I'll just pop upstairs to check out the collectables – see you anon!' He gave a dinky little wave and wiggled out, key in hand.

'You didn't have to invite him,' I snapped when he was out of earshot. 'You're just desperate for the martyr's crown now, aren't you?'

Nick sighed wearily. 'Oh, what's one more fun guy at my dinner table, Polly, and actually, contrary to what you might think, I rather like Bruce – at least he's genuine. He's a genuine poof and a genuine antiques enthusiast – fine, you know where you are. It's all these bloody phoneys swanning around pretending to be something they're not that irritates me.' He pushed his chair back and got to his feet. 'Anyway, I trust you'll be rustling up something predictably delicious for tonight's little gathering?' He grabbed his flat cap from the dresser. 'Can't wait,' he muttered grimly, before striding out of the back door, slamming it behind him.

I stared after him for a second, then, in a moment of blind fury, leaped to my feet, ran to the saucepan cupboard, pulled out the biggest one I could find and hurled it after him with a vengeance.

'AAAAARRRRGH!'

It went straight through the window next to the back door, smashing it to smithereens. My hand flew to my mouth. Oh God. I stared at the hole, aghast.

Nick was back in a moment, his face white with anger. 'Clear up this mess, Polly, and get someone in to fix the window,' he said quietly, 'and in future, if you've got something to say, try to express it with words rather than resorting to primeval urges and hurling things through windows. It's rather an expensive way of communicating.'

'I – I didn't mean it to go through the –'

'JUST FIX IT!' he thundered, and slammed out again, making the door frame shudder.

I shut my eyes tight, clenched everything in my entire body – teeth, fists, toes, buttocks – and when I was sure he was out of earshot, let rip.

'SHIT SHIT BUGGER SHIT!' I shrieked, expressing myself – I thought – extremely clearly.

Then, all sworn out, I slumped in a heap at the kitchen table, snarling into the stripped pine and thinking murderous thoughts. After a while I roused myself, poured a glass of wine and slammed around the kitchen, sweeping up the glass and muttering darkly. Why did he always have to be so *right*, I seethed, banging the dustpan on the floor. Why? Why couldn't he be wrong, just for a change, and let *me* be right? And what the hell was I going to cook tonight, eh? Eh, Delia? I pulled her roughly from the shelf and blew the dust off her spine. I flipped miserably through the pages, staring vacantly at photographs of beef stroganoff and chicken à la king, all of which were apparently foolproof, but not, of course, Polly-proof.

I looked up and stared miserably at the broken window. He'd spoiled everything, the bastard. How was I supposed to enjoy myself tonight with this little débâcle hanging over my head? How dare he speak to me like that, how *dare* he, and, more to the point, what the hell was I going to *cook*? I hurled Delia on to the floor, again expressing myself, I thought, very succinctly. She struck me as being just a bit too bleeding perfect, actually, hard to hack at the best of times but insupportable when I was feeling so incredibly imperfect myself.

I slumped down at the kitchen table again and bit the skin around my nails, hoping for a brainwave. Surprisingly, one crashed over my head remarkably quickly. Yes, of course! I ran to the phone and punched out a number.

'Sarah? Hi, it's me. Listen, are you and Tim doing anything tonight . . . ? You're not? Well, why don't you come for supper? Nick and I are having some of the film people over, should be quite a laugh . . . Great! Listen, the only thing is, I was just wondering if you could sort of give me a hand, only . . . Oh, no, no, not the whole thing, I wouldn't hear of it, but . . . Really? You don't mind? Well, that would be terrific! Yes, if you could do the main course I'll do a pudding and a starter . . . Brilliant! Thanks so much, you've saved my life as usual, we'll be eight, by the way . . . See you then! Bye!'

I grinned and replaced the receiver. My star of a sister-in-law. She knew my limitations and, after all, she had to eat the food, so she might as well make sure it was edible. All I had to do now was nip into Helston for some smoked salmon, some wildly extravagant out-of-season strawberries, a few tubs of Häagen Dazs ice cream, and Bob was undoubtedly my uncle.

With a skip of pleasure and forgetting entirely about the little business of getting the window fixed, I pranced out of the back door, car keys in hand, feeling positively buoyant again.

Bugger Nick, I decided as I leaped a flowerbed, I was damned if he was going to spoil my few days of fun – oh Christ, there he was, coming out of the potting shed. I immediately dropped the skippy routine and adopted the obligatory sober walk – head hung low, face contrite, et cetera, et cetera. I could feel his eyes boring into my back, radiating disapproval. What the hell was he doing sneaking up on me all the time? He was like something out of the Gestapo.

I trudged meekly round the car, shoulders hunched, and slumped disconsolately into the driving seat. I had a quick peek, caught his eye and looked forlornly away. I drove sedately past him down the drive, but as I turned into the lane and was sure he couldn't see me I snapped u2 into the cassette player, gave a whoop of pleasure, and shot off to Helston, singing at the top of my voice.

Chapter Eight

The next time I saw Nick I was charging downstairs at seven thirty to organize supper. He grabbed my arm as I sped past.

'What the hell's that?'

'What?' I followed his incredulous gaze downwards.

'That pink thing round your bottom.'

'It's a skirt, of course.'

'But, Polly, I can see your knickers!'

'No you can't, only if I bend over. I've practised in the mirror.'

'Oh well, that's a relief. Let's just hope you don't drop your napkin. Are you seriously wearing it tonight?'

'Yes, of course, why not?'

Nick raised his eyebrows. 'Oh, no reason, don't mind me, I'm obviously way out of touch. I had no idea the jail-bait look was in this season.' He shook his head in disbelief and carried on upstairs.

I treated this remark with the contempt it deserved and ran on down to the kitchen. Sarah was just staggering through the back door with an enormous pheasant casserole which she dumped gratefully on the kitchen table. She was followed by a startlingly attractive girl bearing a large vegetable dish, which she too deposited.

'Oh, Polly,' gasped Sarah, collapsing in a chair, 'you'll

116

never guess what, I walked past your film crew in the bottom field and ran into Amanda here. She's the art director and she was at school with me! We were in the same dorm! I've asked her for supper, hope you don't mind.'

'Not at all, not at all!' After all, I could hardly object when she'd cooked the thing, could I? 'Where's Tim?'

'Oh, he'll be a bit late, I'm afraid, digging potatoes.'

I smiled at Amanda, who was blinking shyly. 'Typical farmer, always late. Here, grab a chair, I'll get you a drink.'

'Thanks.' She smiled and sat down, flicking back her dark silky hair which was swept off her face in a velvet hairband. She had small, perfect features, a pink and white complexion and pale-blue eyes. She was wearing a navy-blue skirt, a sleeveless puffa jacket and pearl earrings. Very pretty, and very Sloaney, I decided.

'So you were at Benenden with Sarah?'

'Yeah, for me sins,' she said in an exaggerated Cockney accent. I'm a sucker for a silly voice myself.

'Bi' of a dump then, was it?' I bandied back.

'Yeah, couldn't wait to get out of there.' She nodded round the kitchen. 'Nice place you got 'ere, Polly.'

'Oh, ta ever so, we like it.'

'Wodja call this then – a manor?'

'Well, it's a bloody great mansion really, innit?'

'Bet it cost a bob or two. Me dad's got a place a bit like this down Purley way.'

'Purley, eh? Nice part of the world that, me nan came from Purley – 'ere,' I said, passing her a glass of wine, 'get that down yer Gregory Peck.'

I poured one for Sarah too, but when I passed it to her

I noticed she'd gone very pale behind her freckles. She shook her head at me slowly. Suddenly I had a most unpleasant feeling in my tubes. Oh God.

Amanda got up and clutched her bag. 'Can I use yer lav, Polly?'

'Um, yes – yeah,' I mumbled, 'first on the left.'

'Ta.' She withdrew.

Sarah rounded on me. 'You berk!' she hissed. 'That's how she speaks!'

'Well, I realize that now,' I hissed back, 'but how was I to know? You said she was at Benenden with you, for God's sake!'

'Only for the last year. Her father made a fortune in wet fish and sent her there to iron out her vowels!'

'Didn't work, did it?' I groaned. 'Oh no, I'll have to talk like that all night now.'

Sarah was appalled. 'Polly, you can't!'

'I'll have to, otherwise she'll think I'm taking the piss – oh, er, 'ello again, found the karsy orright, did yer?'

'Yeah, thanks.'

She slipped her bag off her shoulder and started helping me arrange the smoked salmon on to plates. I noticed she'd applied some more lipstick to her rosebud mouth. She certainly was very beautiful.

'Sam coming, is 'e?' she asked nonchalantly.

'Yeah, he should be 'ere soon. Know him well, do yer?'

Sarah moaned softly and tiptoed from the room.

'Yeah, I've worked wiv him a bit over the years.'

'Nice bloke, is 'e?'

She blushed and looked a bit uncomfortable. 'He's all right,' she said shortly.

She avoided my eyes and busied herself arranging slices of lemon on the plates. I wondered if she fancied him. We worked in silence for a minute and I tried desperately to think if I knew anything about Purley or wet fish that I could use as an opening gambit, but luckily I was saved from making a complete idiot of myself by a sharp rap on the back door. We both swung round and in strode Sam, his face almost completely obscured by an enormous bunch of flowers, closely followed by Pippa, Josh and Bruce. Sam popped his head over the top of the flowers and grinned.

'And I didn't nick them from your garden either, although I must say I was sorely tempted when I saw the display out there. Touch of coals to Newcastle, I'm afraid!' He thrust them into my hands.

I laughed, feeling unaccountably flustered. 'Thanks! They're beautiful, it's a long time since anyone brought me flowers.' I hurried to a cupboard and busied myself finding a vase.

'Oh, come now,' he said, leaning lazily against the dresser and watching me closely as I arranged them too hurriedly, 'I don't believe that for one moment. Surely the farmer sits down to breakfast with a rose between his teeth every morning?' His hazel eyes twinkled.

'Hardly!' I laughed. Suddenly I remembered Amanda. 'Not on your bleedin' nellie, actually – hah hah!' I cackled like a fishwife.

My guests eyed me curiously. There was a slight pause.

'Where d'you want us then?' asked Pippa eventually. 'Shall we get out of your way?'

I nodded furiously, grinning inanely. Surely if I stuck to nodding and grinning Sam wouldn't think I was unspeakably 'cor blimey', and Amanda wouldn't think I was taking the mickey? I wasn't really enjoying this; I felt a bit clammy under the arms.

'Yes?' Pippa raised her eyebrows enquiringly, head on one side. 'Shall we get out of your way? Go-in-the-drawing-room?' She enunciated it slowly as if I was brain dead.

I nodded enthusiastically and ran to the door, gesturing like a demented traffic policeman for them to pass through. They trooped past me, looking slightly mystified, and Pippa paused to hiss in my ear, 'We're going to have to get you up to London pretty damn quickly, Polly. You've obviously been stuck in the country far too long – you're behaving like the village idiot!'

'I'll explain later,' I muttered out of the corner of my mouth. 'There's method in my madness.'

Whilst everyone else was drinking in the drawing room I slipped away and hurriedly wrote out some place cards, putting Amanda as far away from me as possible next to Nick at the far end, and Sam as close as possible, on my right. By the time I'd slipped back into the drawing room the noise level had reached a pitch that suggested that thus far, at least, the party could be deemed to be a success. Nick was leaning up against the fireplace laughing and joking with Sarah and Amanda; Josh and Pippa were screaming with laughter at something outrageous Bruce had said, and Sam was beside him, egging him on. Suddenly I felt unaccountably happy. I stood in the doorway watching for a moment. This was more like it. This was what you might call a social life. After a moment I clapped my hands and yelled at everyone to come and sit down.

We all trooped through and as everyone jostled into their places I noticed Amanda glance over and catch Sam's eye. He smiled but she looked away quickly. She's definitely got the hots for him, I thought as I shook out my napkin, either that or they've had a ding-dong in the past.

'So, Polly,' said Sam as he settled down next to me with a grin, 'tell me, what does a married lady get up to on a vast estate like this? A tinkle on the pianoforte, perhaps? A visit to the neighbours with your calling card? A slow amble round the gardens with your parasol before collapsing on the chaise longue with the vapours? Am I close?'

I laughed, but was aware he was mocking me slightly. 'Heavens, no, I wish you were! No, I'd love to play at lady of the manor but unfortunately I'm much too busy.'

'Oh really?'

'Oh yes, this place keeps me –' I broke off, suddenly recalling Pippa grilling me in a similar vein a couple of weeks ago. I wasn't going to get caught out twice. I licked my lips. 'This place keeps me pretty occupied, but I also have a – a hobby, which is terrifically time-consuming.'

'Oh? What's that?'

'Oh, it's terribly boring.' I gulped and gripped my wine glass.

'Try me.'

I caught my breath and looked wildly around the room for inspiration. Wallpaper-hanging? Carpet-laying? Table-laying? Luckily my eye caught the serried ranks of silver photograph frames arranged on the cabinet in the corner.

'Well, it's photography, actually,' I blurted. 'I'm absolutely mad about it. Snap, snap, snap, I'm at it all day!' After all, anyone can take a picture, can't they?

'No, really? How extraordinary, it's one of my passions too. What camera do you have?'

'Oh, er, well, I use all sorts really, a Canon, an Olympus, a Brownie –'

'A Brownie?' He looked astonished.

'Yes, you see, I'm a great believer in not getting too attached to one particular camera, I like to think I can get equally good results whichever one I use. It's much more of a challenge if the art is down to the photographer rather than his tools, don't you agree?' Gosh, was that *my* mouth talking? I quickly popped some smoked salmon into it before it said anything else. Its capacity to perform in public without consulting me first was getting seriously out of hand. I chewed hard.

Sam looked puzzled. 'Well, it's an interesting thought, but I must say I've always tended to use the camera that gives me the best results.' He sipped his wine thoughtfully. 'You have a dark room here, I suppose?'

'Sorry?'

'You develop them yourself?'

'Oh, good Lord no, this may be deepest Cornwall but we're not that backward, no. I take them into Helston, Boots does a very good twenty-four-hour service.'

'Oh!'

'More wine?'

'Er, yes, thanks very much.' Sam looked amused, obviously enjoying my company.

'And are these your pictures?' he asked, indicating the extremely average happy holiday snaps arranged on the cabinet.

'Oh no, Nick took most of those.' An awful lot of

them featured Nick, but I didn't let that bother me. 'No, mine are all upstairs. I'm rather shy about displaying them, actually.'

'Oh, come now, you mustn't be shy!' Sam scraped his chair back a bit and rested his arm on the back of my chair. 'I'd love to see them.' He held my gaze for just a little longer than was strictly necessary.

Christ! I took a great gulp of wine and quite a lot went down my chin. Gosh, this was so exciting. He was flirting *outrageously* with me, wasn't he? He obviously fancied me something rotten.

'Oh, they're frightfully ordinary,' I warbled, desperate to get off the subject of my fascinating camera technique. 'You wouldn't be very interested – but tell me,' I cupped my chin in my hands and gave him what I hoped was a ravishing smile, 'what I really want to know is how did you get into directing?'

He smiled. 'Oh, that's a long and boring story.'

'Rubbish, I'm interested, go on.'

Sam sighed. 'Well, I suppose I worked my way up from the bottom really. It's the only way in the film world; nobody's terribly impressed by degrees or exam results. I started off as a runner when I left school – ran my little legs off, in fact – then I got a job as a second assistant, which led to first assistant, then finally someone gave me a chance to direct my first commercial. That led fairly naturally to films, of course, but I tell you it was a hard slog getting there – you have to be prepared to work very long hours. Sally was marvellous about it but it can't have been much fun for her.'

'Sally?'

'My wife. We'd only just got married and the last thing we wanted to do was spend our evenings apart. I missed her like mad, so in the end she used to come and watch me work, sit there reading or sewing or something while I fiddled around with a camera. Then we'd go out and have a late supper. It was the only way to get on in those days: you had to put in the hours and learn how to do things practically, learn how to focus properly, how to get the lighting right, that sort of thing. Of course, being a photographer in my spare time helped enormously. It's very much a natural progression, as I'm sure you're aware, Polly.' He smiled.

I stared at him blankly. I'd been thinking about Sally. What was a natural progression?

'Oh! Oh yes, of course, it is, isn't it? Yes, I'm terribly interested in filming myself, always catch the latest directors – Visconti, Coppola, Capoletti – I've seen them all, never miss a chance to see something avant-garde.'

'Capoletti? I'm not sure I know him.'

Heavens, did I mean Capoletti, or was that a kind of pasta? Luckily, there was a slight pause as Mrs Bradshaw, whom I'd enlisted to help for the evening, replaced our empty salmon plates with pheasant. 'Oh, er, well, he's a bit of an acquired taste really, does, um, spaghetti westerns, that kind of thing.'

'Really? Well, you certainly have eclectic tastes. Do they cater for that sort of thing down here?'

'Oh yes, we have a marvellous cinema in Helston' – the fact that it showed *The Jungle Book* pretty much continuously was neither here nor there – 'marvellous, but you know what really interests me, Sam, is the actual technique of film-making. That's why I was so keen for you all to come down here. I want to immerse myself in the finer nuances, get the smell of greasepaint up my nose.'

Sam smiled ruefully. 'I'm afraid it's only a commercial, Polly.'

'Oh, I know, but I've got to start somewhere, haven't I? And it's such a shame you're shooting the final day in London! I only found that out from Pippa earlier on today. I would have loved to have seen it through to the end, appreciated it as a whole entity and –'

I jumped as an arm went round my shoulders and a head came between me and Sam.

'I don't know what she's telling you but I wouldn't believe it if I were you. It's bound to be lies, every word of it!'

'Tim! You made it at last!' I blushed, wishing he hadn't hit the nail quite so firmly on the head. 'Sam, this is my brother-in-law Tim Penhalligan; Tim, this is Sam Weston, the director.'

Tim smiled and held out his hand. He was a smaller, softer version of Nick, nice-looking but with none of Nick's stature and presence.

'I can't believe you got my brother to agree to this commercial,' he said to Sam incredulously. 'You must have asked him at a very weak moment.'

'Well, you'll have to ask Polly about that – she engineered the whole thing.'

'I bet she did!' Tim grinned widely. 'Exactly how devious and Machiavellian did you have to be, Polly?'

'Now, Tim, don't be like that, go and sit down next to Pippa, there's a good boy. Your wife's made the most delicious pheasanty thing and it's getting cold.' I shooed him away before he had a chance to elaborate on my engineering skills.

I turned back to Sam and smiled winningly, wondering what we could talk about next. Would he be interested in the organization of the village fête, I wondered?

'So, why don't you then?' he asked with a smile.

I jumped. 'Sorry? What?'

'The commercial, you said you'd like to see it through to the end. Why don't you come up to London for the studio shoot? Frankly, there's a lot of waiting around and not much action, but, if you're interested, by all means come and watch – you'd be more than welcome.'

'Oh! Oh, well, I don't know, I mean it's quite a long way to go just to watch a commercial being shot, isn't it?'

'Sure, absolutely.' He nodded. 'I just thought I'd offer, but you're right – it's a hell of a drive just to stand around in a draughty studio.' He smiled and cupped his ear at Bruce, who was shouting something at him across the table. 'What? Missed that, Bruce.'

I stared at his profile, then down at my pheasant. Well done, Polly, you handled that beautifully, you moron. I watched him chatting and laughing with Bruce, so easy, so self-assured, so urbane, so . . . London. Suddenly I wanted to stand around in a draughty studio more than anything else in the world. I tried to catch his eye but he was deep in discussion. Bruce was waxing lyrical about the porcelain.

'You really should see it, Sam, it's out of this world!'

'So you said earlier, Brucey, but to be honest it's not really my scene.'

'Don't you like antiques?' I asked, trying to crowbar my way back into the conversation.

He turned and looked at me for a moment. 'In the right setting, yes, I do, and they look perfect here, but personally I'm more at home with the minimalist look. I'm not very keen on clutter – I like very clean lines.' He laughed. 'I'm probably a bit of a philistine but if truth be told I like everything to be bang up to date. I'm not a great one for living in the past and being surrounded by relics.'

'Oh, but these Meissen figurines are different,' gushed Bruce. 'They're mind-blowing, they belong in a museum. They must be worth a fortune, Polly!'

'Probably,' I said ruefully, 'and don't get me wrong, I love them too, but sometimes I think I'd love the money more. We need it so badly at the moment but Nick won't hear of selling anything; they've been in the family for generations, you see.'

'Oh, you couldn't sell them!' said Bruce, shocked.

Mrs Bradshaw momentarily obscured Bruce from view as she leaned in to serve some vegetables. I seized my chance.

'Sam, actually,' I murmured, leaning towards him and blushing slightly, 'I'd love to come. You're right, it would be a tremendous opportunity.'

'Really?' He grinned. 'What made you change your mind?'

'Oh, I don't know . . .' I faltered, wishing he wouldn't look at me like that. 'I – I would have said yes in the first place but I suppose I'm not used to having things sprung on me like that.'

'It's always as well to say yes to things, rather than no,' he said softly. 'It's a bit of a philosophy with me.'

'Oh, I couldn't agree more,' I said quickly, thinking I'd say yes to absolutely everything from now on.

'Good, well, I'm delighted you're coming. The last day's really quite fun. We usually go out for a few drinks after the shoot, have something to eat.'

'Oh!' I exclaimed. 'A wrap party! I've heard about those!'

'Well, not quite, we're making a Doggy Chocs commercial, not *Ben Hur*, but budget permitting we should have a few laughs.' He took a sip of wine, smiled at me over his glass, then turned to talk to Sarah, who was momentarily on her own.

I drank my wine thoughtfully and wondered what his wife was like. Stunningly beautiful, I suspected, but perhaps in a rather hard way. Sharp little power suits, a dark geometric bob and bright-red Paloma Picasso lips, no doubt. Really high-powered and successful, another media whiz kid or something big in PR. I wondered what she did while her man was away shooting? Did she pine, or was she even now twinkling away in a similar vein at an elegant dinner party in London, besotting a barrister or mesmerizing a management consultant – it certainly seemed to be the way the chattering classes behaved these days, and why not? It was obviously totally harmless, and great fun. Gosh, I was so out of touch. But I wondered if I'd mind if Nick chatted up the birds quite so vociferously. I watched him at the other end of the table laughing and joking with Pippa. Now, that really was harmless. He caught my eye and smiled. I smiled back, relieved that we were at least on smiling terms again.

'Nick can spare you for a couple of days, can he?' asked Sam with a grin, clearly witnessing this touching exchange of teeth.

'A – couple of days?'

He saw my face. 'Well, it's not really worth driving there and back in one day, you'll be whacked, but of course if you'd rather just come up for the morning or –'

'No, no! No, I wouldn't! I mean, you're absolutely right, I'll stay with Pippa. Yes, of course he can spare me; I don't have to ask permission, you know!'

He laughed. 'I'm sure you don't.'

'And, um, where shall I meet you?' I asked, leaning back and rummaging in the sideboard drawer behind me for paper and a pencil. 'Where do I have to go? What time?' I flipped open a pad.

Sam laughed. 'You're so efficient, Polly. I could do with a secretary like you! To be honest, I'm not absolutely sure. I haven't actually used the studio before, but I think it's somewhere in Chalk Farm. I'm sure Pippa will fill you in on the details.'

'Oh sure, I'll ask her later,' I said, nonchalantly flinging the pad and paper over my shoulder on to the floor, as if I couldn't be more relaxed about where and when I was next going to see him. I tucked into my supper and turned to chat to Bruce for a while.

After a bit, Mrs Bradshaw appeared to take more plates away. It was too much for her to carry in one go so I got to my feet and held out my hands. 'Here, let me help you.'

She stared incredulously at me and stalked past, holding on firmly to the dirty dishes. I flushed unattractively and sat down in confusion. Sam gave her a winning smile as she collected his and, to my surprise, she smiled back.

'God, that was blood out of a stone,' he muttered. 'Where did you find her, Central Casting?'

I sighed ruefully, 'Unfortunately I inherited her with the house.'

'Well, I should disinherit her if I were you. Life's too short to be bossed around in your own home.'

I stared at him. He didn't care what he said, did he? For all he knew she might be a faithful and valued old retainer. But he was right, and it was about time I said what I thought for a change too, instead of pussyfooting around people's feelings and getting my own crushed in the process. It was about time I stood up for myself. I watched as he chatted to Sarah, not quite as flirtatiously as he had with me, I was pleased to see, but still charm itself, asking questions and listening attentively to the answers as if she were the only person in the room with anything worthwhile to say.

Sarah caught my eye when he'd turned back to Bruce and did a mock swoon. 'Divine,' she mouthed, rolling her eyes.

I grinned, but felt ridiculously proprietorial. He was *my* film director, making a commercial in *my* house, so I got to be chatted up, OK? My turn came again soon enough and I made the most of it, laughing uproariously at all his jokes, twinkling merrily into his eyes and doing a great deal of crossing and uncrossing of legs, even once – in a very daring moment and hoping to God Nick hadn't seen – retrieving a deliberately dropped napkin from the floor. It was the best fun I'd had in ages.

Later that evening when everyone had gone, I took the coffee cups through to the kitchen where Mrs Bradshaw was washing up. I closed the door behind me.

'That's OK, Mrs Bradshaw, I'll do the rest, you get off home.'

She didn't budge from her position at the sink, neither did she acknowledge my remark. She simply took the cups from my hands without even looking at me and carried on washing up. I bit my lip and moved to the side of the sink where she could see me.

'I said leave it, really, I'll finish up here.'

'I'm here now, aren't I?' she growled.

'Look, I don't think you understand. I don't want you to do any more. In fact I don't want you to do anything for me ever again.'

She looked up sharply. 'What d'you mean?'

'I mean I'm letting you go, Mrs Bradshaw.'

'You can't do that!'

'Of course I can. I'll give you a month's wages, of course, but I honestly think it's best for all concerned if you leave now. You obviously don't enjoy working here and, to be perfectly honest, I don't enjoy having you. Goodnight, Mrs Bradshaw.' I turned and left her staring open-mouthed into the soap suds.

I closed the kitchen door softly behind me and went upstairs to the bedroom. I smiled. Yes, I was sorting my life out. It was really beginning to take shape. Nick was already in bed. I climbed in beside him.

'I've fired Mrs Bradshaw,' I whispered.

''Bout time too,' he murmured back.

'You don't mind?'

'Course not. I said you should do it. What made you suddenly decide?'

'Oh, just something Sam said. It's such a relief, I must say.'

There was a pause. 'Good,' he said gruffly. 'Anything else? Or can I go to sleep now, I've got to be up in a few hours.'

'Well . . . there is, actually. D'you mind if I go to London for a couple of days?'

'Of course not, why?'

'Well, I thought it would be fun to see the rest of the commercial being made. Sam suggested it and I'd really quite like to.' This last bit came out in a bit of a rush. There was another pause.

'Fine,' said Nick slowly, 'although I'm surprised, Polly. I thought you would have had enough of commercials from your advertising days.'

'Oh, well, yes, I certainly typed a few, but I never actually made it to a shoot, did I?'

'My fault, I'm sure,' he said drily. 'When are you off?'

'On Thursday.'

'Right. Anything else?'

'No, I don't think so.'

'Good.'

'Oh, yes,' I said a few moments later, 'I thought I might buy a camera.'

Nick made no response.

Chapter Nine

I was awoken the following morning by a scrunch of wheels on the gravel, followed by a terrific barking. I sat up in bed with a jolt. For some extraordinary reason I'd been having an erotic dream about Val Doonican, and we'd ended up in a precarious position in his rocking chair with one of his woolly cardies thrown over us, rocking for England, as it were. Understandably, I was in something of a fluster when I flew out of bed and ran to the window, not least because it had been strangely pleasurable . . . Perhaps Pippa was right about older men?

I peered out, loins still twanging perceptibly, to see a large green van parked outside on the drive. The deafening barking was coming from within and the van itself looked possessed, jumping up and down of its own accord as its canine occupants hurled themselves against the sides, howling their heads off, desperate for their liberty. I shivered and grabbed Val's cardie – I mean my dressing gown – and watched as a little pixie of a man with a green cap on jumped down from the cab and ran round to open the door at the back.

The moment he'd turned the handle the door flew open and out leaped ten or twelve dogs of various shapes and sizes, all thoroughly overexcited and barking their heads off furiously. I was relieved to see that they were all on leads and attached to two or three formidable Barbara

Woodhouse-type minders who were fairly dragged out of the van after them, yelling at them in foghorn, county voices.

'Quiet, Bracken!'

'Pipe down, Sasha! PIPE DOWN, I SAY!'

'Steady, Victor! Steady!'

There were labradors, retrievers, an Alsatian, a couple of Dalmatians and God knows what else, but all of them seemed to me to be on the huge and enormous side. What was wrong with a couple of Yorkshire terriers? I gulped in alarm, threw some clothes on and ran down to the kitchen.

Nick was at the kitchen window, taking in the canine scene in a somewhat tight-lipped fashion. The noise was unreal.

'It's the doggy bit today,' I said nervously as I put the kettle on.

'Really, Polly? I'd never have guessed.'

He grabbed hold of Badger who was leaping up at the back door, barking his head off in an ecstatic, demented fashion, totally over the moon that well over a dozen dogs had suddenly got it into their heads to come and play at *his* house today.

'I'm putting Badger in his kennel,' he said grimly, dragging a wildly protesting Badger in the opposite direction to that of his playmates. 'Don't want him joining in.'

I breathed deeply as he went, exhaling slowly. Oh Lord. I did hope everything was going to go smoothly. Perhaps I should go back to bed until it was all over? I made myself a piece of toast and Marmite and stood munching it at the window, watching as the dogs charged off towards the bottom field, dragging their minders behind them, still hysterical with excitement. A moment later there was a tap at the kitchen door. Sam stuck his head round.

'I know they sound outrageous, but I promise you, when it comes to the crunch, they're incredibly well behaved. They've been specially trained for this sort of thing.'

'I'm glad to hear it,' I said nervously. 'They certainly make enough noise.'

'They're just a little overexcited, but don't you worry, I'm well aware that you've got livestock here and we're going to keep a really close eye on these hounds. All they've got to do is run across a field, leap a little stone wall and run towards some dog bowls. It's a cinch. We might even get it in one take, then they'll be back in the van and off home. You won't even know they've been here.' He grinned. 'Smile, Polly.'

I grinned back. 'OK, if you say so.'

'I do. Coming down to watch? I can get you a VIP seat.'

'Sure, why not?'

'See you later then, don't be too long.' He winked, then disappeared round the door.

Suddenly any misgivings I might previously have had about this morning's activity were totally forgotten. I shoved the toast in my mouth and ran upstairs in a flurry of excitement. A frantic dressing and undressing saga then took place until the bed was piled high with clothes and I was dressed in the very first outfit I'd originally thought of. I stared at my reflection. Right, make-up. I drew a line under my eyes – quite carefully for me – then added lipstick, blusher and – hang on. I eyed my reflection guiltily as the blusher brush skimmed over my cheek-bones. What are you doing, Polly? I tried to meet my eyes.

Nothing, I retorted sharply, snapping the compact shut, I'm simply making the best of myself, anything wrong with that? And yes, OK, I'm enjoying myself too, anything wrong with that either? I raised my eyebrows quizzically at my reflection. God, they could do with a pluck. I hurriedly pulled some tweezers from a drawer and launched a frenzied attack, taking too much from one and having to even up the other, then taking too much from that one – and so it went on until my eyebrows had all but disappeared. It was an absorbing, painful and time-consuming exercise and by the time I'd finished and looked out of the window again I was surprised to see that the dogs were already lined up in the bottom field, ready for the off.

There they sat, all in a row with their minders standing behind them, looking, I had to admit, remarkably quiet and well behaved. Even so, I'd be glad when it was all over.

I grabbed a jacket, ran downstairs and was about to go out when I decided I couldn't possibly take another step until I'd had a cup of coffee and a cigarette. I gulped down a scalding mug of Nescafé and was just taking the last drag of nicotine down to my Docksiders when the most terrific howling made me dash to the window.

The scene that greeted my eyes is one I hope never to see again as long as I live. First I dropped my cigarette then my jaw. I gaped incredulously. A dozen or so sup-posedly impeccably behaved dogs were indeed charging. But they were charging the wrong way. They were charg-ing this way, my way, my house way. A sea of rolling eyes, open mouths, flapping ears and lolling tongues was galloping towards me, a howling mass of totally out-of-control and extremely mad dogs, and behind them, furiously giving chase, were the minders, pounding along, waving their arms, shaking their fists and making almost as much noise, but all to no avail.

Because there was no stopping these dogs. They moved as one, as a back-to-the-wilds pack, pounding along hell-for-leather and destroying everything that got in their way: hedges, fences, gates – you name it, they crashed through it, scattering chickens, geese and ducks, and leaving a cloud of feathers in their wake. I couldn't move. I was literally rooted to the spot, paralysed with fear and disbelief.

They'd almost made it to the garden, just one more fence and – sorry, one more *broken* fence – and they were in, it was the work of a moment. Through they crashed, and behind them crashed the minders, still waving their arms about and screaming futilely into the wind at the tops of their voices. In the midst of this second, human pack, I spotted a familiar figure. Nick was running like the blazes, fists clenched, face purple with fury. It was a terrifying sight. My hand flew to my mouth. 'Shit!' My intestines very nearly obeyed, they certainly curdled nastily. I clenched my buttocks guardedly.

My first, and on reflection probably best inclination was to hide. I looked around wildly – what about the cupboard under the sink? Or maybe I had time to make it down to the cellar? I could stay there for days, weeks even, sneaking up at night for food and water. Nick would never find me. I dithered, but stupidly resisted the temptation, and instead – mad impulsive fool that I am – darted to the back door.

As I opened it I screamed and leaped about a foot in the air as a small, bedraggled creature raced in, swept over my feet and fled through the kitchen. Christ, a rat! I scuttled quickly outside and ran down the path to the vegetable garden.

The marauding dogs had reached the front lawn now, or, rather, the rose garden. I could see the whites of their eyes as they galloped recklessly through it, scattering roses and trampling carefully tended lavender bushes, madness in their eyes, rose petals and saliva dripping copiously from their mouths. I waved my arms around timidly; surely they'd stop when they saw me?

'Steady, boys, steady now!' I quavered nervously.

They didn't seem to be steadying at all, if anything they seemed to be gaining momentum. Any minute now I'd be mown down, flattened by a pack of marauding dogs, but I had to stand my ground. Better to die with paw prints on my face than to face the wrath of Nick, whose livid purple features were even now bearing down on me. If anything, it was a more terrifying sight than the dogs. As he crashed through the rose garden he yelled something about a door, but I couldn't quite hear.

'WHAT?' I yelled back.

The dogs shot past me, missing me by inches, and in their midst I spotted a familiar black figure, pink tongue hanging out, galloping joyously – Badger. For a moment he gave a naughty glance in my direction, then, with mad rolling eyes, thundered on by with the others.

'I SAID SHUT THE BACK DOOR!' screamed Nick, as he raced up the lawn.

I swung round but – too late. The last of the bunch, a

panting golden retriever, flashed inside and out of sight. I moaned low. Ooohhhh . . . divorce. Nick shot past me.

'WHY DIDN'T YOU SHUT THE BLOODY DOOR?'

'I – I didn't hear you, didn't think . . .' I stammered, but he'd gone.

He tore into the kitchen followed by the minders. One of them grabbed my arm as he went past.

'Polly!'

'Bruce!' He was as white as a sheet, his eyes wide with fear.

'Have you seen Munchkin?' he shrieked.

'Munchkin? No, not unless she was amongst that lot – Bruce, what the hell's going on? They've all gone absolutely crazy! Nick's going to kill me, it's going to be all my fault, I just know it is!'

'It's Munchkin,' wailed Bruce, wringing his hands, 'she's on heat and I completely forgot! I took her down to watch the big doggy-boys doing their stuff, thought she'd really enjoy it, you see, and – and they just went berserk! One whiff and they completely forgot what they were supposed to be doing; they just wanted to get at her! She jumped out of my arms, poor mite, and fled – she even swam through a stream – and now I don't know where she is, probably being raped and pillaged by one of those brutish hounds at this very moment! Oh God, I can't bear it!' He wrung his hands in despair.

'Oh! Oh wait, hang on a minute! I thought it was a rat but it must have been Munchkin, yes it was, soaked through – she's in the house! Quick!'

We ran inside where a trail of destruction greeted us.

Chairs and tables had been tipped over, vases were smashed, pictures were askew, plants were spewing out of their pots and carpets were covered in mud. I felt physically sick and very nearly made for the cellar right there and then, but somehow I managed to get a grip and follow Bruce and the paw marks as he raced upstairs towards the frantic howling and baying that was coming from the spare bedroom.

'Oh, Munchkin! Oh my poor baby, Daddy's coming!' he gasped as we tore down the corridor and flew into the room at the end of the passage.

In this very small spare bedroom, about fourteen large dogs were going completely demented. They'd got a wardrobe surrounded and were barking and howling like crazy, scratching frantically at the carpet, climbing on top of each other, desperately trying to shove their noses underneath. Nick and one or two burly women had most of them by their collars and were doing their best to haul them off.

'I think there's a rat or something under the wardrobe,' yelled Nick above the noise, dragging a couple of dogs away. 'I had a look and I can see a couple of eyes. I'll get my gun.'

'NO!' shrieked Bruce, as he fell on Nick's arm. 'No, no! Don't! It's Munchkin!'

Nick frowned. 'Munchkin?'

'My little dog!' Bruce looked around quickly to see who was listening before confiding quietly, 'It's – it's her special time of the month, you see.'

'Her what?'

'Her delicate ladies' time. You know,' he whispered, 'her cursey-wursey.'

Nick stared at him. 'Are you trying to tell me she's on heat?'
'Exactly.'

Nick groaned. 'Oh, Bruce, it's a wonder she hasn't been raped – she's sending these boys absolutely crazy!'

Bruce tightened his grip on Nick's arm. 'You don't think she has been raped, do you? You don't think one of these brutes has had his evil, wicked way with her?' he whimpered, his voice cracking.

Nick regarded the sex-crazed hounds surrounding us, still baying their heads off.

'Well, it would be an interesting combination, wouldn't it? What d'you fancy, Bruce, Chihuahua-Dalmatian or Chihuahua-Great Dane?'

'Oh God!' gasped Bruce, clutching his mouth. 'My poor darling!'

'Relax,' went on Nick darkly, 'unless one of these boys had the nous to hoist her up on to a chair and slip it in before she shot under the wardrobe I think it's highly unlikely.' He turned to the minders. 'Come on, let's get them out of here. Polly, you could lend a hand too if you can tear yourself away from the curtains.'

Oh God, he'd spotted me. I crept meekly out from my hiding place and grabbed a couple of labradors. Nick found a piece of rope and we managed to make some leads so the minders could drag them, protesting wildly, downstairs and back to the fields.

Bruce then spent half an hour lying on the floor trying to coax a terrified Munchkin out from under the wardrobe.

'Come on, Munchy, come on, Boofles, come to Daddy! The nasty rough boys have all gone home now, come to Daddy-kins!'

I would have liked to have stayed safely up in the bedroom with Bruce and Munchkin but Nick jerked his head curtly in the direction of the door and I meekly fell in behind him. We walked downstairs in silence and surveyed the mayhem around us. My spouse's lips were tightening by the moment and a look of furious horror and outrage was passing over his face. I had a feeling he wasn't going to be able to quell it. I was right.

'This is intolerable, Polly,' he seethed, 'absolutely intolerable!'

'But, Nick, it wasn't my fault,' I quavered pathetically. 'I mean, Munchkin is Bruce's dog; she's nothing to do with me, all I did was –'

'All you did was leave the bloody door open, which I think you'll agree was really quite a contributing factor to the destruction of our house,' he seethed. 'If I were you, Polly, I wouldn't say another word on the subject, because I have a feeling I may not be able to control my temper, and I don't want to have to kill you.'

Grateful for the warning, I confined myself to surveying the debris. I dreaded to think how much it might cost to repair, but in the light of Nick's last remark thought it best not to broach the subject. Josh did it for me. He came racing through the front hall and skidded to a halt at the foot of the stairs.

'I've just heard,' he gasped. 'I'm terribly sorry – this is appalling!'

'Isn't it just,' muttered Nick darkly.

'Now look, don't worry about a thing, it'll all be put straight in a twinkling. I'll get on to our insurance company straight away, they'll be round here just as soon as I've briefed them.'

'They'd better be,' said Nick curtly. 'That vase down there in a million pieces was a very old Royal Doulton.'

'Everything will be replaced – I give you my word.'

'Something like that is irreplaceable.'

'Oh dear.' Josh scratched his head. 'I am extremely sorry, but it really wasn't our fault. Apparently Bruce's little bitch got them all sexed up and –'

'So I gather,' snapped Nick, picking up a small tripod table and setting it straight. 'Well, please see what can be done about the superficial mess and get the house tidied up. I'll look into the more serious damage outside. Excuse me while I go and round up any animals that might have escaped to the next village and mend a few miles of fencing.' He stalked off, leaving Josh and me to cringe deeply at each other.

In the event, it was only the Royal Doulton vase that had actually been irrevocably smashed. Thankfully, everything else could be picked up, put back together, sponged down or washed. I dragged a much-scolded and sheepish Badger back to his kennel, tying him up firmly this time. He gave me a pathetic, pleading look but I didn't melt. If I was in the dog house, so was he. Various crew members arrived to clean the stair carpet, wash down the walls and generally pick up the pieces. Pippa and I rolled up our sleeves and set to work in the kitchen. We'd just finished washing the kitchen floor when Sam stuck his head round the door. His eyes were shining and a mischievous grin lit up his face.

'Where's the irate husband?' he whispered.

'He's gone to cool down.'

'Is he absolutely livid?'

'Steaming.'

'Out for blood?'

I giggled. 'Mine in particular, but probably yours too.'

'Oh hell.' He crept in, unable to keep the radiance from his smile. 'I'm terribly sorry, dreadful thing to happen, but the thing is, you see, we got the most incredible shot of the dogs! Tony managed to swing the camera round and we got them charging hell-for-leather. It looked absolutely amazing on the monitor, you should have seen it.'

'I did,' I said grimly, 'together with the whites of their eyes. I was on the receiving end of the magic.'

'Gosh, how awful, poor you. I am sorry.' Actually, he did look genuinely sorry. 'And I gather they made a bit of a mess in here – anything I can do to help? Sponge a few walls? Wash the floor, perhaps?' He looked innocently at the now gleaming, damp flagstones. 'Oh dear, I see I'm too late.'

I grinned. 'Just a touch. Don't worry, everything's under control now. To be honest, it looked worse than it was.'

'Oh, what a relief. Well, I just came to tell you that since we got the charging scene in the can so quickly we'll be off pretty soon. We're leaving Bruce behind for a couple of days to tie up a few loose ends – he wants to see his mother anyway – and he'll liaise with the insurance company for you. He'll be staying in Helston if you need him, but the rest of us will be getting out of your hair and shooting back to London in' – he looked at his watch – 'oh, about an hour's time, I suppose.'

'Oh!' My spirits sank into my boots. 'So soon?'

He smiled ruefully. I could feel Pippa's eyes on me. ''Fraid so, but we'll see you again in London, won't we? You're still on for that?'

'Oh yes, of course! Yes, I'll see you then.' My spirits made a miraculous recovery, rocketing from my ankles to my armpits in seconds. I was all smiles again, transparent or what?

He grinned. 'Good, look forward to it. See you then, Polly, and thanks again for the hospitality.'

'My pleasure,' I whispered as he pecked me on the cheek.

I watched as he disappeared round the back door and down through the garden.

Pippa stood up, put her bucket and mop in the broom cupboard, pulled her sleeves down and folded her arms in a businesslike manner. She turned to face me.

'He's married, Polly,' she said grimly.

I stared at her. 'Don't be ridiculous!' I gasped. 'So am I, happily, thanks very much!' I could feel myself blushing.

'I know, and that's why I don't want you to spoil things. I know you're a bit bored, but don't – you know – dabble, will you, Poll? It's simply not worth it.'

I gaped. 'Bloody hell!' I spluttered eventually. 'That's rich coming from you!'

'But that's precisely why I'm telling you this, don't you see?' she said earnestly. 'My situation is not a happy one. I'd give anything not to have fallen for a married man, and apart from anything else Sam's not a patch on Nick.'

'Pippa!' I exploded. 'You're way off beam here. I have *not* fallen for a married man! Just because I'm enjoying myself for a change – God, you were the one who told me to have a bit of fun, get my act together, lose weight, go blonde, shorten my skirts, get up to London – and now that I'm doing all that you go off the deep end!'

Pippa shook her head sagely. 'Polly, I know when you've got the hots for someone – you get that look in your eye.'

'What look?'

'That sort of glazed goldfish look. Also your boobs heave around like nobody's business and you hold your tummy in – come on, you definitely fancy him, any fool can see that.'

'Well, OK, maybe I do, so what? Doesn't mean I'm going to do anything about it, does it? I mean, I fancy Jeremy Paxman but I don't sniff around the *Newsnight* studio waiting for him to emerge, do I? I quite fancy the sheep-shearer in the next village in a bit-of-rough sort of way, but I don't make myself available to him every time he gets to grips with our sheep. So what if I fancy Sam? So what if I indulge in a little harmless banter, flirt with him even, where's the harm in that? Married people are allowed to talk to each other, you know, it doesn't mean we're about to embark on a full-blooded sex romp.'

'No, but –'

'Pippa, you see adultery at every corner. You live with it so you automatically assume everyone's up to it.'

Pippa opened her mouth to argue – then hesitated. She sat down at the kitchen table and sighed. Her lips compressed and she gazed past me.

'Maybe you're right,' she said softly, 'perhaps it's me. I'm so obsessed with a married man I think everyone else must be too. I'm sorry, Polly.' She looked down and abruptly covered her face with her hands. 'Oh God, what am I going to do?' she whispered.

I sat down next to her and put my arm round her. Even though it was upsetting for her I was relieved we'd got off the subject of me and were talking about her suddenly. I sighed.

'I don't know, I don't know what you're going to do. I just know it must be awful for you.'

'It's not awful, it's hell!' she snapped, looking up for a second. 'It's an absolute living hell!' She sighed and looked down again, 'Oh, Polly, I don't even like myself any more. I don't like what I'm doing but I just can't help it. It's so destructive – for Josh, for his wife, not to mention me – God, it's tearing me apart!' She gulped. 'Look at me, I'm falling to pieces here, and for what? He's never going to leave her, is he?' She looked at me pleadingly, willing me to say he might.

I hesitated. 'Well . . . put it this way, Pipps, I wouldn't set your heart on it.' Her face crumpled. 'Isn't there any-one else?' I said quickly. 'Anyone – you know – single? Charles was lovely, what happened to him?'

'Charles?' She looked wistful for a moment, then shook her head. 'Oh, I don't know, I suppose I bished it up as usual. You just don't know how lucky you are, Polly, you don't know what it's like to be still out there, still on the market, still sitting on the shelf and getting staler by the minute.'

'Pippa! You don't think like that, do you?'

'Not usually, no, but in my darker moments I do. I see

myself as a stale old bun with a few mouldy currants on top. Only for a second, of course, then I pick myself up, brush myself off, read a few "think positive about being single" articles in women's magazines, remember my great job, my friends, my sort-of relationship with my sort-of boyfriend, and I'm all right for a bit. But it's still there, you know, however much I disguise it, that nagging feeling that I haven't quite got life in the bag.'

'You mean a man in the bag.'

'I suppose so,' she mumbled. 'Christ, not very feminist, is it? What would the editor of *Cosmo* say?'

'I won't tell on you.'

'Thanks. But, you see, that's why I find it so hard to see how two married people like you and Sam can be just good mates. I think all married people are secretly looking for a bit on the side. But I suppose that's just me being jaundiced – sorry.'

'Forget it.' I squeezed her hand. 'I have.'

I poured her a glass of wine and she downed it practically in one. Then she looked at her watch. 'God, is that the time? I must go, Josh will kill me if I'm late.'

She quickly put on some lipstick and dragged a brush through her hair, then we hugged each other and she went on her way, off to join the crew and then back to London.

When she'd gone I got up and moved slowly round the kitchen, thinking about what she'd said. I put a few things away and wiped the last traces of dirty dog tails from the walls. I poured myself a drink. Nick came in from the farm.

'Everything all right?' His lips were still quite tight.

'Well, they've gone, thank God, and everything's

shipshape and tidy again – very little damage, actually, just the vase,' I breezed as brightly as I could.

'Good,' he said shortly. 'Well done for clearing up.'

'Oh, it didn't take long.'

We smiled politely at each other, then Nick went upstairs for a bath, taking the newspaper with him. I felt guiltily glad to be on my own. I sat at the table, smoking one cigarette after another, trying hard not to think too much.

Chapter Ten

Two days later I set off for London. Nick heaved my heavy case downstairs and round to the car in the drive.

'God, how long are you going for, Polly, a fortnight?'

'Don't be silly, just a couple of days, but I couldn't decide what clothes to take so I ended up packing half my wardrobe.'

'So I see.' He slammed the boot shut. 'I hadn't realized it was a fashion parade. You'll be back by Saturday morning, won't you?'

'I'm not sure, why?'

He sighed. 'Don't you remember? I asked you to make sure you were. Foxtons are delivering a whole load of corn and feed at nine o'clock and Larry and I won't be here to check it. You know what Foxtons are like – they're bound to short-change us if no one's around, and it takes months to get them to deliver again.'

'But where will you be?'

'I told you, Polly,' he said patiently. 'Larry and I are going to Yorkshire to look at some stock. We'll have to stay over on Friday night. I told you all this yesterday while we were having supper, don't you remember?'

'Er . . . well it sort of rings a bell now you mention it.'

Nick shook his head. 'Sometimes I really wonder about you. You're in another world half the time, aren't you?'

He had a point there, though it was actually more like

three-quarters of the time. And, funnily enough, the other world I'd been inhabiting lately was the glamorous world of stage and screen.

You see, in the space of just two short days I'd graduated from being spotted by Sam to star in his dog-food commercial to taking the leading role in his latest blockbusting feature film. Of course, he'd taken a major gamble casting an unknown newcomer in the starring role, but my goodness it had paid off. The film – a sort of arty-farty English thing with lots of twirling parasols and bags of good taste, the sort of thing Helena Bonham-Whatsername does – had been a phenomenal success, so I now lived a glamorous peripatetic life flitting back and forth between Hollywood, London and Cornwall, still madly in love with my divine husband, of course, but now the darling of the film world too.

Sam, naturally, had fallen headlong at my feet, but I made sure I kept him at arm's length. Obviously we still had to go to expensive restaurants and I had to lean over tiny little tables looking beautiful and sexy to discuss scripts and things, but whilst he tried desperately to look down my top – no, too tacky – to gaze into my eyes, I remained friendly but aloof, maintaining a purely professional relationship with him at all times.

Eventually he poured out his heart to the tabloids – 'The love I can't have' by Sam Webster, 'The Forbidden Fruit I crave' by Sam Webster – but I kept a dignified silence. I tried gently to discourage him and was only ever seen on the arm of my incredibly good-looking husband – attending first nights, accepting awards, holidaying in Antigua – the sort of thing one sees in *Hello!*, though of course we'd never stoop to that. Well, I suppose we *might* just consider one photograph in the drawing room at Trewarren with me reclining gracefully on the sofa in a gorgeous white silk affair, Nick standing proprietorially behind me, his hands resting protectively on my shoulders and two or three enchanting children playing at our feet . . . Ah yes, the children. I sighed. Even in my fantasies that was quite a stumbling block. Nick seemed to be saying something.

'Polly? Are you with me?' He knocked on my head. 'Is anyone at home?'

'Sorry, what?'

'I said, what's this?' He picked up a black leather box from the front seat of the car.

'Oh, that's my new camera, I bought it in Truro yesterday.'

'Really? I didn't know. You should have said – I'd have come with you to choose it.' He took it out of its case and turned it around. 'Is it a good one?'

'Oh yes, it's brilliant, the man in the shop said so, and I know Sam's got one exactly the same.'

'Ah.' Nick put it back and snapped the case shut. 'I see.' He put it down on the front seat again. He seemed strangely silent.

'See you on Saturday then?' I ventured cheerily, and went to peck him on the cheek.

'Sure.' He kissed me back, but as I turned to get in the car he suddenly grabbed hold of me and held me tight. I looked up in surprise. His face seemed troubled.

'What's wrong?'

'Nothing.' He shook his head.

I gave him a hug. 'Have a good time in Yorkshire, give my love to the cows!'

'Will do. Listen, Polly, I'm sorry if I've been rather – well, bad-tempered lately. I've blamed you for everything that's gone wrong around here and it hasn't all been entirely your fault. Sorry. You know me and my short fuse.'

I looked at him incredulously. Good grief, whatever had come over him? 'That's all right, don't be silly. Most of it was most definitely my fault, and anyway, as you well know, it's water off a duck's back with me. Most of the time I don't even listen to you.'

'I know, but . . .' He bit his lip and frowned. 'Look, Poll, are you bored down here?' He looked searchingly at me. 'Because if you are there's nothing to stop you from doing something. I'd go along with it wholeheartedly, you know I would. I remember when you first came down you said the shops round here were lousy and talked about opening a boutique or something – you could still do that, you know. I could raise a bit of money if I had to, it wouldn't be that much of a problem, we could always sell something.'

I was amazed, and very touched. Sell something? Nick?

'That's sweet, Nick, but honestly I went off that idea ages ago. I think I'd be even more bored sitting in a shop waiting for customers. But thanks anyway.'

His brow puckered. 'So you are bored?'

'No! No, of course not, I didn't mean it like that. It's just – well, I don't want to start another career really – not that I had much of one in the first place. I suppose some-how I thought . . . well, I think I thought I'd be doing something else by now.'

I paused and looked at the ground, kicking a bit of gravel around with my foot. I didn't want to bang on about it. Nick nodded and looked at the ground too.

'I know. Babies.' He put his arms round me again. 'It'll happen, Polly, really it will, there's nothing wrong with either of us and there's no reason why we shouldn't have a whole brood one day. We just have to be patient, that's all.'

'I know.'

We held each other silently. I felt rather choked up. Eventually we disentangled ourselves, Nick kissed me hard on the mouth and deposited me in the front seat. I buzzed down the window.

'See you then.'

He smiled. 'Will do. Drive carefully.'

'I will.'

I let the clutch in and moved off slowly, looking in my rear-view mirror at him standing there. He watched until I was out of sight. I waved as I rounded the corner into the lane, still feeling rather choked. Gosh, he could be sweet, couldn't he? I flicked a cassette on. Simply Red blared into action. I flicked it off. I didn't feel like that quite yet. I lit a cigarette. Odd, Nick had seemed strange, emotional . . . troubled, even, so unlike him. Usually he was so – well, pragmatic. I shook my head, perhaps I was imagining it. I gave Simply Red a second chance, put my foot down and headed for the London road.

When I eventually arrived in London I made straight

for the centre of the universe, Harrods car park. I had absolutely no idea where Chalk Farm was but it was bound to be somewhere central; there was no way a man like Sam would shoot a commercial in the back of beyond, was there? I dumped the car at vast expense and whizzed into Rymans for an *A to Z*. Blimey, Chalk Farm was in the back of beyond. I suddenly remembered Pippa saying something about it being a bugger to get to and it was best to drive, but I couldn't possibly get the car out now, having invested a fortune in its installation, so I dived down the Underground steps and headed north.

An hour and a half later, I emerged from beneath the ground, panting, swearing and hoping to God I was somewhere in the region of Camden Town. It had indeed been a bugger of a journey. First a suicidal commuter had to be prized from the rails three stops down before we could even begin our journey, and then our driver had taken it into his head to do a funeral crawl, perhaps as some sort of misguided mark of respect. If anything was designed to make people speak ill of the dead, it was this, and the mutterings around me ranged from 'Odd how they always choose the rush hour to top themselves,' to 'selfish, inconsiderate bastard'. I must say, by the end of the journey I was very much lining up with the sentiments of the latter.

I trudged the last half a mile on foot and eventually arrived at the impossibly difficult-to-find location, which, far from the glamorous studio I'd imagined, seemed to be more of an enormous converted garage next to a fish and chip shop. Frankly, by this stage I couldn't have cared if they were shooting the commercial in a human abattoir I was so exhausted, and I crashed through the double doors like a thing possessed, crazy for a seat and even crazier for a cup of tea.

'Hi!' I gasped, stumbling into a gloomy cavernous room with one very bright spotlight shining at the other end. 'Ooof!' I collapsed gratefully on to the nearest chair, brushing off a few tapes and things so I could sit down.

'Phew! Bloody hell, Pippa, you weren't joking, were you, that was a hell of a trip!' I cried, peering around in the darkness for her.

'Ssshhhhhh!' hissed someone furiously.

'Christ, who the hell's that?'

'CUT! Damn it!'

I gulped and slid down in my chair. Oh no, they hadn't been shooting, had they? At the far end of the room the very bright light snapped off.

'Shit,' said somebody.

I gulped again. They had. An overhead light flicked on and about twenty people turned to look at me. I felt a boiling blush unfolding from my feet.

'Oh it's *you*, Polly!' cried Pippa, appearing from the back of the room. 'Didn't you see the red light?'

'Er, sorry, what red light?'

'The one we put outside to let people know if we're shooting! Oh well, never mind, you weren't to know, you're not used to this sort of thing, but next time – oh my goodness, you look dreadful!' She peered at me. 'Look at you, you're all hot and sweaty, and look at your hair! You didn't walk here, did you? I *told* you not to walk. Honestly, you're such a moron, you never listen, do you?'

By now the entire crew, actors, technicians, Josh, and

of course Sam, had turned to look at this hot, sweaty moron who never listened and had terrible hair. Vowing to disembowel Pippa later, I blustered, 'Of course I *drove*, Pippa, I'm not that stupid. I've been here *millions* of times!'

'Have you? When?'

'When I worked for Nick, of course.'

'But I thought he never took you to a —'

'Sam! Gosh, sorry I'm late, and sorry for barging in like that.' I jumped up, brushing brusquely past Pippa with a mighty glare, and gave Sam my very best smile as he came over to greet me.

He gave me a resounding kiss on the cheek, ruffled my already extremely ruffled hair and grinned.

'Not to worry, although I must say I was beginning to get worried. This is a hellish place to find, but somehow I thought you might know it from your advertising days.'

'Of course, of course! I was just saying to Pippa, I've driven here millions of times. No, the reason I'm a bit late is I stopped off on the way to shoot a couple of rolls of film!'

I indicated the camera swinging jauntily from my neck.

'Oh, excellent,' beamed Sam, 'got to seize the moment, a good shot doesn't wait for anyone.'

'Absolutely, and you see there was this marvellously surly London Transport guard who I just couldn't resist, bags of character, so I just — well, as you said, seized the moment!'

'But I thought you drove here?'

'Oh! Oh yes, I did, but luckily he just happened to be standing *outside* the station, probably getting some fresh air – after all, it's awfully muggy on the Underground – so when I drove past and spotted him, I leaped out, and snapped away – like this –'

I stepped back and took a quick shot of Sam at an artistic angle, then flexed my fingers in a professional manner.

'Thanks, Sam, I think that was a good one.' I patted my camera knowingly and pursed my lips. 'Yep, bags of depth.'

'Er, yes, that's the idea, although you'll probably get more depth if you take the lens cap off.'

Sam reached over and pulled it off for me, but before I had time to take this crushing blow on board he was steering me in the direction of a group of people standing by a camera.

'Now,' he went on, 'who d'you know out of this little lot? Josh and Tony, of course, and Tim who was our lighting cameraman in Cornwall, but I don't think you've met the actresses we're using in the kitchen scene – the non-canine variety, of course! This is Susan Tyler . . .'

I smiled and shook hands with a wholesome, motherly type holding a can of dog food.

'Hi.' She returned my smile.

'And this,' Sam went on, 'is our glamorous leading lady, in as much as you can have a leading lady in a dog-food commercial!'

Out of the shadows emerged an undoubtedly glamorous but also extremely familiar figure. I stepped back and gasped.

'Well, well,' she drawled. 'Hello, Polly, fancy seeing you here.'

'Serena!'

Sam raised his eyebrows and looked from me to Serena. 'You two know each other?'

'Oh sure,' purred Serena, 'we're old buddies. In fact Polly married one of my cast-offs, didn't you, Polly?'

There was an embarrassed silence. Serena stood watching me, looking as devastating as ever. Her slanty green eyes shot off at angles over her high cheekbones and her short blond hair gleamed almost white. She swept it back in a practised manner, a mocking smile playing about her perfect mouth. She fair took your breath away in more ways than one. Eventually I stopped gasping at her audacity and found some wind.

'If I remember rightly,' I snapped, 'he cast *you* off, not vice versa!'

Serena's irritating girly laugh tinkled around the studio. 'Gol-ly, calm down!' she tittered. 'I'm only winding you up. I see you're still as hot-headed as ever. Anyway, I seem to recall there was very little love lost between either party at the end of our relationship. But tell me, how is Nick? Still playing at being a farmer?'

I clenched my fists. 'There's no playing about it; it's a serious business, as you well know, and he's extremely well, thank you!'

'Phew!' Serena fanned her perfectly made-up face and backed away. 'You don't half heat up quickly, Polly. Try exercising a little self-control now and again.'

'I'm perfectly in control, thank you very much,' I snarled between gritted teeth, 'and I must say I'm a little surprised to see you here, Serena – a dog-food commercial? Slumming it a bit, aren't you? Hardly Oscar-winning stuff, is it, or has your career been put on the back burner for a while?'

Serena threw back her pretty blonde head and tinkled merrily into the rafters. 'You're showing your ignorance, darling, I should keep quiet if I were you. When one has a chance to work with a director like Sam, one would do anything, simply anything – a video, a commercial, a feature film – just for the experience. It's all in the direction, you see, but I don't expect you to understand that.' She lit a cigarette, narrowed her eyes and blew the smoke into my face. 'But tell me, what about you? What brings you all the way from the sticks on your little ownsome? Don't tell me you're bored with rural life already? Got a bit of time on your hands? Planted all your cabbages? Or is Nick neglecting you, perhaps – no trouble at home, I hope?'

I was just about to biff her smartly on the nose when Sam cut in hastily. 'Er, Polly's come up to watch the commercial being made. We filmed the first day on her farm and she's very interested in camera technique, so she's here to see the conclusion.' He looked totally baffled by the shrapnel that was flying around.

Serena raised her eyebrows. 'So you filmed the first day at Trewarren? How amusing!' She turned to Sam. 'Nick and I were briefly engaged, you see, but thank God I saw the light and got out, otherwise it might have been me living in that run-down old farmhouse, can you imagine!'

I was speechless with rage and shock now. She took advantage of this and steamrollered on as I gasped for breath.

'So you're a film groupie now, are you, Polly? How extraordinary, you really must be bored. Got a bit of a taste for the high life when they were shooting down on the farm, did you? What was it that caught your eye, I wonder, or should I say,' she winked at Sam, '*who* was it? Camera technique indeed!' She threw back her head and tinkled again, before leaning forward and confiding, in an incredibly loud whisper, 'He's married, you know – happily – and she's absolutely *sweet*. I do hope you're not making a fool of yourself again?'

'Bl– Je– Wha–!' I spluttered incredulously and incoherently, before eventually managing, 'Don't be so bloody ridiculous!' What I really wanted to do was spit in her eye and kick her shins very hard. 'God, Serena, you're unreal! You're absolutely unreal! If you think for one moment I'm –'

'Er, Serena, I think you're wanted in make-up.' Sam slid between us, arms outstretched. 'And, Polly, if you come this way, I'll show you the monitor. I think you'll find it interesting.'

He took me firmly by the arm while the make-up girl quickly appeared to lead Serena in the other direction. I was spitting with fury.

'Bloody hell! She's a bitch! She's an absolute bitch!'

'I know, I know,' soothed Sam, 'she loves to bait, I'm afraid.'

'Don't I know it,' I seethed. 'We're old sparring partners. She used to go out with Nick but he turned her down in favour of me.' I knew it sounded childish but I wanted to set the record straight.

'Ah, I see. Yes, I got the impression you'd come to blows in the past.'

'She's utterly poisonous. She tried to pretend she was

getting married to Nick in order to get rid of me, and she even got an old boyfriend of mine to try to lure me away from him. She'd stop at nothing to get her own way; she's the sort of person who should have a government health warning stamped on her forehead!'

Sam scratched his head. 'Well, I must say, from the little I know of her I'm inclined to agree with you. I thought it was rather a coup to get her for this commercial, because, as you know, she's done some pretty classy films –'

'Mostly naked,' I spat venomously.

'Well, yes, I suppose some of them required her to take her clothes off – but she's very difficult to direct. I wanted to try her out in this with a view to having her in my next film, but to tell you the truth I'm having second thoughts. She's only got one line but you'd think she was playing Lady Macbeth the way she argues with me about it.'

'I should fire her now,' I said decisively. 'Tell her to pack her bags and get out – go on.'

I'm not normally remotely bitchy but I can really pull the stops out when it comes to Serena. Sam looked taken aback.

'Well, I can't exactly do that now. She's signed a contract and it is after all only a commercial.' He smiled. 'Anyway, let's forget about her, shall we? She's not worth it.'

The smile was desperately winning. I smiled back in what I hoped was an equally winning fashion.

'No, you're absolutely right, she's not worth it.' I put my head to one side, rested my chin on one finger and tried to look intelligent and creative.

'Sam, I was wondering if I might pick your brains on

filters, only I do feel they're an integral part of photo-graphy, don't you?'

He threw his head back and laughed. 'Oh, Polly, I think you're absolutely right, filters are an integral part and I'd love to stand here all day and gas about them, but unfor-tunately I've got to get on. But listen, do wander around and don't be afraid to ask the crew questions; they love an enthusiastic amateur. Tony's particularly patient and amenable.' He nodded over to Tony, who I recognized from Cornwall. 'Oh, incidentally, you're still on for the party at Quaglino's tomorrow, aren't you?'

My heart sank. 'Tomorrow? I thought it was tonight.'

'No, we couldn't get a table for tonight so we booked it for tomorrow. Is that a problem?'

'No, it's just . . . well, I promised Nick I'd be back by Saturday morning. He's away and I've got to check a deliv-ery for him. I can't drive back after dinner, it'll take forever and I'm bound to be pissed – damn.' I bit my lip miserably.

'Oh dear, what a shame.' Sam frowned. 'Well, hang on, why don't you leave the car in London and get the sleeper at about midnight? You could come up by train another day and pick the car up then, couldn't you?'

I stared at him, joy and incredulity surging within me. My goodness, he really wanted me to come, didn't he?

I gulped. 'Well – well, yes, I suppose I could – yes, why not? I'll come! And I'll pop back next week and pick up the car!' I breezed, as if popping back took a matter of minutes.

'Excellent!' He beamed. 'That's the spirit. And now if you'll excuse me' – he looked at his watch – 'I must get on.

I've got loads to do and I'll have to go and placate the sulky star first – see you later, Polly!'

He whizzed off. I watched him go in a trance. He was obviously absolutely mad about me. Totally infatuated. Out of his mind with desire for my body. I gulped. I'd have to be very careful, have to play it cool, mustn't lead him on, mustn't, under any circumstances, encourage him. I was, after all, a married woman. He suddenly turned, saw me watching him and smiled. I gave him an enormous wink back, quite forgetting how cool I was going to be.

Pippa dashed by, clutching a clipboard and looking important. I seized her arm.

'Pippa, I'm coming with you!' I gabbled.

'Where?'

'To Quaglino's tomorrow! I'll leave the car in London and get the sleeper.'

'Really? Well, great, that's great.' She looked around distractedly. 'Have you seen Serena? She needs this.' She held up a dog-food can and peered around.

'Yes, she's in make-up – oh, and that's another thing, Pippa, you didn't tell me *she* was in this. Why didn't you warn me?'

Pippa stared at me for a moment, then it dawned. 'Oh God, I'm so sorry, Polly, I completely forgot about all that business with her and Nick. I've worked with her quite a lot, you see, and all that seems so long ago now.'

'Not to me it doesn't,' I said grimly. 'I can remember her throwing her weight around at Trewarren only too well. Honestly, you might have said something.'

'Well, you'd still have come, wouldn't you?'

'Well, yes, but – well, I might have been a bit more pre-pared, made more of an effort clothes-wise so she didn't think I'd become a country bumpkin.'

'Oh, right.' Pippa gazed doubtfully at my suit. 'Yes, I see what you mean, sorry.'

I gasped. She was supposed to say I looked great. 'What d'you mean? What's wrong with this?' I smoothed down the skirt of my sharp little black suit.

'Oh, nothing, it's lovely, but it's a bit sort of eighties really, isn't it? A bit nipped in and shoulder pads. Anyway, I must get on. I've got heaps of things to do – see you later.'

She wafted off in her long flowing skirt, muslin blouse and bovver boots, leaving me with my mouth open. I shut it thoughtfully. I'd thought she'd looked extraordinary when I'd arrived, but I had to admit the fab look was growing on me; she had a certain groovy charm. I obvi-ously needed a sartorial refresher course and I resolved to buy *Vogue* on the way home.

I wandered around happily, looking at the set, chatting to Tony, marvelling at the realistic rustic kitchen made entirely from cardboard, and pausing to pat the little cocker spaniel in his basket, the only dog in this scene. I couldn't quite believe it was going to take a whole day to shoot ten seconds of commercial. Heaven knows how long it must have taken to shoot *Gone With the Wind* or something epic. It seemed to me there was an awful lot of standing around and very little action, and when there was any action Serena certainly seemed to do her damnedest to make things as difficult as possible for everybody.

In the middle of the final take she put her hands on her hips and resolutely refused to do what Sam asked her.

'I'm not kissing that bloody spaniel,' she stormed, 'it'll ruin my credibility!'

'Whatever that means,' muttered Tony, who was standing beside me.

'Serena, please,' said Sam, quickly leading her off the set and taking her over to the side, 'it's only a very short take and it would look marvellous. Apart from anything else the advertising agency have specifically asked us to do it. Couldn't you just –'

'No!' She glared at him. 'It's too much of a risk to my career. I didn't get where I am today by kissing spaniels, you know – why can't Susan do it?'

'Serena, please be reasonable,' said Sam quietly. 'I'm sure Susan would be very happy to do it, but to have a middle-aged woman kissing a dog as the end frame isn't really sexy advertising, is it? Whereas if *you* did it we could get a nice close-up on those beautiful lips all puckered and pursed and then freeze-frame on your lovely face for – oooh . . . a good three seconds while we slip the pack shot in.' He shrugged and made as if to walk away. 'But of course if you insist on Susan having the final frame I'll just go and ask her if she'll –'

'Oh, all right, I'll do it!' snapped Serena quickly. 'Although why I have to kiss a bloody dog I don't know. I usually kiss leading men, handsome ones too – although,' she sniggered in my direction, 'I suppose I have kissed a dog or two in my time.' She sneered and flounced past us, leaving me with my mouth gaping yet again.

'Was that a reference to my husband perchance?' I gasped. 'She's got a sodding –'

'Let her go.' Sam held me back as I went to go after her.

'She's not worth bothering about; she's just a spoiled child.'

'You're telling me!' I fumed.

But he was right, she wasn't worth the effort. She didn't strike me as being particularly good at her job either. I watched as she fluffed her only line time after time. She sulked and flounced around, saying the words were stupid, and had to be constantly cajoled by Sam, who eventually got the result he wanted on about take fifteen. Finally she kissed the dog and there were sighs of relief all round as Sam declared a wrap. Serena grabbed her bag and stormed out immediately without saying goodbye to anyone.

'Stuck-up bitch,' muttered Tony.

The crew began to pack up and I followed Sam, Josh and Pippa out from the gloom of the studio into even more gloom outside. It was pouring with rain. Sam had an umbrella and we huddled underneath it, looking at the sheets of water which hit the ground and bounced back over our feet.

'We'd better make a run for the car,' said Pippa, turning up her collar. 'I'm going back to the office first, so I'll see you at home, Polly.'

'Oh, OK.' I was going to get soaked. I was just about to make a dash for the Tube when Sam caught my arm.

'Where are you parked?'

I gasped. Oh Christ. I had a car, didn't I? I'd clean forgotten.

'Oh, er . . . not far away, just down the road a bit.'

'Down which road?' We seemed to be at something of a crossroads. I looked around wildly and picked one.

'That one.'

'That's where we are, come on, let's go.'

'But –'

'Come on!'

Pippa and I huddled under the brolly and the two men ran on ahead. Two seconds later we were all gathered at Sam's Range Rover.

'Bye then!' I warbled, giving a cheery wave and making to trot on. Sam seized my arm.

'Don't be silly, it's pissing down. I'll just let these two in, then I'll walk you with the umbrella.'

'There's really no need. It's not very far, I can easily –'

'I insist, hang on.' He opened the door for the others, still holding on to my arm.

'Where is your car anyway, Polly?' asked Pippa, climbing in and looking around.

'Oh, a bit further on.'

'I can't see it.' She screwed up her eyes and peered down the road.

'Well, to tell you the truth, it's quite a *bit* further on. I couldn't park any closer so it's a few minutes' walk, but I feel like a walk so I'll see you later, bye.'

I wriggled free and made another spirited attempt to escape but was once again intercepted by Sam, who grabbed my other arm.

'For goodness' sake, it's bucketing down. Hop in, we'll drive you to it.'

'No – no, really –'

'Don't be silly, Polly, you'll get soaked,' snapped Pippa. 'Just get in.'

My mouth felt dry and my toes began to curl. 'But I like

the rain . . .' I bleated in a small voice as the authoritative film director and my best friend – who was rapidly being demoted – bundled me forcibly into the front seat. Sam ran round and jumped up the other side. He snapped his seat belt on, indicated, and pulled out.

'Now, where to?'

I gulped. He might well ask.

'Um . . . just a bit further down here . . . sort of.'

We went quite a bit further, so far in fact that we came to a junction.

He looked at me. 'Which way?'

'Er, it's . . . right here.' My tongue seemed to be stuck to the roof of my mouth. My hands felt clammy. I gazed stupefied at the cars lining the residential street as we purred along at about five miles an hour. Sam looked at me again and raised his eyebrows.

'Further?'

'Um, yes, a bit further,' I croaked.

'Blimey, you did have a walk.'

'Mmmm . . .'

We drove on in agonizing silence.

'And we're looking for a red BMW, right?' he asked, peering from side to side.

I had in fact been looking for that very thing, not mine of course, somebody else's, to borrow, as it were, but red BMWs seemed to be an endangered species in North London and I had a feeling we'd never find a spare one.

'Er, no, we're not actually.'

'We're not?'

'No, you see, it broke down so I borrowed Larry's.'

'Oh! Oh, OK, so what's that?'

'Well, I'm not too sure, to tell you the truth, but I'll recognize it when I see it.'

'You're not too sure?' Sam's mouth twitched. 'Any clues? A colour, perhaps?'

'Oh, yes, well it's sort of . . . white. Whitish-cream. Or grey.' Like my face probably, I thought, feeling rather sick and wondering if we might just pull over so I could puke out of the window. Why had I started this?

He grinned. 'Whitish-creamish-grey. Right.'

We drove on. The silence was excruciating. Sam looked at me enquiringly from time to time. I bit my lip and frowned at the mass of parked cars, concentrating like mad and willing myself to pick one.

'Oh, for heaven's sake, Polly,' snapped Pippa, exasperated, 'you haven't a clue where we are, have you? You've gone and lost the bloody car. This is just typical of Polly, Sam, absolutely typical!'

'It is not!' I stormed. How dare she? I'd have a few words with her about loyalty later. 'I know exactly where we are and I know precisely where the car is, it's – it's that one!' I cried, pointing to an innocent little whitish, creamish-grey car sitting at the side of the road minding its own business.

Sam pulled up. I jumped out thankfully.

'Bye then!' I cried, with what I hoped was a degree of finality. I slammed the door firmly.

Sam buzzed down the window. He made no move to drive on and they all watched as, despite the torrential rain, I walked very slowly to the car. Go away, I muttered to myself, as I walked around it, just damn well go *away*. But they didn't.

I pulled my keys out of my bag and waved them in the air triumphantly. 'It's all right, I've got them!' I yelled. 'Bye now!' Still they watched.

I dumped my handbag proprietorially on the roof and made a great show of finding the right key and pretending to put it in the lock. A good thirty seconds later I looked up, aware that I was sweating. Three pairs of eyes met mine.

'Always sticks a bit, nothing to worry about though! See you tomorrow!' I waved again.

Still they sat on the tarmac, staring, mesmerized, it seemed. I began to panic. Didn't they have anything better to do? Surely this was about as exciting as watching paint dry, and far nosier. Go away. Just sod off, why don't you, can't a girl even get into her car on her own?

'Everything all right?' called Sam, in a I-could-be-over-to-help-you-in-a-jiffy sort of voice. Christ, was that his door opening even now?

'Fine! Fine!' I cried.

In desperation, I straightened up and caught Pippa's eye. I looked straight at her, tilted my head to one side, opened my eyes wide until they were enormous with meaning, pursed my lips, raised my eyebrows to heaven and shook my head very slowly. It was a momentous look. She stared at me for a moment in amazement, then the penny dropped. She blanched perceptively, quickly leaned forward, and whispered something in Sam's ear. He raised his eyebrows in surprise, shunted into first gear, and they moved off.

I keeled over and slumped on to the little car, joy and relief flooding within me. 'Oh, thank you, God, thank you, thank you!' I whispered to the car roof, shutting my eyes and kissing the dirty paintwork. 'Thank you a million times!'

Suddenly I jumped about a foot in the air as a large hand seized my shoulder from behind. I swung around. A huge, burly great thug of a man was towering over me. He was totally bald, with bulging pale-blue eyes and bulging forearms.

'Just what the hell d'you think you're doing!' he thundered. 'That's my car you're breaking into!'

'Oh no, is it? I mean, I – I'm terribly sorry, I thought it was mine!'

'Oh you did, did you?' He lowered his moon-like face and positioned it inches from mine. The bulging eyes nearly popped out on to the pavement. 'So where's your car then, eh? Tell me that, darlin', where's yours?'

'Well, it's, it must be –' I gesticulated wildly down the road. 'It must be a bit further down! I obviously haven't walked far enough – so silly of me, I do apologize, but it's incredibly similar to this one, almost identical in fact! I've even got those lovely fluffy things hanging from the mirror and – and that adorable froggy air freshener on the dashboard! Extraordinary, isn't it?'

'Oh yeah? And I suppose you've got "Toot if you think I'm sexy" on the back window too, have you?' He jerked his head towards the witty little sticker. I groaned inwardly. I did hope Sam hadn't seen that.

'No, no, I haven't actually.' I shook my head regretfully. 'But it's awfully good, very amusing. I must look out for one of those, I like a jokey little remark on the back of –'

'Oh, just bugger off, you silly tart – go on, bugger off!' he bellowed, giving me what for him was probably a little shove but which jolly nearly propelled me under the wheels of a passing taxi. What I wouldn't have done to be propelled into it. He advanced as I groped for my footing.

'If it wasn't pissing with rain, I'd drag you down to the police station right now, and if I catch you anywhere near my car again I'll set the dog on you – Sergeant!'

On command, Sergeant, the biggest Dobermann I'd ever seen, came bounding out of the adjacent house, knocked a couple of gnomes over and threw himself against what was, happily for me, a very high wrought-iron fence. He barked furiously, baring razor-sharp teeth.

'And he doesn't take prisoners either!' bellowed my new friend as I backed away hastily. 'Just you remember that!'

'Oh I will, I will! So sorry, just a silly misunderstanding!' I turned, put my head down and galloped off down the road. I pounded along the pavements in the torrential rain and didn't stop running until I reached the Tube station.

An hour or so later I squelched miserably through Pippa's hall, soaked to the skin, my suit clinging to me, shivering like a wet puppy. Despite popping into the office, Pippa had beaten me back. She was lying with her feet up on the sofa, reading *Tatler* and watching *LA Law*. She gazed in astonishment as I dripped slowly by.

'Blimey! What happened to you?'

'Don't ask,' I said wearily, kicking my shoes off and squelching on upstairs. 'Be an angel and fetch me a large gin, would you?'

I fell into the bathroom, peeled off my sodden clothes

and turned on the taps. A few minutes later she appeared, a gin in each hand. She handed me one, and put the top of the loo seat down and sat on it.

'That wasn't your car, was it?'

I sighed. 'No, but I'm too tired and pissed off to explain. All I can say was it seemed like a good idea at the time.'

I sank back into the warm, Radoxy waters with a sigh of relief. I looked up at her.

'What did you say to Sam?'

'I said you were an extremely nervous driver and you'd be scared shitless at the prospect of us all watching you emerge from a tight parking space. I said most of the surrounding cars, including his, were in imminent danger and would probably be written off. He moved off pretty sharpish, I can tell you.'

I brought the gin to my grateful lips, took a slug and groaned. 'Oh God, now he must think I'm completely mad.'

'Probably,' said Pippa, regarding me coolly, 'but what does it matter?'

I avoided her eye and buried my face in my gin.

Chapter Eleven

I spent about two hours getting ready for the party at Quaglino's. Luckily I'd brought plenty of clothes, but for some reason nothing seemed quite right. Every so often I'd fling something on and run into Pippa's bedroom, where she was lying on her bed reading and eating an apple.

'What about this?'

Pippa looked up laconically and appraised me in my neat little black skirt with red linen jacket. She bit into her apple and shook her head.

'No. You look like a secretary.'

'Really? It's Joseph, you know, and the skirt's quite short.'

'You still look like a secretary.'

She went back to her book and I ran out, wondering if Pippa recalled that not so long ago we'd both actually been gainfully employed as secretaries. A few minutes later I was back.

'What about this then?'

She raised her eyes from her book, stuck her finger in her place and looked me up and down in my very best navy-blue suit complete with vivid red silk scarf tied jauntily at the neck.

She shook her head. 'Uh, uh.'

'Why?'

'Come fly with me.'

'Really?'

'Definitely.'

'Oh Christ!'

I ran out again and ripped it off. When I returned I had on the shocking pink micro mini and a nipped-in black velvet jacket with nothing on underneath. I was grinning confidently, I looked terrific. Pippa took one look, sighed, and got off the bed.

'Polly, where have you been?'

'Sorry? What d'you mean?'

'That sort of look went out with the ark, no one's wearing that sort of tarty power thing any more.'

'Aren't they? Oh! Well it hasn't got any shoulder pads – look.' I squished the shoulders down to prove it.

'Doesn't matter, it still looks naff – here, try these on.'

She delved in her wardrobe and threw me a bundle of clothes. I shook them out.

'What's this – a swimming costume? And . . . flares!'

'It's a body, you goon, and flares are back. I'll lend you some platforms to go with them.'

I collapsed on her bed in a heap. 'Platforms? You must be joking!'

'No, I'm not, now get it all on quickly then we can share a bottle of wine before we go.'

I ran into my bedroom, giggling, and dutifully obeyed, wriggling into the clinging Lycra.

'D'you wear pants with this body thing?' I yelled as I shimmied into it.

'Oh, Polly, for goodness' sake!'

I stared down doubtfully at the garment as it hung,

unclasped, between my legs. For goodness' sake yes, or for goodness' sake no? I didn't like to ask her to be more specific for fear of incurring more incredulity about my spell in a sartorial time warp, so in the end I left the pants off, feeling more than a little outré.

Twenty minutes later, with a bottle of hastily guzzled Sancerre inside us, we piled into a taxi, looking, I thought, like a couple of born-again hippies. Pippa even had a long sleeveless cardigan on – I drew the line at that, but had added a string of beads just to show willing.

Quaglino's was already throbbing mightily when we arrived and I felt a surge of excitement as we clumped precariously down the steps in our platforms and then waded through the packed tables, turning heads as we went. Sam stood up as soon as he saw us and kissed us both roundly on the cheeks.

'Wow! You both look terrific! I like the kit, although it makes me feel incredibly old – I was wearing all that the first time around. Take a pew. You know everyone here, don't you, Polly?'

I had a quick glance around the table. I certainly knew most, Josh, Tony, Tim, Amanda – oh God, don't let me be next to her, I couldn't take the strain of dropping my aitches and crucifying my vowels all evening – Amanda's copywriter Chris, a few other crew members, Susan, but thank goodness, no Serena.

'Here, sit next to me.' Sam had obviously got one or two warmers into the bank already; he was looking decidedly pink about the cheeks and his eyes were shining. He pulled out a chair and patted it. 'I've been saving it for you,' he murmured with a wicked wink.

'Thanks.' I sat down, delighted. Pippa slipped in next to Josh.

'No Serena?' I asked as I shook out my napkin.

'No, isn't it a blessed relief? She had a more important party to go to, more star-studded, no doubt, but she's no loss.'

I grinned. 'I couldn't agree more.'

'Now – a drink? I ordered you a gin and tonic because I seemed to recall it was your tipple, but I can change it if you like.'

'No, that's fine!' He remembered my drink? I smiled up at him. He smiled back and held my eyes for an inordinately long time. Suddenly I looked away. Steady, Polly, have a good time but take it easy; you're a married woman, remember? And for goodness' sake don't get drunk. My gin and tonic arrived, I took a huge gulp out of nerves and excitement and nearly collapsed on the floor. It was practically neat gin.

'Christ!' I spluttered.

Sam patted my back as I coughed and snorted attractively into the crudités. 'All right?' he enquired.

'Yes thanks,' I croaked, 'bit strong, that's all.'

'They do make a rather mean cocktail here. D'you want some more tonic?'

'No! No, it's fine.' I took another hefty gulp just to prove it. I smiled nonchalantly. 'I've been drinking mean cocktails since I was a babe in arms.'

He grinned back. 'I rather imagined you had . . . your health, Polly.'

Our glasses gently collided, and so again did our eyes, and this time I had the nerve to return his gaze. I mean, what the hell, we were only looking, weren't we? Just window-shopping, and in a crowded restaurant what's more, with me to be deposited on a train at midnight like Cinderella – what could be safer? I looked a bit more. God, he was attractive, in a kind of Mel Gibson playing an Argentinian polo player sort of way. I licked my lips wantonly.

'I'm so glad you decided to come this evening,' he murmured into my ear. 'It really wouldn't have been the same without you.' His lips brushed briefly against my hair.

I felt a frisson of excitement and leaned forward to come back with something equally suave yet titillating, but for some reason my tongue seemed to be well and truly tied. I wrestled with it, but we were talking bondage here.

'Th-thanks, it was nice of you to ask me,' I squeaked at last, a deep blush accompanying this incredibly sexy riposte.

Sam smiled, but politely rather than lecherously, and turned to his other side to talk to Susan, who'd plucked at his sleeve and asked him something urgently. He replied at length, giving her the benefit of his hazel eyes, and me his back.

I was furious with myself. For heaven's sake, Polly, buck up! What's happened to your sexy banter, your winning smile, your flirty little ways? Nice of you to ask me? Hell's teeth, you'll be saying thank you for having me next!

Truth was, of course, I was chronically out of practice. Not much call for sexy banter in Helston, but all I needed was a little refresher course, and speaking of refreshment – I picked up my gin and hoovered it back in one. I put the glass down and shuddered. Wow, that was strong, but it should do the trick. I had a quick look around and, managing to avoid Pippa's rather censorial eye, surreptitiously popped open a couple of buttons on my top, took a huge gulp of wine and – *voilà*! I grinned. Tongue and buttons well loosened, I was raring to go.

I practised a smoulder and murmured 'Well, hello' to myself once or twice, just to make sure my voice was deep and sexy, then turned to muscle in on the conversation Sam was having with Susan. It was quite hard because Sam had his back to me now, so I had to sort of peer round and try to catch Susan's eye. She wouldn't look at me, so I listened closely, watched her teeth and laughed when they laughed.

'Ah ha ha! Very good!' I roared.

No response. I leaned round again and smiled sweetly at Susan, who saw but didn't smile back. Cow, I thought, a huge frozen smile on my face, how could I ever have thought she was wholesome? She was about as wholesome as a packet of pork scratchings.

Determined not to be beaten I tried again and this time leaned forward until my head was practically resting on the table. *Chariots of Fire* cropped up.

'Oh, that's *such* a good film, isn't it?' I enthused loudly. 'Oh, Nigel Havers, yes, he's *fabulous*, isn't he . . . ? Oh, you know him, do you, Susan? . . . Yes, yes, *marvellous* soundtrack, simply *marvellous*, by that Greek guy – whatsisname, well anyway, *very* memorable . . .'

I roared on thus but they chatted on regardless. I flushed, hot with embarrassment now. Damn it. Quite apart from anything else I was the only person at the table not talking to anyone. How incredibly galling, had anyone noticed? I had a quick look around. Everyone but me was engrossed. Something had to be done. Quick as a flash and thinking on my feet as usual, I pulled off an earring, dropped it on the floor, then slid off my chair and disappeared under the table on a spurious errand to retrieve it. I salivated slightly at the sight of Sam's glorious long Armani-clad legs, then emerged, smiling and waving the earring triumphantly.

'Got it!' I announced to anyone who was interested. I awaited attention. Nothing. Help.

I blushed some more and nervously quaffed my wine. My spaghetti with some kind of clam and lobster sauce arrived. I frowned with intense concentration and made a great show of expertly winding it on to my fork as if I really couldn't possibly have coped with talking to anyone anyway, seeing as how I had such a delicate operation to attend to. But there's only so much attention one can give to a plateful of spaghetti and when I'd masticated every tiny morsel I put my fork down and turned to Tony next to me, eyes wide and desperate now. Not a chance, he was deep in conference with Josh. I tried to catch Pippa's eye across the table, but she was too far away. Hell. There was nothing else for it, I'd have to turn to drink.

I summoned a passing waiter, commandeered a bottle of red and treated it as my own private supply, steadily emptying and refilling my glass, as if finishing the bottle were some sort of gargantuan task I'd set myself. By the time Sam eventually turned back to me a good fifteen minutes later I was so plastered I was practically nose-diving into my crème brûlée.

'Sorry,' he muttered in my ear, 'I didn't mean to abandon

you but Susan's having a bit of a confidence crisis at the moment. I had to reassure her – you know what actresses are like.'

'S'quite all right, don't mind me,' I slurred, with more than a hint of pissed petulance in my voice.

She was having a confidence crisis, what did he think I was having, sitting here like a lemon? But at least I had his attention, and just enough sobriety to realize that now was not the time to sulk, but rather to put my skills into action.

I pulled my hair free from behind my ears and let it fall sexily into my eyes, then I nuzzled towards him, lowering my lashes and speaking softly so he had to lean in close to hear.

'Sorry? What was that?'

'I said I really admired the way you handled Serena at the shoot,' I murmured. 'It can't be easy having temperamental actresses flouncing around on the set.'

He laughed. 'That's nothing – you should see them on a feature film. Sometimes they lock themselves in their caravans and refuse to come out for days, and not just the women. The men are just as bad, if not worse. You need to be a nanny, psychiatrist and film director all rolled into one sometimes.'

'Well, you do it awfully well,' I husked admiringly, swaying slightly in my seat as I gazed up at him. I steadied myself on the table and ran my tongue over my teeth as they stuck to my lips. Sam rested his arm round the back of my chair and regarded me thoughtfully.

'Tell me, Polly, have you ever thought about taking filming seriously? I think you have all the right instincts for it and I think you'd probably take a very fresh approach.'

I clenched my toes. This was it, this was *it*! He was going to ask me to audition for his next film – I was about to be discovered! I smiled coyly and played with some breadcrumbs on the table.

'Well, I must admit I did a fair amount of acting at school, in fact I was a bit of a star, in a very small way, of course.' I smiled modestly.

He nodded. 'Good, so you know the basics. That's terribly important – so many young directors these days don't know a thing about acting and it helps enormously. There's a marvellous film-making course at one of the polys in London, why don't you sign up for it?'

'Er, yes, bit of a hike from Cornwall, isn't it?' I said weakly, neglecting to add that somehow I'd imagined myself on the other side of the camera.

'Well, what's to stop you being a weekly commuter? You could always stay with Pippa during the week and go home at weekends.' He raised his eyebrows enquiringly.

I gasped and took a slug of wine. Wow! He obviously wanted me all to himself during the week! Was he hot for me or what? And was it my imagination or weren't those hazel eyes just sparkling with depravity? Play it cool, Polly, I thought, blushing into my *brûlée*, he's mad about you all right, but for God's sake play it cool.

'What d'you think?' he asked.

'Well, Sam, I'm flattered, really I am, but to stay all week in London, I'm not sure how Nick would –'

'Look, Polly,' he put his hand on my arm, 'I hope you don't think I'm coming on strong or anything, it's just that – well, I find you so refreshing, so gloriously unspoiled. And I'm not bullshitting you about the directing either,

I do think you'd bring a fresh approach, but I must admit I have a selfish motive too. I'd really like to see more of you, in – well, in a purely platonic way of course.' He shook his head and looked slightly bewildered. 'I don't know, I just find you so –' He paused and struggled for the right word.

Golly, what? What was I? I was absolutely agog now and leaned forward, eager not to miss a syllable of this tantalizing observation, but unfortunately he never got to the end of it because I inadvertently put my elbow on the edge of his plate and catapulted a great dollop of gooseberry fool up on to my chest.

'Damn!' I squeaked. 'Oh God, what a mess!'

'Here – let me.'

Sam reached quickly for a napkin, dipped it in some Perrier and began mopping my top, perilously close to a couple of my larger erogenous zones. I clutched the table for support and moaned softly, trying desperately to imagine he was Roy Hattersley or someone.

'Thanks!' I gasped at last. 'Silly of me!'

'Easily done,' he said, still mopping away in the lower armpit region. He grinned. 'Not making you nervous, am I?'

'God, no!' I trilled, feeling decidedly light-headed with drink and excitement. 'Me? Nervous? Not at all, don't be ridiculous.'

'Good,' he said quietly. He stopped mopping and his hand came to rest next to mine on the table. Our fingers touched and I could almost feel mine vibrate with excitement. I swallowed hard and stared at him. He held my gaze.

'Um . . . look, Sam . . .' I began, but quite forgot what I was going to say as his hand covered mine and held it. I felt powerless to take it away. My head said no, but my body was all for it, no self-control as Nick would say – Nick! I gulped. Would he sense that I'd indulged in guilty gazing? That I'd been mopped to within an inch of my erogenous zones? That I'd done a bit of extra-curricular hand-holding? Drunk or not, alarm bells rang loud in my head and with a staggering flash of sobriety I realized I had to act fast. Perhaps Sam had forgotten he too had a spouse? Certainly it had temporarily escaped me. His hand held mine and his eyes were getting more dangerous by the second. I had to remind him.

'And how – how is your wife?' I enquired desperately.

Sam looked surprised.

'My wife?'

'Yes, your, um, wife. Sally, isn't it?'

Sam's mouth began to twitch at the corners. He took his hand away, threw back his head and laughed out loud. He roared away for quite some time before eventually slumping back in his seat. He wiped his eyes and groaned, shaking his head.

'Oh God, Polly, you do make me laugh. That's what I like about you, you have absolutely no guile at all, do you? You just say exactly what comes into your head. My wife is fine and you're absolutely right – I'm getting way out of line here. Sorry, I've probably had one too many of these,' he indicated his gin, 'and I have to admit, I do find you incredibly attractive.' He shrugged and gave me a lopsided smile. 'Sorry, but there it is, can't help myself. If it's not too corny, you're a real breath of fresh air in this fuggy, pseudo-sophisticated London atmosphere. I can't tell you what a glorious change it is to talk to someone like you after the luvvie people I spend my time with, but, believe me, that's as far as it goes. I've never cheated on my wife in my life and I don't intend to start now, even,' he grinned and winked, 'with someone as delectable and enticing as yourself.' He raised his glass enquiringly at me. 'OK? Friends?'

I grinned back and raised my glass. I wasn't sure about the lack of guile, I'd always thought I'd had buckets of it, but this was much better, this I could cope with. 'Friends,' I agreed, 'and I'm sorry I brought your wife up in such a cack-handed manner, but I did just think it might be as well to – you know – keep our matrimonial obligations to the forefront of our minds and not to forget that we do owe it to our partners to –'

'Hey, hey, enough!' Sam was grinning and backing away in mock terror now. He held up his hands. 'I promise I'll never so much as smile at you again, I'll never even glance in your general direction! Dib dib dib, dob dob dob, scout's honour, you've made your point, Polly!' He wiped his mouth on his napkin and got to his feet. 'In fact I'm backing off right now.'

'Oh!' I felt suddenly disappointed. 'Wh-where are you going?'

He grinned. 'To the loo. I'll be right back.'

'Ah.' I smiled. 'Right, good.'

He went. I leaned back in my seat and sighed. Shame. Pity I'd had to nip him in the bud like that, but it had to be done. I frowned as I cradled my wine glass, taking the occasional sip. Odd that there really didn't seem to be any middle ground with this flirting lark. As far as men were concerned it was very definitely a means to an end and not an art to be savoured and perfected. Such a waste, and so unlike France, where it's practically a national pastime. I mean look at that Cointreau ad. That smoothie Frenchman's been at it for years – stroking crystal glasses suggestively, giving his bird smouldering, sexy looks over the dinner table, banging on about an inimitable blend of 'erbs and spices – it's never got him anywhere but he still seems to be enjoying himself. What a pity the English are so – I jumped as someone tapped my shoulder.

'Eh? What?' I swung around.

'Wake up, Polly, there's a plan afoot to move on.'

Sam was smiling down at me from behind my chair. I looked around dreamily. Everyone else appeared to be standing up too but they weren't smiling. Coats were on, bags were on shoulders, hands were in pockets, in fact the entire table were standing behind their chairs looking at me in a rather disapproving manner.

'Wh-what? What's going on?' I enquired from my slumped position. It occurred to me that I couldn't even begin to move without some help, I was positively welded to my chair. I spotted someone familiar.

'Where are we going, Pippa?' Her face swam in and out of focus.

'Well, one or two people are going on to Annabel's, but personally I'm going home to bed, and I think perhaps you should come too, Polly, and get the train in the morning.' She looked at me meaningfully.

I giggled. 'What, with you and Josh? Three in a bed, you mean?'

I sniggered. Gosh, I was on form tonight. Then I saw her face. It was white, ashen even. Oh Christ. I stumbled to my feet and crashed towards her, knocking over a couple of chairs on the way.

'Pippa! Oh, Pippa, I'm so sorry, I didn't mean to say that, it just slipped out!'

'I've no idea what you're talking about,' hissed Pippa, 'but I'm going home – on my own – right now. Are you coming?'

'Oh, Pippa, I'm so sorry, I completely forgot no one was supposed to know!' I wailed, making it much worse, but Pippa was already halfway out of the restaurant with Josh stalking out behind her. I went to go after her but Sam put a restraining hand on my arm.

'Leave her – wait till she's calmed down a bit.'

'She hates me!' I wailed.

'Course she doesn't. Besides, it's no big deal; we all knew anyway.'

'Really?'

'Sure, it's been going on for months, and it's probably a good thing it's out in the open now, certainly from Pippa's point of view.'

I considered this. He was right. I cheered up immeasurably.

'Yes, of course, you're right. Gosh, she'll probably even thank me tomorrow!'

'Exactly. Now come on, forget about Pippa and Josh, let's go dancing.'

'Really? Now?' I peered at my watch. 'I've got to get a train at some point.'

The point was, when? I couldn't actually see what the devil the big and little hands were up to; they seemed to be rotating at an alarming rate. I knew I should have gone for digital. I turned to Sam for assistance.

'Er, any idea what the time is?'

'Oh, it's quite early. You'll make it easily, don't worry.'

'Will I?' I lurched and clung to his arm to steady myself. 'Will I really?'

'I'll personally put you on the train myself. Now come on, let's go and get a taxi.'

'What a dominant man you are,' I murmured, knocking back the remains of my wine and clinging to his arm like a limpet as we ascended the perilous staircase to the front door. 'I like my men like that, dominant and forceful, mmmmm . . . lovely, only – shhhh,' I held a wobbly finger to my lips and it slipped attractively up my nose as I stumbled on the steps, 'keep it shtum. We girls aren't supposed to like that cave-man-hunter-gatherer bit any more; we're supposed to go weak at the knees for the caring-sharing lark. Well, stuff that for a game of soldiers, give me a great big dominant man any time, only' – I looked around for fear of being overheard – 'for God's sake keep it quiet,' I hissed. 'If any of those open-toed feminists found out, there'd be hell to pay, know what I mean?'

Sam grinned and guided me through the door. 'Your secret is safe with me, Polly. I won't breathe a word.'

He bundled me into a purring taxi and I fell into a bucket seat. Amanda, Chris and Sam made up the party. I looked around.

'What – just us? Isn't anyone else coming?'

'They've all dun a bunk,' grinned Amanda. 'Couldn't 'ack the pace, most likely.'

I groaned inwardly. Oh no, Amanda again. 'Yeah, well blimey, wot a load of par'y poopers, eh? Gorblimey, the night's still bleedin' well young, innit? Wot the 'ell are they playin' at, eh? I mean, lawks a mercy, apples an' pears, whistle an' flute –' Suddenly I felt weak, I couldn't keep it up.

'Um, listen, Amanda.' I leaned forward – a huge mistake in the bucket seat of a taxi – and nose-dived into her lap. She helped me up and deftly swapped places with me.

''Ere, you sit 'ere, you need it more than I do.'

'Thanks – I mean, ta – I mean, listen, Amanda, I've got a terrible confession to make.'

'Oh yeah?'

'Yeah – yes. You see, the thing is I'm not really like you at all.'

'Come again?'

'I mean, I don't – you know – speak like you do, actually. I'm sorry, but the thing is I'm really quite posh, well, a little bit posh, and I'm certainly not a Cockney – not that you are either, of course.'

Even in my highly intoxicated state I was dimly aware that making fun of someone's regional accent was neither politically nor socially correct, but it was a very dim awareness, and anyway, it was out now.

There was a terrible silence. Chris and Sam stared at their feet, Amanda stared at me. I gulped. Oh hell, what was she going to do, punch me on the nose? Or perhaps something altogether more sinister? I clutched my kneecaps possessively. After all, she could well be related to the Kray twins.

Suddenly she let out a bellow of laughter. She threw her head back and roared into the roof of the taxi.

'It's all right, I sussed you! You were so bad at it. I mean, blimey, I might be an East London girl but I'm not the blinkin' Pearly Queen, you know!'

More raucous laughter followed this declaration and I joined in, nervously at first, but then wholeheartedly, and then of course I couldn't stop. In fact the pair of us didn't stop roaring and gasping until we fell out of the taxi at Berkeley Square, helpless with hysteria.

Sam gripped my arm and steadied me as I lurched around on the pavement, holding my stomach.

'Here we are, girls,' he said, ushering us down the steps. 'Steady now, Polly, you'll rupture something if you're not careful.'

'Oh God, that was so funny,' I gasped weakly as Sam held the door open for me. 'It's made me positively thirsty!'

'Er, d'you think perhaps you should have something soft, Polly, maybe a Perrier?' said Sam, following me rather anxiously as I headed in a determined, if not entirely straight line for the bar.

'Water? Don't be ridiculous. I want to drink it, not swim in it – waiter! Oi, waiter, one large gin and tonic please!' I yelled, totally out of control now. I banged the bar and tried to climb on to a stool but it was awfully high and I fell off.

'Waiter!' I shouted, trying to scramble up the stool again.

'Er, it's OK, Polly, I'll get the drinks,' said Sam, prizing me off the stool as I clambered up the side and steering me towards a little table. 'You sit down here.'

'So dominant, so charming,' I muttered, giving him a winning smile as I lowered myself rather precariously into a chair.

He turned to Amanda. 'Amanda, what would you like?'

'No thanks, Sam, actually I've just spotted some really old mates of mine over there, d'you mind if I go and join them for a sec?'

'No, no, fine, we'll see you later.'

She disappeared with Chris in tow.

Sam returned from the bar with our drinks and sat down opposite me. 'So . . . just the two of us.' He smiled. 'Perfect. Cheers.'

I smiled back, but had the feeling it was more of a drunken leer, so I buried my face in my gin. This one hadn't even been near a tonic bottle but luckily my taste buds were totally anaesthetized so I knocked it back without a problem. The only problem seemed to be coming from my loins. I staggered to my feet.

'Got to go to the loo,' I mumbled, and off I stumbled, knocking over a couple of chairs on the way and cannoning into quite a few people who didn't seem to be able to walk in straight lines.

It took me ages to find the ladies' and when I did I was a little taken aback to see a couple of men already *in situ*. They looked equally surprised to see me, so I gave them an icy glare and made a mental note to inform the management that whilst mixed loos might be a liberated concept I didn't think it would work until men could be trained not to pee in the basins like that. Disgusting. Not being such an exhibitionist myself I crashed into a cubicle to relieve myself, but once relieved, I encountered a problem. Getting the Lycra body unpopped at the crutch had been simple enough, but getting it done up again was a different matter. I had to half crouch down and sort of lean forward and peer, and then for some reason my fingers wouldn't work the poppers.

'Oh come on, come on,' I whispered urgently, but it was no good. All manual dexterity had deserted me. Not only that, but every time I adopted the obligatory skiing position needed to get to grips with the thing, the blood would rush to my head and I'd cannon forward, hitting my head violently on the loo door. When this had happened more than twice a plummy male voice enquired from without – rather impertinently I thought – 'Are you all right in there?'

'Fine, thank you,' I informed him icily. Christ, can't a girl even snap her knickers together in peace?

Eventually I gave up and just tucked the tails hastily inside my trousers, thinking that whoever had invented this extraordinary bit of kit had a lot to answer for. I lurched out of the door to a wash basin and steadied myself on the porcelain. More men were wandering around now, giving me the oddest looks, but I expect they just fancied me. I ignored them all disdainfully and studied my reflection. Heavens, I looked terrible. My hair was all over the place and the bloods of my eyes were only slightly whiteshot. I dragged a comb through my hair, added some lipstick which conveniently matched my eyes, then stumbled out again, bursting back into the nightclub like an unguided missile and cannoning straight into warm human flesh.

'Look out!'

'Ooops, sorry!' I steadied myself against the female I'd embraced. She had a beautiful face with large brown eyes and long dark silky hair, and by golly she looked familiar.

'Polly!'

I tried desperately to focus. 'Good grief.' I squinted. 'Lottie!'

'What on earth are you doing here, and why were you in the men's? Heavens, you look terrible!'

'Do I? Oh well, never mind.' I grinned up at my erst-while flatmate and hugged her warmly, grateful for something friendly to hang on to. 'I'm having a terrific time!'

We wobbled precariously. 'Hey, steady – gosh, you look completely plastered. Are you all right? Is Nick with you?' She looked around for my husband.

'No, no, I'm with Sham, he's a film director,' I confided happily.

Lottie frowned. 'Sham? But where's Nick?'

'Oh, he's busy farming. Now, don't you worry, it's not like that, Lottie – it's all strictly above board. It's just that he thinks I've got hidden talents, you see, thinks I've got the makings of a marvellous director, so he's giving me the benefit of his vast expertise.'

'I bet he is,' she said drily.

'Oh, Lottie, don't be like that, come and meet him!' I dragged her bodily over to our table. 'Sam,' I called loudly, perhaps too loudly, because quite a few people turned round. 'Hey, Sam, stand up please, I want you to meet one of my very best friends in the whole world, Lottie – shit, I've forgotten your name.'

'Parker,' she put in helpfully, 'and don't shout, Polly.'

'Parker, that's it, she got married, you see, lost her real name which was why I couldn't remember it, oh, and Lottie, this is Sam Weston, an *extremely* famous film director, you've heard of him, of course, haven't you?'

'Well –'

'Oh God, Lottie, you're *hopeless*, he's done *loads* of things, haven't you, Sam? Come on, what have you done?' I bellowed. 'Tell her what you've done! Come on!'

Suddenly I had to grip hold of the back of a chair as I swayed violently and experienced a rush of blood to the head. Too much shouting, probably. I wondered if I could possibly walk around the front of the chair and get my bottom on to its seat.

Sam was on his feet now, shaking Lottie by the hand. 'I assure you I haven't done anything remotely memorable; there's no reason why you should have heard of me.'

Lottie smiled. 'I'm afraid I don't get to the cinema much these days.'

'I don't blame you – most of it's rubbish.'

'Hey, Lottie, sit down!' I'd finally managed to park my own bottom and was keen for others to join me. It was making me dizzy looking up at them. 'Sam, oi, Sam, how about getting a drink for Lottie, where are your manners, eh?' I yelled. The people at the next table turned to stare at me.

'Er, sure – what can I get you, Lottie?'

'Oh no, not for me,' said Lottie, waving her hand. 'I've

195

got one over there; I'm with a party from the office – oh, here's one of them. Polly, you remember Peggy, don't you?'

An extremely large American colleague of Lottie's came bounding up, fairly shaking the floorboards as she bounced to a halt. Remember her? I'd nearly fallen asleep on her. Nick and I had once spent a mind-numbing evening in her company at a party of Lottie's where she'd singlehandedly bored for America. All night long we'd been treated to her views on IKEA furniture, Marks and Spencer pre-cooked meals, Benetton jumpers, Sainsbury's crème fraiche and the joys of Mars Bar ice creams. Now I can shop till I'm sick, but this girl had me beaten into a paper bag. Nick and I had finally escaped, reeling and gasping into the night, vowing never again to accept an invitation without having a full dossier on the other guests first. She grinned toothily at me.

'Polly, hi! How y'doing? Hey, I love your beads. You must tell me where you got them, I'd love to take some back to the States. You wouldn't believe it but it's just impossible to get hold of that kind of thing out there, weird, isn't it? What d'you think of this dress, by the way?' She glanced down at the snot-green tent affair she was wearing. 'Bet you can't guess where I got it?' she asked gleefully.

'Harvey Nicks?' I hazarded meekly, knowing full well that that was what she wanted to hear but that Oxfam was nearer the mark.

'Wrong! Marks and Spencer, fourteen ninety-nine, don't you think that's just incredible value?'

'Incredible,' I agreed weakly.

Peggy smiled with satisfaction and looked around ominously, as if searching for somewhere to park her heavily upholstered derrière and continue this fascinating retail discussion. Sam looked alarmed, as well he might. Luckily I was alive to the situation.

'Oh, er, Lottie, is that the rest of your crowd from the office over there?' I asked, peering into the middle distance. 'I think they're waving to us,' I lied.

'Where?' Lottie strained to see.

'There, behind that pillar, they're beckoning to you, I think.'

'Really? I can't see, but perhaps we'd better go – they'll be wondering where we are. Come on, Peggy.' She seized Peggy's huge arm and bent down to peck me on the cheek.

'Listen, are you really all right, Polly?' she hissed in my ear.

'Yes, of course, why?'

'Because you look absolutely out of your head, that's why. D'you want me to get you a taxi or anything?' She looked worried.

'Don't be ridiculous, I'm having a whale of a time!'

'Really?'

'Bloody hell, Lottie, I haven't had so much fun in ages!'

'Well, if you're sure . . .' She looked doubtful. 'Only I know you . . .'

'Course I'm sure, now get back to the rest of your crowd – go on!'

She laughed. 'Bugger off, you mean. All right, but take it easy, OK?'

I grinned and waved her on her way, winking conspiratorially at Sam as she went. We settled down into another cosy gaze. This time I tried out a sort of come-hither one, complete with languid licking of lips. It was a huge success, I think, judging by the way he guffawed with pleasure. I wriggled happily in my seat. This was bliss. It was weeks, months – no, years even – since I'd felt this way. Silly, light-headed, frivolous, irresponsible – drunk, even – but why not? I was still young, wasn't I?

Sam leaned forward, looking a bit concerned. 'Polly, would you rather make a move now? Your train's not for a while yet, but I'll wait with you at the station if you like. We could get a cup of coffee?'

'But we've only just got here. There's still bags of time, isn't there?'

'Sure, but you look a bit tired.'

'Me? Tired? Rubbish, I'm having a brilliant time!'

He smiled and looked at his watch. 'OK, if you're sure, but you'd better not have any more to drink. I just hope yours is the last stop on the line because I can't see you waking up for it. I'll have to hang a notice round your neck – "Wake me up at Truro".'

'Like Paddington Bear.'

He smiled and took my hand. 'Just like a little bear.'

I let him take my hand. That was OK, I decided. After all, we'd held hands before, so we weren't breaking new ground. I sighed blissfully as he stroked my fingers. God, he was attractive. If I wasn't married and in love with Nick . . . He smiled and I smiled back. I couldn't think why I hadn't thought of this before, I mean, the world must be full of gorgeous married men, why stop at this one? Why not find some more? There must be loads of them with time on their hands, ready and willing for a bit of innocuous eye contact and platonic hand-holding, why not make it a pastime? A sort of hobby? I wondered if Nick would be prepared to put some money into a little scheme if I went into business. Set myself up as an expert, give lessons, that sort of thing – after all, he'd offered to set me up in a shop, hadn't he? I was just idly wondering if a council grant would be possible when I found myself being dragged to my feet. Neither my feet nor the rest of my body wanted to move an inch.

'Come on,' said a voice in my ear, 'just one dance then I'll put you on that train. I just want to hold you once in my arms before you go.'

I couldn't even speak now, let alone put up any resistance, so I let myself be half dragged, half carried to the dance floor. Once there, I fell into his arms. I didn't like to tell him it was a mistake but I knew it was, I'd felt much better sitting down. People seemed to be cannoning into us from all over the place, so I hung on tight and buried my face in his shoulder.

I felt awfully sick but didn't like to open my mouth to tell him so in case I gave a practical demonstration. Coloured lights were swirling horribly above me and the music was unbearably loud. I shut my eyes tight. I was dimly aware that the tails of my body had crept out and were hanging down on the wrong side of my trousers, but there was absolutely nothing I could do about it. Sartorial elegance be damned, I had more important things to contend with, like how to stay upright.

Whitney Houston pounded urgently into my ears. My

head was throbbing. Sam held me close and stroked my hair. If only I was sober enough to enjoy it, but I really did feel terribly ill.

'Sam, I . . .' I whispered into the pounding music, looking up into his face.

He smiled down at me and I realized that he must have thought I was lifting my face to be kissed. He bent his head and his lips brushed mine, warm and soft, but definitely unwelcome in the light of my condition. I gritted my teeth. Please don't let me be sick now, oh please God, not now! It was important that he didn't kiss me again so I kept my head buried in his shoulder, praying that the dance would end soon and we could get far enough away from the pounding music for me to tell him how ill I felt. All of a sudden I knew I couldn't wait till the end of the record. I had to act fast or I was going to disgrace myself in a very big way and make a terrible mess all over the dance floor.

'Sam, I feel awful,' I muttered, 'I must –' I made an almighty effort to wrench myself free of his arms but, sadly, simultaneously lost the fight. The one I'd been waging to stay upright. The flashing lights fell from the ceiling in a dazzling display of colour and the dance floor came up to meet them. Ceiling and floor collided with an almighty flash of white. After that, there was nothing. Just blackness.

Chapter Twelve

When I came to, I was lying in a bed that wasn't mine, in a room I didn't recognise. My head was throbbing like a waiting taxi and my eyes ached in their sockets. I opened them slowly. Where the hell was I? Battling through a wave of pain and nausea I tried to work it out. The curtains were drawn, but it was light. I narrowed my eyes. Too light. I peered around nervously. The room was smart, a tasteful grey and white colour scheme prevailed, but it was tomb-like, impersonal, and it smacked of efficiency – a hospital perhaps? Private, of course, I thought, glancing down at the inch-thick carpet. I hoped to God Nick had kept up the BUPA payments. Two seconds later I realized that glancing at the carpet had been a huge mistake, as my tummy rose to my throat like a high-speed lift and I clutched my mouth.

'Nurse, nurse!' I yelled, looking around wildly. I was about to be very ill and I needed a bowl, or preferably a bucket, right now.

'NURSE!' I shrieked in panic.

No nurse, and no handy red button with which to summon one. Damn. Still clutching my mouth, I sat up and swung my legs over the side of the bed. There was a door, slightly ajar, to my left. A bathroom? I bolted towards it, hoping it wasn't a wardrobe as it had been on one disastrous occasion at a house party in Scotland, but happily, instead of encountering a row of shining Churchill brogues, I encountered a shining marble bathroom instead. I made it to the loo with seconds to spare and was violently, and repeatedly, sick.

I clutched the porcelain to steady myself and sank down gingerly on to the cold tiled floor. I shivered. It occurred to me that I hadn't a stitch on. I grabbed a towel from a rail and pulled it around me, shaking now and feeling extremely ill. This was extraordinary. Where on earth was I, and why was I naked? It was a pretty rum sort of hospital that liked their patients starkers, wasn't it? I looked around, desperate for clues.

The bathroom was a riot of marble and chrome, with so many gleaming surfaces and sparkling taps it made your eyes ache to look at it. Perhaps this doubled as an operating theatre? The lights were certainly bright enough and there were plenty of marble slabs for surgery, handy really, because I was going to need some in my brain quite soon. 'Oooooh . . . Christ!' I moaned and clutched my head.

Holding it carefully, as if bits might spill out, I hobbled gingerly back to bed. I lay down and turned on my side. Surely a nurse would come soon, to check I was OK. I hoped so, I certainly couldn't go looking for one in my condition. I stared at the hygienic-looking bedside table beside me. Nine o'clock, said my watch.

Through the table's glass top I spotted a little black Bible. I blinked. Heavens, that was a bit pessimistic, wasn't it? Was it handily placed there for the last rites, perhaps? Didn't give one much faith in the medical team, did it? I stared at the spine of the book underneath it. *A Guide To London's Night Spots*. I blinked again. Wow. One minute the inmates were on their deathbeds and the next they were dancing round their handbags. Talk about kill or cure.

Suddenly I had a nasty thought. I sat bolt upright and stared at the dressing table. There was a tray with a teapot on it, and some cups, two cups, and round the rim of the cups something was written in green – The Royal . . . something . . . Hotel. Oh! I gulped. A hotel! Not a hospital at all, but – what was I doing in a hotel? How had I got here? I racked my addled brain and tried desperately to piece together the happenings of the previous night.

Well, first we'd all gone out to dinner, that much was clear, then a few of us had gone on to Annabel's, and then . . . what next? I frowned. Somewhere along the line I remembered getting stupendously drunk and dancing with Sam, but then what? Well, then I'd woken up in a hotel bedroom with no clothes on, that's what. I froze. Oh my God! I clapped my hand over my mouth. Had I slept with him? Had I? My eyes grew huge with fear. No! No, I couldn't have, because if I had – well, where was he now?

I sprang from the bed with hitherto unimaginable alacrity, rushed to the wardrobe and flung it open. Empty. I ran to the curtains and swept them aside, hastily shutting them again as a startled passer-by got a full-frontal. No, he definitely wasn't here, which was a rattling good sign, because if, *if* by any catastrophic chance anything untoward *had* occurred – God forbid – well, then he'd certainly be here now, wouldn't he? Being even more untoward? I mean, who forks out for a hotel room for only one bunk-up, for heaven's sake? Hardly worth the effort, is it? No, he'd definitely still be here, demanding his early-morning rights.

I paced nervously round the room, looking for clues. I sorted out my clothes which were scattered about. No boxer shorts amongst them – good. I peeked cautiously in the waste-paper basket – nothing rubber and unspeakable in there. Excellent, things were looking up. I sat down on the bed, relief flooding over me. Yes, of course, I'd obviously missed the last train and had been parked here by some good samaritan to sleep off my alcoholic stupor – what a relief!

I flopped back thankfully on the bed, and as I did so a piece of paper flew off the bedside table. It fluttered about in the breeze my flop had created and then spiralled slowly down to the floor like a sycamore seed. I watched as it landed. My heart just about stopped beating. I jumped off the bed and fell on it. My hand shook as I spread it out.

Saturday, 7.00 a.m.

Darling Polly,

Thank you for a wonderful evening. Sorry you missed your train, but it was worth it, wasn't it? Had to dash off early this morning but I'll ring you soon.

Love always, Sam.

I stared at the paper in disbelief. I read it again. Seven a.m., it said, so he'd been here . . . all night. My hand flew to my mouth and something cold gripped my heart. I'd slept with him. I must have done. My stomach curdled with revulsion. I dropped the piece of paper and it fluttered down to the carpet again. I stared at it, stunned.

Then I picked it up again. 'It was worth it, wasn't it?' The words swam in and out of focus. I tried to think what that meant. Did it necessarily mean that . . . yes, of *course* it did, Polly, what else *could* it mean? Oh God! I sank to my knees on the carpet, hid my face in my hands and doubled up in agony like a footballer who's been kneed in the groin. How could I? How *could* I have gone to bed with him? Had I really been that drunk, was it possible?

I lay down on my side, holding myself, shivering with cold and self-pity. I pulled my towel around me and stared at the grey carpet, which was getting less tasteful by the minute. I felt numb. I simply couldn't believe I'd done it. As I lay there, something green and shiny caught my eye. It was sticking out from under the bed, right by my shoes. I pulled it out. It was an empty champagne bottle. I sat up and looked around. Sure enough, sitting on the dressing table was a champagne glass. I glanced wildly around the room and there, on the windowsill, just behind the curtain, was another. Only this one had lipstick on the rim. I got shakily to my feet, walked over and picked it up. Pink lipstick. My lipstick. Clearly these had been our pre-, and possibly post-, coital drinks.

I sat down on the little stool by the dressing table, put my head in my hands and wept. I hated myself. I just wanted to die. Tears streamed down my face and I let them fall unchecked. I'd broken my marriage vows, I'd been unfaithful to Nick, I'd – Nick! Suddenly I froze. I sat bolt upright like a pin in a bowling alley and my tears stopped in mid-stream. Hell! No! It was Saturday! Saturday morning, and I should be in Cornwall, not dying gracefully in a London hotel room! I should be checking the Foxtons delivery, Nick would kill me – Jesus!

I scrambled to my feet and raced to my bundle of clothes, grabbing bra, body, trousers, shirt and – oh God, platforms. I scrambled into them. Infidelity might find me doubled up on the floor in agony but the impending wrath of my husband had me throwing my clothes on, grabbing my handbag, dragging a comb through my hair and bolting out of that room in three minutes flat.

I tore along the corridor and down the stairs, nearly breaking my ankle in my ridiculous shoes. Should I go by train or collect the car? But the car was – heavens, where was the car? I racked my brain as I hobbled down the stairs. Oh Lord, the car was still in Harrods car park, wasn't it? I couldn't possibly go and get it now. I probably owed them about a million pounds! No, I'd just have to ring later and explain I'd had a terrible accident, been hit by a truck in Knightsbridge or – no, a Bentley – and hadn't been able to pick it up. It would take much too long to go along and lie my way out of it now, though. I'd get the train.

I ran through the lobby, looking straight ahead and hoping to God I'd be spared the indignity of being stopped to pay the bill. No one batted an eyelid so I pushed through the revolving doors and ran out into the sunlit street. Cars screeched around me, honking their horns madly.

'Taxi!' I yelled, as a proximate one nearly bowled me over.

'Jesus Christ!' bellowed the driver. 'You want to die?'

'Wouldn't mind,' I muttered, climbing in. 'Paddington, please, I'm in a tearing hurry.'

'So I see.'

I sank back in the black leather and caught my breath. I

looked around. Mayfair. Definitely Mayfair. A discreet yet expensive little hotel just off Dover Street, a stone's throw from Annabel's – he probably used it all the time, the bastard. I ground my teeth miserably. It was all becoming horribly plain. He'd deliberately got me plastered – hadn't he been tipping gin down my throat all evening? Then he'd got rid of everyone else, and just when I was more or less unconscious he'd taken me back to a hotel and violated me – raped me even!

'Rape!' I yelped, clutching my mouth. The taxi driver looked at me in horror in his rear-view mirror.

'I never bleedin' touched you!'

'Oh, no, no, it's all right, not you, um, someone else.'

'Blimey,' he said shortly. A second later he looked in the mirror again. 'What, you mean you've been . . . ?' he asked nervously.

'No, no, forget it,' I said quickly. 'I'm rehearsing for a play, learning my lines; forget I said anything.'

'Ah.' He looked faintly reassured.

I stared out of the window, wishing it were true, but this was no rehearsal, this was real life. Perhaps I should go to the police? Get him arrested, bound over, imprisoned – anything to keep him off the streets, to keep him from doing it again. I frowned. From doing what again? What exactly had happened?

I rummaged around in my bag and pulled the note out. 'It was worth it, wasn't it?' Crikey. That sounded very much as if I'd been a willing participant, as if I'd enjoyed it. Would that stand up in court? I mean, I couldn't remember a damn thing, so perhaps I had enjoyed it? And had he really been tipping gin down my throat? I had one or two hazy recollections of him actually trying to restrain my alcohol intake. I hastily stuffed the note back in my bag. Perhaps I wouldn't go to the police after all. And perhaps I'd burn that note, or eat it even, before it was used in evidence against me.

At Paddington I bought a ticket, raced over to a kiosk for some cigarettes, and belted over to platform six. By some lucky chance a train had just pulled in and was throbbing away impatiently, waiting to set off again. I climbed aboard. It was relatively empty so I found a window seat and sank down into a corner. The train chugged slowly out of the station.

With shaking hands I took a cigarette from my pack, lit it, and managed to spill the rest of the packet on the floor. As I scrambled around under seats picking them up, someone tapped me on the shoulder.

'No smoking in here, young lady!'

I looked up from beneath a seat. A bumptious little man in half-moon glasses was glaring over his pinstriped stomach at me, thumbs lodged in waistcoat pockets. He was a dead ringer for Captain Mainwaring. I stared at him. This was no ordinary cigarette – this was keeping me from throwing myself off a moving train, didn't he know that?

'I'm an addict,' I informed him. 'Have to have one every ten minutes or I pass out; I've got a doctor's certificate to prove it.'

He looked a little taken aback, but soon recovered. 'Well, you shouldn't be travelling by train then, should you? Go on,' he waved his hand imperiously, 'put it out.'

'I also get very sick – it's the withdrawal symptoms, you see.'

He went purple. 'Just put the blasted thing out or I'll have you thrown off the train!'

He probably would, too. 'Well, don't blame me if I throw up on your shoes,' I warned icily.

He flinched but sat down opposite to spy on me, tucking his highly polished shoes well under the seat. I took one last, lingering, defiant drag, then threw it out of the window. I glared at him. Yet another member of the smoking police with nothing better to do than persecute people who just wanted a quiet fag in peace. Unbelievable. He shook his *Telegraph* out noisily and peered over it every now and then just to make sure I hadn't lit another.

I ignored him and stared out of the window. My mind boomeranged back to Sam. What the devil was his game? Wasn't he supposed to be a happily married man? What about his sacred marriage vows? I mean, for goodness' sake, it had just been a harmless little flirtation, not a full-blown adulterous wham-bam-thank-you-ma'am, hadn't he realized that? Hadn't he? I squirmed in my seat. I had a nasty feeling in my waters. Had it, I wondered, been in any way my fault? Had I, perhaps . . . led him on? I'd certainly been aware that he fancied me and – well, yes, OK, I probably *had* led him on, but had I led him on so far that it was inconceivable we wouldn't go all the way? Was I in fact . . . to blame?

'Oh God . . .' I groaned, and hid my face in my hands.

Tears began to trickle down my nose. I let them fall unchecked. I peered through my fingers. Captain Mainwaring was spying on me, looking rather alarmed. Yes, I thought savagely, this is what you've done to me, this is what an addict looks like deprived of her fix. I'll be having a cold chicken next, or a turkey, or whatever it's called. I hope you're thoroughly ashamed of yourself.

I stared out of the window, my cheeks sopping wet. Would Nick guess? Would he find out? And, if he did, would he ever feel the same way about me again? And even if he didn't find out, it would still be hanging over us, wouldn't it, because I'd know. I gazed out at the tower blocks, the graffiti, the inner-city decay. It all swept by in the drizzling rain.

Odd, I reflected, resting my forehead on the window, how one night can change your entire life, especially one you can't even remember. Yesterday I hadn't a care in the world, now I had a truckload. I felt numb with shock, with shame, and with the pain that was still rattling around in my head. I also felt desperately tired, which was odd, considering I'd just woken up. Clearly, it had been an eventful night. I shut my eyes and listened to the wheels rattling beneath me. Faster than fairies, faster than witches . . . I let my mind go blank and let sleep wash over me, a defence mechanism I've always been able to employ, no matter how dire the circumstances.

I think I must have slept for a long time because when I woke up there had been quite a dramatic scene change. Inside the carriage Captain Mainwaring had disappeared, and outside the rain had stopped and the sky was clear and blue, with only the odd wispy little cloud racing through it. Green hills swept up from the track, horses nodded and flicked flies with their tails, cows tugged at the wet grass. It looked a lot more like home. Suddenly London and all its horrors seemed a long way away. I sat up. My head had stopped throbbing and I didn't feel sick any more. In actual fact I felt a lot better. I got the note out of my handbag again and spread it on my knee. I dissected it word by word.

'7.00 a.m.,' it read. Yes, well, OK, there was no escaping the fact that he'd spent the night with me, but *how* exactly? Shouldn't we be careful not to jump to conclusions here? Shouldn't we, in fact, read between the lines just a smidgen more? For example, thus:

'Darling Polly' – well he would call me darling, wouldn't he? I mean, all those luvvie types do, look at Richard Attenborough, he probably calls the milkman darling, so nothing odd about that. 'Thank you for a wonderful evening' – evening, mind, not night – why hadn't I noticed that before? My heart lifted a millimetre. 'Sorry you missed your train, but it was worth it, wasn't it?' – i.e., the fun we'd had that *evening*, the party at Quaglino's, the dancing at Annabel's, the laughs, the jokes. 'Had to dash off early this morning' – no inclination to stay, note – 'but I'll ring you soon. Love always' – luvvie language again – 'Sam.'

I stared at the paper as if I'd never seen it before. No mention of a night of debauchery, no mention of sex, no mention of anything other than the fact that we'd had a good evening. I'd missed the train and he'd kindly deposited me in a hotel room and stayed with me. Why had I automatically assumed the worst? I mean, after all, if I couldn't remember doing anything, it was pretty unlikely, wasn't it?

Well! I sank back in my seat, quite weak with relief. What on earth had I been worrying about? Nothing had happened and Sam – bless him – had been an absolute saint! What else could he have done? He could hardly have taken me home, could he, burst in at midnight and called up the stairs to the wife – 'Sorry, darling, this is Polly, we've been in Annabel's having a mild flirtation, she's a bit plastered and she's missed her train, all right if she kips on the sofa?'

No, no, that wouldn't have gone down at all well, so naturally he'd booked me into a hotel and then stayed with me, just in case – well, just in case I swallowed my tongue, or some puke, or anything else that comatose drunks are wont to swallow.

I smiled, I beamed, I almost laughed! Oh joy! It was all so simple! Sam had been a white knight! Why, if it hadn't been for him I might have woken up on a bench at Paddington station with all the other inebriates. I had a great deal to thank him for, a great deal. I'd write, yes, I'd write him a little note when I got home, just to say thanks. I'd send it to his office, though, I thought hastily, didn't want his wife to get the wrong end of the stick.

At long last the train chugged into Truro station. With a much lighter heart I jumped off and dashed across to another platform, where I caught a slow, chugging, comforting train to Helston and then, eventually, a taxi home.

As the taxi rounded the stone gates to Trewarren and swept up the gravel drive, I peered nervously over the driver's shoulder from the back seat. Was Nick's Range Rover in the drive? I hoped not. He wasn't due back until this evening, but it was already four o'clock and you never quite knew with Nick. He was so bloody efficient; he could have gone to Yorkshire, bought the cattle and been back by yesterday lunch time. I breathed a huge sigh of relief as I saw the empty drive. Thank goodness.

I leaped out of the taxi and ran up the stone steps two

at a time. The front door was still double locked so he definitely wasn't back, good. Feeling decidedly carefree for a girl who not so long ago had been perilously close to suicide, I raced around the house, turning lights on, drawing curtains and rolling around on beds. Then I threw bits of food on the kitchen floor, pulled all the loo paper off the rolls, flushed it down the loos, left the empty rolls hanging and generally made it look as if I'd been back for hours.

When the house looked suitably chaotic I grabbed a Barbour from the back hall and scampered down to the farm to check the delivery. I swung back the huge Dutch barn door and flicked on the light. The whole place was piled high with sacks of grain, corn and maize and great black bags full of silage. I found the list that Nick had left me, pulled it off the nail in the wall and began the long, tedious task of counting the sacks and checking everything off.

Half an hour later I emerged beaming and confident into the early-evening sunshine. All present and correct for once, definitely a first for Foxtons and a hell of a relief for me. I slammed the barn door behind me and skipped back to the house.

In a fit of enthusiasm I got a couple of chicken breasts out of the freezer, defrosted them in the microwave, then poured a tin of tomatoes, a few mushrooms and a slug of wine over the top of them and shoved them back in the microwave. Could be interesting. Then I mashed up some bananas, poured cream on top, gave it a layer of sugar and browned it under the grill. Terrific! Gosh, cooking was tiring, though. I was just sitting down at the kitchen table and helping myself to a glass of wine, when the back door gave a familiar rattle. It stuck, as usual, then flew open and in walked Nick.

'Darling!' I sprang up much too guiltily and knocked over my glass of wine.

'Careful!' Nick grabbed it before it rolled off and smashed on the floor.

'Sorry,' I said breathlessly, mopping it up with newspapers. 'I'm just so pleased to see you!'

I threw my arms round his neck and hugged him hard, burying my face in his jacket and breathing in its gorgeous tweedy, Nick-like smell. I reached up and kissed his mouth.

'Well, what a welcome!' laughed Nick, giving me a hug. 'I shall have to go away more often if it provokes such a homecoming. What's the matter, didn't you enjoy your little jaunt to London?'

'Oh, it was OK,' I said, turning away and busying myself peeling some potatoes, 'but I really think I've had it with London, you know. I mean, restaurants and nightclubs are all very fine now and again, but I don't think it's really me. I'm much happier in the country, couldn't wait to get home, actually.'

'Well, you know my feelings on that score,' said Nick, sitting down and helping himself to a glass of wine. 'I wouldn't care if I never saw the inside of a nightclub again as long as I lived. Which one did you go to?'

I felt my colour rising. 'Which what?' I peeled potatoes furiously.

'Which nightclub?'

'Oh . . . er, Annabel's.'

'What, on Thursday?'

'Y-yes, Thursday – ouch!' I'd cut myself with the knife. Blood spurted out. I sucked my finger. Nick reached up and pulled the first-aid box off the top of the dresser. He took out a plaster.

'Come here, idiot.'

I held out my hand.

'So who's a member then, not Pippa, surely?'

I met his eyes briefly as he bandaged my finger, then looked down. 'Um, no, not Pippa. Sam, I suppose.'

'Ah. Sam.'

I looked at him quickly. 'What does that mean? Ah, Sam?'

He grinned and put the box away. 'Nothing really, it's just his name crops up quite a lot these days, doesn't it? God, what's this?' He was peering into the microwave now.

'Oh, it's just a chicken casserole thing I made.' What did he mean about Sam? Did he suspect anything?

'*Just* a chicken casserole thing? Blimey. Chicken on its own is a major breakthrough in this kitchen and a casserole thing is positively a gastronomic delight. What's happened to the fish fingers? Did they finally get up and walk away? And what's this?' He stuck his finger in the bowl of bananas and looked amazed. 'Pudding? Good heavens, Polly, what have you been up to? Haven't got a guilty conscience by any chance, have you? Any minute now the doorbell's going to ring and a man from Interflora will thrust some roses into my hands!'

'Don't be silly!' I blustered, pink with indignation and horror. 'I just felt a bit peckish, that's all. Aren't you hungry?' I put the casserole on the table.

'Starving,' he said, sitting down and helping himself to

a chicken breast. He grinned. 'Just winding you up, Poll, can't you take it any more?'

'Course I can!' I declared, slipping in opposite him and helping myself with a cheery grin. I chewed grimly. Bit close to the bone, that's all, I thought.

After supper I collapsed on the sofa in the sitting room and flicked on the TV. I put my feet up and let the cathode rays wash over me. It had been a busy old day one way and another. Nick lit a fire. It was early May, but it cheered the room. A film had just started about a blind woman left alone in an enormous house, fumbling from room to room whilst unbeknown to her a serial killer with a penchant for the partially sighted crept around after her, moving things so she tripped up and making creepy noises. It was right up my street, although I watched most of it from behind a cushion. I found half a bar of stale Fruit and Nut tucked down the side of the sofa and nibbled away at it, waiting nervously for the murderer to pounce. Nick watched for five minutes, pronounced it utter drivel, and went upstairs to have a bath.

A few minutes later he was down again. The murderer had just cornered the blind woman in the airing cupboard, so I was well and truly glued to my cushion. I turned round and saw Nick's face. It was as white as a sheet.

'It's all right,' I whispered, 'her brother's just arrived in his car, he's got a gun.'

Nick didn't seem to register this. He looked most peculiar. I put my cushion down and sat up.

'What's wrong?'

He stared at me, his face ghostly. 'We've been burgled,' he said.

Chapter Thirteen

I dropped the cushion. 'What!'

'We've been burgled. I walked past the blue room upstairs and the door was wide open. When I went in I noticed the cabinet was open too. It's completely empty, cleared out, every single piece of porcelain has gone.' His voice was odd, strained.

'No! I don't believe it!'

'Go and see for yourself.' He sat down rather abruptly on the sofa opposite. He looked shattered.

I stared at him. 'Nick, how appalling! Has anything else gone?'

'I don't know. I daren't look.'

He put his head in his hands. I jumped up and sat beside him, putting my hand on his knee. I'd never seen him like this.

'You must phone the police,' I urged.

He raised his head and stared at me, looking a bit dazed. He didn't seem to hear.

'Nick —'

'Yes, yes, of course, you're right, I'll do it now.'

He jumped up, suddenly back to his normal, assertive self, and disappeared into the hall. I followed him, feeling suddenly cold. I pulled my jumper down over my hands and folded my arms tightly across my chest as I listened to him briefing the local police station. Fat lot of good they'd be, I thought bitterly. Directing the traffic in Helston was pretty much beyond them. Nick put the receiver down.

'Right, well they're on their way. We'd better go and see what else is missing. Come on.'

He turned and led the way upstairs, still white as a sheet. I scurried after him. Gosh, how awful. Quite apart from being extremely valuable, the porcelain had been in the Penhalligan family for generations. Nick's great-grandfather had started the collection by giving a figurine to his wife as a wedding present, and every year after that he'd presented her with a different piece. Each one had a provenance and usually a fascinating story about how and where he'd managed to acquire it. In terms of sentimental value they were priceless. I felt sick to my stomach, so heaven knows how Nick must be feeling. What on earth would his mother say?

'What will Hetty say?' I whispered as we went into the blue room together.

'God only knows,' he said grimly. 'Bastards, look at this.' He pointed to the empty cabinet. The door was wide open.

'My God, there must have been about thirty pieces in there!'

'Thirty-two.'

'But how did they get the door open? Was the lock smashed?' I went up to look.

'Don't touch it!' Nick grabbed my arm. 'Just in case there are fingerprints on it. No, look, the key's still in the lock.'

'What! They had the key? But – there are only two keys, aren't there?'

'Exactly. Mum's, and this one which is ours, it's got the blue ribbon on it.'

'So they took it from the jug?'

He shrugged. 'Must have done.'

'So it's someone we know, someone who knows where we keep it. Nick, how awful, how creepy!'

'Or someone who's heard about where we keep it – let's face it, the blue jug on the dresser isn't exactly the safest place in the world.' He shook his head. 'God, I could kick myself. I kept meaning to put it back in the safe but I just never got round to it.'

He started prowling around the room, pulling open cupboards and searching through drawers. This was the room where anything remotely valuable was kept. I followed tentatively.

'Anything else missing?' I asked, anxiously peering over his shoulder as he rifled through a drawer.

'Nope, not as far as I can tell. The watches are still here and they haven't touched the stamp collection – go and check your jewellery, Polly, oh, and the silver downstairs.' He had a clenched calmness now; he was back in control.

I ran down the corridor and into our bedroom with a hammering heart. How beastly, and how horrid to think someone had been rooting around in our house, our home, going through our things. It made me feel sick just thinking about it. I pulled my jewellery box out of a drawer and opened it. I don't really have much, but I'm desperately attached to the few pieces Nick has given me and one or two brooches of Granny's. Thank goodness, it was all there. I put it back in the drawer and ran down to the dining room.

The silver candlesticks were still in the middle of the table and the usual array of odds and ends was all present and correct on the sideboard. I was just looking through the cutlery when the doorbell rang. I dropped the knives and forks and ran to the front door. Two rather bored-looking policemen stood on the doorstep, one of them leaning against a pillar.

'Mrs Penhalligan?' enquired the elder of the two.

'Yes, thank goodness you're here,' I gasped. 'Quick, come in, we've been burgled, isn't it awful!'

The pair moved slowly through the hall, gazing around and taking in all the portraits and the huge chandelier.

'There's a lot of it about, madam,' observed the elder one lugubriously. 'In here?' He indicated the drawing room.

'Yes, yes, go in. My husband's just checking to see if anything else has been taken; he'll be down in a minute.' I followed hard on their heels. 'What d'you mean, there's a lot of it about? Has there been a spate of burglaries in the area or something? Have you any idea who it is? Is it a gang? D'you think we'll ever get our stuff back?'

They made straight for the fire, toasting their bottoms and looking around the room with interest.

'It's a little early to answer all those questions, madam, certainly without more detailed information,' said the elder man pompously. 'We'll start when your husband gets down, shall we?' He picked up a little silver snuff box from a table, looked at it with interest, turned it around and put it down again.

'You've got some nice stuff here, Mrs Penhalligan,' he observed.

'Yes, yes, we have, um, you said there's a lot of it about —
round here, d'you mean?' I persisted.

'All I meant, madam,' he said with weary indifference, 'is
that burglary is a very common occurrence these days.' He
pursed his lips, clasped his hands behind his back, rocked
back on his heels and resumed his appraisal of the room.

'Not for us it isn't,' I retorted darkly, 'and not when it's
thirty-odd pieces of priceless porcelain either. I do hope
you're not going to write that off as a common occurrence. This collection has been in the family for centuries;
we must get it back — it's absolutely imperative!' My voice
rose rather hysterically.

I felt a hand on my shoulder. 'Take it easy, Polly, come
and sit down.' Nick led me over to a sofa.

The policemen sat opposite us. I glared at them.

'My wife and I are in need of a drink, but I don't suppose you'll join us?'

'No thank you, sir,' declined the elder one, taking off his
cap, 'not whilst we're on duty, got to keep our wits about
us, you see!' He grinned moronically.

Yes, that must be a full-time job, I thought sardonically
as Nick handed me a large gin. What hope did we have of
getting our loot back with this pair of country bobbies?
God, the younger one was even stifling a yawn now, not
too keen on night duty, perhaps? Missing the football on
the telly, maybe? Well, bad luck, Ploddie, I thought, eyeing
him grimly, you've got work to do now.

Plod the elder wearily took a notebook from his top
pocket, then he patted a few more pockets and eventually
extracted a pencil. He licked the end and slowly flicked
through his little black book.

'Now. Suppose you tell me exactly when you discovered that the collection was missing, sir?'

'Just now,' said Nick patiently, 'just before I telephoned you.'

'What, just before? Or about five minutes before?'

'Er, well, yes, about then.'

'Shall I write ten o'clock then, sir?' he asked, pencil poised, eyebrows raised.

'No, it was about three weeks ago actually,' I burst in angrily, 'but we've only just got around to telephoning you, been too busy, you see. For goodness' sake, what difference does it make?'

'OK, Polly,' Nick said gently, 'I'll deal with this.' He took my hand. I was trembling.

The Plods stared at me open-mouthed. Eventually Plod the elder cleared his throat. 'We have to go through the formalities, madam,' he said stiffly, 'for our notes, you see.' He indicated his little book.

'Well, be a bit quicker about it, can't you?' I muttered.

He turned his watery gaze on Nick. 'What exactly did you discover was missing, sir?'

'Thirty-two pieces of antique Meissen, mostly figurines. I can give you a more detailed description later.'

'Valuable?'

'Very,' said Nick through clenched teeth.

'And, er, was this said collection in a safe?'

'Well, no, it was in a glass cabinet, actually.'

'A glass cabinet?' He raised his eyebrows.

'Yes, I know that probably sounds a bit crazy to you but they've always been kept there, so that we can see them.

Not much point in having beautiful objects if you can't look at them, is there?'

'That's a matter of opinion really, sir,' murmured Plod the elder, exchanging a knowing look with his gormless companion. 'And, er, was this said cabinet, by any happy coincidence, locked?'

Nick flushed. 'Of course it was.'

'And the lock had been smashed?'

'No, the key was in the lock. Whoever it was had found our key and used it.'

At this, Plod the younger raised his head. He awoke from his dream and turned his sleepy eyes on his partner. One of them flickered ever so slightly as if he were alive.

'Ah ha!' he murmured knowingly. Heavens, he could speak.

His partner nodded sagely and, leaning in, confided to Nick in a conspiratorial whisper, 'It's too early to say for certain, sir, but what you've told us so far gives us reason to believe that this was an inside job, someone who knew the house, who knew where the key was kept.'

'Oh, brilliant!' I snapped scathingly. 'Truly amazing deduction. Funnily enough we'd come to the same staggering conclusion ourselves in about two seconds flat!' God, these people were morons, where were MI5, CID – where was Morse when we needed him most? The policeman looked at me in amazement.

'OK, Poll,' soothed Nick, 'calm down, they're just doing their job.'

I ground my teeth but managed to hold my tongue.

The Plods turned away, pointedly excluding me, and addressed themselves exclusively to the man of the house.

'Anything else missing, sir?' purred Plod the elder.

'Not as far as I can tell, but I'll have to have a thorough look later.'

'And as far as you've been able to check – no broken windows? Signs of forced entry?'

'No, nothing, although the downstairs loo window was slightly ajar, but that's not unusual and it's too small for anyone to get through anyway.'

Plod the elder pursed his lips. 'Hrmmm . . .' He jotted something down, murmuring 'Open . . . win . . . dow' as he wrote. He looked up sharply. 'Now. Burglar alarm?'

'Er, no.'

'Locks on the windows?'

Nick shifted awkwardly. 'Well, most of them don't shut properly anyway, they're so old, so it would be a waste of time locking them.'

The policeman stared. 'Don't shut properly? Really?' He gave a sardonic little smile. 'I wonder, sir, you didn't actually leave the front door open for them, did you?'

I was on my feet in an instant. 'Oh, so it's our fault, is it?' I stormed. 'Because we don't live in a house with bars on the windows and Rottweilers circling the grounds, it's our fault if our property is violated, is that it? Well, funnily enough, we choose to live like this, in a home, not a prison, and why shouldn't we, it's a free country, isn't it!'

'Polly –' Nick put his hand on my arm.

'Well, honestly, it's ridiculous! They've been here about twenty minutes now and all they've done is yawn, state the bleeding obvious and blame us!' I rounded on them. 'You should be after them! Giving chase, radioing for help, pursuing them across country, climbing over walls, jumping ditches, instead of sitting here on your bums scratching your heads and taking notes!' I couldn't help it, I couldn't bear to see them make Nick feel so guilty, knowing how desperately upset he was.

The Plods declined even to acknowledge this outburst. They politely examined their notebooks as if the mad wife had unfortunately, and embarrassingly, escaped from the West Wing. They focused their attention even more pointedly on Nick, shifting their bottoms as they turned towards him. I fumed silently.

'Now, sir,' went on Plod the elder, 'you've been here all day, I take it?'

'No, I've been away for a couple of days on a business trip, I got back at about six o'clock tonight. My wife has also been away, but she got back last night.'

Suddenly my fumes evaporated. I sat very still. Plod the elder turned to me.

'Is that right, Mrs Penhalligan? You got back last night?'

My tongue seemed to be welded to the roof of my mouth. I unstuck it, it tasted rather as I imagined dog poo would. 'Er . . . yes,' I whispered, 'last night.'

'I'm sorry? I didn't quite catch that.'

I cleared my throat. 'Sorry. Yes, I got back last night.'

'And you'd been away for . . . ?'

'J-just one night. Thursday.'

'And were you also away Thursday night, sir?'

'No, I was here. I left on Friday at about lunchtime. You see, that's what I don't understand: the house was only empty on Friday afternoon and I can't believe anyone would have had the nerve to break in in broad daylight, especially with our various farm hands wandering around, but I suppose they must have done, unless it happened last night while Polly was asleep. What an awful thought, darling.' He took my hand.

'Awful,' I murmured. The whole thing was awful, appalling, actually. I felt hot all over, I seemed to have been ambushed by pints of red-hot blood and every part of my anatomy was either burning like fire or wet and clammy, except my mouth, of course, which was extremely dry. Plod the elder turned to me.

'At about what time did you go to bed on Friday night, madam?'

'I – I'm not sure.'

'Approximately, darling,' coaxed Nick gently. 'I know it's horrible to imagine someone prowling around while you slept, but do try and remember. Was it about ten? Or eleven?'

'Er, yes. About ten. Or eleven. About ten thirty,' I whispered, pulling a cushion on to my lap and using it to wipe the perspiration from my hands.

'And nothing disturbed you all night?' Plod the elder's eyes bored into mine. How could I ever have found them watery and insipid? They seemed to burn like laser beams, and his questions, which had previously seemed so banal and inconsequential, now seemed terrifyingly probing and inquisitorial.

'You didn't get up to go to the bathroom? Or go downstairs for a glass of water? Nothing like that?'

'No, nothing like that,' I whispered. Was he trying to trap me?

'You stayed in bed all night?'

I licked my lips. 'Yes, all night.'

Well, that was true enough, wasn't it? I thought desperately. I had been in bed all night. All right, it hadn't been *my* bed, but it had been a bed. Another man's bed. I felt sick for the umpteenth time that day. Nick's precious porcelain collection had been stolen whilst I lay next to another man in a hotel bedroom, and now I was lying like a dog to save my own miserable skin. Even by my extremely low standards this was unspeakably shameful. I stared at my shoes. Guilt seemed to be leaking out of them, all over the polished floorboards and the Persian carpet. I daren't look up. My toes were sliding around in my Docksiders now, slippy with perspiration. Was this what was known as perjury? I wondered. Lying to the law like this? Was it a treasonable offence? Could I be arrested?

The navy-blue legs opposite me were straightening. The Plods were getting to their feet, notebooks were snapping shut and, thank God, they appeared to be talking to Nick rather than me. I took advantage of this brief respite and wiped a few beads of sweat from my forehead. My hair was frizzing dramatically.

'Now, sir,' Plod the elder was saying, 'we'd like to have a look around in a minute if we may – check the windows, look at the cabinet, that sort of thing – but first of all, could you tell me who exactly has a key to this house?'

'Well, aside from ourselves there's my mother, Hetty Penhalligan, she lives in Gweek, and my brother Tim, whose farm is next door to ours. I think that's it.'

'No, Mrs Bradshaw has one,' I muttered.

'Oh yes, our daily.'

'Ex-daily,' I reminded him.

Plod the elder raised his eyebrows. 'Ex?'

'Yes, I fired her last week.'

'Did you now? And she still has a key?'

'I suppose she has. I certainly don't remember asking for it back.'

'Ah ha!' He pursed his lips and nodded importantly. Revenge Motive flashed like a neon sign on his forehead.

'I really can't see Mrs Bradshaw taking a cabinetful of antique china,' said Nick wearily. 'If she felt like taking something out of spite – and I'm quite sure she wouldn't – she'd be far more likely to nick the video, something she could sell.'

'Well, we have to explore every possibility, sir, follow every lead. In our line of work, no stone can be left unrolled or it won't gather moss. If you want to see the trees in the woods, you've got to be alive to every possibility,' he said pompously, comprehensively mixing every single metaphor he could think of.

He pocketed his notebook. 'And now, if you'd be so kind as to furnish me with Mrs Bradshaw's address, I'll have one of my men interview her just as soon as possible.'

He made it sound as if he had a force of thousands at his disposal, whereas in actual fact one or other of these two goons would be round at her house dunking a digestive in a cup of tea and discussing The Mad Woman of Trewarren just as soon as they'd finished here.

Nick showed them around the rest of the house, then saw them to the front door. I was very relieved to see them go. He came back from the hall looking pale and drawn. He stood with his back to the fire, massaged his eyes with the heels of his hands, yawned widely and shoved his fists despondently in his pockets.

'I'm knackered.'

I reached out and touched his arm. 'Me too. Let's go to bed.'

'Good idea. We'll sleep on it.'

We turned out the lights and went slowly upstairs. Nick shut the blue-room door as we passed. We undressed in silence, got into bed and lay still, our minds whirring. I stared into the darkness.

'Odd, isn't it, that nothing else is missing,' mused Nick eventually.

'Mmmm . . . I mean, it's not as if the silver isn't valuable, or the stamps. You'd think if someone was going to go to the trouble of breaking in they'd snap up as many goodies as possible.'

'Unless they were particularly interested in the porcelain and knew where they could sell it on. It's incredibly difficult to get rid of a collection like that unless you have contacts and you know the antique world. You can't just leak thirty-odd pieces of Meissen on to the market; people in the know would immediately smell a rat.'

'So . . .' I said, thinking aloud, 'it's got to be someone who knows the antique world . . . who knew where the key was kept . . . and who also knew that we were away!' I raised myself up on to my elbows, feeling quite excited.

'Who knew *I* was away,' corrected Nick.

'I – I mean, who knew you were away,' I stammered, flushing in the darkness and lowering myself hastily back on to my pillow. That'll teach you to be a smart arse, Polly.

'But you must admit,' I went on a moment or two later, 'it sounds very much like someone who knows us.'

Nick sighed wearily. 'Not necessarily. Word spreads very quickly in the country, especially in a small village. Mrs Bradshaw might inadvertently have let it slip that the key was kept in the jug and then somebody could easily have overheard in the pub that Larry and I were going to look at cattle for a couple of days. They've only got to put two and two together, and bingo.'

'I bet Mrs Bradshaw's thrilled to bits,' I said bitterly. 'Word will have reached the village by now and she'll be rubbing her hands with glee, revelling in our misfortune.'

'Don't be silly,' said Nick, turning over to go to sleep. 'Mrs Bradshaw might be a sour old bag but she's always been tremendously loyal. I'm sure she'll be horrified when she hears.'

'Don't you believe it,' I said grimly.

'We'll see. G'night.'

'Night.'

I turned over and shut my eyes, but for once my defence mechanism failed me. Sleep evaded me, and I tossed and turned fitfully, eventually resorting to my secret supply of Curly Wurlys under the bed. I sucked one after another, shut my eyes tight and eventually, in the early hours, drifted off to sleep. Despite my fitful sleep I managed to have quite a good dream which involved me rescuing Prince Harry from under the wheels of a speeding taxi in Pall Mall. As a result I became Princess Diana's new b.f. and had loads of chummy lunches with her in San Lorenzo's. Prince Charles was also incredibly grateful and I became his new confidante too – apparently he found me a refreshing change from Laurens van der Post. I was just trying to patch things between him and Diana, when the doorbell rang.

'Oh Lord,' I murmured sleepily, raising my eyebrows at Charles, 'I do hope it's not that blasted Camilla again.'

'There's someone at the door,' said an equally sleepy voice in my ear.

'What? Charles? Nick? Oh God, what time is it?' I rolled over and peered at the clock.

'Seven o'clock. I'll go,' groaned Nick. He sat up, yawned, scratched his head vigorously, then threw on some clothes and went downstairs.

I lay very still, straining to hear and hoping to God it wasn't the police again, wanting to know if I'd kindly accompany them to the station. A few minutes later I heard my mother-in-law's unmistakably deep baritone voice resounding confidently and emphatically up from the kitchen. Hetty! I felt quite weak with relief.

I gave Nick a few minutes to break the news then put on my dressing gown and went downstairs to greet her. I hoped she wasn't going to be too upset; I was extremely fond of her. I needn't have worried – Hetty was as unpredictable as ever.

'Polly, darling!' she boomed as I shuffled sleepily into the kitchen. 'Wonderful news! I heard at six thirty this morning; it's absolutely the talk of the village. Isn't it simply marvellous!'

I blinked. Hetty was perched on our kitchen table, swinging her legs excitedly, her dark eyes and dark bobbed hair shining brightly. She was dressed, as usual, in her own alternative, inimitable style. Today she'd chosen a pair of corduroy knickerbockers, an England rugby shirt, a red silk scarf for her neck and a tweed Baker Boys cap for her head. A cigarette was poised in her bejewelled fingers and she carried the whole arresting ensemble off with effortless style and panache. I groped around in the larder, searching for a new box of tea bags.

'Er, marvellous, Hetty? Are you sure?'

'Of course, it's fabulous news!'

'Don't be ridiculous, Mum,' snapped Nick, banging the kettle on the Aga. 'How can it be?'

'Well, think about it, darling,' she boomed, flicking ash nonchalantly into a saucer. 'There's no way you'd ever have sold all that ghastly old china, and quite right, you can't sell off the family silver, I wouldn't have done either, although your father and I were sorely tempted at times – but, well! Now that it's been *stolen*, that's *quite* a different matter, isn't it?'

'Is it?' I poured boiling water into the teapot with a rather unsteady hand.

'Well, of *course* it is,' insisted Hetty, 'don't you see? It must be insured for *thousands*, so this way you get all the loot, with none of the guilt – terrific!' She kicked her heels up gleefully and beamed triumphantly.

I grinned. I had to admit she had a point. We'd never have sold the porcelain, but now that it had gone walkabout – well! How much was it insured for? I wondered. I raised my eyebrows enquiringly at Nick.

'Don't be absurd, Mum,' he snapped. 'I'd much rather have the porcelain, and I'm going to make every effort to get it back!'

'Oh well, suit yourself,' sighed Hetty with a shrug. 'I

personally think it's a blessing in disguise, couldn't bear the stuff, actually; it took so bloody long to dust, and just when you'd finished you had to start all over again. I'd much rather have had the money, would have used it for something fun – a gazebo perhaps, or an amusing statue in the garden.' She took a sip of tea. 'Yuck!' She made a face. 'Revolting – any coffee going, Polly? I need something strong and dark in the mornings, can't be doing with this Earl Grey chappie; he wouldn't have been my type at all, insipid and chinless, I bet.'

'Oh, sorry, Hetty, here –' I threw some Nescafé into a mug, poured boiling water on and handed it to her.

'Marvellous, darling – spot of brandy, perhaps? Awfully chill for May, isn't it?'

I giggled and added a splash of cooking brandy.

Nick raised his eyebrows. 'It's only seven o'clock, Mum.'

'Don't be a boring old fart, darling, the French would have knocked back a couple of cognacs by now – cheers! Here's to the insurance money!' She winked and I stifled another giggle.

'Now' – she lit another cigarette while the previous one was still smoking in the saucer and leaned forward conspiratorially – 'any ideas? Any inkling as to who it might be? I gather the key was used so it must be someone from around here, don't you think? Someone local who knew the house? Shall we make a list? Isn't it thrilling!'

'Hardly,' said Nick grimly. 'It's bloody irritating and pretty unpleasant too. D'you realize Polly could have been badly hurt? As far as we can tell it happened on Friday night while Polly was alone here. I hate to think what might have happened if she'd disturbed them.'

'My dear!' Hetty turned to me in surprise. 'You were here? I had no idea! I thought you were in London!'

'Er, no, I got back on Friday evening,' I mumbled into my tea.

'Really?' Hetty looked puzzled. 'That's odd. I rang on Friday night, but there was no answer. What time did you get back?'

'Oh, er, about nine,' I muttered, pitching it fairly late.

'But I rang at about quarter to ten! There was this marvellous programme on the television. I wanted you to watch it so I –'

'Oh, I was – having a bath. I heard the telephone but couldn't be bothered to get out to answer it.' I buried my flushing face in my mug. This was horrible, just horrible.

'Oh, what a shame, you'd have loved this, it was a David Attenborough thing all about the praying mantis – fascinating. Did you know, for example, that after they've had nooky, the female *eats* the male? Just pops him in her mouth and swallows him whole – isn't that terrific! You see, once he's done the business he's totally redundant as far as she's concerned, so she just has him for her supper, a little post-coital snackette, as it were – isn't it killing! I think I shall have to ring Harrods pet department and order a couple!'

I tried to grin, but my mouth twitched with terror. This was awful. These were really dirty lies now, not just the harmless little whitish-grey ones I'm wont to pepper my life with – no, these were thumping great black ones. I busied myself slicing some bread, my hand shaking. Luckily Hetty started prattling away again. I turned to get some bacon out of the fridge, keeping my eyes down, and, when

I deemed it safe, turned to Nick and said as normally as possible, 'Bacon sandwich, darling?'

'Please.'

Was it my imagination or did he give me the strangest look? No, I was getting paranoid. The telephone rang and Nick went to the hall to answer it. Good. Phew, this was getting much too hairy for my liking. I fried the bacon and listened whilst Hetty outlined her list of prime suspects.

'Well, for a start there's Tom Rawlings at the butcher's, I wouldn't put it past him at all. He knows the house and he's delivered here loads of times so he could *easily* have seen the key in the jug, *and* he absolutely loathes us because I caught him fiddling the bill once and switched the account to the butcher's in Helston, *and* his silly fool of a wife likes to think she dabbles in antiques although in actual fact she wouldn't know a Queen Anne cachepot from a Victorian piss-pot – oh yes, the pair of them are high on my list of possibilities.' She nodded sagely, narrowed her eyes and took a long drag from her cigarette.

'*Then* of course' – she looked for the saucer, couldn't find it so leaned back and flicked her ash in the sink – 'there's Mrs Bradshaw, who I was *delighted* to hear you'd fired! Should have done it myself long ago – sour old bag – it was only loyalty to her poor old henpecked husband who worked on the farm that made me keep her on. Mind you, she drove him to an early grave; he probably would have thanked me if I'd given her the boot. Yes,' she mused, taking another long, thoughtful drag, 'Mrs Bradshaw, a little too obvious at first glance, perhaps, but . . .' She sat up straight suddenly. 'How about this – suppose she put someone up to it? Eh, Polly? What d'you think?'

'Er, sorry? What did you say?' I gave her an ashtray. I was finding it hard to concentrate.

'Mrs Bradshaw, suppose she put someone up to it?'

'Well, yes, I suppose it's a possibility.'

'Of course it is! A very distinct one at that, and shall I tell you who that someone might be?'

'Do, Hetty,' I said, sitting down wearily and putting three bacon sandwiches on the table.

She leaned forward eagerly. 'Ted Simpson,' she whispered.

'What, that enormous great chap from the hardware shop?'

'Exactly. And d'you know why?' I shook my head and bit into my sandwich. 'Well, I'll tell you. Not only is he practically bankrupt, but *apparently* he used to work for a house-clearance company in London so he's got plenty of contacts in the antiques world, but even more pertinent – and get this – word in the village is that Simpson and Mrs Bradshaw are having a ding-dong!'

'No!' I abandoned my sandwich, agog now. 'But he's enormous, and she's so tiny!'

'Precisely! Isn't it disgusting? That hideous great whale of a man with that shrivelled little prune of a woman – imagine! How d'you think they do it – with her perched on top like a little gnat, or with him on top squashing the life out of her? Or do you suppose he suspends himself from some sort of trapeze from the ceiling so as not to crush her, or even – goodness, what's the matter, darling?'

She broke off as Nick came back into the kitchen. His face looked strange, twisted almost.

'Nick, what is it?' I quickly got up and went to him but

he seemed almost to back away. He thrust his hands in his pockets, he wouldn't look at me.

'That was Tim. He'd heard, of course, from one of his farm hands, he was ringing to commiserate. But he said he was here on Saturday morning, Polly, he brought us some vegetables, early, at about seven thirty. He rang the door-bell but no one answered. Then he came back about an hour later, just in case you'd been asleep, there was still no answer. Eventually he used his key to get in and left the vegetables in the pantry. He said the house was deserted.' At last he turned to look at me, his eyes full of pain. 'Where were you, Poll?'

Chapter Fourteen

I was a rat and his eyes were the trap. He pinned me with them. I looked at the floor, and then rather desperately at the skirting boards, hoping perhaps for a handy little rat hole through which to slip, but there was no escape. The eyes had me.

'Well, Polly?'

I licked my lips. 'It's a long story,' I whispered.

There was a terrible silence.

'Oooohhh!' breathed someone excitedly to my left. 'You naughty girl, Polly, what *have* you been up to?'

Hetty had blown her cover. For a moment there I think both Nick and I had actually forgotten about her. Her eyes were wide with wonder, her face agog.

'Come on, Mum, we'll see you later,' said Nick, thrusting her latest handbag, a tartan rucksack affair, into her arms and hustling her towards the door.

Hetty pouted and dug her heels in. 'But, darling, I want to hear where Polly was, oh come on, don't be a spoilsport,' she wailed as she was dragged across the floor, physically outmanoeuvred.

'Polly, do tell, where were you?' she asked breathlessly, swivelling her head round a hundred and eighty degrees as she was bundled past me.

'Come on,' said Nick, holding her in a vicelike grip with one hand and reaching for the door handle with the other.

But, just as he was about to grab it, the door flew open of its own accord. Sarah stuck her head round.

'Hello there, thought I'd pop in for coffee. I say, terrible news about the burglary, who d'you think it was? Any theories?' She raised her eyebrows and looked from one face to another – one guilty, one grim, one bursting with excitement – then she took in the half-nelson grip Nick had on his mother.

'Bad moment?' she ventured.

'Not great,' agreed Nick. 'Mum was just leaving, actually, and Polly and I have something we want to discuss. Could you come back later, Sarah?'

'Sure, no problem,' she said, not moving an inch. 'What d'you need to discuss? Is it the burglary?'

'No, they're having a domestic!' hissed Hetty loudly. 'Nick's just found out that Polly stayed out all Friday night, imagine!'

'Really?' Sarah's eyes grew round. 'Goodness, Polly, where were you?'

'Out, please!' said Nick, depositing Hetty on the doorstep and bundling Sarah off with her. 'Out, out, OUT!'

'Pop round later, Polly!' yelled Hetty as the door shut on the pair of them – slammed, actually.

Through the glass I saw them give one last lingering look in our direction before turning away, heads bent together, whispering furiously as they went down the path. What I wouldn't have given to have been on the other side of that door, whispering with them. I began to clear the table, frantically burying my head in the dishes.

'Now,' said Nick calmly, turning to face me, 'if it's not too much to ask, perhaps you'd be good enough to let me be the first to know what the hell's going on here, before Mum and Sarah spread tidings of our impending divorce throughout the county!'

'Oh, don't be silly, they wouldn't do that!' I said, desperately trying to change the subject. 'They're very well meaning really, and if their tongues do tend to wag a bit it's only because they're taking an interest and –'

'Terrific, so am I,' interrupted Nick, grabbing my arm and turning me round to face him. 'Come on,' he said grimly, 'spill the beans.'

I started to tremble. I was holding a pile of dirty plates which began to clatter uncontrollably.

'Just let me get rid of these,' I muttered, 'before I spill them instead.'

I bent down to load the dishwasher, hiding my flushing face in its stainless-steel depths and desperately playing for time. When I stood up I had a feeling my time had run out, but I had one last shot.

'Look, Nick, it's an awfully long story and I'm feeling so hot and bothered, would you mind terribly if I just had a quick bath first and then I could –'

'Get your story straight? Think of a few lies with which to embellish it? No, Polly, you couldn't, I want it NOW!' He banged the table with his fist, his face livid. 'Where were you?' he asked in a dangerously quiet way.

I sat down, it was a must, my legs just wouldn't do their supporting act any longer.

'Sit down,' I mumbled. I couldn't possibly look up at that man-mountain towering above me. He sat. I licked my lips, they were like sandpaper.

'I was . . . still in London.'

'At Pippa's?' he asked, somewhat hopefully.

I hesitated, sensing an escape route here. It would be the work of a moment to ring Pippa and make her corroborate, but something stopped me – Nick's face. It was deadly, but at the same time vulnerable, frightened even. I couldn't lie to him any more. After all, as far as I knew I hadn't done anything wrong. In fact, I was convinced I was totally in the clear – nothing had happened at all. I'd tell him everything, he'd just have to understand, of course he would. He loved me, didn't he, and didn't he always say honesty was the best policy?

'No, not at Pippa's – look, Nick, I'm going to tell you exactly what happened and I swear to God this is the truth, OK?'

'Fire away,' he said, tight-lipped.

'But it's most important you believe me,' I urged. 'Promise me you will, because – well, what I'm going to say may not exactly *sound* like the truth.'

He looked at me squarely. I tried to look back equally squarely but ended up looking all sort of sideways.

'Get on with it, Polly.'

'And if I look shifty now it's only because you make me very nerv–'

'Just get on with it, will you!'

'OK, OK.' I gulped and pulled my dressing gown around me. 'Right.' I licked my hellishly dehydrated lips. 'Well, there was this party in a restaurant, you see, on the Friday night, after the shoot.'

Nick looked puzzled. 'Which you went to?'

'Well, yes I did, actually, but only because everyone kept asking me to go. I was sort of – persuaded into it.'

'But you were supposed to be back here on Friday night, you knew that.'

I nodded. 'To check the delivery on Saturday morning, I know, I know, but – well, I had this brainwave, you see!' I looked at him eagerly, hoping he'd share my enthusiasm. 'I thought – why not leave the car in London, get the sleeper after the party and still be back in time to check the stock on Saturday! Brilliant, eh?'

Nick looked more incredulous than enthusiastic. 'You left the car in London? I thought you'd just put it away in the garage or something – Christ, Polly, you must have wanted to go to this party very badly.'

'Well, yes,' I shifted uncomfortably. 'I suppose I did, but – only because it was going to be such *fun*.' I grabbed his hand, desperate for him to understand. 'And it was so long since I'd been to anything remotely like that, and I've missed that part of my life a bit – not much, of course, not much at all, in fact, but just a bit – and I thought, well, just for once – damn it, why not?'

Nick pulled his hand away. 'Why not indeed,' he said drily. 'I had no idea you were suffering such withdrawal symptoms for your good-time-girl days.' He looked pained.

'Oh no, I'm not! No, not at all really, it's just that now and again – well, obviously I can see how superficial it all is but sometimes I miss that buzz, that little thrill of excitement, that feeling you get when you're out with loads of people having a good time; there's something so –'

'Polly, could we debate the pros and cons of London's social scene some other time? Just get to the point. You went to the party, and . . . ?'

I sighed and lit my third cigarette of the morning. 'Well, after that, a few of us went on to Annabel's.'

'I thought you said that was Thursday night?'

I dredged up yet more saliva.

'I lied,' I said in a small voice.

'I see,' he said in an icy one.

I swallowed hard. This was going very badly, very badly indeed, and I hadn't even got to the horrendous bit. I desperately wanted to get it over and done with so I speeded up.

'So as I said, we went on to Annabel's – me, Amanda, Chris and S-Sam.' There, I'd said it. I hurried on. 'And of course there was lots of dancing and drinking and that sort of thing and – oh yes, *lots* of drinking, actually, I got incredibly drunk, Nick, absolutely steaming, in fact I was –'

'How unusual,' he cut in sarcastically.

'No, but I was really *spectacularly* drunk.' It was imperative he understood I was in no way responsible for my actions. 'To the point where I was' – I looked down at my hands – 'practically unconscious.'

'Really.' I felt his eyes burn into me. 'And then?'

I twisted my hands together miserably. 'Well, that's just it, I don't know, I've got absolutely no idea how what happened next actually . . . happened.'

'How d'you mean? What did happen next?'

'I don't know!' I gazed at him desperately, willing him to understand. 'Because the next thing I knew, I was waking up in bed the next morning.'

'Where?'

'In a . . . hotel bedroom,' I whispered.

There was a horrible silence.

'With Sam?' His voice was weird, strangled.

I dared not look at him. I pulled at a thread in my towelling dressing gown.

'No, not with Sam, but – well, he'd obviously been there. At some point. There was a note, you see . . .' I trailed off miserably.

'Give it to me.'

With a hand like blancmange I reached behind me to the dresser, pulled my handbag down, rummaged around for the crumpled note and handed it to him. He spread it out on the table. I watched his face as he read it. It went white. He handed it back to me.

'I see.' He got up and went towards the door.

'Wh-where are you going?' I stammered.

'Out.'

'But I haven't finished! I have to tell you why I –'

'You mean there's more!' Nick swung around. His face was like a mask, like someone else's face, not my husband's.

'Still more?' he whispered. 'Jesus, Polly, you really know how to kick a man when he's down, don't you? I don't believe this, I just don't believe it!'

'But you don't understand!' I wailed. 'I didn't do it!'

He just stared at me.

'Don't you see?' I pleaded. 'I don't *remember* anything, nothing at all! I just woke up and found this on the bedside table, so – so if I don't remember, well, I can't have done anything wrong, can I?'

'So – what, you expect me to believe he raped you while you lay there unconscious? D'you want me to phone the police, Polly?'

'No, but –'

'Or – or perhaps nothing happened at all? Maybe he tucked you up in bed, read you a bedtime story, made you some cocoa and then curled up quietly on the floor. Is that more to your liking?'

'Well, perhaps not on the floor, but –'

'Oh, on the bed? But no funny business? Ah, I see, there's a sporting chance he just lay down beside you, is there? Oh yes, of course, it's all becoming crystal clear now, a platonic little sleep-in, babes in the wood, a kind of mixed dorm, is that it?'

I felt his tone lacked a certain conviction. I shifted uncomfortably.

'Well, it's possible, isn't it?'

'Oh, quite possible, quite possible, and tell me, Polly, the "wonderful evening" he refers to – what are your theories on that? Was he perhaps referring to your sparkling conversation? Your witty line in repartee? Or do you have any other ideas?'

'Well,' I whispered, 'I wondered perhaps if it was . . .'

'Yes? Go on, I'm keen to learn.'

'Well, a combination really, you know – chatting, laughing, joking, dancing –'

'Dancing! Yes, of course, why not? You've always created quite a stir on the dance floor, haven't you? Your dancing! Why not indeed?'

'Oh, Nick,' I said desperately, 'I know it all sounds a bit odd, but –'

'A bit odd? A BIT ODD!' he bellowed.

He leaned his hands on the table and stuck his face close to mine. I shrank down in my seat.

'Polly, I just don't believe this. You sit down at the

breakfast table one Sunday morning and cool as a cucumber tell me a story about how you spent the night in a hotel room with a man I very much suspected you had the hots for anyway –'

'Now that's not –'

'Let me finish!' he yelled. I gulped. 'You tell me you woke up the next morning and found this note' – he flicked it across the table as if it were a piece of dog shit – 'saying what a wonderful lover you were and what a marvellous time you'd given him –'

'But it doesn't –'

'Yes it *does*, Polly, clear as daylight I'm afraid, and then you expect me to believe you had convenient amnesia between the hours of midnight and seven a.m. and that because you don't *remember* anything, nothing actually happened? D'you honestly expect me to swallow that?'

His incredulous face was inches from mine now. I'd never seen him so angry, not even back in the bad old days of Penhalligan and Waters when he was my exacting boss and I was his useless secretary and he bawled me out on a regular basis. Nothing had ever remotely prepared me for this. I quaked in my slippers and tried desperately to defend myself.

'Well, I know it *sounds* a little far-fetched, a little unbelievable even –'

'A little far-fetched? Polly, it's downright lies and you know it!'

His eyes had me pinned again. I shrank, I slithered, I ducked and weaved, but there was no getting out of the line of fire.

'Don't forget, Polly, I know you,' he hissed. 'I know you

inside out, and God knows you've told some whoppers in your time, but this really is the biggest, isn't it? This really takes the biscuit. Tell me, I'm genuinely intrigued, what exactly were you wearing when you woke up?'

'Wh-what was I wearing?'

'Yes, do tell.'

'Well . . . I was . . .'

'Naked?'

I hung my head, shame overwhelming me now, filling every crevice, every nook, every toenail.

'I see. And you still don't know what happened?'

I shook my head miserably.

'Well, let me enlighten you, Polly, let me fill you in. It's like this. You went to bed with him. You went to bed with Sam. You took advantage of the fact that your husband was away on a business trip and you bonked another man whom you'd fancied for some time. Not a very original scenario, I grant you, and a pretty cheap and nasty one at that, but one that you obviously had no qualms about participating in. In fact I'd go so far as to say you almost planned the whole thing.'

I couldn't look at him, this seemed so unfair, and yet, what could I say? Had I? Had I done it? I stared at the floor, my eyes filling with hot tears. Nick saw my shamed face and took it as an admission of guilt. He straightened up and shook his head slowly.

'Jesus,' he whispered. His face, which had been firm and furious up to now, suddenly wobbled precariously. His mouth trembled, his eyes watered.

'This time, you've just gone too far,' he said in a shaky voice.

He got up and walked out of the kitchen, banging the back door behind him. I stared at the door for a second, then my head dropped on to the table and I burst into tears. My heart broke into the stripped pine. After the few first terrible convulsions, I dragged myself up and ran after him. Sobbing and heaving, I flung open the back door and raced down the garden path, dressing gown flying, but he was striding fast. I ran through the vegetable patch in my bare feet and eventually caught up with him in the lettuces. I grabbed his sleeve.

'No! No!' I sobbed, clinging to his arm. 'It wasn't like that, really it wasn't, you don't understand, you must let me explain! I don't *know* what happened, but it wasn't that! I know I'm a terrible liar, but, Nick, I promise I'm not lying this time, I'm not, you *must* believe me, I'm telling the truth, I'm telling the truth!'

He tried to shake me off but I clung to his arm like a puppy with a rubber toy, tenacious, desperate, sobbing. Eventually he prised my fingers off one by one and pushed me away. Not hard, but definitely away. We stood facing each other a few feet apart. The tears were streaming down my face now, my shoulders were shaking and my breath was coming in gasps. I'm not sure, but I think he was crying too.

'Nick, please . . .' I sobbed, holding out my hand.

'I'll be staying at Tim's tonight. We'll make other arrangements later,' he whispered.

With that he turned on his heel and left me standing there. I watched him go, then covered my face with my hands and sank to my knees in the lettuces.

Chapter Fifteen

I must have sat there for some time, because when I tried to get up my legs were stiff and numb from being doubled up beneath me and my dressing gown was sopping wet and covered in mud. I pulled it around me, shaking with cold and misery. As I knotted the cord, I noticed a tiny black spider scrambling furiously along it, frantic and lost amongst a mass of blue towelling. I flicked him on to the mud and he sped away on more familiar terrain, just a wrong turning in an otherwise ordinary day. As I turned and stumbled back to the house I saw Larry mending a fence in the far field. He looked up, waved and smiled, just an ordinary day for him too. Life, for the rest of the planet, seemed to be going on as normal, why was mine falling apart?

I went into the kitchen and sat down carefully, holding myself tightly. I rested my head on the table. I couldn't even cry now. I stared at the remains of the breakfast things in front of me. The blue teapot was inches from my nose. Was it only this morning I'd been pouring tea from it? Funny, it seemed like days ago. It had a crack, I saw, just at the top, by the handle. Odd, I'd never noticed that before. I shut my eyes and heard Nick's voice in my head. 'I'll be staying at Tim's tonight. We'll make other arrangements later.' What other arrangements? What did that mean? Separate rooms? Separate houses? Separate lives?

I turned my head, leaned my other cheek on the table and stared at the fridge minus its magnets. Minus its finger paintings. I felt my guts knot themselves into a tight little ball and my face buckled. Did I say I was all cried out? The tears flowed silently down my cheeks. This was so unreal, I just couldn't believe it was happening. Nick . . . my Nick, was I losing him? Had I lost him already? It was something I'd never, ever envisaged. I'd assumed we'd be together forever, have children together, grow old together, and now, in the space of just a few days, it was all over. What had happened?

I buried my head in my arms and groaned. I'd cocked it up, that's what. A loving husband, a beautiful house, security, love, happiness – it hadn't been enough for me, had it? No, I'd wanted more. Not much more, of course, just a little bit, nothing big enough to trouble the happy home, but enough to bring a small frisson of excitement now and then. A secret, something to think about in quiet, private moments – when I was drying my hair, or driving to the shops, or listening to a slushy record, or before I went to sleep at night – something to hug to myself or, more precisely, someone. And someone to be thinking about me too.

And of course, if that someone had ever got out of hand, if Sam had come on a bit strong, for instance, why then I'd have been wide-eyed with innocent amazement.

'Heavens, Sam, you mean you thought that you and I might one day . . . oh! Golly, so sorry to have misled you, to have wasted your time, but you see I've got this husband . . .

Love him? I adore him! Worship the ploughed fields he tramples on – didn't I mention it?'

I probably would have shot him one last hot look full of the promise of what might have been, given a tantalizing flick of the long blonde hair that never lay on his pillow and then left him to stew in his own frustrated juices, longing for me, lusting after me. Yes, that had been about the size of it, hadn't it, Polly? Hadn't that been the big idea? Well, blow me if it hadn't backfired in one hell of a big way.

I dragged myself up from the table and moved slowly through the kitchen to the hall. I went to go upstairs but the mirror at the foot of the banisters stopped me. I stared. God, I looked like I'd been beaten up. My jaw wobbled and another tear made its way rather self-consciously down my cheek. I brushed it away roughly and scowled fiercely at my reflection.

'Oh, for heaven's sake, get a grip,' I hissed. 'Who are you to feel sorry for yourself – you've brought it all on yourself, haven't you? Shut *up*, you silly fool, stop blubbing and bloody well *do* something about it, all right?'

But what? I rested my burning face against the mirror. My head felt so thick, so gummed up, I couldn't even begin to think. I had to make Nick believe me, that much was clear – he'd never forgive me, not in a million years, so I had to make him believe me. I turned my forehead against the cool glass. If only I could remember what had actually happened, if only I hadn't been so out of it, so drunk. I mean, if I didn't know, how on earth could Nick be expected to?

Suddenly I froze and eyeballed myself in the mirror.

A gem of an idea was scuttling across my retina. Blimey. Of course! Yes, of course, you idiot, ask Sam, just jolly well *ask* him! And if it transpires that you did indulge in any naughtiness – as I was rapidly coming to suspect I had – well then, just get him to lie! Get him to ring Nick and say it hadn't happened at all, that I'd fallen asleep and he hadn't laid a finger on me!

I frowned and bit the skin around my thumbnail. But why should he do that, why should he lie? I thought hard. Because – because if he didn't, I'd – I'd tell his wife! I gasped and clapped my hand over my mouth, my eyes huge with horror, stunned by my own treachery. Goodness, Polly, what an awful person you've become! I gazed in wonder at my reflection, wondering if it showed. I hesitated, but only for a moment. No, damn it, this was no time to be moral and whimsical – my marriage was at stake. It was a brilliant idea, absolutely brilliant.

Today was Sunday and I couldn't possibly ring Sam at home, but I'd do it tomorrow morning. Yes, absolutely first thing, just as soon as he got into his office. I set my mouth in a determined line and regarded my reflection. Things were looking distinctly upward. Well, all right, not distinctly, but marginally, because you see I had a plan, and there's nothing I like more in a crisis than a plan.

The following morning I woke up alone. I had a brief sob into the pillow about this sorry state of affairs, then I remembered my plan. I sat up straight and forced myself to think positive. I looked at the clock. Eight thirty. At nine o'clock I'd phone. I grabbed my muddy dressing gown from the floor, pulled it around my shoulders and sat watching the minutes tick by. I lit a cigarette – couldn't find an ashtray so commandeered the top of a deodorant spray and wedged it precariously in the bedding. I took one deep, thoughtful drag and murmured a brief rehearsal of what I might say to Sam on the phone.

'Er, hello there, Sam, it's Polly . . . Fine thanks, and you? . . . Good. Sorry to bother you but there's something I'd like to clear up. Did we do it last Friday night? . . . Ah, we did, I rather suspected as much. Listen, old boy, sorry to be a nuisance, but get on the blower and lie through your teeth to my husband, would you, or before you can say alimony I'll be round at your place spilling the beans to her indoors, all right?'

I gulped and took another deep drag of nicotine. Well, something like that anyway. My cigarette-holding fingers were shaking violently, bad sign. I suspected this was going to be rather an awkward phone call, but on the other hand it had to be done. At nine o'clock on the dot I bit my lip and punched out Sam's work number. A rather plummy receptionist answered.

'Eu, helleu, Rocket Productions?'

'Yes, could I speak to Sam Weston, please?'

'Aim afraid he's not in the office today, he's aight shooting.'

'Oh! Where's he shooting? Can you give me the number?'

'Aim afraid Mr Weston doesn't like to be disturbed on a shoot.'

'I'm sure he won't mind under the circumstances,' I purred sweetly. 'We're making a film together. Could you put me through to his office, please? I'll speak to his assistant.'

'Jarst one moment,' she said icily.

There were a few clicks and gurgles, then another girl answered.

'Production?'

'Hello,' I said briskly, 'look, sorry to bother you, but it's imperative I get hold of Sam Weston right away, I'm making a war-torn documentary about the Bosnian Kurds and I need to discuss the rushes with him immediately. Could you get his telephone number for me, please, it's rather urgent. My name's Kate Adie, by the way.'

There was a pause. 'Polly?'

'Pippa! Oh, Pippa, it's you, I didn't recognize you, oh, thank goodness. Listen, I must speak to Sam, where is he?'

'Sam's on location at the moment.' She sounded hostile, even more hostile than the receptionist, in fact. Crikey. I frowned, then suddenly remembered.

'Oh gosh, Pippa, I'm so sorry!' I gasped. 'I'm so sorry about what I said in the restaurant about you and Josh, but you see I was incredibly drunk! It was stupid and – and horrid, I know that, but, Pippa, I was out of my tree, and so many awful things have happened to me since then that I just completely forgot to ring and apologize, please forgive me, please!'

'It was totally out of order, I've never been so embarrassed in all my life.' Her voice was icy.

'Oh, I know, I know,' I wailed, 'but it'll never happen again, honestly, please forgive me, Pipps, please?'

There was a pause, and then a sigh. 'You really are a dickhead, aren't you, Polly?'

She forgave me. 'Oh thank you, thank you! And you're

right, I am a dickhead, I really am, and you're so sweet, so —'

'Oh, all right. Spare me the effusive gushing, just *think* next time, OK?'

'OK, OK!' I agreed wholeheartedly. 'And thank you so —'

'Shut *up*, Polly.'

'Right, right.' I cowered. 'Was Josh, um, furious?'

'Livid. He got in his car and raced off without me. I tried to follow in a taxi but I lost him. I don't know where he went but it wasn't home. I sat outside his house for ages waiting for his car to draw up, but he never appeared.'

'Oh, Pipps, I'm so sorry,' I said in a small voice.

She sighed. 'Well, actually, as it turned out it wasn't so terrible. When I got into work everyone said they couldn't understand what the fuss was all about because they all knew anyway. It doesn't make things any easier but I suppose at least we can be a bit more open about things here; I don't have to skulk around quite so much.'

'You see! Oh good, I'm so glad! So it's all turned out rather well then?'

'I wouldn't go as far as that,' snapped Pippa tersely. 'I'm certainly not about to thank you, if that's what you mean!'

'No, no, of course not,' I muttered meekly.

'But what happened to you? Did you get your train?'

I groaned. 'Oh, Pippa, it's awful, simply awful, so much has happened I just can't tell you. Nick hates me — I think he's leaving me, in fact, and he's right, I'm a ghastly person, rotten through and through, a liar, a cheat, a —'

'*What!* He's leaving you? But he knew all that stuff when

he married you, didn't he? The cheating and the lying and –'

'Oh yes, of course, but he didn't know I was an adulteress, did he? He didn't know I'd go to bed with Sam, he didn't know about my nasty, rotten, conniving –'

'YOU WHAT! You went to bed with Sam? Polly, what the hell's going on?'

Out tumbled the whole sordid story, punctuated by much sniffing, sobbing, nose-blowing and pauses to light more cigarettes. When I'd finished there was a silence at the other end.

'Pippa? Are you still there?'

'Yes, I'm still here, but I'm practically on the floor. God, you've really gone and done it this time, haven't you?'

'I know, I know!' I wailed.

'What on earth are you going to do?'

'Well, first of all I've got to speak to Sam and find out exactly what happened.'

'I should have thought that was fairly obvious.'

'Well, yes, OK, but – I wondered if he could be persuaded to pretend otherwise.'

'What, to lie?'

'Er, sort of, yes.'

'To Nick? Heavens, Polly, talk about a tangled web and all that. Why don't you just come clean for once?'

'Oh yes, brilliant,' I snapped. 'I came clean yesterday and look where it got me, practically in the divorce courts. No, I've got to speak to him, it's the only way.'

'Well, you've got a slight problem; he's somewhere on the Nile.'

'The Nile! What the hell's he doing there?'

'Shooting a commercial for Turkish delight. He'll be back in about two weeks.'

'I can't wait that long, I could be divorced by then!'

'Well, I've got a few telephone numbers, but they're moving around a lot and it might be quite difficult to trace him.'

'Give them to me,' I said desperately. 'I'll try them all.'

'Cost you a fortune, Polly,' said Pippa dubiously.

'Oh, what does money matter when my marriage is at stake!' I cried dramatically.

I wrote down all the numbers and promised to report back if I had any news. A couple of hours later, when my index finger was numb from punching out twenty-digit numbers and my voice hoarse from shouting at ignorant Egyptian hotel receptionists who couldn't even speak the Queen's English for heaven's sake, I finally put the phone down in despair. I traipsed miserably downstairs, poured myself a large gin and tonic, cut some cucumber slices for my puffy little eyes and trailed back to bed again. It was quite clear that getting hold of Sam was going to be very tricky. I'd tried every hotel between Aswan and Cairo and the answer was always the same. 'He not due here till next week,' or, 'He been, he gone now, he go yesterday.' Eventually, knocked out by the mother's ruin and soothed by the cucumber eye patches, I went back to sleep, resolving that in the afternoon, with a rested brain and finger, I'd track him down if it was the last thing I did.

Unfortunately, as I discovered later, this was not to be. After shrieking at a whole new batch of receptionists and then reporting back to Pippa, it transpired that there'd been a complete change of plan and the entire film crew was now actually *on* the Nile, on a boat which stopped whenever and wherever the director felt like filming, but with no firm schedule.

'How can he do this to me?' I screeched to Pippa. 'I need to speak to him right now!'

'Well, he'll definitely be in Cairo in a couple of weeks,' soothed Pippa, 'no question about it. They're shooting the pack shot there and that's where the client's waiting, complete with pristine box of Turkish delight in his hot little hand. So don't worry, you'll get hold of him then. Just for once in your life be patient, Polly, OK?'

Easy for her to say, I thought gloomily, putting the phone down. It wasn't her life that was in the balance here, was it?

The next two weeks were purgatory. Nick worked on the farm but slept and ate at Tim and Sarah's. I never saw him. I stayed inside and basically took to my bed, just popping down to the kitchen now and then for supplies, which I then squirrelled away in a little store under my bed. I curled up miserably under the duvet, mentally ticked the days off as they went by and generally felt that there was nothing much to live for, let alone get up for. I tried to diet but seemed to put on more weight than ever, which might have had something to do with the fact that the only exercise I got was reaching for my cigarettes.

Apart from smoking a lot, I cried a lot and talked tearfully on the phone to Pippa, who did her best to console me, but who, I could tell, felt that the dice were not exactly loaded in my favour. Sarah, I knew, felt much the same. She crept over to see me every day, feeling horribly divided between Nick and me.

She'd assured me on her first visit that the whole village knew of the marital tiff and were on tenterhooks, dying to know the outcome – would he come back? Paul, the news-agent, had even opened a book on it. Apparently the odds were against me, but that could have had something to do with the fact that the current story sweeping the village was that I'd got out of my head on Ecstasy at an acid house party and then bonked an entire rugger team.

As Sarah was one of the few people privy to a conver-sation with Nick these days, I awaited her daily visits with bated breath. One day, at the beginning of the third week, she crept in as usual at around eleven o'clock. I sat up eagerly, wrapped my distinctly grubby dressing gown around me and peered through the dark glasses which hid my puffy eyes.

'How is he?' I whispered, before she'd even got a foot through the door. 'Pining for me yet, d'you think?'

''Fraid not, Polly,' she said, a mite too cheerfully for my liking, brushing some ash off the bed cover before she sat down. 'He was up with the lark this morning and ate a hearty breakfast. Actually he was on quite good form for a change. Of course,' she added quickly, seeing my face fall, 'he's probably faking it, he's probably eating his heart out, but you know Nick, he'd never show it.'

I nodded dumbly. 'Sure.' I slumped back down on the pillows and stared out of the window.

Sarah got up and swept some crumbs on to the floor. 'God, this bed's disgusting, crumbs and ash and – oh yuck, toenails too! You are a slob, Polly, when did you last change the duvet cover?'

'Oh, I don't know,' I muttered miserably, reaching down

beside my bed for the Coco Pops packet and pulling out a handful of cereal. I crunched away gloomily. 'Last month, I think. Does he mention me, Sarah?'

'Christ,' she muttered, moving hastily on to a chair. 'Er, well, not exactly, but then I think that's pretty significant, don't you? It's as if he can't bear to mention your name in case – well, in case it hurts too much.'

'Or in case he pukes,' I muttered. 'What's in the Le Creuset thing?' I'd spotted a casserole dish by her feet.

'Oh, I thought you probably weren't eating properly so I brought you a stew, we had some last night.'

'Stew? On a weekday? Gosh, he'll never come back if he gets used to your cooking. Give him beans on toast every night like I do. You're an angel for bringing it, Sarah, but honestly, I'm trying to diet. I'm getting so fat.'

'Well, it's hardly surprising since you live on Coco Pops – and what's that aerosol thing you keep squirting in your mouth?'

'Whipped cream,' I said, giving my tonsils a quick squirt. 'Easier than going downstairs to get the milk. These are my staples. Sarah, just a little cereal and cream every day. I'm cutting out all the frivolous luxuries like bread and –'

'Fruit and vegetables, yes, I know. It's no wonder you're putting on weight – and look at all these empty chocolate boxes!' She cruelly swept the duvet aside to reveal my secret store.

'They're not all empty,' I protested sulkily. 'Here, have one.' I pushed a box in her direction.

'No thanks. I know you – if it's still sitting there it'll be because it's marzipan or something disgusting and it'll have a chunk out of it where you've tried it and put it back. Anyway, I thought you hadn't got out of bed for ages. Where did you get them from?' She giggled. 'Secret admirer? Someone who goes in for the distressed-bag-lady look, eh?'

'Very funny, and for your information I did actually get out of bed one day last week. I went into Helston to get my split ends cut.' I sniffed. 'I felt so lonely and miserable I just had to have some sort of physical contact, even if it was only with a complete stranger who stroked my hair and snipped the ends off.' I turned to face the wall. 'And guess who I ran into as I was coming out of the salon?'

'Who?'

'Nick,' I whispered. 'We practically bumped into each other. He didn't say a word. I opened my mouth to say hello but I shut it when I saw his eyes. Cold and hard. He just looked straight through me and walked on by without saying anything.' I pulled my hanky out from under my pillow and snuffled into it. 'What have I got to live for, Sarah? Just tell me that, eh?'

Sarah sighed. 'Look, Polly, he's bound to be feeling like that at the moment – just give him some time, OK? And you know something?'

'What?'

'You'd feel much better if you got up and got your act together. You could clear up this pigsty of a room for a start. I mean, look at it!' She swept her hand around in disgust. 'You can hardly move for dirty washing and over-flowing ashtrays. I've never seen so many cigarette butts in one room – and look at all these empty Mr Kipling boxes! I don't know how you can bear to live like this! And look at that dressing gown you're still wearing – it's filthy, why don't you wash it?'

'Washing machine's broken,' I said gloomily.

'Well, get a plumber!'

I bit my nail. 'Don't scold me, Sarah. I'm just not up to it.'

'Take it off and give it to me,' she sighed. 'I'll wash it and give it back to you tomorrow.'

I dutifully slipped out of it and handed it to her. She took it gingerly and bundled it up by the door ready to take. I huddled under the duvet with nothing on and watched as she began sweeping all the debris into the waste-paper basket, emptying ashtrays and picking up clothes. She stubbed out a couple of cigarette ends smouldering peacefully away in the top of the deodorant spray.

'Apart from anything else you'll go up in flames if you're not careful!' she scolded.

'And who would care?' I retorted. 'Who would care if I died right now, certainly not Nick. He hasn't even bothered to enquire how I am; I could be dead already and he wouldn't even know about it!'

Sarah stooped to pick up a mouldy banana skin that was nestling in one of my suede shoes. She straightened up and looked at me rather impatiently.

'If you don't mind me saying so, Polly, I think you're taking this self-indulgent bit a mite too far. I mean, no one can actually blame Nick for avoiding you, seeing as you were the one who opted for the extra-marital sex in the first place.'

'Whose side are you on, Sarah?'

'No one's, but you must admit he's got a point, and

anyway, you wouldn't want him to come and see you now, would you? Imagine if he walked in and found you in this revolting state.'

'Well, he's not going to, is he? I mean, let's face it, Sarah, he's never going to come back, is he?' My voice cracked.

Sarah busied herself grinding out more cigarettes. She didn't look at me.

'Well, is he?' I pleaded.

She sighed. 'I don't know. I really don't, Poll. I think he's talked to Tim but Tim won't tell me anything because he thinks it'll go straight back to you, which it probably would.'

I was shocked. 'There's no probably about it, Sarah, of course it would!'

'All right, all right, of course it would. But you're right, he's not going to walk back in just like that. Nick's got some pretty uncompromising views about the sanctity of marriage.' She picked up a mug with two inches of solid blue mould at the bottom. 'Shall I soak this for you?'

'Oh, throw it away,' I said miserably, 'it'll never come off.'

Sarah ignored this directive and put it in my washbasin, running the hot tap over it. I groaned and bashed my head on the pillow.

'You know, Sarah, everything would be all right if I could just talk to Sam and find out what happened! I've got to speak to him in Cairo, I've just got to!'

'And if he says you did sleep together you're still going to ask him to lie through his teeth?'

'You bet,' I said grimly, 'it's the only way.'

Sarah sighed and folded her arms. 'Well, you know my

views on that topic. I mean, wouldn't it be easier to just – well, to just sort of – stick to the truth?' She had the grace to ask this somewhat hesitantly, knowing how diametrically it went against the grain.

'Oh sure, *easier*,' I scoffed, 'but hopelessly ineffectual, and anyway, sometimes,' I went on piously, 'one has to take the hard route in life, however unpleasant it might be. One can't always take the easy way out, you'll learn that one day. No, no, this calls for some carefully thought-out subterfuge.'

She shrugged and threw open a window. 'Oh well, you know best. Phew, that's better. God, you can hardly see for smoke in here!'

'Atmosphere,' I mumbled.

'And what are you doing with these binoculars?' She picked them up off the windowsill.

'Oh, that's so I can see Nick when he's working in the fields. It's the only time I get to catch a glimpse of him now, and to think, I used to be able to see him every minute of the day!' My voice rose dramatically and I sniffed into my hanky, poking it up under my dark glasses to dab my eyes.

Sarah sighed and sat down patiently on the bed beside me. 'Oh dear, you are in a bad way, aren't you?'

I nodded miserably, sniffing wildly. She patted my hand, then looked at her watch. She shook her head.

'Listen, I'm really sorry, Poll, but I must go in a sec. I've got a new showjumping pupil arriving at the stables soon. Will you be all right?'

'Yes, I'll be fine,' I whispered, smiling bravely. 'Oh, and er – leave the stew if you like, Sarah,' I added quickly, seeing her tuck it under her arm. 'You never know, I might feel up to it a bit later on.'

'That's the spirit,' she said, putting it on a chest of drawers. 'It'll do you good. And just think, Polly, tomorrow you'll be able to speak to Sam and sort out exactly what happened. Odd the way these film people change their schedules all the time. I thought he was supposed to be in Cairo today?'

'No, it was always tomorrow. He arrives at the hotel on Tuesday.'

'But it's Tuesday today, Polly.'

I went pale. 'Don't be silly, it's Monday.'

'No.' Sarah shook her head emphatically. She pulled a diary out of her handbag, flipped through, then brandished it in my face. 'Look, definitely Tuesday.' I nearly fainted with shock.

'My God! It can't be true! You mean I'm sitting here wasting precious hours gabbling to you when I could be talking to him?'

'You've been in bed too long, Poll. Lost a day along the way somewhere.'

'Out! Out!' I screamed, shooing her away. 'I've got to ring him right now, quick, Sarah, go away!'

'All right, I'm going, I'm going,' she said, making hastily for the door. One hand was already on the phone, the other scrabbling around on my bedside table for the important piece of paper I'd scribbled the number on.

Sarah picked up the dirty dressing gown and scuttled out, but a second later her head popped back round the door. 'Oh, and you will let me know how it goes, won't you?' she said eagerly.

'Yes!' I screeched. 'Just go!'

She went.

With a very shaky hand I punched out the number. I listened nervously as it rang and rang. Eventually someone answered.

''Allo?'

'Yes, I'd like to speak to Mr Sam Weston, please,' I said breathlessly. 'I believe he's staying with you.'

'Heh? Speak up?' It was a terrible line.

'MR SAM WESTON!' I shouted.

'Ah yes, he in his room.'

I sat bolt upright. 'He is? Terrific! Put me through, please!'

'Ah no, he resting, he say he no want to be disturbed.'

'Do you know who I am?' I screeched.

'Heh?' The line was getting worse.

'DO YOU KNOW WHO I AM?'

'No, but Meester Weston, he say –'

'I don't give a damn what he say! I'm Helena Bleeding-Bonham-Carter, that's who, Mr Weston's leading lady no less, and if you don't put me through right now I shall abandon Mr Weston's picture and go to Hollywood and make one with Harrison Ford and Great Britain will hold you personally responsible for the collapse of its film industry! You'll find yourself impaled on top of one of your precious pyramids if you're not careful. Now put me through!'

I thought I might have gone slightly over the top as far as the old prima donna bit was concerned, but it certainly did the trick. It scared the living daylights out of Abdul and two seconds later Sam answered his phone.

'Sam Weston?' The line was even worse. 'Hello, Sam? It's me, Polly, can you hear me?'

'Hello? Who's that?'

'It's me! POLLY!' I yelled, almost eating the mouthpiece.

'Polly! Darling, listen, I'm so sorry I had to dash off like that the other morning, do forgive me, I'd much rather have woken up beside you but I had to go to the office to organize this blasted shoot!'

'Doesn't matter, doesn't matter at all – listen, Sam, are you on your own? Can you talk?'

'What? Speak up, Polly, this line is appalling, you want to what?'

'TALK! It's about that night at the hotel. It's very important, Sam. I need to know what happened, because you see I can't remember!'

'Become a member? Darling, it's a hotel, not a club. Very smart, I agree, but –'

'NO!' I screeched, feeling rather faint from shouting. 'I said I can't remember! Did we do it, Sam?'

'What?'

'DID WE DO IT?'

'Darling, I want to do it too, I'm aching for you right now, absolutely aching! And Polly, let's see each other the moment I'm back, we've been apart too long already. I can't wait to take you in my arms and –'

'NO!' I screeched, feeling sick with both fear and a strained larynx. 'I don't want to do it again, I want to know if we did it at all! If we made LOVE!'

'Ah, love.' He sighed. 'D'you know it felt very much like that for me too, isn't it extraordinary? I've never in my life strayed out of my marriage, Polly, and to be honest I expected to wake up the next morning with terrible feelings of guilt and awful misgivings, but I didn't. I can't help it, I just didn't, and now I can't stop thinking about you. When am I likely to see you again – can I phone? I haven't liked to in case Nick answered but –'

I groaned and bashed my head against the headboard a few times. The way this convoluted conversation was going there seemed little doubt that I should essentially fear the worst and slit my wrists right now, but, call me old-fashioned, I still wanted confirmation that the evening had indeed been consummated. I got the mouthpiece so close it was practically nudging my tonsils and yelled, 'DID WE HAVE SEX?'

'Sorry?'

'SEX, damn you, SEX SEX SEX!'

As I screeched these last few words I heard a faint click behind me. I turned around to see Nick standing in the doorway. I stared at him aghast, and simultaneously heard a voice in my right ear saying, 'Oh, sex! Yes, of course we did, darling, you were tremendous! It was absolutely wonderful, I've never felt so close to someone in my entire life, I just wish I wasn't a million miles away and could –'

I gasped and slammed down the phone. Nick was staring at me, ashen-faced, a muscle twitching away in his left cheek. It seemed to me that my last, highly compromising words were still echoing round the room. I jumped up and ran to him.

'Oh no, Nick, it's not what you think!'

He shook me off and pulled a case down from the top of the wardrobe. He began to fill it with clothes.

'No? I take it that was Sam?'

'Y-yes, it was, but –'

'But what, Polly?' he said, throwing things in the case. 'God, I had no idea you were so frustrated, you've obviously got a problem.'

'But you don't understand, I –'

'Oh really?' He turned to face me, his face white and deadly. 'I walk into my bedroom to get some more clothes and find you sitting up in bed, stark naked, screaming, "Sex! Sex! Sex!" down the phone to some guy you bedded a couple of weeks ago. What do you expect me to think?' He shook his head grimly. 'I obviously haven't been able to satisfy you, Polly. I had no idea you were so highly sexed.'

I groaned and fell to my knees on the floor, clutching my head and bashing it on the carpet.

'No!' I groaned. 'No, it's not like that, really it isn't! For a start, the only reason I've got nothing on is because my dressing gown is filthy and Sarah's taken it away to – WHAT ARE YOU DOING!'

I screamed as he reached into the back of the wardrobe and pulled out a gun. I ducked, covering my head with my hands.

'Don't be bloody silly, Polly, it's for the rats in the barn, not the rat in the house.'

I gulped, peering through my fingers. He rested it against the wall while he snapped his case shut. Heavens, for a moment there I thought I was going to be on the receiving end of a *crime passionnel*. Then he picked up the case in one hand and the gun in the other and marched to the door.

'Oh, Nick, please . . .' I whispered, as he walked away.

'Oh, Nick, please what?' he hissed, suddenly turning on his heel.

I tried to meet his eyes but couldn't. I stared down at my bare knees, lost for words. There was a silence.

'Nothing to say?' he asked softly. He walked back. 'Well, perhaps while I'm here you could explain our phone bill which I picked up from the hall table not a few moments ago.' He took it out of his pocket and threw it on the floor beside me. 'No less than fourteen itemised phone calls and all of them to Egypt. Is that where your boyfriend is at the moment?'

'Nick, he's not my –'

'IS THAT WHERE HE IS?'

'Yes, but you don't understand,' I wailed. 'I was just trying to get hold of him, to ask him something. I wasn't trying to –'

'I understand perfectly, Polly,' he interrupted icily. 'I understand that this was anything but a one-night stand and that you're speaking to him constantly and probably thinking about him every minute. You're infatuated with him, aren't you? God, you're nothing but a nasty, cheap little cheat.'

'Nick, I –'

'Yes you are, Polly, and you know it.' He sat down slowly on the arm of a chair and shook his head. 'You know,' he said softly, looking past me, 'when I married you, I have to admit I found your cock-eyed view of life rather endearing. Call me foolish, but I always thought your propensity to be so economical with the truth was just a harmless, quirky trait in your character.' He shrugged. 'If anything,

I found it rather charming and lovable, I certainly didn't see it as anything sinister. But this isn't charming and lovable, Polly, this is just downright devious.' He narrowed his eyes at me. I tried to meet them but had to look away. 'You're corrupt, Polly, you know that? You slip from one lie to the next without even knowing what the truth is half the time. You go through life in a haze of half-truths, white lies, and now downright deception. Well, I've had enough. I'm getting out. I've had it with your nasty, cruel little games. Go and inflict them on someone else. I'm sure Sam would be a willing partner – he's obviously cheating on his wife too.'

'You're wrong, Nick, you're so wrong,' I whispered. 'If you could just let me explain for one moment I could –'

'Polly, no!' he snapped fiercely. 'Enough! I've told you, I just don't want to *hear* any more! I'm quite sure you could fabricate your way out of this one like you've fabricated your way out of everything else, but to be honest just hearing your voice, just hearing you *attempt* it, makes me feel sick now!'

His face screwed up in disgust and I gazed at him in horror. I could feel the tears rushing to my eyes. I made him feel sick. I actually made him feel physically sick.

'Now what I propose,' said Nick, rearranging his features with difficulty and speaking calmly, 'is that you should find yourself somewhere else to live. There's no rush, and you don't have to start looking immediately, but start thinking about it, please. I'm quite happy to stay with Tim and Sarah for as long as it takes, but you must see that we can't live together any more. You're entitled to a decent-sized place, so don't go looking at hovels. Somehow, I'll find the money to run two houses.' He paused. 'If it means I have to sell this place,' he went on, slightly shakily, 'then so be it.'

I gasped. My God. He hated me so much that he was prepared to sell his beloved house just to get rid of me. There was no holding the tears now, they streamed down my cheeks, and splashed on to my bare knees.

'No histrionics please, Polly,' said Nick quietly, getting to his feet. 'I dare say you won't be short of places to stay. I'm quite sure your boyfriend will look after you.' He walked to the door and made as if to go out, but before he did he turned. Our eyes met. His hard, but nonetheless hurt and haunted, mine streaming with tears.

'Shame on you, Polly,' he whispered, 'shame on you.' And, with that, he walked out.

Chapter Sixteen

I don't remember much about the next couple of days. I lay in bed and lurched from one bout of crying to the next, feeling shocked and dazed. I couldn't actually believe this was happening to me. I stayed in my room and drew the curtains, staring into space, sleeping a bit, but eating nothing. I didn't answer the telephone and I didn't answer the doorbell. I just lay there, hugging my pillow, my face turned to the wall.

Sarah had a key so she still came to see me, but she didn't say much on these visits. There wasn't an awful lot to say. She just sat by the bed and patted my hand. Now and again she tried to get me to eat, but they were half-hearted attempts because even she knew it was useless. My marriage was over and I just wasn't up to eating. She'd heard the news from Tim and she knew it was final. Nick wasn't a man to make idle threats so there was no point in trying to make me think positive and I didn't ask her to.

We sat in silence most of the time, except when I cried, but after a while she began to make tentative suggestions about places I might go and look at with a view to living in. She'd seen a nice cottage for sale in Polzeath, apparently, but just mentioning moving out only provoked a fresh bout of tears, so eventually she gave up on that too. She simply arrived, made sympathetic noises, cleared up my room and left food parcels by the bed as if I were a little old lady and she were Meals on Wheels.

On one such day, about a week after Nick's dreadful pronouncement, she was creeping round the room, stooping to pick up tear-sodden tissues and cigarette ends, when she suddenly straightened.

'Oh, I almost forgot why I came today, I mean apart from trying to tidy up and get you to eat a bit. I've got some news!'

I turned my head away from the wall and looked at her with blank eyes. 'Is it Nick?' I whispered. 'Has he said something?'

'Oh, er, no, 'fraid not, Polly, it's not Nick. No, it's about the burglary.'

'Oh, that.' I turned away again. Gosh, all that seemed so long ago now, and so unimportant.

'Don't you want to know?'

'Go on then,' I sighed, 'tell me.'

'Well, apparently they've arrested someone!'

I turned back and raised myself up very slightly on my pillows. 'Really? Who?'

'Ah, you see!' said Sarah gleefully. 'You *are* interested.'

'Only because it took place in my – my husband's house,' I said shakily. 'Go on, Sarah, spill the beans, who is it?'

'Well, it's one of those film-crew people, you know, who came here. I think he actually came to supper that time. I'm just trying to think of his name.' She frowned.

I sat up a bit more. 'Really? God, who is it?'

Her face cleared. She snapped her fingers. 'I remember now! It's that poofy guy, Australian name . . .'

I sat bolt upright. 'Not Bruce!'

'That's it, Bruce!'

'Oh no.' I shook my head. 'No, you must have got it wrong, Sarah.'

'No, it's definitely Bruce the police have got, I heard Nick talking to the police last night and he was amazed too, he kept saying – Bruce? Surely not! So there you go, quite a piece of news, eh?' She grinned, clearly delighted she'd managed to get some sort of reaction from the corpse in the bed aside from more tears or a noncommittal whisper. They arrested him a couple of days ago apparently. I think they're holding him in London, but – oh, I know, Polly, why don't you ring Hetty? She knows all about it and I know she's dying to speak to you.'

'No, I couldn't,' I said, shaking my head and sinking back into my pillows again. 'Not Hetty.'

'Look,' said Sarah gently, sitting down beside me, 'please speak to her. You and I both know that Hetty is the last person to take sides. She loves you, Polly, she really does, and not just because you married her son, and she's desperate to talk to you, to comfort you. Please give her a ring; she's too afraid to ring here.'

I sighed. 'I'd like to speak to her too,' I said softly, 'but not about me and Nick. I can't discuss that.'

'Well, say that then, say you just want to talk about the burglary. Honestly, Polly, you've got to get out of bed at some point – you can't stay here forever.'

'I'm not staying in bed forever. I'm getting up the day after tomorrow. I'm going to London.'

'Oh?' She looked amazed. 'Why?'

'Sam's back, that's why. I'm going to give it one last shot.'

'What – get him to lie about that night? Polly, I honestly think that even if you *can* get him to talk to Nick, Nick's gone beyond the point of listening to anything. He's going to guess it's all a huge invention dreamed up between the two of you and –'

'But it's worth a try, isn't it?' I cut in desperately. 'I mean, anything's worth a try. I know it's hopeless but I've got to have one last attempt to save my marriage.'

'OK, OK,' she said hastily, seeing my eyes water. 'Have a go, see what he says, at least it will get you out of bed. But please, Polly, do talk to Hetty, you've got no quarrel with her, have you? And she's so worried about you.' She gazed at me beseechingly.

I sighed. 'OK,' I muttered, 'I'll ring her when you've gone.'

'Brilliant,' beamed Sarah, hastily making for the door before I could change my mind. 'Now don't forget, will you, do it now.'

The door shut behind her and I heard her running downstairs. Bruce. Blimey, who would have thought? And why? I wondered. I bit the skin round my thumbnail, then reached for the phone. I hesitated. Hetty was the kindest, wackiest and most sublime of mothers-in-law, but she was nonetheless my mother-in-law. How was I supposed to explain that the reason her son had walked out on me was that I'd been up to no good with another man?

Suddenly I grabbed the receiver decisively. No, I had to do it. I couldn't lie in bed and hide from people forever. I punched out her number. She answered straight away in her dark-brown throaty voice.

'Hello?'

'Hetty, it's me, Polly,' I said somewhat shakily.

'Polly! Darling, how lovely, I've been dying to ring but – well, you know, haven't liked to, what with one thing and another.'

'I know, and it's my fault. I should have rung you sooner, but I felt awkward. Listen, I'd love to come and see you, but would you mind awfully if we didn't talk about me and Nick?'

'Of course! I couldn't agree more, too boring for words, and anyway I think he's behaved abysmally. Fancy moving out lock, stock and barrel after only one tiny little indiscretion on your part, I mean, really! Incidentally, hate to be nosy, but this indiscretion, it wasn't really a whole rugby team, was it? Only Mrs Parker at the dairy swears it was but I told her it was far more likely to be one of those glamorous film people. I can't really see you as the rugger-bugger type and I don't honestly think you've got the stamina for a whole team of virile young –'

'Hetty,' I interrupted sternly.

'What? Ah, yes, right. Sorry, darling, I'll try to mind my own business, shall I?' She sighed wistfully. 'Awfully hard though.'

'I can imagine,' I sympathized. 'I'd be the same and, just for the record, no it was not a rugger team. But look – what I do want to talk to you about is the burglary.'

'My dear! Isn't it too exciting? Come over at once and I'll tell all.'

Half an hour later, having washed my hair and put on make-up for the first time in weeks, I borrowed Larry's car and drove over to Hetty's cottage.

Hetty had moved out of Trewarren just after Nick's

father had died. The house had been left to Nick on her death, but she'd asked him to take over immediately, saying it was much too big for her and that she found it too sad and empty now that her husband had gone. Much to Nick and Tim's horror she'd found herself a tumbledown cottage just outside Gweek and insisted on buying it. No surveyor in Cornwall would swing a plumb line at it, it was so rotten and derelict, but Hetty had been adamant and within a twinkling had bought it. In fact, it was a sensible decision. She'd needed to do something with her grief and had poured all her energy into lovingly restoring it until she'd transformed it into the house it was today – the showpiece of the village.

There it stood at the bottom of the hill, a welcoming sight as one approached the village. The new wing that she'd so cleverly added looked as if it had been there forever, the brand-new thatched roof was weathering nicely, sparkling leaded windows poked out from under the eaves and the whole thing was painted the palest shade of putty. It was surrounded by a beautiful cottage garden full of lupins, delphiniums, honeysuckle and climbing roses.

Inside, the original warren of tiny dark rooms had become one enormous, bright, airy ground floor, and upstairs had likewise said goodbye to its dividing walls to become a huge circular gallery with all the bedrooms and bathrooms running into each other. There were no doors to speak of and any staying guests had to leave their inhibitions firmly at home, but as Hetty said – who needs doors?

I peered through the bay window and rapped on the stable door – no bell, of course.

'Hetty, coo-ee!'

'Come in!' she yelled from within.

I stepped in and was simultaneously taken aback. All the rugs on the floor had gone and in their place were green floorboards. Actually they were clearly in the throes of being painted green, because in the far corner of the room I spotted Hetty, crouching low and eagerly covering what remained of the wood with copious amounts of emerald paint. She was dressed in a rather elegant Noël Coward silk paisley dressing gown, a pair of trainers and a New York Yankees baseball cap. I don't think I've ever seen Hetty without a hat; she probably wears one to bed. As usual, most of the ensemble was spattered with paint.

'Darling!' She turned around, beamed and waved her paintbrush in the air. 'Be with you in a minute, but I must just finish this bit of grass.'

She bent down again and carefully added what was obviously a crucial finishing touch.

'There!' She straightened up. 'Like it?' she asked proudly, cocking her head to one side and eyeing her handiwork.

'Er . . . well, it's certainly unusual, Hetty. All right to step on it or is it still wet?' I gingerly tiptoed in.

'Oh no, that bit's dry, I did it yesterday. Isn't it divine? I'm going to add some daisies later, and a few poppies, just scatter them liberally around. It'll be just like strolling through a summer meadow,' she said dreamily.

I looked down doubtfully. 'I suppose it will, but won't it get a bit chipped? With people walking on it?'

'Oh yes, possibly,' she said airily, wiping her hands on her dressing gown, 'but I'll probably be bored with it by then so I'll change it to something else – a beach, maybe, with shells and a spot of seaweed. Anyway, sit down, darling, and I'll get us both a large drinky – God, I could use it, I'm exhausted!'

She strode off to what passed as the kitchen but was actually a stove, a sink and a few cupboards in the far corner. A woman after my own heart, Hetty thought cooking was wildly overrated and didn't believe in setting aside a whole room for it. I meanwhile installed myself in a large, squashy blue sofa, by the fire which Hetty lit – for colour, darling – even in August. I glanced around and couldn't help noticing that the grass seemed to be growing up the side of most of the furniture too.

'So what's he like, this Bruce chap?' foghorned Hetty from what was effectively the other side of the house, but then she'd never been one to let a little thing like distance come between her and conversation.

'Terribly nice,' I yelled back, but my voice doesn't have quite the same resonance, as her answer confirmed.

'What? A complete bastard? I bet he is. I'm so disappointed I didn't meet him. Everyone in the village is asking me about him and I'm having to make it up, rather like you do, Polly.' She marched back armed with two hefty gins and handed one to me.

'Oh, thanks very much!' I said indignantly.

She flopped down at the other end of the sofa and opened her eyes wide.

'Oh, but I'm right behind you, darling. I mean, why tell the boring truth when you can get away with a good lie? But do tell, is he mean and conniving? Has he got a pinched, sly little face and slitty, piggy eyes like this' – she twisted her features accordingly – 'only that's how I'm pitching it to everyone at the moment.'

'Well don't,' I said, sipping my gin, 'because he's not like that at all. He's got a lovely face – angelic even, with big blue eyes. He's such a waste. When I first saw him I couldn't stop hitching my skirt up and sucking my cheeks in until I realized the only cheeks he was interested in were the ones in Nick's jeans.'

'Ah yes, I gathered he was a poof. Awfully amusing company on the whole, but they can be a bit sly, you know,' observed Hetty sagely, as if she were describing a completely different species.

'No, but he's not, that's just it. When you elbow your way through his rather whimsical ways you realize he's an absolute darling underneath, very kind and sincere, and actually if anything rather insecure. Nick and I both really liked him and Nick spent quite a bit of time with him.' I shook my head. 'I really can't believe he's done this. The police down here must have got it wrong. You know their alarming propensity to get everything wrapped round their necks.'

'Not this time.' Hetty pursed her lips. 'No, for once they've done their homework. They've got conclusive proof. You see, apparently he was stupid enough to give a piece of the porcelain to his mother for a birthday present – I mean, for heaven's sake!'

'What!'

'I promise you it's true. His mother's in a hospice some-where near here –'

'In Truro; she used to live in Penrith.'

'Precisely, well it turns out she was rather grand at one

time and had an amazing porcelain collection – not as amazing as ours, of course, but, still, quite good stuff – but when Bruce's father died she was clobbered by death duties and had to sell it all.'

'D'you know, I think Bruce mentioned that,' I said slowly, suddenly remembering.

'Exactly, which is why it all makes sense. You see, according to Mrs Parker –'

'The fount of all knowledge and inventor of rugby anecdotes,' I put in sourly.

'Well, quite, but no, this time it's gospel. According to her the poor old dear is absolutely riddled with cancer and your chap Bruce is beside himself with grief. She's clearly dying, so Bruce thinks – wouldn't it be wonderful to give her something really special on what will obviously be her last birthday, something beautiful that she can hold in her hands and get some sort of final pleasure from? So what does the poor silly boy go and do? He visits her in hospital and gives her a piece of the porcelain he's nicked from us – sorry, darling, from you – the week before.'

'Good grief, he must be mad!'

'Totally, but wait, there's more.' Hetty leaned in eagerly and took an enthusiastic drag from her cigarette, thrilled to have such a captive audience.

'Presumably he told her to keep very quiet about it, to hide it and keep it a secret, but of course as soon as he'd gone she couldn't resist showing it off around the ward. Well, eventually one of the nurses saw it and suspected it might be worth a bit. She'd also read about the burglary at our place in the local paper, so she put two and two together and tipped off the police. They arrived hotfoot, checked it out and Bruce was arrested that afternoon at his flat in London.' Hetty sat back looking frightfully smug. 'You see? Caught red-handed, in flagrante, fingers in the till and absolutely with his trousers down – what further proof do you need?' She raised her eyebrows and stubbed her cigarette out triumphantly in the geranium pot behind her.

I shook my head incredulously. 'God, I just can't believe it, it's ludicrous, how could he have been so stupid? And what on earth made him take the whole lot, Hetty? Surely if all he wanted was one piece to give to his mother before she died he could have slipped that away easily. We probably wouldn't have noticed for ages.'

'Ah, but you see it *wasn't* enough – he needed the rest of it too.'

'Why?'

'Because' – Hetty leaned forward eagerly to deliver her *pièce de résistance* – 'he was being blackmailed!' she hissed.

'What!'

'I promise you it's true. The police searched his flat and found all these blackmail notes – you know, letters cut out of newspapers and stuck on to Basildon Bond paper, that sort of unspeakable stuff.'

'God, how horrid! What did they say?'

'Oh, ghastly things about how perverted his sexual preferences were and how disgusting it was that he was gay, but the main thrust of it was – if you'll excuse the expression – that if he didn't cough up with some money soon, his mother would be told.'

'What, that he was gay? Surely she knew that?'

'Apparently not. According to Mrs Parker's niece who

lives in Penrith' – I rolled my eyes to heaven but she swept on – 'Bruce is an only child, and was a very late arrival. So just imagine, right? He's got elderly parents who absolutely dote on him – the child they thought they'd never have and all that – and then, *quelle horreur*! He discovers he's gay! Now how d'you think a sweet old couple living in the depths of conservative Cornwall are going to take that piece of news? Not quite on the chin, I can assure you. So, naturally, Bruce keeps quiet. His gay world is up in London so there's no reason why they should ever find out, and when he comes to visit them at weekends he plays the dutiful bachelor son, presumably dropping all his camp ways, and they're none the wiser.' Hetty took a quick swig of gin and licked her lips. 'Of course, the father's dead now so there's only the mother, and now *she's* dying too, so why shatter her illusions when she's only got weeks to live?'

I nodded. 'I couldn't agree more, but – God, how ghastly, you mean some vile bastard is threatening to spill the beans while she's on her deathbed?'

'Precisely. Isn't it unspeakable?'

'It's horrendous.'

We both sank into our gins. I stared at the fire. Poor Bruce, sitting in a prison cell somewhere with all this hanging over his head. Somehow it seemed to eclipse even my own monumental problems.

'But you see, what I want to know,' said Hetty, cradling her gin thoughtfully, 'is how he got into the cabinet in the first place without breaking the lock? How on earth did he know where the key was kept?'

'Oh, that's easy,' I said miserably. 'Nick and I practically showed him where it was. He was very interested in the porcelain so Nick let him go up and look at it on his own. In fact, if I remember rightly, Nick even took the key down from the dresser in front of him.' I shook my head. 'Gosh, we practically talked him into it. I'm surprised we didn't help him pack his swag bag.'

'Nonsense,' said Hetty briskly, 'you just trusted him, that's all. How were you to know he was up there pricing it all with his *Miller's Guide* with a view to selling it on?'

'He did have a *Miller's Guide* too,' I remembered gloomily. I took another gulp of gin. 'Poor Bruce. I almost wish he'd got away with it.'

'Polly!'

'Well, he obviously needed that china more than we did.'

She sighed. 'That's true, I suppose.'

We were silent for a while, staring at the fire as it crackled away in the grate. I shifted position, tucking my feet up under me.

'But how do the police think he got into the house? Have they worked that one out? There was no sign of what they so pompously call "a forced entry", was there?'

Hetty stubbed her cigarette out. 'Well, I think they're still working on that one but apparently they've got enough conclusive proof without it to lock him up for quite some time.'

'Where have they got him at the moment?'

'Oh, he's not behind bars yet, he's out on bail. He's got to wait for his court case to come up first.'

'Oh! So he's not in a cell or anything?'

'Oh no, I imagine he's at home, sweating it out. I think

he's free to come and go as he pleases as long as he doesn't leave the country or anything.'

I stared at her and put my gin down slowly on the table. 'I'll go and see him then,' I said suddenly.

'Polly!' Hetty looked alarmed. 'You can't do that, he's – well, he's a hardened criminal. I mean, he stole from you, after all.'

'Yes, but it's totally understandable, isn't it, Hetty? I mean, think about it, if you had some awful secret which you knew would break your mother's heart and some bastard was threatening to break it to her on her deathbed, you'd move heaven and earth to do something about it, wouldn't you? You might even steal, I know I would. God, I think it's outrageous!'

I quickly collected my cigarettes and lighter from the table and popped them in the pocket of my denim shirt.

'No, I must go and see him, tell him I understand – especially since it was me he stole from. At least if he knows I'm on his side and I forgive him it might make him feel a little bit better.' I got up to go.

Hetty looked up at me anxiously. 'Polly, I'm really not sure you should. I'm sure burglar and burgled don't usually fraternize before the court case.'

'Maybe not usually, but this is an unusual case. In fact – I think I'll go up today. I was going to go the day after tomorrow anyway to see Sa–' Hetty's eyes glinted with excitement, she held her breath. 'Er – well, to see someone else,' I finished.

Hetty looked disappointed. She stood up and pulled her dressing gown around her. 'Ah. Oh well, if you were going anyway – but do be careful, my dear, he might be feeling awfully bitter and resentful – you don't want him to take it out on you.'

'Don't worry, I can take care of myself. I'll ring him up first and if he sounds murderously inclined I won't go.'

We walked to the door. Hetty took my arm.

'D'you know, Hetty,' I said with a smile, 'I feel a bit better now. It's probably an awful thing to say but other people's problems can sort of put yours into perspective, can't they? For the first time in over two weeks I've got something positive to do.' I pecked her on the cheek. 'Thanks for the drink. I'm glad I came.'

'You'll let me know what happens, won't you?' she said anxiously, opening the stable door for me. 'And don't go to his flat or anything; meet him in a bar, or a restaurant – somewhere public.'

'Don't worry, I'll be fine.' I smiled and shut the bottom half of the stable door after me. Hetty leaned over it.

'Oh, and good luck with your other little assignation too,' she said slyly. 'Who did you say you were meeting in London?'

I grinned. 'I didn't. Bye, Hetty.' I waved cheerily and ran off down the garden path.

Hetty stood and watched as I got into the car. I drove off and she waved till I was out of sight. As I roared back to Trewarren I delved around in the glove compartment and found an ancient bag of Opal Fruits. I sucked one thoughtfully. It was true. Strangely enough, I did feel a bit better now that I had something other than myself to focus on and, anyway, I shifted uncomfortably in my seat, being in bed for so long had practically given me bed sores.

When I got home I ran upstairs to the bedroom to pack a bag, but as I pulled a case off the top of the wardrobe, for some reason I suddenly had to drop it and sit down very quickly on the floor. God. Yuck. I put my head between my knees. I felt most peculiar, rather woozy and sort of – sick. I sat there for a minute or two, then, when I deemed it safe, got up and had a glass of water. I steadied myself on the basin. Clearly my body wasn't used to all this frenzied activity, having spent such a long time horizontal on a mattress.

After a moment I felt better so I flung open the case and ran around the room, throwing things in – as usual I packed for about a month, much preferring to travel heavy in case of a sartorial emergency. Then I sat on it, snapped it shut and ran downstairs to ring Pippa. She wasn't at her desk – out at a meeting or something important – so I left a message to say I was coming to stay. Then I rang Sarah and told her I was going away for a few days.

'What shall I tell Nick?' she asked doubtfully.

'What's it got to do with him?' I snapped. 'I mean, he's left me, hasn't he? I can come and go as I please now, can't I?' As I said it I remembered Hetty had said exactly the same about Bruce. So I was out on bail too, was I? Conditional discharge pending the court case. The divorce court case. I saw red.

'Tell him to go to hell!' I stormed.

Sarah gasped. 'Oh, Polly, you don't mean that!'

I sat down on the hall chair and bit my lip miserably. 'No, you're right. I don't.' My eyes filled with tears and I fiddled with my wedding ring. I sighed. 'OK,' I said after a while, 'tell him I've gone to see Bruce, that I've taken the old Renault, and tell him . . . tell him I love him very much.'

There was a pause. 'He's just come in actually, Polly, you could tell him yourself if you like,' she said quietly.

I hesitated. 'No. No, he won't want to speak to me. You do it for me, Sarah. Bye.'

I put the receiver down, brushed away a rogue tear that had somehow escaped down my cheek and pulled myself together. Right. No time for that sort of nonsense now. I had things to do, places to go, people to – oh, shut up, Polly, just get a move on. I grabbed my car keys from the hall table, picked up my case and ran down to the farm to get the car.

As I beetled down the muddy track to the yard I smiled fondly. For there, mouldering away quietly under a tree, was Rusty, my dear old green Renault. He heralded from my single, girl-about-town days and we'd had some good times together. He was retired now, of course, and his principal role in life these days was to transport chickens and ducks to market. I patted his old bonnet and jumped in. I instantly jumped out again. The nauseating pong of chicken shit was enough to make anyone gag, but with the BMW in London needs must. I brushed half a ton of straw and muck off the driver's seat, then I held my breath, got in, turned the poor old engine over and rattled off to London.

Even in his heyday Rusty had never been much of a speed merchant, but sitting in a wet field with only the occasional trip to market had really taken the edge off him. We vibrated our way precariously up the M4 with me urging him on, cajoling just a few more miles an hour out of him whilst he complained noisily.

When I eventually arrived at Pippa's house it was way after midnight and I was exhausted. I parked the car without bothering to lock it, tottered gratefully up the path, delighted I'd made it in one piece, and rang the bell.

Pippa was yawning away in her dressing gown when she opened the door. She looked very bleary-eyed.

'I thought you were never coming,' she said. 'I was just about to leave a note on the door saying "The key's under the flowerpot" but then I thought that was probably a bit silly.'

'Just a bit, unless you want the whole of Kensington hopping into bed with you.'

'I wouldn't mind,' she said gloomily as I followed her into the sitting room. 'It would certainly make a change. No one's hopped into my bed for about two weeks now.' She flopped down dejectedly on a sofa.

'What, no Josh?' I threw off my jacket and curled up next to her.

'No, he's making himself very scarce these days – family problems, so he says.'

She grimaced and poured out a couple of glasses of wine from a half-empty bottle. I noticed there was already an empty Frascati bottle nestling on the sofa beside her, which would explain the bloodshot eyes. She handed me a glass.

'Here, help me finish this. Actually, I think his wife suspects and now he's showing his true colours and running home with his tail between his legs every night. Bastard.' She knocked back her drink in a couple of gulps and poured herself another one.

I looked at her admiringly. 'Atta-girl, Pippa, looks like you've finally seen the light.'

She sighed. 'Not really, I know he's a pig all right but I'm still in love with him, so it doesn't really help much, does it?' She gave me a sad little smile. 'And anyway,' she went on defensively, 'he does actually have some family problems, it's not a complete lie, his sister isn't well at all.'

I pulled a long face. 'Bit weak, isn't it?'

'Well, no, she's really ill actually, and they're twins so he's very close to her. In fact,' she looked around furtively as if someone might be listening, 'it's a deadly secret, but apparently she might have AIDS.'

'AIDS! Blimey, do be careful, Pippa!'

'What?' She looked blank for a second then rolled her eyes to heaven. 'Oh, for goodness' sake, you're not one of those people who still thinks you can get it from loo seats, are you?'

'Er, no, don't be silly, of course not, but – well, all the same.' I hastily took a slug of wine. 'How did she get it?'

Pippa shrugged. 'Who knows? Someone at work said it was a blood transfusion – it's not the sort of thing you ask, is it, especially since I'm not really supposed to know. Anyway, enough about me, what about poor old Bruce? Have you heard?'

'Yes, Hetty told me – that's why I've come up. Isn't it awful?'

Pippa shook her head. 'Dreadful.'

'How is he?'

'Well, when I spoke to him yesterday he sounded practically hysterical. I could hardly make out what he was saying he was crying so much.'

'Crying?'

She nodded. 'I hate it when men cry, don't you?'

I thought of Nick with tears in his eyes and gulped. 'Yes, but then Bruce isn't really – you know, macho, is he?'

'No, but he's still a man.' She sighed. 'Anyway, at least he's not in a ghastly cell or anything. Sam and Josh put up the bail for him, ten grand they had to find.'

'Really? That much? Gosh, that was nice of them.'

'Well, everyone's terribly fond of Bruce, you know. We rang Sam in Egypt and he's coming back a day early to see him. He instructed the bank to make the money available and apparently he knows a brilliant barrister who's going to act for him.'

'Oh well, that's something. Bruce is going to need all the help he can get.' I sipped my wine thoughtfully. 'So Sam's coming back tomorrow, is he?' I sat up straight and compressed my lips. 'Right. I'll go and see him.'

Pippa gave me a strange look. 'Polly, you're not still . . .'

'What?'

'Well, you're not still keen on him or anything, are you?'

'Aarrrhh!' I shrieked and nearly hurled my wine glass across the room. Instead I threw a cushion. 'No, I'm not bloody keen on him! I'm keen on my husband and I'm keen on saving my marriage, actually! I told you, I've got to go and see him to get him to talk to Nick and – oooohh!' Suddenly I doubled up and clutched my tummy.

Pippa jumped up in alarm. 'God, I'm sorry, I didn't mean to upset you, honestly – heavens, Polly, what's wrong?'

I stuck my head between my knees. 'I don't know,' I mumbled from somewhere near my ankles. 'I just feel a bit odd. It's been happening quite a bit lately.'

'What sort of odd?' Pippa knelt down beside me.

'Sort of . . . faint. And sick. Very sick, actually — ooohh . . .' I moaned again and swooned sideways.

Pippa straightened up beside me and pulled her dressing gown around her. She narrowed her eyes. 'Faint and sick, eh? Really. And how long have you been feeling like this?'

'Oh, I don't know, just a couple of days really. In the mornings mostly, when I get up.'

There was a silence. I eyeballed the carpet for a moment, then slowly brought my head up from between my knees. I looked at her.

'Oh, Pippa, you don't think . . .'

'When's your period due, are you late?'

'Oh God, I don't know!'

'Well think, should it be about now?'

'Well, I'm not sure, I'd have to check — oh God, I feel really sick now — quick, get me a calendar!' I clutched my mouth.

Pippa looked doubtful. 'Polly, if you're going to be sick I really don't think a colander's quite the thing to catch the —'

'No, not a colander, you berk, a calendar — get me a calendar so I can check my dates!'

Pippa got up hastily and ran to the kitchen. A second later she was back with a diary. She rammed it under my nose — 'Here.'

I flicked frantically through the pages, counting back and then counting forward again. I threw it on the floor and groaned.

'Oh my God!' I held my head.

'What?'

'I'm ten days late!'

'Ten days! Really? But that's brilliant, Polly! You must be pregnant!' She bent down and hugged me enthusiastically. 'Gosh, how fantastic, oh I'm so pleased! Imagine, you're going to have a baby!'

I hid my face in my hands and groaned again.

She frowned. 'What's the matter? Aren't you pleased? I thought it's what you wanted, you've been banging on about it for ages.'

'Yes, I do, I *do* want it, I'd love to have a baby.' I looked up at her desperately. 'But, Pippa, don't you see? If I'm pregnant, well then – whose is it?'

She stared at me for a moment, aghast. 'Oh God . . . you mean it could be . . .'

'Exactly!'

'Oh!'

Chapter Seventeen

Pippa looked aghast. 'You mean . . .'

'It might not be Nick's,' I whispered, 'it might be Sam's.'

'Oh!'

She stared at me for a moment, then grabbed my hand urgently. 'Think back, Polly, think back about four weeks ago, could it be Nick's? Did you two see any action around that time?'

I frowned, desperately trying to remember. It would have been just before I came up to London. We weren't getting on desperately well, but even so . . . I shrugged.

'I'm not sure, yes, quite possibly, but I can't really remember – oh, please let it be his!' I wailed, wringing my hands.

'And when did you go to bed with Sam?' urged Pippa. 'Think, Polly, that would have been about . . . ?'

I gulped and nodded. 'Just over three weeks ago.' I put my head in my hands.

Pippa put her arms round me and gave me a squeeze. 'Now don't you worry, that doesn't necessarily mean it's his – it could easily be Nick's. We'll sort this out, you'll see. Everything will be fine.' She was doing her best to sound convincing but failing miserably.

I stared at the carpet in a daze. Suddenly I looked up at her. 'I don't want to get rid of it,' I said quickly. 'I've wanted this baby for too long. I'm not having an abortion!'

'Of course you won't have to get rid of it,' she said staunchly. Then she hesitated. 'But suppose – I mean, what if you knew for sure that it was Sam's, would you then?'

'Oh God, I don't know, I just don't know! I mean, what if it grew up to look just like Sam? Totally different from Nick or me – wouldn't that be awful? Nick would be sure to guess and he'd hate the child and hate me, although of course he hates me anyway and it's not as if he's coming back, but if he did – oh Christ, what a mess!' I burst into noisy tears at the thought of this ghastly scenario.

'Well, that's why I was wondering if it wouldn't be better to –'

'No! No, I can't get rid of it!' I wailed. 'I can't possibly – what if it is Nick's after all? What if I'm carrying his baby and I pull the plug on it, that would be totally horrendous too!' I sniffed hard and wiped my nose on my sleeve. 'Oh God, I need a hanky,' I muttered.

Pippa jumped up and came back a second later brandishing a loo roll. I pulled off about nine sheets, wrapped them round my hand and blew my nose noisily.

'You know, Pippa,' I muttered, stuffing the paper up my sleeve, 'this has got to be about the worst thing that's ever happened to me and, let's face it, some pretty dire things have happened over the years.' I rummaged in my bag for a cigarette and fumbled with the packet but my fingers were shaking too much for me to get one out.

'Light one for me would you, Pipps, and pour me another drink while you're at it.'

Pippa looked doubtful. 'Er . . . well, you shouldn't really, you know.'

'Shouldn't what?'

'Do either. Drink or smoke. I mean, in your condition.'

I looked at her, appalled. 'Really? Oh no, no of course not, you're right, how frightful!' This really was a shaker, almost as bad as being pregnant. I struggled to come to terms with it. 'How will I ever survive? They're my only pleasures in life at the moment.'

'Well, have one quick fag to steady your nerves, but make that the last one you have.'

'Right.'

She lit one for me but I only took a couple of drags before I was overcome with guilt.

'Poor little thing,' I muttered, stubbing it out, 'it's going to have enough problems without me adding to them before it's even born.'

I sighed gloomily as Pippa poured the last of the Frascati into her glass.

'Of course,' she said, sipping it thoughtfully, 'you are only ten days late, maybe you're not pregnant at all.'

'No such luck,' I said darkly. 'I'm always bang on time. I'm like bloody Big Ben, never a second late.'

'Even so, just in case – hang on a minute.' Pippa stubbed her cigarette out, jumped up and ran out of the room. I heard her thumping away up the stairs and running along the corridor to her room. I sank back in the sofa and rested my throbbing head, which felt as if it were going to explode. I closed my eyes. What a nightmare . . . what a complete and utter nightmare. Perhaps if I shut my eyes for long enough I'd fall asleep and the whole ghastly problem would go away . . .

A second later I heard her thumping downstairs again.

I opened my eyes to see her standing over me waving a magic wand, a huge grin on her face.

'Look what I've found!'

'Don't tell me,' I said bitterly, 'you've joined the Magic Circle and now you're going to cast a few spells and make a baby disappear.'

'Don't be silly. It's a pregnancy test, you just pee on it and if you're pregnant it goes bright blue in about a nano-second.'

'So what are you doing with it?'

'Oh, I had a scare a few weeks ago. It was negative, thank God. I'm telling you, Polly, it would be my worst nightmare, a baby – imagine!' She rolled her eyes in horror then saw my face darken. 'Oh! Oh, sorry, I didn't mean it like that, of course a baby would be lovely at, um, at the right time, it's just that – well, you know, Josh being married and everything . . .' She trailed off.

'So is Sam,' I said grimly, grabbing the wand from her and stalking down the passage to the loo, 'and so am I, and so is Nick and – oh God, this is awful!'

I slammed the door and looked doubtfully at the stick in my hand. I opened the door again.

'Pippa?'

'What?'

'Is this the same stick you used?'

'Oh, don't be an idiot, you get two sticks in the box. I haven't given you a part-worn pregnancy test!'

'Oh. Right.'

I shut the door and got on with it. Sure enough it went bright blue before I'd even had a chance to pull my knickers up. I dragged my feet back to the sitting room.

'They don't give you much time to get used to the idea, do they?' I said gloomily. 'I thought I'd at least have time to plan the nursery, think of a colour scheme, decide on a theme for the borders – you know, ducks or teddies, pink or blue, that kind of thing.' I stuck the wand under her nose. 'Positive?'

'Positive, couldn't be bluer. You're up the duff, Polly, no doubt about that!' she confirmed cheerfully.

I sank into a chair and groaned. 'No wonder I feel so lousy. Honestly, this pregnancy lark isn't all it's cracked up to be at all, talk about propaganda. I'm supposed to be blooming, aren't I? Well, all I feel is blooming sick and blooming tired. Unbelievably tired actually, lie-down-on-the-pavement tired – and just look at my boobs! I wondered why I'd turned into Samantha Fox overnight. I tell you my heart goes out to her now – lugging these pendulous melons around is no joke.'

Pippa peered at me. 'You don't look any bigger than normal.'

'Oh, Pippa, I'm huge! Absolutely huge! I'm practically busting my bra here, can't you see? I'll have to go to Peter Jones tomorrow and get a new one.'

'I should wait a bit,' said Pippa knowingly. 'They're going to get an awful lot bigger than that, you know.'

'Are they?' I asked, glancing down in horror.

'Oh yes.' She nodded sagely. 'It's one of the occupational hazards. By the time you're about nine months you'll be carting them around in a hammock; you won't be able to see your feet for bosoms.'

'Oh, thanks very much,' I snapped. 'Since when did you become such an authority? And, incidentally, d'you think you could put your cigarette out? It's making me feel a bit queasy.' It wasn't, but it was making me feel awfully envious.

'Gosh, sorry,' she said, quickly stubbing it out. She looked at me in concern. 'Hey, are you sure you're all right? Not going to be sick, are you? D'you want to put your feet up or anything?'

'Oh, don't be so rid—' I stopped abruptly. 'Well . . . yes actually, now you come to mention it, perhaps I am feeling a little delicate – yes, if you could just pull that stool up for my feet . . . thanks – oh, and that cushion, for behind my head . . . bit to the left . . . down a bit . . . perfect, thanks.' I leaned back in the chair, hands resting delicately on my tummy, looking pained and wan.

Pippa hovered over me anxiously. 'Cup of tea? I think I've got rosehip somewhere, isn't that what pregnant women drink? I'd have to hunt around a bit but I don't mind.'

'Would you? You are an angel, Pippa, thanks so much . . .' I muttered weakly. Pippa trotted off dutifully.

'Oh – and a piece of toast and honey would be lovely if you could manage it,' I called feebly after her, 'and three sugars in my tea, please, got to keep my strength up.'

I settled back into my cushions. This at least was some compensation for my ghastly predicament. I'd no idea pregnant women got such perks. I wondered if I could get a tea-and-toast-bearing punka wallah on the National Health. I shut my eyes and tried to think. What on earth was I going to do about all this? I simply had to have a plan. By the time Pippa came back laden with tea and toast a few minutes later, I had at least formed what you might call a quarter-baked one. I sat up.

'I'm going to go and see Sam tomorrow,' I said decisively. 'First thing.'

Pippa put down the tray and sighed. 'Is there really any point? I mean, I know you've set your heart on him phoning Nick and telling him nothing happened that night, but d'you really think he's going to want to get involved?'

'Well sure, he may not *want* to get involved, but . . .' I hesitated.

Pippa stiffened. 'Polly! You're not going to tell him you're pregnant, are you?'

I shifted uncomfortably. 'Er, it had occurred to me. Don't you think I should?' I hazarded guiltily.

'No. I don't,' she said firmly. 'It would certainly get him on the phone double-quick denying all responsibility, but –'

'Exactly!' I interrupted, eyes shining. 'My thoughts exactly!'

'*But*,' she carried on sternly, 'what if it *is* his? What if it's his baby after all?' She shook her head firmly. 'No, Polly, you can't do that. You'd just be fooling yourself, fooling him, fooling everybody, in fact. No, you've got to wait until you know for sure who the father of this child is. Don't breathe a word of this to Sam *or* Nick, until you know.' She leaned forward and took a bite out of my toast.

'But how am I ever going to find out?' I wailed, dropping my toast and feeling sick with fear now. 'It's all very well for you to say that, but how am I ever going to know?'

She helped herself to my abandoned toast and chewed away, looking rather blank for once. We gazed at each other. We were a bit out of our depth here. None of our friends were even remotely pregnant yet. I was very much a trailblazer.

'Can they tell before it's born, d'you think?' I said hopefully. 'Do blood tests or something? Or what about this new DNA thing, isn't that supposed to sort out who you are?'

'I think that's more to do with fingerprints,' said Pippa doubtfully, 'and I'm not sure a three-week-old foetus even has fingers, let alone prints, and, anyway, how would you get to them?'

'Well, all right,' I conceded, 'perhaps not DNA, but blood tests then, or urine samples or – yes I know – one of those scan things.'

Pippa looked at me incredulously. 'Those "scan things" just show you an ultrasound picture of the baby. You don't think you're going to spot a family resemblance, do you?'

'Well, Nick's got an awfully big nose – that's bound to show up.'

'Oh, don't be ridiculous! He grew that much later! He probably didn't have it as a baby, let alone as a foetus.'

'Well, you think of something then!' I cried desperately, on the verge of hysteria now.

Pippa licked some honey off her fingers thoughtfully. 'Trouble is . . .' she said slowly, 'I may be way off beam here, but I have an awful feeling they can't really tell until it's actually born.'

'No! Don't say that – that can't be true! Think of all the things they can do with unborn babies these days – heart surgery in the womb with laser beams, kidney transplants – all that kind of thing. There was a programme about it the other night. I mean, if they can do that then surely they can discover a tiny little thing like who the father is, surely that's not too much to –'

'Oh!' Pippa suddenly grabbed my hand. She went a bit bug-eyed and trance-like. 'Hang on!'

'What? What is it?' I pounced eagerly.

'I've got a brilliant idea! Of course, I don't know why I didn't think of it before.'

'What?'

'Go and see Mr Taylor!'

'Who's Mr Taylor?'

'He's the most divine gynae in the whole world. I went to see him ages ago when I had a dodgy smear test – he's fabulous, Polly – you'll adore him. He looks just like Peter Bowles!' Her eyes glazed over with lust.

I groaned. 'Pippa, I'm not really in the market for falling for Peter Bowles lookalikes, I just want to know who the father of my unborn child is.'

'Well, if anyone can tell you, he can. He's written loads of books about infertility and that sort of thing; he's a real authority –'

'Pippa, I'm not infertile – I'm sodding pregnant!'

'I know, but same field, honestly, Poll. I promise you he's brilliant. He'll probably be able to tell just by glancing at you. I'm sure if you can work out the exact dates you had sex with both Nick and Sam he'll be able to tell whose it is just from the size of the foetus.'

I went cold. 'You mean . . . I'll have to tell him? About – you know – there being two men and everything?'

'Well, how else are you going to find out?'

I cringed. 'He'll think I'm a dreadful tart.'

'Probably, but you'll never see him again so what does it matter?' She lit a cigarette and blew the smoke out airily. God, it was all right for her.

'Where is he then?' I asked suspiciously. 'Croydon or somewhere?'

I had visions of a ghastly back-street abortionist, right at the top of some dirty lino-covered stairs, probably with one of those beaded curtains for a door. Inside a grotty little room with peeling wallpaper would be a low rickety bed covered in a blood-red blanket, and all around the room, hanging from the walls, would be a glistening array of lethal-looking tools of the trade. I shuddered.

'Don't be silly. He's in Harley Street, he's absolutely kosher. I'll make an appointment for you tomorrow.'

I sighed. 'OK. I suppose I ought to go anyway to find out when it's due and what I ought to be doing. I expect he'll say I have to stay in bed and eat most of the time, won't he? I probably should be eating now – you know, for two and all that. Got any biscuits, Pippa?'

'I haven't actually, and anyway,' she said doubtfully, 'I'm not sure that's right. I have a feeling they like you to exercise these days rather than lie around. My cousin went up Scafell Pike when she was six months pregnant.'

'Really?' I sat up in alarm. 'Christ, I'm not doing that!'

'You don't *have* to, you idiot, it's not compulsory, she just wanted to.'

'Oh, right.'

'Anyway,' she said briskly, getting to her feet and pulling her dressing gown around her, 'go along and see Taylor. He'll tell you all you need to know. Meanwhile, I'm going to bed, and so should you, it's nearly two o'clock, you know.'

'Is it? Gosh.' I looked at my watch. 'So it is.' I got up wearily. 'Thanks, Pippa. I don't know what I'd do without you.'

She grinned and put her arm round my shoulders. 'Don't mention it, all part of the service at this exclusive little hotel.'

We went slowly upstairs.

'You know, Pippa, this should have been one of the happiest days of my life. Of our lives,' I added quietly. 'Nick and I have been waiting for this for so long. Imagine how thrilled he'd have been if – well, if everything had been different.'

She gave me a hug at the top of the stairs as we got to the spare room. 'I know, but try not to think about that, just get some sleep. Everything's going to be fine, really it is.'

I nodded gloomily, wishing I could share her optimism. I crawled under the duvet and shut my eyes, and as usual drifted off to sleep almost immediately, but unfortunately it wasn't the deep, peaceful, dreamless sleep I'd hoped for. In fact it was a complete nightmare.

I dreamed I was in the kitchen at Trewarren – at least, I think it was me, I was so huge with pregnancy I hardly recognized myself – but yes, there I was, an immense, bloated monster of a woman, staggering and reeling around the kitchen, one hand lodged in the small of my back, the other clutching on to the furniture. We were talking *big* with child. As I manoeuvred my enormous bulk around I suddenly stopped short, gasped, clutched my huge stomach and sank with a piercing shriek into a ginormous heap of blubber on the kitchen floor.

'Help!' I bleated. 'Somebody help! I'm having contractions!'

Sure enough a ghastly rumbling sound like Mount Vesuvius about to erupt heralded a shuddering and shaking from my enormously swollen belly. It began to vibrate violently like a washing machine on final spin.

'H-e-l-p!' I shrieked feebly, holding on to the table leg as I vibrated around the kitchen floor. 'Help me, I'm having a baby! Somebody *help*!'

Just then I heard the back door fly open behind me – thank God! Someone was here! I peered over my shoulder, but – oh no, it was Mrs Bradshaw! She stood over me, arms folded, eyes glinting dangerously, as I bounced around painfully on the quarry-tiled floor.

'What seems to be the trouble, Mrs Penhalligan? Tummy ache? Something you've eaten, perhaps?'

'N-no!' I gasped, throbbing away like a pneumatic drill now and hanging on to both table legs for fear of shuddering right out of the back door. 'I'm h-having a b-baby!'

'Oh, is that all?' she said with a sardonic little smile. 'Let's have a look then.'

She knelt down and rolled up her sleeves in a business-like manner. A horrifically loud rumble greeted her as the tummy mountain went into vibration overdrive. It looked like a huge possessed blancmange that any minute now would explode and decorate the walls in a riot of glorious technicolour.

'Help! Get it out!' I shrieked.

'Now hold still, Mrs Penhalligan,' she said, hoicking up

the marquee that passed as my skirt. 'Let's see what we've got in here.'

I shut my eyes tight.

'Brace yourself!' she cried cheerfully as, like a magician producing a rabbit from a hat, she reached up and pulled something out.

'Aaargh!' I shrieked.

'Oh look,' she observed, dangling it under my nose by its feet, 'it's a little boy!'

I stared. It was indeed a little boy, but little only as compared to a grown man. This boy was about six years old, dressed from head to toe in prep-school uniform complete with cap and satchel, and the living image of Sam Weston.

'Aaagh!'

'Now now,' admonished Mrs Bradshaw, 'he's just a mite overdue, that's all. Let's have a bit of stiff upper lip, shall we. You're not the first woman in the world to have a baby, you know – oops, hold still, I think there's another one in here!'

Sure enough, within a twinkling, she'd produced another identical six-year-old.

'Twins!' she announced joyfully, before thrusting her hand up again. 'Triplets!' She pulled out another. 'Quads!' And then another, and another, until eventually the whole kitchen was knee deep in grinning mini Sam Weston lookalikes.

'No!' I screamed. 'No more! No more!'

'Oh yes,' Mrs Bradshaw assured me, eyes gleaming sadistically, 'plenty more where they came from.'

'No! Please, no more!' I shouted as my shoulders began to vibrate too. I felt as if my head was going to pop off.

I opened my eyes and found myself staring at Pippa who had me by the shoulders and was shaking me awake.

'Polly! Polly, wake up!'

I was sitting up in bed, screaming like a banshee.

'What's wrong, what is it?' she cried.

'Oh God,' I groaned, flopping down on to my pillows, 'what a nightmare! I've just given birth to twenty-four Sam Westons!'

'Good Lord, you never do things by halves, do you, Polly? Never mind, you just lie down and take it easy, I'll go and get you a cup of tea.'

She disappeared and I pushed the covers off. I was boiling hot but sopping wet. A few minutes later she returned with the tea.

'Bad dream then?' she said cheerfully.

'You could say that,' I muttered, hoovering up the tea gratefully. My mouth was totally devoid of saliva and I felt as if someone had squirted my eyeballs with vinegar.

'You're dressed,' I observed, eyeing her smart suit and make-up incredulously.

'Well, it is nine o'clock,' she said, looking at her watch, 'and, actually, I really must go. I've got a meeting this morning and I'm going to be late. How d'you feel?'

'Oh, awful,' I groaned, 'absolutely awful. Wrung out, knackered, exhausted.'

Pippa looked puzzled. 'But you've only just woken up, how can you be tired?'

'Pippa, you'd be tired if you'd just given birth twenty-four times, and of course I am pregnant, remember, so naturally I feel sick too.' I lay back on the pillow looking weak and delicate.

She frowned. 'Polly, you don't think you're getting this pregnancy lark a bit out of proportion, do you? I mean, you're effectively only a few weeks pregnant, you don't think your symptoms might be, well – psychosomatic? I seem to remember my cousin didn't feel sick until she was at least –'

'Oh, your bloody cousin!' I stormed, sitting up abruptly. 'I expect she was scampering up Everest, baking flapjacks and running a multi-million-pound conglomerate at the same time as giving birth, well, bully for her, but we're not all superwomen, you know – in fact, if you don't mind I'd rather not hear any more about your sodding cousin; she's making me feel worse by the minute.' I flopped back down on the bed, feeling extremely sorry for myself.

Pippa didn't even bother to answer. She smoothed her skirt down, then adjusted her hair in the mirror. 'Right, well, I've got to go to work now, but I'll ring you from the office and arrange for you to see Taylor, OK?'

'And Sam,' I whispered, gazing up at her beseechingly, 'I've got to see Sam.'

'OK, and Sam. I'll try to put lunch with you in his diary. Oh, and don't forget why you came up in the first place, will you?'

'Why?'

'To see Bruce, of course.'

'Oh help,' I groaned, 'I'd forgotten about him.'

'Well, do try to see him. It would really help him a lot.'

I raised my eyebrows at her. 'Oh, it would, would it?' I dragged myself wearily out of my pit. 'Oh well, I'm glad about that. I'm glad I've got time in my fun-packed life to lend a helping hand where it's needed. It's really not important that my own little world is falling to pieces around me, no no, there are plenty of other people with far more screwed-up lives – poor deserving souls – and help them I must. Dib dib dib, dob dob dob, lend a hand, Mother bleeding Teresa, that's me.'

I staggered to the bathroom and brushed my teeth with a vengeance, spitting the toothpaste out viciously. Pippa was already thumping away downstairs, sensibly ignoring my tirade.

'Have fun!' she yelled cheerfully, slamming the door behind her. I scowled into the mirror.

An hour or so later the telephone rang. I dragged myself out of a hot bath, grabbed a towel and ran dripping down the stairs to answer it. It was Pippa with my itinerary for the day.

'Right, got a pen?' she barked. God, she was efficient.

'Er, yes.' I scrabbled around in my bag on the hall chair and found my eyeliner.

'Good, now listen. Mr Taylor will see you at three o'clock, seventy-two Harley Street, got that?'

'Today? Already?' I scribbled away in black kohl. 'Not exactly in demand then, is he? Hasn't exactly got all the pregnant women in London beating a path to his door.'

'He had a cancellation,' said Pippa patiently. 'It's either today or in three weeks' time, take it or leave it.'

'OK, OK,' I mumbled. I was dimly aware I was behaving badly. 'Thanks, Pipps.'

'And Sam's in a meeting at the moment, but he says he'll meet you for lunch. One o'clock, Daphne's, Draycott Avenue, OK?'

'Really? He agreed? Did you tell him why?'

'Oh yes, I said you were carrying his unborn child and

you had some paternity papers you'd like him to sign – of course I bloody didn't, what do you take me for?'

'All right, all right – and Bruce?'

'Forty-two Sugden Street, W6.' She reeled off a telephone number. 'Got that?'

'Yep.'

'Got to fly now, see you tonight. Busy day, eh?'

'Just a bit,' I said grimly. 'Thanks, though.'

I put the receiver down. Right. I looked at the names and places on the piece of paper in front of me and sighed. I really didn't feel like coping with any of it this morning. I made a cup of coffee, then threw it down the sink in case caffeine was bad for the bump, and made some disgusting rosehip tea instead. I took a sip, gagged, threw that down the sink too, then looked at the piece of paper again. Bruce had to be dealt with first. I picked up the phone and dialled his number.

It rang for ages and ages and I began to feel heady with relief. He wasn't in, he wasn't there, but at least I'd tried. I was just about to put it down when he answered. Damn.

'Yes? Who is it?' he bleated in a tearful whisper. I softened immediately. He was in a bad way.

'Bruce? It's Polly, Polly Penhalligan.'

'Polly!' He gave a strangled sob and then burst into tears. 'Oh, Polly, please don't hate me, it's all a terrible mistake, please don't hate me!'

'I don't hate you, Bruce,' I said gently. 'Calm down. I just wondered if I could come and see you, to see how you are. Would that be all right? Would you like that?'

There was a pause. 'Really? You want to see me? Yes, I'd like that, I would.'

'D'you want to meet me somewhere? For a coffee or something?'

'Um, I'd rather not, Polly, only I don't like to go out much at the moment. I feel safer here, you see. Could you possibly come to the flat?'

'Sure, no problem,' I said, forgetting what I'd promised Hetty. 'I'll be over in about an hour then, shall I?'

'OK. Oh – but Polly, n-no bully boys or anything like that? Just you?' He was frightened, really frightened. I remembered the ghastly threatening letters.

'Of course not, Bruce, just me. Get the coffee on, or even something stronger. I have a feeling we're both going to need it.'

Chapter Eighteen

It took me ages to find Bruce's flat. There was a tennis tournament at Queen's Club and West Kensington was choked with traffic, so I had to leave the car miles away and perform – even by my standards – some pretty creative parking. The space I eventually found would have been more suitable for a three-year-old's tricycle, and I got very wet under the armpits as I pulled and pushed at the wheel, desperately trying to squeeze Rusty in. Eventually I succeeded – albeit with two wheels on the pavement – got out, slammed the door and legged it, keen to distance myself as quickly as possible from the improbably parked heap of rust.

With an *A to Z* under my nose I then map-read my way round a labyrinth of roads; through a mews, down an alley, under an arch, round a corner and, finally, up what looked like some fire-escape steps to the third floor of a dismal-looking block of flats. Taking the lift had been an option, but when the doors had slid back to reveal a menacing-looking steel box of alarmingly beaten up and graffitied proportions and stinking thoroughly of urine, I'd instantly opted for the climb.

I then made my way cautiously along the outside concrete walkway, keeping an eye out for pit bulls and Alsatians. I wasn't too keen to meet one but I was keen to give the tenants the benefit of the doubt apropos the

pong in the lift. This was definitely not the most salubri-
ous of establishments. Was it council? I wondered. Every
flat had the same blue door with a small pane of re-
inforced glass and at each window a net curtain seemed to
twitch as I passed. Eventually I came to Bruce's door,
number 42. I pressed the bell. His curtain twitched briefly
too and I caught a quick glimpse of his face. A second
later he opened the door.

He looked awful. His eyes were huge and sunken, with
enormous dark circles underneath, and his normally
golden face was ashen and unshaven. He clutched at the
lapels of his blue silk dressing gown, which aside from
some rather dirty pink mules was all he appeared to be
wearing. He blinked nervously.

'Come in,' he whispered, glancing furtively over my
shoulder as if to check no one else was with me. He
quickly ushered me in.

'I won't kiss you,' he said, shutting the door behind me.
'I'm a bit of a mess this morning.'

I smiled and kissed him warmly on the cheek anyway.
'You look fine, Bruce, if a little tired.'

'Here, let me take your jacket.'

'Thanks.'

I let him take it off my shoulders while I looked around.
The front door led directly into the sitting room, which
also seemed to be the dining room, and judging by the
large silk screen emblazoned with peacocks sectioning off
the far end of the room, possibly the bedroom too.

I stared. It was an extraordinary place. The whole room
was literally full of childhood memorabilia. There were
teddy bears everywhere: sitting on chairs, perched on

shelves and all over the wallpaper and curtains. Hanging from the picture rails were rows of string puppets – clowns, Pinocchios, harlequins – all with their limbs dangling and their heads lolling as if their necks were broken. There was also a staggering display of china animals – again, mostly teddies, but with a fair sprinkling of dogs, cats and rabbits thrown in for good measure. These were displayed on what I believe are known as 'occasional tables', except that in this instance there was nothing occasional about them, in fact at a conservative estimate I'd say there were no fewer than fifteen dotted about the room.

I blinked in astonishment. My limited experience of gays, gained chiefly from my advertising days, had led me to believe they were a predominantly tasteful lot, given rather to the minimalist and the trendy, but this place couldn't have been more kitsch if it tried. It was also, somehow, terribly sad, as if a little boy had never grown up. Bruce was hovering next to me. I had the feeling some sort of reaction was called for.

'What a . . . lovely room!' I gasped eventually, totally at a loss.

'Thank you,' he whispered. 'Come and sit down.'

He weaved expertly through a sea of clutter and scooped Munchkin up from the only comfortable-looking chair, by the gas fire. He patted the seat.

'Sit here. I'll go and get some coffee.'

'Thanks.'

I clutched my handbag nervously to my chest, tucked my bottom in – I'm nowhere near as sylph-like as Bruce – and weaved precariously around the obstacle course of tiny, ornament-laden tables, hoping my broad beam wasn't going to send something flying. Bruce watched my progress with an expert's eye and then padded out in his slippers to what was obviously a galley kitchen.

I sat down and watched him go. How odd. He'd seemed so flamboyant, so glamorous, so – well, gay – in Cornwall, yet here in this melancholy little flat he just seemed rather small and forlorn.

I looked around. Fighting for space amongst the china animals on the table beside me were a few photographs. They were all of a sweet-looking elderly couple, sometimes with Bruce smiling beside them, sometimes without. I picked one up and looked at it. Bruce came back with the coffee.

'Mummy and Daddy,' he said, handing me a mug. His hand was shaking.

'I thought so.' I smiled and put the photo down. 'You're very like your mother. How is she?' I asked gently.

He shuffled into a seat opposite and tugged his dressing gown down over his bony knees.

'Not good,' he said with a sigh, 'not good at all. Of course, all this business has made her much worse.'

'She knows?'

'Some of it. Not all of it, she doesn't know for instance that I might go to prison.' His eyes filled with tears and he stared into his coffee.

I looked away, giving him a second to wrestle with his lower lip. Something else was different about him too, but I couldn't quite put my finger on it. Then I realized – of course, his voice! All the campness had gone and there were no effete little mannerisms either. He was a different person – more like half a person, in fact, and now I understood why his parents had never known. I reached across and touched his arm gently.

'It may not come to that, Bruce. I mean, there were some incredibly – whassicalled – mitigating circumstances, weren't there? After all, you were being blackmailed, the court's bound to take that into consideration; you might just get a fine or be let off with a caution, and of course it was only your first offence, wasn't it?'

Bruce raised his eyes from his coffee and stared at me. 'No, Polly, it wasn't my first offence, because I didn't do it. Why doesn't anyone believe me!' His voice rose hysterically.

I shifted uncomfortably in my seat. 'Well, it's not that we don't believe you, it's just that – well, the thing is, Bruce, your fingerprints were all over the cabinet, the police said so, and –'

'Of course they were!' he broke in angrily. 'I was probably the last person to look at the stuff, before the burglary, I mean. Don't you remember? Nick gave me the key and said I could help myself –' He blushed at his unfortunate phrase. 'I mean, have a look.'

'Yes, I know, but' – I hesitated – 'that also means that you were one of the few people who knew where the key was kept, and the key was definitely used, so, um . . .' I trailed off nervously.

'Oh, come on, anyone with half a brain could have found it in that jug and, besides, there must have been other people who knew where it was kept.'

'Well, yes, Nick and me, of course, and Hetty and Tim – oh, and Sarah.'

'No one else? Please think, Polly,' he urged. 'It might just help me.'

'Well, Mrs Bradshaw knew.'

'Who's she?'

'My old daily.'

'Well then? Why does everyone automatically assume it has to be me?'

'Well' – I licked my lips nervously – 'perhaps it's got something to do with the piece of porcelain you gave to your mother? I mean, you must admit, that's pretty incriminating, isn't it?' I asked hesitantly.

'But I didn't give it to her! Honestly, Polly, you've got to believe me!'

'You didn't? Oh, so um . . . how did it get there, d'you think?' I asked, trying hard not to sound interrogative.

'I don't know!' he wailed, frantically twisting his fingers together. 'I just don't know! The first I heard of it – before I even knew about the burglary and before the police had arrested me – was when Mummy rang to thank me for some piece of china she'd found. She kept rabbiting on about how she'd woken up about an hour after I'd left her and there it was, sitting on her bedside table, all wrapped up with "Love from Bruce" written on a tag in my handwriting. She kept thanking me over and over again, one minute saying it was too much and the next saying how beautiful it was – she was nearly crying she was so pleased.

'I didn't have a clue what she was talking about; I didn't even know it was a piece of your porcelain. To be honest I thought she'd gone completely doolally – she is getting rather senile these days – and in the end, just to calm her down – because she was getting so agitated and confused when I denied it – I said yes, OK, I had given it to her after all. She was delighted, of course, and I thought no more about it – thought I'd just ring back later and have a quiet word with one of the nurses and sort it out. I even wondered if one of them had bought it, wrapped it up and sent it from me, because I'd only given her some chocolates for her birthday – well, there's not a great deal she needs in there, you see.' He paused for breath and took a gulp of his coffee.

'Well, of course I completely forgot about it, and the next thing I knew the police were banging on my door, telling me I had the right to remain silent but anything I did say would be taken down and used in evidence against me!' His voice rose to a hysterical sob. 'I simply couldn't believe it! They wouldn't even let me speak to her – still won't, even now – it's one of the conditions of my bail. They say I'll try to persuade her to lie, to say it wasn't me, but all I want to do is to find out the truth.' He gazed at me, his pained, hollow eyes wide with anguish. Then, abruptly, he hung his head and looked down at his pink slippers.

'But none of this really matters you know, Polly,' he whispered sadly. 'I could handle all of it, the whole ghastly mess, if it weren't for the fact that she's dying and they won't let me see her. Suppose she asks for me and they won't let me go and I'm not there when she – oh God, it's just too awful to contemplate!' He gave a strangled sob and broke down completely, clutching Munchkin to his chest and sobbing into her fur.

I dashed over and knelt beside him, putting my arm around him. I could feel his bony shoulders shaking and heaving under his dressing gown. Munchkin whimpered as he held her too tightly but made no effort to escape. Eventually Bruce shuddered to a halt and started to sniff. He released his grip on Munchkin, who frantically licked his hand, and I sat back as he rummaged for a hanky down the side of his chair. He pulled one out and blew his nose noisily.

'Someone hates me very much, don't they, Polly?' he muttered, staring at me with red-rimmed eyes. 'Someone's really got it in for me, first the letters and now this.'

'Well yes.' I licked my lips, I had to tread carefully here. 'The letters are awful, simply horrid, but you see, Bruce, that's one of the reasons the police think you did it, because you were being blackmailed. They think you needed the money.'

'Well, I did need money, yes of course I did, but I'd never *steal* for it.' He looked at me in amazement. 'Never! And certainly not from people like you and Nick whom I like and respect – what do you take me for?'

I gulped and sat on my hands, feeling ashamed. 'I'm sorry, Bruce, it's just . . . well, it's so terribly difficult wh-when all the evidence sort of points to you.'

Bruce compressed his lips and sniffed huffily. 'Maybe so, but it would be nice to think people would have a little more faith in one, regardless of the evidence.'

He wiped his nose with his hanky, regarding me reproachfully over the top of it. I looked away guiltily. We were both silent for a moment. I gazed down at the carpet, a ghastly, patterned nylon affair. I looked up quickly, hating myself for noticing it. I racked my weary brains, trying desperately to think of a way out for him.

'I suppose the nurses didn't see anyone else lurking around her bed that day, did they?' I asked tentatively. 'Anyone suspicious?'

He shook his head. 'No one. The only people who visit are me and a few old ladies from her village, neighbours, that sort of thing. Anyone else would stand out like a sore thumb and they say there was no one unusual that day.'

He gave a deep sigh and sank back in his chair, picking abstractedly at some stuffing that was coming out of the upholstered arm. Then he looked up and gave me a wry little smile.

'It's very simple, Polly. I've been framed. Quite comprehensively and cleverly framed, and there's not a damn thing I can do about it.'

I frowned. 'Oh, Bruce, surely not, there's no one who hates you that much, is there? Enough to let you take the rap for this?'

He shrugged and looked down at Munchkin's head as he stroked it with his finger.

'Hard to say really. No one exactly springs to mind but you'd be surprised at the number of people who hate people like me.' He found my eyes. 'Queers, I mean. Shit-shovellers, uphill gardeners, whatever you want to call us.'

I winced and looked away, embarrassed by his blatancy. He sat up straight and rearranged his dressing gown, suddenly composed.

'Oh yes, we know what people think of us. A lot of people still think Hitler had the right idea; they'd like to see us herded into gas chambers and incinerators. And I don't necessarily mean loony extremists, I mean normal, everyday, common or garden people who pretend to be terribly liberated and free-thinking but who would secretly like to see all of us dirty, AIDS-ridden buggers extermi-nated once and for all. Wiped out.'

'Oh come on, Bruce,' I muttered uncomfortably, 'not in this day and age.'

'You'd be surprised. Decent people like you will find it hard to believe but I can assure you it's true.' He smiled sadly. 'That's why, when you ask me if I can think of any-one in particular, it's rather hard to be specific.'

I gazed up at him from the floor where I was kneeling. All of a sudden he'd acquired a certain dignity, dressed even as he was in his dressing gown and slippers. I looked down abruptly, feeling momentarily ashamed of the arro-gance of my own heterosexual community. There must have been times when I'd giggled at Bruce, ridiculed him even, because – well, he set himself *up* to be ridiculed. But seeing him now, in this heart-rendingly childish flat, sens-ing the chaos and turbulence that must have been within him from an early age as he struggled to come to terms with his sexuality and, when he finally did, his bravery in sparing his elderly parents that particular confession, I felt rather small. And his outrageously camp behaviour which he could evidently turn on and off – it was almost as if he put that on to give other people an excuse to laugh at him, to make *them* feel better, not him. It was a defence mech-anism all right, but in defence of whom? I looked at his feet in their pink mules, so white and cold-looking, so vul-nerable.

A silence fell. I tried to think of something that might help him. Anything.

I cleared my throat. 'I don't suppose you've got an alibi for that Friday night, have you?' I ventured hopefully.

He smiled ruefully. 'No such luck. I was fast asleep in bed at the boarding house where I was staying, but the police say I could easily have slipped out and got back in again because the landlady had given me a key.' He grinned suddenly. 'It's a great shame you're such a sound sleeper, Polly. If only you'd woken up you might have seen it wasn't me!'

'Er, yes, quite,' I said nervously and quickly rummaged around for a change of subject. I didn't particularly want to get embroiled in my whereabouts on that Friday night.

'Um, is there anything I can get you, Bruce? Anything I can do, some shopping perhaps?'

He leaned forward. 'There is something, actually.'

Oh Lord, I'd rather imagined I was enquiring rhetorically. I hoped it wasn't going to be anything too demanding, I had rather a lot on my plate at the moment. 'Er, yes, of course, what is it?'

'Well, if I do – you know – go away, would you look after Munchkin for me? Only, if she can't be with me I'd like her to be in the country where she's got lots of space to run around, with people who like animals. Would you mind, Polly?'

I gulped. 'No, of course not, Bruce. I'd be glad to have her.'

I wasn't too sure what a dog of Munchkin's size was going to do with a thousand acres of Cornish countryside, but since Nick would undoubtedly have kicked me out by then anyway, it was purely academic.

'Good, I know you'll look after her properly, but do

remember she's got an awfully delicate tummy. She's allergic to eggs – they make her frightfully sick – but she's rather partial to a little poached chicken – oh, and lightly grilled fish. I'll give you her diet sheet, of course.'

'Super,' I said weakly.

Oh, this was terrific. Absolutely marvellous. Not only would I be a homeless, single parent with a baby to look after but I'd also have a dog with a delicate tummy and a propensity to puke, so not only would I be covered in baby sick but chihuahua icky-poo too. I'd obviously just have to wear a plastic mac all day and sponge myself down at regular intervals, when I wasn't poaching chicken for one or breastfeeding the other, of course. I simply couldn't wait.

And where were we all supposed to live? Eh? Would somebody like to answer me that one, please? It was all very well Nick saying I should go and look at houses, but there was no way I was going to live in Cornwall if I couldn't live with Nick at Trewarren, no way! And since there was also no way he could possibly afford to buy me anything in London without selling Trewarren – which I would never in a million years allow him to do – that left me up the creek without a home really, didn't it? Perhaps I should just get a Sainsbury's trolley to put baby, dog and belongings in, then I could drift around London in my puke-covered mac looking for suitable bus shelters. I sighed and leaned back on the heels of my hands, staring miserably at the teddies on the shelf above me.

Then I had an idea. Oh! I sat up abruptly. Hang on a minute – I had a quick look around – on second thoughts, perhaps we could live here. I wouldn't have to decorate because it already looked exactly like a nursery, so Junior would get the right vibes, Munchkin wouldn't have to be uprooted – an experience which would no doubt play havoc with her delicate digestive system – and Nick could perhaps pay Bruce a small amount of rent which would come in jolly handy when he came out of the clink! Yes, all in all it would suit us very well! A perfect little pied-à-terre for three homeless waifs and strays. I sat up eagerly.

'Bruce?'

'Hmmm?' He turned to me with sorrow-laden eyes.

I sat back again. 'Er . . . nothing.'

One peek at those eyes made me hold my tongue. Some other time perhaps. It might, after all, look a trifle callous to ask for the keys to his flat before he was even banged up.

Once more we lapsed into gloomy silence, both pre-occupied with our respective shattered lives. Eventually I looked at my watch and sighed.

'I must go, Bruce. I'm meeting Sam in half an hour.'

He nodded and got to his feet, retying his dressing-gown cord with something that smacked vaguely of determination.

'And I must get dressed,' he said decisively. 'For the first time in three days actually, awful I know, but up to now I haven't really felt there was much to get dressed for. Talking to you has made me feel a lot better, Polly. You're a real tonic.'

'Oh good,' I said, dragging myself up from the floor. 'I'm glad about that.'

The mere fact that it had depressed the hell out of me was neither here nor there, of course. What did it matter that I felt even more like sticking my head in an oven if one poor soul felt like removing his?

'Actually I know the feeling,' I said, suddenly wanting to out-gloom him. 'I didn't get dressed for about two weeks recently, didn't even get out of bed,' I bragged, as I weaved my way back through the tables.

'Really? Why?' He opened the door for me.

'Oh, er, it's a long story,' I muttered, back-pedalling like mad. 'I won't bore you with the details; I think you've got enough to contend with at the moment.' I smiled. 'Chin up, Bruce, I'll give you a ring in a couple of days, OK?'

He nodded. 'Thanks, Polly. Oh, and give my love to Sam, won't you? He guaranteed my bail, you know. Tell him I'm seeing his barrister tomorrow.'

I pecked his unshaven cheek. 'I will. Now you take care, and ring me if you need anything, I'm staying with Pippa.'

'Will do. Thanks for bothering to come and see me.' His voice cracked slightly at this and tears, I noticed with alarm, were surfacing again.

I hurriedly gave him a hug and then without looking back moved smartly down the walkway to the stairs, giving a cheery little backwards wave as I went. I simply couldn't cope with any more waterworks today, his, mine or anybody else's. I clattered quickly down the fire-escape steps, feeling horribly guilty but desperate to get as far away as possible from that sad little flat. God, poor Bruce, talk about a shedful of problems, and far from lightening my own load it seemed to have added a couple of tons to it. In fact it made me want to hire an articulated lorry in which to cart it around.

I jumped the last few steps and ran to the end of the

street, grateful to be out in the sunshine again. As I ran along I groped in my bag for my *A to Z* and peered at the grid reference for my next little rendezvous, my tête-à-tête with Sam. Draycott Avenue, off Walton Street, Brompton Cross end. It wasn't too far from Pippa's, so I'd dump the car at her house and get the Tube. There was no way I'd be able to park in Draycott Avenue. Right. I snapped the *A to Z* shut and sighed grimly. Oh yes, I was under no illusions about this little débâcle. If I'd thought the encounter with Bruce had been a headache, I was well aware that it was nothing to the severe migraine this one was going to induce. Nevertheless, I trotted dutifully off to my car, shooting only the occasional reproachful glance at the open blue skies above me as I went. Why me, God, why me?

Chapter Nineteen

Sam was already sitting at a corner table when I walked into the restaurant twenty minutes late. He didn't see me come in and I caught him glancing at his watch as I made my way towards him. He looked up, saw me and got eagerly to his feet, knocking his chair over backwards as he did so. He looked a bit embarrassed at his lack of cool and laughed as he picked it up and kissed me roundly on the cheek.

'Just wrecking the joint. It's great to see you!'

His face was tanned from his Egypt trip, his eyes with their amber flecks sparkled brilliantly and his hair was streaked with gold. He certainly looked devilishly handsome and terribly boyish, but I was pleased to note that my heart didn't even miss a semiquaver.

I smiled. 'Good to see you too, Sam.'

'Here, let me.' He rushed round to pull my chair out and took my jacket as I wriggled out of it. He hung it on the back of my chair.

'Thanks.' I sat down.

'Drink?' he asked eagerly, sitting down opposite me again and indicating the carafe of red on the table.

'Please.'

The burgundy liquid glugged delightfully into my glass. It was very definitely just what I needed right now, but as I raised it greedily to my lips I realized it was also very definitely just what I shouldn't be having. I took a miserable little sip then put it down. Christ. How on earth was I supposed to get through a lunch of such awesomely tricky proportions without a cigarette or a drink? It occurred to me that Sam was looking more than a little keen and that I might have to give him the heave-ho, something I hadn't really contemplated. Not only that, but I was also going to have to ask him to do some pretty outrageous lying. I seized my paper napkin and began shredding it maniacally.

'So!' began Sam joyfully, folding his arms on the table and leaning across. 'How've you been? How's tricks, as they say?' He beamed. 'You look terrific, incidentally!'

'God, I look a mess' – I ran my hands through my hair – 'but I'm fine, fine,' I nodded, cranking up a nervous smile.

'Good.' Sam leaned over the table and grabbed my hand enthusiastically, nearly knocking a vase of flowers over. 'It's wonderful to see you again, Polly, it's been so long!'

'I – I know, Sam, it's been ages. Um, how – how was Egypt?' I asked, desperately wanting to get off the subject of our long separation.

He sat back and sighed. 'Oh, so-so. Hard work and incredibly hot.' He shook his head. 'Too hot, in fact, and I'm not sure I got the result I was after. It's impossible to work in those sorts of conditions.'

'I can imagine. Still, you look well,' I observed, 'got a good tan.'

He grinned. 'Well, it's pretty hard to keep out of the sun – you get a tan whether you want one or not.'

'Yes, um . . . I suppose you do.'

I followed up this sparkling piece of repartee with a festive smile and then buried my head in the menu. When I looked up Sam was watching me carefully. I had the impression he knew all was not well. I scrunched the remains of my napkin into a tight ball and wished to God I'd rehearsed just one tiny sentence of what I was going to say before I'd got here. How idiotic of me not to have thought this through. I desperately rooted around for another inconsequential gambit, just one more, then I'd come to the point, really I would. Our voices clashed.

'Sorry I was a bit –' I began.

'Look, Polly –' he started.

We laughed.

'Go on, what were you . . . ?'

'No, no, you first,' he insisted.

'Well, I was just going to say sorry if I was a bit late. I went to see Bruce and I got rather held up, stayed longer than I meant to but it was jolly difficult to get away.'

'God, I can imagine. Good for you for going, though. I'm not sure I could have faced it. Poor Bruce, how is he?'

'Desperate. Frightened out of his mind, and I don't blame him either.'

'No, absolutely, I'd be terrified.' Sam shook his head in horror. 'Awful business, simply ghastly. Apart from anything else, I can't think what possessed him to *do* it. I mean, it's just so unlike old Bruce; he's the last person in the world one would imagine doing something dodgy, and if he was so short of money he could have come to me. I'm sure we could have sorted something out, an advance on his salary or something. I had no idea he had money problems.'

'Oh, I don't think he did, and I don't think he did it either.'

'What?'

'I don't think he stole the porcelain.'

'Really? But I thought the police were more or less convinced – didn't he leave fingerprints all over the place, and Pippa said something about giving a piece to his mother?'

'Oh that,' I said dismissively, 'no no, that's nonsense. He doesn't know anything about it – it was obviously planted there by someone else to get him into trouble.'

Sam looked surprised. 'Really? Is that what the police think?'

'No, but it's what I think.'

'Gosh, well I just hope you're right, for Bruce's sake. I must say, I had my doubts about the whole thing all along, couldn't *believe* it when I heard. Old Bruce just hasn't got the nerve – he'd run a mile from anything that smacked of trouble.'

'Exactly, and I'm sure it'll all come out in court and he'll be completely vindicated. I gather you've got him a brilliant barrister, is that right?'

'Peter Summers, yes, he's a friend of mine and by all accounts he's shit hot. Bruce wanted some idiot of a hack lawyer to take the case, someone his father had known who's about ninety years old now and hasn't practised for years, but I wouldn't hear of it.'

'Quite right, he needs the best defence he can get, and you've put up the bail too?'

'Well, the company's guaranteed it but at the end of the day it's my dosh, I suppose – well, mine and Josh's since he's the other shareholder.' He frowned. 'Had a bit of a job persuading old Josh, actually.'

'Really? Why?'

'Oh, I don't know. I suppose he thought ten grand was a bit steep, and it's not as if he and Bruce are bosom pals either.'

'Oh? I didn't know.'

'Oh, it's nothing drastic, just a bit of a personality clash, that's all. Josh thinks Bruce is a bit of a pain in the arse – in more ways than one, if you know what I mean!' He grinned. 'But, anyway, we're not really here to talk about Bruce, are we? Don't we have more personal matters to discuss?' His smile was warm. He leaned across the table and took my hand. 'Polly, I –'

'Look, Sam,' I said, interrupting him abruptly, 'd'you mind if I go first? Only – well I've got a few things I need to say, to – you know, get off my chest.'

'Sure, sure! Go ahead.' He sat back in surprise.

I took a deep breath and leaned forward. 'Well, the thing is . . . the thing is, I – I think you're a terrific guy. Really I do.' I nodded emphatically. 'But I'm afraid I'm just not on for any of this.'

'Any of what?'

'Any of this – well, any of this adultery lark. You see, in the first place I never actually intended to do it, can't think what possessed me, as a matter of fact, and in the second place – well, I just love my husband too much; it's as simple as that. Oh God, I'm awfully sorry, Sam, this is all coming out wrong, but the bottom line is I'm afraid it just can't go on.'

There was a silence. Beautifully put, Polly, beautifully put.

Sam licked his lips. 'I see,' he said quietly, playing with the stem of his wine glass. 'A one-night stand, is that it?'

'Sam, I'm sorry but you must see that it's just not right! You're married, and I'm married – although I'm not so sure about that any more, but that's another story – but the point is, well, the point is it was just a moment of madness really, wasn't it?' I pleaded.

He looked slightly pained. 'What a lovely turn of phrase you have, Polly,' he muttered.

'Oh Lord, I'm sorry. I'm not doing this very well – I don't mean to sound so heartless.' I took a deep breath and started again. 'What I mean is that it's got nothing whatsoever to do with you. If you were the sexiest, handsomest, most divine man in the world – which of course you are,' I added hastily, 'but even if you were Mel Gibson or – or that divine English actor with the floppy hair, Hugh someone, for example, I'd *still* have to turn you down because I'm just too in love with Nick. I'm just not on for any of this extra-marital stuff.' I shook my head. 'I'm sorry if I'm not being very tactful here, but I don't know how else to say it.'

Sam pursed his lips and stared at the tablecloth. He gave a wry little smile. 'I had a feeling you were going to say something like this, actually,' he said quietly. 'Half expected it in a way, that's why I was nervous about seeing you. And you're right, Polly, you're absolutely right. This *is* madness, but it's a madness I would have continued with, I'm afraid.' He looked up quickly. 'I'm obviously a much weaker character than you are.' He shrugged. 'I'm sorry, I just can't help it, I'm crazy about you.'

He ran his fingers through his hair and continued staring bleakly at the tablecloth.

I gulped. Oh hell. This was much worse than I'd ever envisaged. I clenched my toes. Why the bloody hell had he fallen for me like this?

'Sam, I'm so sorry,' I said softly. 'I had no idea you felt so strongly. I'd never have come barging in and trampled all over your feelings in such a heartless way, but I somehow imagined you'd feel the same. I mean, after all you and Sally –'

'I know,' he interrupted, looking up sharply, 'I know. Sally and I have a terrific marriage and I'm still very much in love with her. I've never done this before, never ever.' He shook his head vigorously. 'This is the first time in our entire marriage I've ever – well, I've ever cheated, that's the only word for it, isn't it? And I know I'm being weak and foolish but . . . God' – he ran his hands through his hair – 'it's been such a long time since I've had this feeling, this incredible buzz of happiness and excitement! And of course it's frightfully addictive. I think I knew it was crazy but I just wanted it to continue for a bit longer.' He took a gulp of wine and gazed at me intently. Suddenly he grinned. 'But you're right, Polly, it can't go on, and sooner or later I would have realized that. I just wanted to prolong my fool's paradise for a while.'

I sighed. 'Oh, Sam –'

He took my hand and shook his head, smiling. 'Don't feel bad – you're right; you're doing the sensible thing. It's much better that we finish it now when it's not too painful, rather than in a year or so's time when it might have been so much harder.'

'Absolutely,' I muttered, nodding hard. I took a huge gulp of wine. A year or so's time! Blimey, he'd had some pretty permanent ideas about the two of us, hadn't he?

He smiled. 'You're a lovely girl, Polly, you know that? You're fresh, beautiful and sometimes just downright hilarious. You made me feel about ten years younger that night – I'll never forget it.'

'Ah yes, well, Sam, that's one of the things I want to talk to you about actually, if you don't mind.'

'What d'you mean?'

'Well, I wondered if you could perhaps shed some light on one or two rather grey areas I have concerning our – um, our encounter. In the hotel.'

'Sure, fire away.' He looked puzzled.

'What happened?'

He frowned. 'Sorry?'

'What happened that night?'

He stared at me. 'What d'you mean?'

'I mean, I can't remember.'

'What . . . not at all? Nothing?' He looked shocked.

'Not a sausage, if you'll excuse the allusion.'

He looked at me in alarm. 'Good grief, Polly, you mean –'

'I mean I have absolutely no recollection of our night of passion, none whatsoever.' I gave this a moment to permeate his boggling brain cells, then leaned in urgently. 'Listen, Sam, the last thing I remember about that night is dancing a clinchy number with you in Annabel's. I remember feeling exceedingly drunk and I remember thinking I wanted to sit down, or go to the loo, or pass out, or *something*, but then all I've got is a complete blank. As far as I'm concerned we then fast forward to the following morning where I wake up alone in a hotel bedroom, the only clue to my recent behaviour being a coded message by my bed.'

He stared at me, aghast. 'That's it?'

'That's it.'

'Heavens,' he muttered, 'good grief, Polly, that's appalling. I feel awful. I mean, I knew you were drunk, plastered even – and so was I – but I had no idea you weren't even remotely compos mentis. I promise you, I'd *never* have taken advantage of –'

'Ah!' I pounced hopefully. 'So you took advantage?'

'Absolutely not!' He looked offended. 'I was going to say I wouldn't have taken advantage of the situation had I known the extent of your inebriation, but I had no idea. Hell, Polly, you were all for it. I mean, you were the one who instigated it, for God's sake!'

My jaw dropped. 'I was?'

'Certainly you were.'

'But I thought – hang on, didn't I faint or something? I could have sworn I went a bit woozy on the dance floor.'

'Oh sure, you did, and I sat you down and got you a glass of water, but you recovered in seconds and that's when you dragged me outside. You hailed a taxi and insisted it took us to a hotel.'

'No!'

'Yes, and you were the one who went for my flies in the back of the cab, you tried to take my trousers off, you even tried to take your own trousers off until I stopped you. The taxi driver nearly threw us out – it was hysterical!'

336

'I don't believe it.'

'I promise you it's true, but – God, does this all come as a complete surprise? What about in the lift at the hotel? Don't you remember trying to re-create that scene in *Fatal Attraction*? You sort of jumped into my arms yelling "Take me, take me!" but I was laughing so much I dropped you – remember? And then in the bedroom – gosh, you made so much *noise*! All that shouting and whooping and waving your bra around your head like a football rattle, shouting "Here we go, here we go!" – Polly, you *must* remember!'

I made a strange retching sound and bit my knuckles. 'No!' I gasped. 'No, I don't. Did I? Gosh, how *awful*! I'm so *sorry*, Sam, how *embarrassing*.'

'Don't be ridiculous, I loved it. I haven't had a night like that for ages. I mean, phew, hot stuff or what, I didn't know if I was coming or going. I was like a boy of eighteen that night – I even impressed myself!' His eyes were shining now. 'It puts my batting average up beyond belief, talk about a personal best, I must have –'

'Yes, thank you, Sam,' I groaned, hiding my burning face in my hands. 'Spare me the score card, would you? I get the idea, you surpassed yourself.'

'Oh Lord, I'm sorry, Polly,' he said quickly, 'I didn't mean to get – you know – crude, but you did ask and it really was the most terrific night. But what a shame you don't remember. What a waste.' He looked slightly hurt, then suddenly his brow puckered as if he were recalling something. 'I suppose,' he said, nodding slowly, 'yes, I suppose if I'm absolutely honest with myself I'd have to admit I was a little surprised when you fell asleep on top of me like that, right in the middle of that last frenzied bout of lovemaking. All of a sudden you just went limp and heavy and started snoring in my ear. I had to prize you off, which was quite difficult under the circumstances, seeing as how we were still very much connected – attached, if you like – and, well, I'm not saying you're a heavy girl, Polly, but I was a bit worried I wouldn't be able to shift you, actually. Thought I'd have to call a porter.'

I gave a faint but audible whimper at this point, seized my wine glass and threw its contents down my throat. It was no good – if I didn't get some alcohol into my bloodstream pretty damn fast I was going to die of shame right here on the spot, and if I went the baby went with me so it might just as well have a drink with me instead. God, how awful! I'd collapsed like a beached whale on *top* of him! Yuck, how repulsive! Sam's mouth was still moving, he was obviously still shedding light. I listened in a daze.

'. . . but up until then you were game for anything. At one point you asked me to get on all fours and make a noise like Thomas the Tank Engine.'

'No!'

'Oh yes,' Sam nodded emphatically, 'definitely Thomas the Tank Engine – you were quite specific.'

'God! And did you?'

'Well, I had a go. I gave a sort of feeble *peep-peep*, which seemed to go down rather well actually. You did quite a bit of toot-tooting back and kind of chugged round the bed a bit. Said you were Gordon.'

'Jesus!'

'Then you wanted to ring room service and send down for some sex food.'

'What the hell's that?'

'You may well ask.' He frowned and scratched his head sheepishly. 'It came as a bit of a surprise to me too. You were babbling a bit by this stage but I seem to recall you thought an assorted fruit bowl might do the trick.'

'No!' I gasped in horror. 'What on earth was I *thinking* of?'

'Lord knows,' he said wistfully, 'but I wish we had, the very idea got me pretty feverish, I can tell you.'

'Oh God,' I groaned. 'Oh, Sam, how awful, what must you think of me?'

He grinned. 'I think you're a pretty game girl actually. It made me realize I'd been leading a frightfully tame love life. Couldn't stop thinking about it the whole time I was in Egypt, but – don't you remember *any* of this?' he asked incredulously.

'No,' I muttered, staring down at my hands, shame filling every part of me.

'And can't you even *imagine* doing all that?'

'Oh yes,' I whispered miserably, 'that's no problem, that's the awful thing. Given the right amount of alcohol and a little encouragement it's all entirely possible, I'm afraid. I'm only surprised I didn't treat you to some naked abseiling or a flying trapeze act.'

He looked at me wistfully. 'Really? I'd have loved that. Still, I think you made up for it. I love that thing you do with your toes, by the way.'

I froze, my eyes huge with terror. 'What thing?' I breathed, paralysed with dread.

'You know,' he winked conspiratorially, 'that . . . thing. Come on, Polly, you must have done it before, it's absolute dynamite.' He grinned salaciously and wiggled his fingers on the tablecloth. 'This little piggy went to –'

'Stop, *stop*!' I shrieked. I shut my eyes tight and stuffed my fingers in my ears. 'No more!'

After a moment I opened my eyes cautiously. His mouth, thank goodness, was firmly shut in a rather hurt little line. I slowly removed my fingers from my ears.

'No more, really, Sam,' I said in a shaky whisper. 'I – I don't want to know.'

'Well, I'm sorry, but you did ask. I was only trying to enlighten you,' he said in a wounded tone.

'And I'm most grateful, really I am, but if it's all right with you I think I'd rather be left in the dark as far as the rest of the evening's concerned. I'm quite sure my imagination can fill in the blanks; it's already boggling out of my earholes as it is.' I drained my wine glass, feeling rather faint. 'Oh, Sam,' I whispered, 'you've no idea how awful this is.'

'Don't be ridiculous, Polly – it was wonderful!'

'No, but . . . you don't understand. I have to think of Nick.'

'Well of course, and I have to think of Sally, but what's done is done; it's no good wishing it had never happened. And look at it this way,' he went on brightly, 'if you can't remember a thing about it then you almost have a clear conscience, don't you? It's almost as if it never happened, practically puts you in the clear, doesn't it?'

'Practically,' I whispered, 'apart from one tiny detail.'

'What's that?'

I gulped. 'Nick knows.'

'What!'

I nodded dumbly. 'He knows.'

Sam's jaw dropped, his eyes grew wide with alarm. 'But – but how on earth did he find out?'

'I . . . told him.'

'You *told* him? Polly! What on earth were you thinking of?'

'Well,' I muttered, avoiding Sam's gaze, which was one of undiluted horror, 'he found out I wasn't at home that night. It was the night of the burglary, you see, and the police were round questioning us, and when they'd gone – well, it just all came out. I *had* to tell him. I suppose I thought he'd understand,' I said miserably. 'I thought he'd believe me when I said I couldn't remember what had happened but – he didn't. He was furious. He's left me actually,' I whispered, 'moved out. I'm on my own.'

Sam could hardly speak 'You told him?' he blustered eventually. 'You actually told him you spent the night with me? Did you say it was me?' he added quickly.

I nodded without looking up.

He shook his head in despair. 'Oh, Polly, *Polly*, what were you *thinking* of?'

'I don't know!' I wailed. 'I know it sounds ridiculous, and obviously in retrospect – well *certainly* in retrospect, particularly now I've found out what happened – I wish I hadn't, but at the time I didn't even know I'd snogged you, for God's sake! Let alone wrestled you to the ground in a lift, got you chuffing round the bed like a steam engine and performed some sort of gruesome Fergie-meets-David-Mellor toe-job on you. I didn't have a clue! And I suppose I thought he'd think the best of me. But he didn't,' I went on in a small voice, 'he thought the worst, and obviously he was right.'

'Jesus,' muttered Sam.

I looked up earnestly. 'So the thing is, Sam, I want you

to talk to him. Please, you've got to – it's the only thing that's going to get me out of this mess. You've got to swear nothing frisky happened, say I passed out or something and – and you just spent the night beside me making sure I was OK. You must,' I pleaded, 'don't you see? He's never going to forgive me and it's the only thing that'll save my marriage now. You're my last hope!'

Tears were springing into my eyes. I could feel them, hot and salty and swimming around at the bottom ready to fall. 'Please!' I begged. 'Please say you'll do it!'

Sam lit a cigarette. He shook his head slowly. 'Polly, you're asking the impossible, you really are. How can I possibly get involved? This is between you and Nick now. You've told him you spent the night with me. I can't just turn round and lie to him, pretend nothing happened. He'd never believe me, I'd feel a complete tosser. Anyway, you wouldn't lie to Sally if I asked you to, would you?'

'Oh yes!' I said eagerly. 'If you wanted me to, I could do it easily, no problem at all, honestly, pop round if you like!'

Sam raised his eyebrows. 'Well, I'm sorry,' he said flatly, 'but it's just not my style. I can't tell a bare-faced lie just like that, I really can't.'

'But it's only a tiny little one,' I pleaded, 'a sort of off-white one, and anyway,' I went on angrily, 'this is no time to be moral, Sam – this is my sodding marriage we're talking about, damn you!'

He began to look huffy. 'There's no need to be like that, Polly.'

'Sorry, sorry,' I said quickly, realizing this was no way to cajole him into anything. 'I'm just a bit desperate, that's all.'

'But – what on earth made you tell him in the first place?' he said, looking mystified. 'I mean, what did you think he'd say, for heaven's sake? Oh never mind, Polly, don't let it happen again? Or – good for you, have one on me?'

'No,' I groaned, 'no, of course not.'

'Or perhaps you thought he'd imagine we just did a bit of innocent hand-holding? Read each other poetry in bed? Played a bit of Scrabble, perhaps? Hell's teeth, he's a *man*, Polly; he knows what goes on. Did you really think he'd give you the benefit of the doubt when you said you were pissed out of your mind and ended up in a hotel bedroom with another man? God, I'm surprised he's not coming after me.' He took a rather feverish drag on his cigarette.

'Well, I –'

'And as for roping me in on this . . .' He shook his head vigorously. 'He's a big chap, your Nick, he'll – he'll knock my teeth into my head, it'll be pistols at dawn, he'll –'

'Oh no, you don't have to see him,' I said quickly, 'just ring him up and explain nicely over the phone. You don't have to come within a hair's breadth of him, but you must understand, my life dep–'

'No, Polly,' he said firmly, cutting me short. 'I'm afraid I'm just not for it. I'm not getting involved and that's that.'

He helped himself to another glass of wine and downed it decisively. He looked rather cross and petulant now.

I stared at him, the tears ready to brim over. 'You mean . . . you won't do it?'

He sighed. 'Oh, Polly, please' – he took my hand – 'don't do that, don't give me the emotional blackmail bit. I'm so

343

fond of you, you know that, but I just can't do it. As far as I'm concerned it happened, it was wonderful – beautiful even – and I'd dearly love for it to happen again. I'm not going to deny it; it makes it so – well, cheap.'

'It was,' I muttered softly.

'Sorry?'

'Nothing. Forget it, I'm sorry, we're obviously both coming at this from completely different angles. You see it as a night to remember and I see it as a night to – well . . . Never mind.'

A silence engulfed us. I stared at the tablecloth in a daze. A few minutes later a waiter materialized beside us.

'So sorry to have kept you waiting, there's been a slight delay in the kitchen,' he purred. 'Can I take your order?'

I don't think it had occurred to either of us that we'd sat there for about half an hour with diddly-squat to eat. Suddenly I didn't feel in the slightest bit hungry, in fact I felt positively sick at the thought, for emotional and biological reasons.

I shook my head. 'I've lost my appetite,' I muttered.

The waiter looked concerned. 'Is madam all right? Can I get you some water, perhaps?'

I looked up. He was a young chap, with a nice open face. He was worried, how sweet.

'No, I – I'm fine,' I faltered, trying to smile.

'Could you give us a moment?' asked Sam. 'You see, I'm not sure we're going to –'

'No, we're not,' I put in decisively, 'at least I'm not.'

'What, nothing at all?' asked Sam, in concern. 'Not even a quick spaghetti?' he suggested.

'Not even a quick anything,' I muttered between clenched

teeth. Then I remembered my manners. 'No thanks, Sam, I'm not really very hungry.'

'I'm sorry,' said Sam to the waiter, 'could I just pay for the wine?'

'Of course, I'll get the bill, sir.'

He took one last look at my pale face, then disappeared. I stared at the tablecloth. Sam shifted around uncomfortably. He cleared his throat and gave a nervous laugh.

'That suits me, actually, I've got so much to do at the office. You know what it's like when you've been away. My desk looks like bloody Snowdonia!'

I nodded dumbly. I couldn't speak.

He leaned over. 'Polly, don't hate me,' he mumbled. 'I'm sorry, but what more can I say? I simply don't want to get involved. You can't blame me for that, surely?'

I didn't look up. I shook my head. 'No . . .' I said slowly, 'I suppose not, but I just sort of thought . . . hoped really . . .'

The waiter came back with the bill. Sam quickly paid in cash and stood up. He helped me on with my jacket and we walked outside.

When we got on to the pavement the light hit me. It was a beautiful day. I blinked hard against the sun and bit my lip; tears were imminent. Sam saw and took me in his arms. He hugged me close.

'I'm sorry I've caused you so much pain,' he muttered. 'It's the last thing in the world I wanted to do.'

A cab cruised past with its light on. I broke away from Sam's embrace and stuck my hand out to stop it. Suddenly I just wanted to get away. It screeched to a halt in front of us and I went to open the door and scramble in. I turned back as I was halfway inside. Sam was standing with his hands thrust in the pockets of his overcoat. He looked hurt, miserable.

'Sorry to rush off, Sam, but there's nothing more to say really, is there?'

He gave a rather bleak smile. 'It would appear not.'

'Um, can I give you a lift? I'm going to Harley – Oxford Street to do some shopping.'

'Well, you could drop me at Knightsbridge Tube if you could bear to sit next to me for another five minutes.' He grinned.

I managed to smile back. 'Don't be ridiculous, of course I could – get in.'

Must we prolong the agony? I thought miserably as he sat down next to me. I felt dumb with despair and I wanted to be alone. The cab pulled away. I was dimly aware that Sam was making a stab at polite conversation but I was unable to concentrate on a word. I stared out of the window as the shops flashed by in all their Knightsbridge glory. I'd lost Nick. Lost him. And it was all my fault. And, much as I hated Sam for refusing to comply, it was crazy of me to blame him – I could see that. I looked up. His face was pale with tension; he was looking at me anxiously.

'Are you all right, Polly? I feel absolutely dreadful, really I do, but –'

'It's OK, Sam,' I said wearily, 'it's not your fault. Don't lose any sleep over it.'

We drove the rest of the way in silence. As we drew up at the Tube station he leaned across to kiss me. I think it would have landed on my lips but the cab lurched to a halt and he missed. We laughed nervously as he ended up somewhere round my ear. He smiled ruefully as he got out of the cab. I pulled down the window.

'Bye then, Polly,' he said. 'Don't think badly of me. I'll certainly always have wonderful memories of you.'

I cranked up a tepid smile. 'Bye, Sam.'

The cab pulled away. If only he knew, I thought bitterly, sinking back into the black leather upholstery, if only he knew I might be carrying his child, he wouldn't be so keen not to get involved then, would he? Oh no, he'd be on the blower to Nick before you could blink, denying all knowledge of our night of passion, disclaiming any sort of responsibility. Or would he? I gazed out of the window. Perhaps I was being too hard on him. After all, he'd wanted to carry on the relationship, perhaps he'd have wanted me big with child too? Who knows. But I wasn't about to find out.

The taxi lurched up to some lights, taking my delicate tummy with it. I breathed in hard through my nose and gulped back the bile. Thankfully, the moment passed and I sighed the sigh of the fated as we trundled north towards my next assignation, the third appointment on my fun-packed agenda. Oh yes, I was in for even more thrills and spills now, because what was my next blind date? A trip to the gynaecologist. As Cilla would say, what a lorra fun that was going to be. I groaned.

'Whereabouts in Oxford Street, love?' yelled the driver, cocking his ear at the glass partition.

'Actually I want Harley Street – hang on, I'll give you the number.'

I reached down to the floor for my bag and it was then that I saw the case. A silver, typically posey, film director's attaché. Oh no, he'd left his case behind! I looked around wildly, almost as if to catch him and fling it out of the window, but of course he was long gone. I leaned back in despair. Christ, now I'd have to *get* it to him somehow, have to bloody *see* him again. I bashed my head hard against the headrest.

'Aaaaargh!'

'Sorry, love? What number was that?'

'Oh, hang on.' I rummaged around for the bit of paper. 'Seventy-two,' I yelled.

I gazed out of the window and it was with a profound sense of relief that it dawned on me. No, I didn't have to see him at all – all I had to do was give the blasted thing to Pippa, who could take it with her to the office in the morning. Phew. Well, thank heavens for small – and we're talking minuscule here – mercies. I sighed as the taxi headed north.

Chapter Twenty

Having skipped lunch I was of course far too early for my appointment with Mr Taylor. I walked aimlessly up and down Harley Street, sat waifishly on doorsteps and eventually trudged dejectedly into number 72 with still about half an hour to spare.

To my surprise the receptionist informed me with a bright, white smile that it was in fact my lucky day. And I'd had no idea! There was I thinking that this was the day to contemplate suicide in more than just a half-hearted fashion, when all the time my luck was in. I questioned her further and it transpired that Mr Taylor was running at least twenty minutes early so I only had about five minutes to kill. Ah. I went gloomily into the oak-panelled waiting room and, as it turned out, killed time quite fittingly by sticking imaginary pins into the only other patient in the room.

The girl in question was about my age and luminous with pregnancy. She had pretty blond curls, a contented, Madonna-like smile on her rosy-cheeked face and was wearing a terribly twee maternity smock, strewn with daisy chains. Every so often she'd stroke her swollen tummy protectively, giving me the benefit of not just a wedding ring and an engagement ring but a serious whopper of an eternity ring too.

I stared at her, sick with jealousy. That should have

been me over there, happily pregnant with a loving husband to go home to, hand heavy with rocks. She looked across and smiled. A nice, comradely, we're-both-in-this-together smile. Now, under normal circumstances I'd have been over there like a shot – comparing morning-sickness bouts, asking her the best place to buy outsized bras, enquiring about the likelihood of piles – but as it was I could only twist my face into what I hoped was a smile but was probably more of a homicidal grimace, make sure my own rings – albeit smaller and fewer – were well on display too and bury my head firmly in *Country Life*. I caught her look of disappointment as the chance of a cosy mother-to-be chat proved not-to-be. God. When did I get to be so mean and twisted?

I flicked miserably through the vast houses for sale at the front of the magazine, remembering how I used to pore over them, salivating with longing, dreaming of living in just such a pile. Of course, now I did, but for how much longer? How much longer would it be before Nick decided he could quite easily live without a cheating, scheming, conniving little hussy and sue for divorce on the grounds of adultery?

Once he discovered I was pregnant of course, that's how long. Nick was no fool, he'd know the baby was Sam's. I mean, let's face it, two years of bonking for Britain with my husband had resulted in absolutely zilch in the way of a bun in the Aga, but one night of steaming sex with a fabulously fertile film director and *wham*! Here I was, up the duff without a paddle and down at the gynae clinic before you could say knife. Knife! I jumped. No. No way. No way was I losing this baby, not while there was still a chance, however remote, that it might be Nick's.

Out of the corner of my eye I spotted a white coat gliding silently towards me. It stopped beside me.

'Mr Taylor will see you now,' murmured a discreet female voice in my ear.

'Thank you,' I muttered nervously.

I got up too quickly and sent at least three magazines flying. As I bent down to pick them up, my bag slipped off my shoulder on to the floor. It flew open and various odds and ends spilled out, including a witty paperback Pippa had lent me to cheer me up, entitled *101 Ways to Have an Orgasm*. I flushed, hurriedly shoved everything back in, straightened up, and as I swung the bag back on to my shoulder again, caught White Coat full in the stomach with it.

'Oof,' she groaned, but faintly and decorously.

'Sorry,' I muttered, puce now.

'Take your time,' she murmured, with enviable composure.

I hid my flushing face and scampered after her as she silently glided away again. As I hurried up the stairs behind her I noticed a ladies' loo on the landing.

'Just popping in here for a moment,' I mumbled.

She nodded politely and I scurried in, principally because it had suddenly occurred to me that I might reek of booze. I'd only had a couple of glasses but judging by the innocent demeanour of Daisy Chain downstairs that was a couple more than the mighty Mr Taylor was used to smelling on his patients' breath, and I did, after all, want to create a good impression.

I rummaged around in my bag, found my Gold Spot and had a good squirt, tugged down my rather too short skirt – what on earth had possessed me to wear it? – and was about to leave when I realized I was so nervous I had to have a quick pee. I rushed into a cubicle, sat down, but – oh hell, there was no loo paper. I rummaged around furiously at the bottom of my bag, aware that white coat was tapping her foot impatiently outside, but also aware that I *had* to have some loo paper, I was having an examination for God's sake. Fortunately, right at the bottom of my bag I found a grotty rolled-up ball of tissue with bits of fluff and gunge stuck to it. It looked as if it had been there for a hundred years. I hurriedly used it and scurried out again.

White Coat was well on her way up to the next landing. 'Mrs Penhalligan to see you, Mr Taylor,' she announced, opening a door.

Blimey, hang on, I thought, bounding after her two at a time. I quickly scuttled past her into the room. She shut the door behind me and I stood there, panting and flustered, not quite making the entrance I'd envisaged.

The room was large and light with a high, heavily corniced ceiling and gracious french windows leading on to a balcony that overlooked the street. Mr Taylor was sitting with his back to the windows behind an enormous leather-topped desk. He stood up and stuck out his hand and I was almost blinded by the simultaneous flash of teeth, cuff links, gold watch, tie pin and silk accessories.

He was indeed a dead ringer for Peter Bowles, and my God was he dapper. His black, military-style moustache gleamed with good health – even Brylcreem perhaps – his immaculate, but slightly too loud pinstriped suit looked fresh from Savile Row, and his yellow silk tie matched his yellow silk handkerchief which I had no doubt matched his yellow silk underpants.

'Mrs Penhalligan,' he beamed, 'delighted . . . do, please,' he purred, indicating for me to sit opposite him.

I sat down nervously, still puffing and blowing a bit, and watched as he rearranged himself in his chair, pulling up his trouser legs before he lowered his bottom, flicking his arms out to push up his sleeves and then adjusting his cuffs so that j-u-s-t the right amount of shirt protruded. Thus arranged, he folded his arms neatly on his desk and leaned forward, brown eyes twinkling.

'So,' he purred smoothly, 'what can I do for you this sunny afternoon?'

I gulped. Bugger. Bugger, bugger, bugger. This was a big mistake, why had I let Pippa talk me into this? Why hadn't I gone to some tweedy old professor who would have listened sympathetically to my tale of woe, patted my hand reassuringly and assured me all would be well, instead of this obvious ladykiller in the flashy suit? How was I supposed to unburden myself to *him*, for heaven's sakc? I mcan, it shouldn't be allowed, he was a *gynaecologist*, for crying out loud, he was going to – well, you know. And look at those eyes. Twinkling away all come-hitherishly – it was obscene. Not that he was my type, of course, not at all, but, still, he had a certain raffish charm and one simply didn't *want* to be charmed, however raffishly, when one's legs were sticking out at undignified angles. One wanted to be as detached as possible from the whole ghastly business – plan one's dinner party, rearrange the furniture, contemplate one's summer wardrobe – that kind of thing.

'Er . . . Mrs Penhalligan?' His expensively coiffured head was cocked enquiringly to one side. 'Are you with me?'

Shit. I crossed my legs in what I hoped was a rather businesslike manner and cleared my throat.

'Yes. Well, the thing is, Mr Taylor, I appear to be pregnant.' Good start, Polly, tell it like it is.

He beamed across at me. 'Excellent, excellent, that's the sort of thing we like to hear in this surgery. That's what we're here for!'

We? I looked around nervously, wondering if more Peter Bowles lookalikes were suddenly going to spring out from behind the furniture.

'Pleased, are you?' he enquired, still beaming. 'Feeling pretty chuffed? Rightly so, rightly so!'

God, he was jolly.

'Er, yes, sort of, but –'

'Jolly good, jolly good! Takes a bit of getting used to, of course, but it's a big event in anyone's life. Husband pleased?'

'Well –'

'Excellent, excellent.' He nodded, and started scribbling away on a pad. He paused, and looked up, pen and eyebrows raised. 'Done a test?'

'Sorry?'

'Pregnancy test, done one yet?'

'Oh, yes – yes I have, actually.'

'Good, when was that?'

'Um, yesterday.'

'Remember which one?'

We were well into clipped, ex-army, staccato speak now, and by God it was catching.

354

'Don't actually, went blue, though, 'bout thirty seconds.'

'Splendid, splendid.' He scribbled furiously then beamed up again.

'Now. Last period, Mrs Penhalligan. Any idea? Got a date? Got a clue?'

'Have actually, wrote it in my diary, April the twenty-sixth.'

'April twenty-sixth!' he exclaimed as if it was some kind of magical date. 'Marvellous! Now, if you'll just bear with me while I have a little . . . look . . .' He picked up a chart and ran a finger down a line of dates. 'That'll be . . . yes! Baby due February third, tremendous!' he declared joyfully. God, anyone would think it was his.

'Third all right?' he enquired.

'Er, yes, fine.' What did he expect me to say? No, actually, I'm having my roots done?

'Good.' He threw the chart in a drawer and shut it with a flourish. 'Now.' He folded his arms and leaned across the desk with a smile. 'How's Mum? Feel OK? No sickness? No gippy tummy?'

'Um, a bit, in the mornings – oh, and evenings sometimes.'

He compressed his lips and nodded, scribbling furiously. 'Only to be expected, dry biscuits, sips of water, don't get up too quickly, soon pass. Four months max. Anything else? Aches and pains?'

'N-no, but –'

'Good, excellent, Charlotte's all right?'

I looked at him in bewilderment. Who the devil was Charlotte and how the hell was I supposed to know how she was?

'Sorry?'

'Queen Charlotte's all right? Got to have it somewhere!'

'Oh! Y-yes, fine.'

'Good, good, book you in then. Now.' He held up his hand and proceeded to tick off on his fingers what were clearly key points. 'No smoking, no drinking – within reason, of course.' He winked. 'Couple of glasses of wine now and then won't hurt you – but no illegal substances, eh? Ha ha! Lots of fresh fruit and veg but go easy on the soft cheese, other than that, life goes on as normal, OK? So! There we are. All seems to be present and correct, Mrs Penhalligan, see you again in six weeks' time!' He beamed, stood up and stuck out his hand. Jesus.

'Th-that's it?' I asked incredulously.

He looked puzzled. 'Sorry?'

'That's it? You're not going to examine me or anything?'

He shuffled his papers busily, shaking his head. 'No, no real need, if your period's late and you've had a positive result from a test, well, Bob's your uncle generally.' He looked up abruptly. 'Unless of course you'd like me to examine you? Feel more reassured, perhaps? Some women do?'

'Well, I –'

'Fine! Fine! No problem, hop up over there in that case.' He indicated a bed with a curtain half drawn round it in the corner. 'No problem at all, let's have a quick look at you.'

Hop up? A quick look? God, this chap was like greased lightning, no wonder he was running early: he only allotted twenty seconds to each patient and then no doubt charged like a wounded rhino. This little interview had probably cost me well over a hundred pounds already, just for telling me what I already knew.

Nevertheless, his alacrity was infectious. He'd really got me going now. I flew behind the curtain, ripped my skirt, tights and pants off in one untidy bundle, threw them on the floor and in double-quick time jumped up and hit the deck, ready for action, so to speak. The curtain swept aside.

'Now . . .' he murmured, and went to a little table to peruse his instruments.

I gulped and shut my eyes, preparing to think of England and hoping to God I wouldn't fart at a crucial moment. I went into my usual gynae-visit deep-breathing exercises and was well on the way to feeling reasonably relaxed, when all of a sudden I had a thought. I opened my eyes. Hang on a minute – this was absurd. I had to tell him why I was here! There were specific things I needed to know – this was no routine check-up and I had to tell him so before he was telling me to hop back down again and it was too late!

'Wait!' I sat bolt upright.

He was poised for action beside me, jacket off, Marigolds on, an instrument of torture poised in his rubber-gloved hand. His eyebrows shot into his hairline. This man was a consummate eyebrow-raiser.

'Sorry?'

I swung my legs over the side of the bed.

'Just wait a minute, please, you're going so fast I can hardly think. You see, there was a specific reason why I came to see you today, not just to confirm my pregnancy but to ask you a very important question.'

'Oh?'

'Yes, only you haven't let me get a word in edgeways!'

He looked abashed and lowered his tool. 'Gosh. So sorry, Mrs Penhalligan, so used to this first visit being purely routine – do go on, I do apologize.'

'Yes, well, thank you,' I said in a peeved tone, rather milking this moment of moral superiority. It was, after all, the only one I was going to get. I cleared my throat.

'The thing is, I need to know something about the baby.'

'Y-e-s' – he folded his arms and nodded slowly and carefully – 'and what is it exactly you need to know? I'm sure it's absolutely fine, by the way, nothing to worry about at all.'

'No, it's not that, it's – well . . .' I bit my lip and shifted around from one cold buttock to the other on the hard bed, staring down at my toes. I looked up. 'It's about the father.'

'The father? Oh! Oh goodness me, yes, fathers are always welcome. Consultations, examinations, scans – oh yes, no problem there, do bring the father.' He beamed and picked up his instrument again. 'Shall we go on?'

'Er, no, no, it's not about bringing the father, it's about . . . knowing who the father is.'

He frowned. 'Rather lost me there, Mrs Penhalligan – I know the father, do I? Is that it? Penhalligan, Penhalligan – army chap, was he? Blues and Royals?'

'N-no, you don't know him.' I licked my incredibly dry lips. 'It's more to do with the fact that – I don't know him.'

He shook his head, bewildered. 'Really losing me completely now, I'm afraid, Mrs P' – heavens, he was even abbreviating my name now – 'you're surely not telling me – no. No, of course not, do excuse me.'

'What? What were you going to say?' I pounced eagerly. Please God let him be the one to say it rather than me.

He nervously smoothed down his moustache and looked embarrassed.

'I – I was going to say . . . surely you're not saying you don't know who the father is?'

'That's it! That's it exactly!'

He stared at me incredulously. 'What . . . not at all?'

I met his eyes and felt myself flushing scarlet with shame. I quickly looked down. My toenails, appropriately enough, were crimson too.

'Well, I've narrowed it down to two,' I whispered.

'Good Lord.' He whistled. 'Yes, I see. Yes, quite a predicament. Quite, um, distressing.' He pursed his lips and frowned, looking hugely embarrassed. 'Dear me, yes, and – well, extraordinary,' he murmured, 'you don't seem . . . anyway.'

I looked up quickly. He was fiddling with his cuff links.

'Don't seem what?' I demanded. 'Don't seem the type? Don't seem like the sort of girl who sleeps around and doesn't know who the father of her child is?' My voice rose hysterically. 'Well, I'm not, Mr Taylor, I'm not! I'll have you know this was a totally uncharacteristic and unprecedented departure from the straight and narrow path I usually stick to, a one-in-a-million drunken encounter with a good-for-nothing bastard who I'm quite convinced took complete advantage of me. I don't love him and he doesn't love me and I hope to goodness this is my husband's child and not his and – oh God, this is all so awful!' I covered my face with my hands and burst into tears.

Within a twinkling a blue and white striped Gieves and Hawkes arm had whizzed around my shoulders and a yellow silk hanky was thrust into my hands.

'There, there, it's all going to be fine,' he murmured. 'You'll see, these things always sort themselves out. It'll be fine.'

Ah, there they were at last, the magic, comforting words they obviously all learn at medical school but are so bloody economical with. What had taken him so long? So soothing, yet so tear-provoking too.

'Oooh, no it *won't*!' I blubbed into the glorious silk hanky which I felt sure had never in its life been used for practical purposes. 'It's such a mess! What on earth am I going to *do*?'

A fresh flood followed this outburst, plus more reassuring shoulder-hugging from Peter Bowles. I sobbed and sniffled into his hanky and all the time I was breaking down part of me couldn't quite believe I was doing it. Heavens, Polly, in front of a suave Harley Street consultant? All over his immaculate pinstripe? Naked from the waist down? – me, not him, of course. But it was no good. The floodgates had never officially been opened on this subject, but now that they were it was damned hard to shut them again.

Eventually, though, the tears subsided enough for me to at least be able to see and the sobs became mere gasps and hiccups. Peter Bowles patted my hand.

'Now you just sit there quietly for a second and I'll be back in just a mo with a nice cuppa tea.'

He disappeared and I tried desperately to get a grip on myself. I blew my nose, wiped my eyes and shoved my hair behind my ears, attempting at least to look a little more presentable, but it was jolly difficult to look even remotely dignified sitting there as I was without my skirt on and with just my T-shirt protecting my vitals. I pulled it down, frantically trying to cover my thighs which are only fit to be seen in the dark and then only fleetingly. I spotted a handy blanket at the end of the bed and hurriedly pulled it across them. By the time Peter Bowles returned bearing hot, sweet tea, I had at least gained some sort of control and composure.

'Thank you,' I whispered, taking the cup and saucer from him and sipping thirstily.

'Now then,' he said kindly, perching beside me on the bed, 'what are we going to do about all this, eh?'

I shook my head. 'I don't know,' I whispered, 'I really don't.'

'Do you want to keep the baby?'

'Oh yes, yes I want to keep it – at least, I'm pretty sure I do. When you've told me who it belongs to I'll know for sure, of course.'

He frowned. 'Sorry?'

'Well, you can do that, can't you? Take a blood test or something? My husband's AB negative which is pretty rare, so if we took some blood from the baby and it turned out to be the same, well, that would be terrific, wouldn't it? Then we'd be almost sure it was his.'

Peter Bowles pursed his lips and looked at the floor. Then he folded his arms and turned to look at me.

'Mrs Penhalligan,' he said gently, 'there is absolutely no

way of knowing who the father of your child is before it's born.'

I stared at him, aghast.

'What?' I whispered. 'No way of knowing? But there must be!'

He shook his head. ''Fraid not.'

'But – but what about all those tests you do – amnio-cen-whatsit and – and all those blood tests and things?'

'Amniocentesis is about extracting fluid, not blood. It tells us if the baby has Down's syndrome and it can also tell us the sex of the child. The blood tests we do are samples of *your* blood, not the baby's, to check for other abnormalities. There isn't one test that is actually done on the baby itself. It would be too dangerous, you see, and we certainly wouldn't attempt anything simply to find out who the father is.'

'So . . . what you're telling me is . . . there's no way of knowing?' I stared at him in horror.

'No way at all, I'm afraid. The only thing we can do is try to work out the date of conception. Did you sleep with both men in the middle of your cycle?'

I cringed deeply. Must he be so basic? I supposed he must. 'Yes,' I whispered.

'Within weeks or days of each other?'

I clenched my toes and squirmed. 'Days,' I breathed, 'possibly two days, I think.' Oh God, please let me die now. I dared not look but I knew the eyebrows were well raised.

'Hmmmmm . . .' he murmured, 'in that case I'm afraid there really is no way of knowing.'

I think I must have looked awfully shaken, because he squeezed my hand.

'Sorry,' he said gently. 'What I suggest you do is make a decision as soon as possible as to whether or not you want to keep the baby. The sooner you make that decision the better it is all round, for you and the foetus. You do see that, don't you?'

I nodded, not trusting myself to speak. Suddenly the baby had become a foetus.

'And if it's all right with you,' he went on, standing up, 'I think I'd still like to make that examination, just to make absolutely sure. Is that OK?' he asked gently, his brisk army manner totally evaporated now.

'Yes, of course, Mr Bowles,' I whispered.

He frowned. 'Taylor, actually.'

'I – I mean Taylor.'

I took the blanket off my thighs, swung my legs back on to the bed again and lay down, dumb with disbelief. No way of knowing? No way at all? What on earth was I going to do?

Peter Bowles put his Marigolds on again and I lay there, staring blankly at the elaborate plaster cornicing on the ceiling. God, what a mess. I sighed. Well, at least I had plenty to think about as he went about his business; I had enough problems to fill an entire woman's magazine. What must he think of me?

I swivelled my head slightly to the left and took a sneaky look at his face. Inscrutable, of course. Another thing they all learn at medical school. How to make a gynaecological examination without betraying the slightest trace of emotion. But, suddenly, he frowned. He seemed to take a closer look, then he reached behind him to a little table and picked up what looked like . . . a pair of tweezers.

Tweezers! What the hell were they for? I raised my head slightly from the bed and watched, fascinated, as he used them to remove something . . . from within my person. Heavens! From inside? Surely not. What the hell was it? Had something fallen out? Had the *baby* fallen out? He turned away, tweezers in hand, and, still frowning, gingerly dropped whatever it was . . . in the waste-paper bin. Bloody hell, in the *bin*? What *was* it?

'Um, wh-what was that?' I ventured querulously.

He shook his head, lips pursed. 'Noo . . . nothing, nothing at all.'

'No, really, I'd like to know. What was it?'

'Nothing of any consequence, nothing to worry about.' He resumed his examination.

I stared at him, incredulous. Nothing of any consequence? He removes something from *inside* me, chucks it in the bin and says it's nothing of any consequence? Jesus!

He straightened up and slipped his gloves off in a businesslike manner.

'All finished, Mrs Penhalligan, and yes, you are most definitely pregnant, cervix very swollen. If you'd like to pop your clothes back on I'll just go and write a few notes. Take your time.'

He slipped around the curtain, drew it back again for me, and disappeared to his desk.

I sat up, slipped off the bed and grabbed my clothes, hurriedly tugging them back on. Then I cocked an ear to the curtain to make sure he wasn't coming back, and tiptoed over to the bin in the corner.

I peered in. It was empty. How extraordinary, empty, except for – wait a minute, a small piece of paper at the bottom. I reached in and picked it out. I turned it over in my hand and stared at it. It was a Green Shield stamp. I frowned, completely foxed. A Green Shield stamp? Up my whatsit? Surely not. Suddenly I went cold. My jaw dropped. I clapped my hand to my mouth. Oh good grief! It must have been stuck to the tissue! The grotty one I'd found at the bottom of my handbag, it must have been stuck to it along with all the other bits of fluff and gunge, probably been there for centuries! Oh God, fancy having a Green Shield stamp up my – what must he think?

I swept the curtain aside and hurried to his desk.

'Mr Taylor, I –'

'Won't keep you a moment . . .' he purred, cutting me short. His dark head was bent low, he was writing studiously. I bit my lip. What did it say? What was he writing? I craned my neck but I couldn't see. I could imagine, though. 'Doesn't . . . know . . . who . . . the . . . father . . . of the . . . child . . . is . . . and keeps Green . . . Shield . . . stamps –' I couldn't bear it.

'L-look, Mr Taylor, about the stamp, you see the thing is, there wasn't any loo paper downstairs so I used an old tissue at the bottom of my handbag and – and I think it must have –'

'No need, Mrs Penhalligan,' he said, shaking his head vehemently, still writing away, 'no need at all, really.'

'No, but –'

'Now then.' He looked up abruptly and gave me a bright smile. 'I'd like to see you again in about another six weeks just to make sure everything's going smoothly, so let's see now, that would be . . .' He consulted his diary.

'But I really would like to explain about the –'

'July the sixteenth. That suit?'

He didn't want to know. He simply didn't want to know, did he? And who could blame him? Wasn't it enough of a shock to an eminent gynaecologist to have a patient who didn't know who the father of her child was without wishing to know why she should feel the need to secrete ancient voucher stamps so snugly about her person? And why did it have to be Green Shield? So naff, so common, so very un-Harley Street?

I bit my lip and stared at my shoes, suffused with shame. Peter Bowles neatly recapped his pen and arranged it, just so, above his papers. He flicked out his arms, realigned his cuffs, folded his arms and smiled in a most professional way.

'Y-e-s, well, that seems to be all for the moment, Mrs Penhalligan. I'll see you again on the sixteenth and, if I don't hear anything to the contrary, I'll book you into Queen Charlotte's, OK? I do hope everything sorts itself out. I'm quite sure – well, I'm quite sure you'll soon come to terms with your rather, ahem, unusual situation.' He coughed nervously. 'Now, any questions? Good, good,' he said, getting smartly to his feet and thus forestalling any other horrendous enquiries I might have. He stuck his hand out. 'Look forward to seeing you on the sixteenth then. Goodbye!'

His smile was kind, but I couldn't meet it. I stared red-faced at his leather-topped desk, like an errant child in a headmaster's study. I nodded and extended my hand, hoping he'd make contact with it without me having to look up. He did.

'Thank you so much,' I whispered when he'd released it, 'see you on the sixteenth.'

I picked up my bag and Sam's case, turned round and shuffled miserably from the room.

Chapter Twenty-one

That evening I was ambushed by a premature attack of morning sickness. I lay on Pippa's sofa with a bucket poised on the carpet beneath me, feeling incredibly sorry for myself. Pippa was on the floor beside me in her dressing gown, painting her toenails with meticulous attention. I watched as her brushstrokes swept slowly up and down.

'Remind me never to take medical advice from you again, Pippa,' I muttered bitterly, 'not even if I'm dying. I'll arrange my own doctors from now on, thanks very much. Incidentally, could you give that a rest for a sec? The fumes are going right up my nose.'

'Nearly finished,' said Pippa, hastily applying a few final strokes. She screwed the top on the varnish and sat up. 'Well, I'm sorry, I was only trying to help, and so what if he is charming? It's better than having some repulsive old toad examine you, isn't it?'

'No, it isn't, give me a repulsive old toad any day. At least it doesn't matter if you make a complete fool of yourself.'

I tried not to gag as she waved her feet in the air to dry them and I got another noxious whiff.

'And if you must do that I'd move away from the bucket if I were you,' I whispered. 'I'm not sure how good my aim is.'

Pippa got up hurriedly and plumped down in an

armchair opposite. She stretched her legs out and surveyed her sparkling red toes.

'I must admit old Taylor is rather yummy, just my type now that I'm into older men. Did he mention me at all? Ask how my blood pressure was or anything? It always seems to rocket when I visit him.'

'No, he didn't,' I snapped, 'we had enough to talk about without getting on to your very minor problems, it wasn't even as if he could solve mine!'

Pippa frowned. 'Yes, I must say that does seem a bit rum. I mean, if they can do all that amazing *in vitro* stuff, you'd think they could sort out a tiny technicality like who the father of your child is, wouldn't you?'

'I have an idea one is supposed to have an inkling one-self, at least that's the impression he gave me,' I said grimly. 'God, what's that revolting smell?'

'It's a packet of crisps, Polly,' she said patiently. 'Can't I even eat a packet of crisps in my own home?'

'Not when they smell like rotting armpits you can't. Please put them away, Pippa, unless you want a technicolour carpet.' I clutched my mouth dramatically and rolled my eyes.

She sighed and screwed the top of the bag shut. 'It's all very well but I'm really hungry, you know. I haven't had supper yet because you can't stand the smell of baked beans, I can't paint my nails, I can't fry sausages –'

'Don't even mention sausages,' I whispered, gulping back the bile.

'But I thought this sickness lark was supposed to be restricted to mornings. How come you get it in the evenings too?'

'I don't know, Pippa,' I groaned, resting my head on the arm of the sofa, 'and I'm sorry, really I am. I know it's frightfully inconvenient of me and I apologize for feeling so lousy, so sick, so tired, so permanently nauseous, so tummy-churningly wretched. It must be awful for you.'

'Oh, it's OK,' said Pippa cheerily, lighting a cigarette and somehow missing my shovel-load of sarcasm, 'I don't really mind. It might be nice to open the fridge door now and then without you collapsing in a heap and shrieking for the smelling salts though. D'you think it would be all right if I did it now? You're not going to smell the salami long-distance, are you, only if I don't make myself a sandwich soon I'll expire.'

'No, no,' I muttered, 'you go and stuff your face, see if I care.'

'D'you want anything?'

'You could bring me a dry biscuit to nibble on, I might just be able to manage that. If it's not too much trouble, of course.'

'No trouble at all!'

She got up with an alacrity that made me wince and bounded off to the kitchen. I groaned and shut my eyes. A few minutes later she was back with a plate piled high with dead meat. She sidled guiltily past, tossing me a biscuit as she went.

'All right if I eat in here?' she asked, ostentatiously scraping her chair right back. 'I mean, right in the corner, practically in the garden?'

'Sure, sure, just don't be surprised if I honk, that's all.'

I moaned low and half closed my eyes. Pippa regarded

me thoughtfully as she munched her salami sandwich. Suddenly she put her plate down.

'Can I have a feel?'

'What?'

'Your tummy, can I feel it?' She jumped up and knelt down beside me, pulling up my jumper.

'Pippa, for goodness' sake, I'm only a few weeks pregnant – you're not going to feel anything!'

'Even so . . .' She put her hand on my tummy. 'Weird, isn't it,' she said after a moment, 'to think there's something in there. How does it feel? D'you feel different? I mean, apart from sick, d'you feel like you're carrying a baby?'

Suddenly I felt rather important. I sat up and adopted a slightly superior tone. 'Well, yes, I suppose one does feel a bit special, rather – you know, chosen.'

'Chosen? God, anyone would think you were the Virgin Mary!'

'Hardly,' I said grimly, 'but all the same, yes, I do feel incredibly blessed.' I smiled serenely and stroked my tummy like the girl in the waiting room had, trying hard to re-create the Madonna look.

'Is that why you're looking so gormless?' Pippa kneaded around with her hand looking for action. 'Is it kicking yet? Can you feel it?'

'No, of course not,' I snapped, dispensing with the blessed look, 'it's only about the size of a pea, for goodness' sake – ouch, geddoff, that hurt! In fact,' I reflected, 'that's how I like to think of it at the moment.'

'What, as a pea?'

'Well, some sort of vegetable, not a baby at any rate, not until I know more about it. A little potato perhaps, or a carrot.'

'Gosh, it would be a bit disappointing to give birth to an eight-pound carrot, wouldn't it? Imagine lugging it around for nine months thinking it was a baby then out pops a carrot.'

'It would come out pretty easily though, wouldn't it? Just the right shape!' We giggled.

Suddenly I frowned and pulled my jumper down. 'And that's another thing, Pippa, this giving-birth lark. I'm not at all sure about it.'

She sat back on her heels. 'What d'you mean?'

'Well, I'm not very good at pain. As a matter of fact I've got an extremely low threshold – some people have, you know.'

'Oh, it'll be a breeze, don't worry about it. All you need is the right birthing partner to spur you on, keep your pecker up.'

'What the hell's a birthing partner?'

'Oh, it's someone who sprays you with water and warms your feet up and brings along sandwiches – oh, and plays soothing music, that kind of thing.'

I frowned. 'Music? What, on a guitar or something?'

'No, idiot, on a tape recorder, unless you particularly want a live guitarist. I'm sure it can be arranged.'

'So who is this person?' I felt none the wiser and had visions of a Cat Stephens lookalike droning away on a guitar in the corner of my delivery room, occasionally pausing to eat a sandwich, fiddle with my feet or spray me with water.

Pippa looked a bit uncomfortable. 'Er, well, actually it's your husband, but of course in your rather unusual situation . . .'

I sat bolt upright. 'Oh help! You mean I haven't got a birthing partner? You're right! I can't have Nick and I certainly don't want Sam – oh, Pippa, what am I going to do? I can't possibly have this baby on my own!'

'Well, don't panic, I'm pretty sure it doesn't necessarily have to be your husband, I'm sure it could be – I know!' Suddenly her eyes shone dangerously. 'It could be me!'

'Er, well, Pippa, I'm not sure if –'

'Yes! Of course, I'd be brilliant . . .' She was gazing rapturously into space now and I could tell she'd already got herself kitted out in the Florence Nightingale garb and was mopping my fevered brow yelling 'PUSH! PUSH!' at the same time as maintaining feverish eye contact with the dreamy white-coated doctor in charge.

'Yes, well, we'll see shall we, Pippa?' I said a trifle nervously. 'Actually I wondered if I might try the whole thing unconscious – some people do that, don't they?'

Pippa frowned. 'I think if you have a Caesarean it's possible, but I'm pretty sure you're only allowed one of those if your pelvis is too small to squeeze the baby out, and I hardly think, Polly' – she looked doubtfully at my distinctly child-bearing hips – 'you'd qualify on that score.'

I sighed. 'Oh well, that's out then. I'll just have to rely on pain relief. They have all sorts of knock-out drops these days, don't they?'

'Oh yes, they'll toss you the occasional aspirin as you writhe around in agony.'

'Aspirin!' I gasped.

'No, idiot, you can have an epidural; it paralyses you from the waist down.'

My eyes grew wide with fear.

'Oh, not permanently, at least not in most cases, although my sister knew someone who –'

'Thank you, Pippa,' I said quickly, 'I'd rather not know.'

'Oh, it's perfectly safe as long as it's put in by a competent anaesthetist, and as long as they can get it *in* in time, of course.'

'What d'you mean?'

'Well, you might not make it to the hospital: you might drop the baby in the back of the car, or on the bus or –'

'Oh thanks, really dignified.'

'Well, don't you remember Jane Hutchinson's sister? Hers popped out in Sainsbury's car park! Luckily the car-park attendant had done a St John Ambulance course so he had a vague idea and managed to sort of pull it out, but God' – she rolled her eyes dramatically – 'she'd have been snookered if it hadn't been for him.'

'Oh terrific, so if I get some oily car-park attendant officiating at what should be the most poignant and moving moment in my life I should count my blessings, is that it?'

'Well, you have to be prepared for all eventualities,' said Pippa sagely. 'I mean, what about Kate Rawlinson?'

'What about Kate Rawlinson?' I said warily. I had the impression Pippa was getting a vicarious kick out of dredging up these horror stories. 'Had hers in a public loo, did she? With the lavatory attendant as her birth partner?'

'Oh no, she was in hospital, but she wasn't on the labour ward because they thought she wasn't going to have it for ages and it was only when a passing doctor stuck his hand up to check everything was OK that he discovered the baby was on its way and the cord was wrapped round its neck!'

'Is that good?'

'Of course not, you idiot, it could strangle itself! No, it was awful, but luckily the doctor managed to slip his fingers under the cord to stop it getting any tighter, but then they had to somehow get her to the labour room which was two floors down!' Pippa's eyes were shining now as she relived the horror. She leaned forward. 'So guess what?'

'What?' I muttered nervously.

'Well, the doctor had to keep his hand right up – literally elbow deep – and they pushed her into the lift with him still attached and then when they got out they had to run really fast down loads of corridors, and she was bouncing around all over the place and this doctor *still* had his hand right –'

'Thank you, Pippa, that will DO!' I screeched with my hands over my ears. 'I simply don't want to *know* about any more nightmare deliveries if it's all right with you. I mean *we're* here for God's sake: our mothers must have done it, there must be some women who have these things without a hitch, mustn't there?'

Pippa pursed her lips and gave this some thought. Eventually she shook her head. 'Not to my knowledge, Polly.'

I sighed. 'Oh well, I'll manage somehow I suppose.'

I sank back on the sofa and had just about rested my head when the phone rang, making me jump. It was right

375

by my ear but I simply didn't have the energy to swing around and get it. Pippa reached over and picked it up.

'Hello? . . . Oh hi! . . . Yes, she is, hang on a minute.' She clamped her hand over the mouthpiece and grinned. 'It's the father of your unborn child!'

I ground my teeth together. 'Which one?' I hissed.

'The married one!' Her grin was getting bigger.

'Pippa . . .' I eyed her dangerously.

'OK, sorry, it's Sam.'

I glared at her as I took the receiver, hauling myself over on to my tummy and up on to my elbows. I felt like I had a sack of potatoes on my head.

'Hello?' I said weakly. Surely we'd said all we had to say?

'Hello, Polly?' He sounded anxious. 'Listen, you haven't by any chance got my case, have you, only I think I left it in the taxi.'

'You did, and I have. It's right here actually.' I eyed the fiercely trendy silver case sitting under the table next to my legs and aimed a vicious little kick at it.

'Oh, thank goodness for that, what a relief, I thought I'd lost it! Thanks for picking it up, could you possibly ask Pippa to bring it in with her tomorrow?'

'Sure, I was going to do that anyway.'

'Great, thanks so much. Oh, and, Polly' – he lowered his voice slightly, 'listen, there's some pretty confidential stuff in there regarding the company, so if you could give it to Pippa in the morning when she leaves, rather than now, I'd be grateful, only I don't really want her to, well –'

'To look? Sam, as if she would!'

'No, no, of course not, silly of me even to mention it, but you know what it's like – some people like to snoop a bit, not Pippa, of course, but – well, you know!' He laughed nervously. 'Thanks, Polly . . .'

'Not at all, goodbye, Sam,' I said, with what I hoped was grim finality.

I put the receiver down, leaned across and picked up the case. I swung it round by its handle. Big mistake, Sam, big mistake.

I grinned across at Pippa. 'Guess what?'

'What?'

'This here case contains some awfully crucial information pertaining to your company, Pipps.'

'Oooh, really? Is that what he said? Hang on, I'll just go and get a yoghurt and then we'll open it, shall we?'

'Thought you might say that.'

She crammed the last of the evil-smelling salami into her mouth and dashed out to the kitchen for some nice sour milk to taunt me with. The moment she'd gone the phone rang again.

'Pippa!' I yelled.

'Can't you get it?' she bellowed from the kitchen, but dashed back, grumbling, to pick it up.

'Hello? . . . Oh hi!' She clamped her hand over the mouthpiece. 'It's the father again.'

'Sam?'

'No! Guess again!' She giggled. I could see she was finding this hard to resist.

'I'm going to kill you later!' I hissed.

She composed herself with difficulty. 'Sorry, it's Nick.'

'Nick!' I felt the blood drain from my face. 'What does he want?'

'Well, I don't know – talk to him, for God's sake. He's not

377

going to eat you!' She rammed the receiver into my trembling hands.

'H-hello?' I whispered.

'Polly? It's me.' He sounded fierce. 'Look, I got some convoluted message from Mum saying you'd gone off to London to investigate the burglary, is that right?'

'Well, I just thought I'd –'

'Well *don't*. For God's sake, it's not for you to poke your nose into this – it's the police's job – and apart from anything else it could be bloody dangerous. She said you had some harebrained idea about going to see Bruce. I couldn't believe it! You haven't seen him yet, have you?'

'Oh, er, no, no, of course not.'

'Good, I absolutely forbid it. Who knows what state of mind he might be in? If he's guilty, he'll be furious at being caught and if he's not guilty he'll be bitter as hell at being arrested. If you go skipping round there offering tea and sympathy, he might just go ballistic, so don't go, OK?'

A tiny glimmer of hope shone out of a very dark sky. 'No, darling, I won't, and sweet of you to worry.'

'Don't push your luck, Polly. I just don't want to have to pick up the pieces, that's all.'

I gulped. 'Oh. Right.'

There was a pause.

'Um, how are you, Nick?'

'I'm fine,' he said shortly. 'Except that a fox got into the chicken run last night and killed most of the laying stock – that didn't improve my temper, I can tell you.'

'Oh dear,' I said lamely.

'Yes, eleven dead and feathers everywhere. Doesn't exactly add to the gaiety of nations, does it? Incidentally,

378

have you found anywhere to live yet? Sarah said there was quite a nice house over at Polzeath.'

I couldn't speak for a moment.

'Polly?'

'Y-yes, that's right, I'll go and look at it when I get back.'

'Good. No rush, but decent houses don't hang around for long, you know – it'll get snapped up. Anyway, remember what I said about Bruce. Goodbye.'

He put the phone down.

I lowered the receiver back into its slot, feeling awfully sick. Tears welled in my eyes.

'What happened, what did he say?'

'He – he asked me if I'd found anywhere to live,' I whispered. The tears began to topple over the brink.

'Oh! Oh dear. Is that why he rang?'

'No, he rang to tell me not to go and see Bruce.'

'Bit late for that.'

'Exactly, but don't tell him. He thought it might be dangerous.'

'Well, that's good news,' Pippa said brightly. 'He obviously cares, don't you think?'

'He might care enough not to want to see me decapitated but he doesn't care enough to want me back, that's for sure,' I whispered. I wiped my wet face with the back of my hand and sighed. 'Said he didn't want to have to pick up the pieces.' I slumped back on the sofa. 'He was awfully terse.'

'Oh well, you know Nick, he's not exactly the gushing type, is he? At least he rang. Now come on, buck up,' said Pippa hastily, trying to ward off a fresh flow of tears. 'Let's have a look at this.'

She picked Sam's case up from under where I'd dropped it, pulled it up on to her lap and flipped the lid open. I watched gloomily as she rifled through the papers. I'd completely lost interest now, and, anyway, it all looked deadly dull to me. Nick, my Nick ... he'd sounded so cold, like a stranger. And he wanted me out of the way as soon as possible. I stared into space, trying to gulp back tears as Pippa flipped through the papers. Every so often she'd exclaim as she came across a new snippet of gossip.

'Oh really? Gosh, that's interesting – a merger's possible apparently ... oh, with Bazooka Films ... Hey it looks like Marion's finally going to be fired, 'bout time too – she's lazy and good-for-nothing. All she does is paint her nails – ooh look, his Filofax. I bet he's lost without this.'

She went to put it back but I grabbed it from her.

'Polly!' She looked shocked.

'What?'

'You're not going to look at it, are you?'

'Well, you're going through his case.'

'That's different, a Filofax is – well, it's like a diary.'

'Oh don't be silly, it's just a notebook really – ooh look, photos.'

'That's Sally,' said Pippa, instantly abandoning her principles and peering round over my shoulder. 'Pretty, don't you think?'

'Very,' I said, staring at the rather shy-looking girl with long blond hair and freckles who smiled back at me from a deckchair in her garden.

'And that's not actually awfully good of her,' said Pippa,

'she's a stunner in the flesh, oh look, there's one tucked in behind it, maybe that's better.'

She pulled out a tiny snapshot. 'Oh!'

'What?' I peered over. 'Oh! Golly.'

It was a photo of Serena Montgomery. We stared at the picture, then at each other.

'How very odd . . .' said Pippa slowly. 'What on earth d'you think he's doing with a picture of her in his wallet?'

'Could it be for casting purposes, or something? I mean he does use her quite a lot in his films, perhaps it's to remind him what she looks like?'

'In his Filofax though? Behind a picture of his wife?'

We gazed at each other.

'Pippa, you don't think . . .'

'Oh no. Surely not. He doesn't even know her that well, at least that's what he says.'

'Makes quite a point of saying it too, doesn't he?' I said slowly. 'Always telling someone how he doesn't know her very well and doesn't like her much either. Odd how she crops up in all his films and commercials though, isn't it? Methinks he doth protest too much.'

Pippa looked shocked. 'But, Polly, he's a happily married man!'

'But is he, Pippa? I mean, the more I think about it the more I wonder. I saw him at lunchtime today and to be honest he was desperate to have an affair with me, and if he'd have one with me, well, why not other girls as well?'

'But I thought he said it had never happened before, that you were the first?'

'He did, but then if you think about it, he would,

wouldn't he? He's not going to admit he's always played around with other women, is he?'

'I suppose not . . . Golly, I always thought he was happily married.'

'I'm beginning to think he's about as happily married as Prince Charles.'

'So you reckon he's cheating on Sally?'

'Well, of course he's cheating on her, we know that much from the high jinks he got up to with me, so why not with Serena too?'

'Crikey. Serena.'

We stared at the photo. Pippa shook her head. 'I don't know, they just seem so unlikely . . .'

'Only because he pretends to bitch about her so much, but when you think about it – glamorous film director, beautiful actress, what could be more obvious?'

Pippa raised her eyebrows. 'What indeed?'

We peered at the photo again. It was a tiny black and white shot of Serena sitting by a pool, no doubt in some exotic location, throwing back her beautiful blonde hair and laughing into the camera, displaying perfect white teeth.

'You've got to admit, she is pretty gorgeous,' said Pippa. 'I suppose he just couldn't resist her. I expect he was bowled over by her when they were away shooting somewhere, just couldn't help himself.'

'Mmm, she's certainly got the capacity to twist men round her little finger. Look what happened to Nick: he went out with her for ages before he saw the light. Still, Serena and Sam. That's quite a turn-up for the books, isn't it? I wonder if his wife knows?'

'Doubt it,' said Pippa. 'I'm sure she thinks he's totally faithful – oh God, there's the phone again, it's like the blasted BT exchange tonight and I bet it's not for me either.' She reached across. 'Hello?'

I tensed up, wondering which of my possible impregnators it might be this time.

'Oh hi, Amanda, how are you?'

I relaxed. Thank goodness. I stared down at the photo again. Sam and Serena. Who would have thought? I had a quick flick through the diary section of the Filofax and, sure enough, now and again I spotted a discreet little 'S' in the lunch and evening sections. And to think, he'd been hoping to pop a little 'P' in as well. He really was a bit of a lad, wasn't he?

'Polly? Yes, she's right here, hang on.'

I looked up. 'For me?' I mouthed. She nodded. I frowned and took the phone.

'Hello?'

'Polly, it's me, Amanda, how you doin'?'

'Er, fine, fine thank you.'

'Good. Listen, I wondered if you'd got time to meet me for a quick drink, only I need to have a little chat with you about this an' that.'

'With me?'

'Yeah, if you don't mind.'

'Er, sure. When did you have in mind?'

'Well, I'm still at work but I'll be driving past Pippa's place at about nine o'clock, so why don't I meet you down the Scarsdale?'

'Tonight? Why not tomorrow or –'

'Can't wait, I'm afraid, for one thing I'm off on location

tomorrow, but apart from anything else I've gotta get something off me chest.'

I froze. Jesus! I swallowed hard. 'Er, righto then, I'll meet you there at nine. Um, what's it about, Amanda?'

'It's about Sam. See you later, Polly.' She rang off.

I replaced the receiver slowly and stared at Pippa.

'What?' she asked.

I licked my rather dry lips. 'She wants to meet me,' I whispered, 'to talk about Sam.'

'What about Sam?'

'Well, I don't know, do I? But – oh God, Pippa, she sounded really odd, really – well, cross actually.'

'But why doesn't she just come here for a drink?'

'I think she wants to see me alone,' I whispered. 'Oh, Pippa, I think I know what this is all about – she's going to kill me, I know she is!'

'Don't be silly, why on earth should she do that?'

'Because I've seen the way she looks at him.'

'At who?'

'At Sam! She's having an affair with him, I'm convinced. Or she's *had* an affair with him and he's spurned her, or she *wants* to have an affair with him or – or something, anyway, I'm absolutely sure of it. She's found out about our night of passion and she's coming to get me!' I went cold. 'Of course! She saw me dancing with him in Annabel's and she probably saw us leave together – oh, Pippa, what am I going to do?'

Pippa looked very confused. 'But . . . I thought we'd decided he was having an affair with Serena?'

'Well, why not Amanda too? I mean, he slotted me in, so why not her as well?'

'But –'

'And don't tell me he's happily married!' I shrieked. 'The man's clearly a sex maniac. He should be in that clinic in Hollywood, the one Michael Douglas went into for sex addiction; he's quite obviously a nymphomaniac!'

Pippa frowned. 'I think only women can be nymphomaniacs.'

'Typical, if it's a woman she's a maniac, if it's a man it's something medical, an addiction – but, oh God, Pippa this is awful, she's coming to sort me out!' I wrung my hands in terror.

'Don't be silly, Amanda's not violent.'

'How d'you know? She's from the East End, isn't she? I mean, that's where her roots are and that's where the underworld is. She's coming to warn me off, fill me in – d'you know what she said? She said she wanted to get something off her chest, that's probably rhyming slang for dead meat or something.'

Pippa frowned. 'Doesn't even rhyme . . .'

'It probably doesn't have to!' I shrieked. I was getting a bit hysterical now. 'The really nasty ones probably don't, to make them more sinister.'

'Now, Polly, you really are overreacting. I'm sure there's some perfectly simple explanation. Just relax, will you?'

'Easy for you to say,' I muttered grimly, 'you're not the one she wants to kneecap.'

Suddenly I had an idea. I curled up defiantly on the sofa and buried my head under a cushion.

'I feel sick.'

Pippa regarded me severely. 'Polly, Amanda is a friend of mine – you can't stand her up. You're meeting her in a crowded pub, for heaven's sake; there's absolutely no way you can come to any harm. You're going, OK?'

I stayed rooted to my cushion for a moment, then stupidly looked up and caught her eye. It was enough. I banged my head on the arm of the sofa and groaned.

'OK,' I muttered, 'I'm going.'

Chapter Twenty-two

Half an hour later, feeling like death in a sweatshirt and clutching a warm tonic water to my chest, I perched nervously in a corner of the crowded pub. I watched the door, wide-eyed with apprehension, and every time it opened I jumped off my chair. After ten minutes of this rather tiring, bottom-numbing gymnastics, I decided I'd had enough. I drained my tonic and looked at my watch. Ten past nine. Surely I'd done my bit? I'd waited a while and she hadn't shown – couldn't I creep off home to bed with impunity now? Two more minutes, my conscience told me, then I'd be away.

I sat back and a couple of likely lads propping up the bar leered over in my general direction. They had to be very desperate or very drunk – I looked like something out of *EastEnders*. I glared back and scratched my chin with my wedding-ring finger, wishing I had a T-shirt with 'Bog off I'm pregnant' written on it. They leered again, had a quick confab and looked perilously close to swaggering over, which frankly was all I needed right now. I glared as icily as I could and was just about to pick my nose to really put them off when the door opened and Amanda walked in. I was almost pleased to see her.

'Sorry I'm late,' she breezed, with not too much of a murderous smile, 'got a bit held up.' She eyed my empty glass. 'Blimey, you've obviously been 'ere ages, sorry 'bout that. Another gin?'

'Er, just a tonic, please.'

She raised her eyebrows. 'Not like you, is it?'

I smiled weakly. 'No, I suppose not.'

She shrugged. 'OK, back in a mo.'

She put her case down, flung her jacket over the back of a chair and elbowed her way determinedly to the bar, taking no nonsense at all from the two grinning idiots supporting it and looking like a woman who was used to pushing people out of the way. I couldn't help noticing that her arms looked awfully strong in her skimpy black T-shirt, in fact she looked worryingly fit all over. I wondered if she worked out? Pumped iron or something?

I reached nervously for a cigarette, not to smoke, you understand, just to fondle. Recently I'd found that it helped just to be in contact with one, to hold it, gaze at it and basically reassure myself that this was just a temporary lull in my smoking career, that they hadn't disappeared from my life forever. I was nervously smelling one and rolling it around in my hands when Amanda came back. She put the drinks down and pulled a lighter out of her pocket.

''Ere.' The flame flickered in my face.

'Er, no, it's OK,' I said, putting the ciggie back in my bag. 'I'll smoke it later.'

She sat down next to me. 'I've got masses if yer short.'

'No, no, I've got loads, it's just that I'm – trying to give up.'

'What's this, Polly, no gin, no fags, not pregnant or anything, are you?'

'No!' I gasped. 'No, good Lord no, of *course* not! No, I'm just on a bit of a health kick at the moment. Pregnant! Ha! What a joke!'

I lifted my tonic water to my nervous lips and realized my hand was shaking perceptibly. You idiot, Polly, for goodness' sake be careful. If she finds out you're carrying Sam's baby she'll probably finish you off right here and now. I surreptitiously sidled round the table a bit, wondering which way I should duck if she took a swing at me.

'So how've you bin?' she asked, convivially enough.

'Fine, fine,' I croaked, cranking up a smile.

She lit a cigarette and I watched enviously as the smoke flew in a perfect straight line over my head. I craned my nostrils skywards and inhaled deeply, hoping to catch a gratuitous whiff.

'A-and you?' I faltered, remembering my manners.

'Oh, not so bad, up to me eyeballs in work, but there you go, better than being bored out of yer skull, innit?'

'Yeah, yeah, I s'pose it is.' Oh no, Polly, don't slip into that again. 'Yah, right,' I brayed hastily, 'absolutely nothing worse than being bored is there? Simply gha-a-stly.'

She looked at me carefully. I gulped. Now she probably thought I was taking the mickey. I flushed and threw back my tonic water, chucking most of it down my sweatshirt. She handed me a hanky.

'Listen, Polly,' she said as I mopped away, 'I wanna ask you something.'

'Oh yes?' I croaked casually, studiously avoiding her eye.

'You might think this is none of my business, but are you havin' an affair wiv Sam?'

I gasped and looked up, eyes – hopefully – full of shock and horror.

'Good Lord, no! Gosh, what a question – with Sam? Good gracious me, no, perish the thought, of course not!'

She eyed me speculatively. 'What about that night in Annabel's then? Or just after, to be more specific?'

'Wh-what about it?'

'Come on, I saw the way you were lookin' at 'im. I saw you dancing wiv 'im too – you'd even started to take yer kit off; yer underwear was hangin' out all over the place.'

'It was a body,' I muttered.

'Well, whatever it was it was all over the shop, and you were definitely overexcited, practically had yer tongue round 'is tonsils. I couldn't bear to watch so I went to the lav and when I came back you'd both dun a bunk. What did you do, slip off to a hotel or something?'

'Oh God, Amanda . . .'

'Well did you? Come on, I'm not gonna spit in your eye or anything. I just need to know, did you go off wiv 'im or what?'

I sighed. I couldn't look at her. I was also beginning to suffer from the rather debilitating effects of sobriety. It had been a good eight hours since I'd had a drink. I picked up a beer mat and twisted it nervously in my hands.

'Look,' I muttered, 'it was a big mistake, all right? I was incredibly drunk – we both were. These things happen.' I licked my lips.

'What things?'

I shrugged miserably. 'You know . . .' I sighed. 'Yes, all right, we did go to a hotel. For the night.' I looked up; her eyes were pinning me to the wall. 'But, honestly, I didn't have a clue what was going on – I was completely out of it. I mean, you were there – you must have seen how drunk I was. I promise you, Amanda, it wasn't my fault!'

My voice sounded shrill, guilty. I avoided her eyes. I knew it, I *knew* it. She was in love with him; she was having an affair with him. She was the other woman, and as far as she was concerned I was the other, *other* woman. Well, the other, other, *other* woman, actually, counting Serena. There seemed to be rather a lot of us about.

She ground her cigarette out in what I considered to be an incredibly threatening manner, leaving both hands free for nail-flexing. I couldn't help noticing that they were long, red and very sharp and I therefore took the precaution of cunningly placing both my feet to one side of my chair, thus poised for a quick getaway.

Amanda narrowed her eyes and nodded thoughtfully. 'We thought it was you.'

I jumped. We? Hang on a minute, just how many other women were there? Did he have a harem or something? How many concubines had I upset here, a dozen or so?

'Drive up from Cornwall a lot, do you?' she asked casually. ''Bout twice a week? Tuesdays and Fridays usually, innit?' She gave a twisted little smile. 'I'll say this for you, Polly, you've certainly got stamina, hell of a long way for a quick bonk.'

She lit a fresh cigarette and blew the smoke over my head, but only just.

'Don't be ridiculous,' I spluttered, coughing a bit under the smoke. 'I don't come up to bonk Sam; I don't usually come up at all actually, and anyway – what's it got to do with you?'

That was brave, Polly, foolhardy more like. I clenched my buttocks and prepared to duck the left hook.

She smiled sardonically. 'Fair enough, but just remember, we've got your number. We know what you're up to.'

It was this *we* business that was so damned intimidating. Any minute now I expected a whole posse of women to appear at the table, fold their arms and glare threateningly at me.

Amanda frowned and shook her head. 'We were really surprised when we found out it was you. I mean, there you are with that lovely bloke of yours and that bloody great house, and you go riskin' it all for some two-bit affair. Whadja wanna do that for? You must be out of your head.'

'I'm not! I don't! For goodness' sake, you've got it all wrong. I'm *not* having an affair with him, and anyway, what's all this *we* lark, who else knows about this?'

'Oh, just me and Sally,' said Amanda calmly.

I gasped. 'Sally? You've told Sally?'

'She guessed.'

'What – about you too?'

She frowned. 'Whadja mean, about me too?'

'Well, you're having an affair with him, aren't you?'

She stared at me. 'What?'

'You and Sam, you're having a ding-dong, aren't you?'

She looked at me in amazement, then abruptly threw back her head and hooted with laughter.

'You must be joking! Me and Sam? Do me a favour, 'e's my idea of a complete tosser!' She hooted some more, then wiped her eyes. 'No, I wouldn't touch 'im with a bargepole, but Sally's me best mate, you see.'

'Your what?'

'Yeah, we were at college together, shared a flat too.'

I stared at her. 'So that's why you kept giving him funny looks, I thought you were after him.'

'After 'im? God, I'd run a mile in the other direction! No, I can't stand the bloke and 'e knows it, which is why 'e goes all shifty when I'm around. 'E's sussed out I'm on to 'im, you see, knows 'e has to be really careful when I'm around. Sally's suspected for ages but 'e's always denied it and she's never been able to catch 'im out. 'E's a clever little bastard, really covers 'is tracks.' She grimaced at me. 'Oh, you're not the first, not by a long shot. Sally reckons 'e's been at it for years but she's never been able to prove it. 'E's never slipped up before, you see, not once. Until now of course, until you.' She blew another line of smoke centimetres above my head. ''E went a bit too far in public this time, didn't 'e? Got a bit overconfident, like. So now we know.'

'Oh no you don't,' I retorted, 'you don't know the half of it! I might have had a ghastly one-night stand with him but that was it! I am not, repeat *not* having an affair with him, you can believe what you damn well like but it's the truth!'

She sighed. 'Look, Polly, I like you, really I do, and I don't wanna interrogate you, but Sally's me mate, right? And she's desperate for some information. You'd do the same in my position, wouldn't you?'

'Well, if it was absolutely necessary, but I'm telling you, Amanda, you're way off the mark here – you've totally lost the plot. *I'm* not having an affair with him, but if you like,' I paused slightly here for dramatic effect, 'I can tell you who is.'

She frowned. 'But I thought you just said you *did* go to a hotel and bonk the living day–'

'Yes, all right, all right – I did, but it was just one night, that's all. If you want to know who's rocking his socks off on a permanent basis, I'll tell you: it's Serena Montgomery.'

'Serena Montgomery? Don't be soft,' she scoffed.

'It's true, I promise you, at least we're pretty sure it is.' I rather enjoyed my own little 'we' there.

'We?'

'Yes, me and Pippa. He was careless enough to leave his Filofax lying around and we found a cute little picture of her in the back, together with a fair smattering of S's in the lunch and dinner sections of his diary. She's definitely your girl, Amanda.'

'But 'e doesn't even like 'er – at least . . .'

'Exactly. As you said, clever little bastard, isn't he? Even goes so far as to pretend he hates her.'

She frowned. 'Now I come to think of it, out in Aswan . . .'

'Come again?'

'At the shoot on the Nile, 'e was always mouthing off at 'er for not knowing 'er lines and then draggin' 'er off for private little rehearsals an' that, raising 'is eyes to heaven as 'e went. But they didn't appear again for hours on end . . .' She stared into her drink. 'And they were always goin' off to check out locations together and – oh yeah, hang on, they both liked early nights, didn't they! Did a lot of ostentatious yawning and then disappeared while the rest of us were still partying – damn, why didn't I think of it before?'

'Because you were too busy thinking it was me, I suppose.'

She looked surprised. 'Yeah, I suppose I was.' She had the grace to look abashed. 'Sorry, Polly, been a bit hasty I suppose, but Sally's in such a state, you see, always crying an' that, and I really wanted to help her nail 'im this time. She's had it up to here with 'is lies, she really has.'

'Would she divorce him then?'

'If she found out the truth, I reckon she might. Sally's big problem has always been that she loves 'im too much, that's why she's never been able to leave 'im. She hides from the truth, see, kids herself 'e's working late when 'e doesn't pitch up till midnight, but just recently she's been toughening up a bit, says she wants to know what 'e's up to. I reckon if she actually had some cast-iron proof she'd do something about it, kick 'im out once and for all.'

'And Sam wouldn't want that? I mean, if he leads this extraordinary double life, why doesn't he just leave anyway? What's the point of staying with Sally?'

'Because Sally's got all the dosh, 'e'd be penniless.'

'What?'

'Yeah, Sam owes so much money it's untrue. Sally's 'is second wife, you see, 'e's still paying maintenance to number one and putting 'is two kids from that marriage through public school.'

'God, I had no idea. He keeps that very quiet.'

'Well 'e would, wouldn't 'e? Sally owns the house, the car, probably even the company. Her old man set Sam up when they got married, so there's no way 'e'd be able to get his hands on that money. 'E'd probably have to pay maintenance too, 'cos Sally's never really worked, and considering 'e's completely stony broke 'e'd be in a bit of a pickle really, wouldn't 'e?'

'But surely his films, his career –'

Amanda scoffed. 'Listen, Sam's career is only going one way at the moment, down the bleedin' plughole. 'E's a nobody in the film world, a washout, a has-been.'

'But I thought – God, I thought he was famous. I mean, he made that film – what was it called?'

'Yeah, *Marengo*, a low-budget, culty little film that was a surprise hit about seven years ago, but 'e's done bugger all since then apart from a series of major flops. Why d'you think 'e makes all these terrible commercials? Not exactly high art, are they? No, 'e's desperate to claw some cash together.'

'Gosh, I had no idea. He comes across as such a groovy film director.'

'Well, that's his image, innit? 'E's got to keep up the front, got to keep the girls in the dark, can't have them knowing 'e's just a sad old has-been, can 'e? I mean, let's face it, that's what you fell for, wasn't it, the famous-film-director bit?'

I looked sheepish. 'I suppose so.'

She shrugged. 'Well, there you go.' She stubbed out her cigarette. 'But it's a long way from the truth. My guess is 'e's up to 'is eyeballs in debt and 'e's absolutely terrified Sally's gonna find out about all 'is indiscretions and haul him off to the divorce courts. Then 'e'd really be up the creek.'

'Serve him right,' I muttered. I remembered how I'd sat opposite him at lunch and listened to him telling me how crazy he was about me, how miserable he'd be without me. What a load of crap, he couldn't care less about me; he'd just wanted a repeat performance of our sex-crazed night together. I shuddered.

'Exactly' – Amanda leaned forward eagerly – 'serve 'im right. Listen, Polly, would you do something for me?'

I eyed her nervously. 'What?'

'Would you go and see Sally? Tell 'er about what happened to you?'

I nearly fell off my chair. 'What! Go and see Sally? Amanda, you must be mad!'

'Look, she's not out for blood or anything, but she's doin' 'er nut trying to find out the truth and you've got – well, you've got first-hand experience, like, haven't you?'

'Yes, but I don't particularly want to share it with his –'

'And you could spill the beans about Serena too. I mean, let's face it, at the moment she thinks you're the one having the ding-dong with 'im so you could at least let yourself off *that* hook, put 'er straight on that score, as it were.' She eyed me carefully. 'I sort of think you owe it to 'er.'

I gasped. 'I do?'

'Well, you wouldn't like it if someone bonked your old man, would you?'

'Well no, but –'

'Well then. Go on, Polly, you can do it.'

'But – why can't you? I mean, couldn't you just report back, say you've seen me and –'

'I'm off to the States tomorrow,' she said briskly, stubbing her cigarette out, 'an' I hardly think she's gonna want to hear all this over the telephone, do you? But I'll tell you what, I'll ring 'er up and let 'er know you're coming to see 'er, how 'bout that?'

'But –'

'Come on, Polly, it's the least you can do.'

I had a nasty feeling this girl was used to getting her own way. Talk about persistent. She fixed my eyes with hers like a couple of drawing pins, nailing them to the wall while the rest of me squirmed around in my seat. Was there no way out of this? Suddenly I spotted one, a tiny little exit sign. I lunged for it.

'OK,' I said, nodding and smiling warmly, 'I'll go and see her.'

'Good on yer, girl!' she said heartily, and went to slap me on the back, but I instinctively ducked when I saw her hand coming and she cuffed me round the head instead.

'Blimey, sorry, you moved!'

'It's OK,' I mumbled, straightening my hair.

'Here's the address,' she said, busily scribbling the name of a smart Chelsea street down on the back of an envelope, '. . . and 'er phone number.'

'Great, great,' I said, picking it up and grinning broadly, still clinging like billyo to my big idea. It was quite a good one as it happened, very simple. You see, I wouldn't go. I just wouldn't go. I'd pretend I would, but I wouldn't. Amanda would be out of the country tomorrow and hopefully, by the time she got back, so would I. Somewhere far-flung, somewhere remote, somewhere incredibly inaccessible, maybe even somewhere hot. I'd like to get something out of this ghastly fiasco, even if it was only a suntan. I pocketed the address, a plastic smile still spread broadly across my face.

'Super, well, I'll go and see her tomorrow then, shall I?' I said brightly, getting to my feet.

She eyed me cautiously. 'You will go, won't you, Polly?'

'Yes, of course I will,' I assured her, 'first thing probably, straight after breakfast, pop round for coffee, get it over and done with. And now' – I looked at my watch and sighed regretfully – 'I'm afraid I really must go because I haven't got a key and I don't want to keep Pippa up too late.'

'Oh right.' She drained her drink. 'Well, I've got to go to the lav, so you go on, don't wait for me.'

'Righto!' I chortled merrily, grabbing my bag and scuttling for the door. I turned and gave her a cheery wave. 'Have a good time in the States then, bye!'

I was out, out and running. I scurried up the dark street, clutching my handbag to my chest, my heart thumping away high up in my ribcage. Heavens, what a nightmare, what a complete and utter nightmare! And what a narrow escape! Lucky I was such a quick thinker. How many other people could have extricated themselves from such a tight spot quite so brilliantly?

I rounded the corner at a canter and set off down the home straight, panting heavily now. I mean, did she think I was mad? Totally stark staring mad? What – go and confess to the wronged wife? Have a quiet word with her indoors? Pop round for coffee and say, 'Oh, by the way, I appear to have rogered your husband, only once, mind, and I can't remember a thing about it, but if you're interested I can give you the name and address of someone who's been *much* naughtier than me, rogered him on a *much* more regular basis – mmm, lovely coffee, is it filter?' Oh no, no thanks, not likely.

I dashed up the path to Pippa's front door, found the

spare key under the geranium pot and bounded up the stairs two at a time, quite forgetting my delicate condition. I threw my clothes on the floor, dived under the duvet and pulled it up high over my head. Oh no, I had quite enough on my plate without tipping that particular can of worms on to it as well, thank you very much. I shut my eyes tight. Sorry, Amanda, nice try an' all that, but sorry, no.

Chapter Twenty-three

I hadn't really been serious about fleeing the country, but the more I thought about it as I lay in bed the next morning, the more I decided it wasn't such a bad idea. What was the point of going home right now? What did I have to look forward to apart from a big empty house and the odd telephone call from Nick enquiring as to whether I'd found a house to live in and how soon could I get out of his? I felt my eyes fill up at this but gulped down the tears determinedly. No, Polly. No more falling apart at the seams. Instead I was going to get away from all this aggro, even if it was only for a week or two. Yes, I'd take a little break, a little holiday. When had I ever needed one more? I asked myself. I couldn't be more tired and run down if I tried. I huddled under the duvet, staring at the cracks in the attic ceiling, warming nicely to my plan.

I'd go somewhere hot, of course, no point whatsoever in going away if I didn't come back with a suntan, but it didn't have to be too remote, just Spain, or maybe Greece, or – hang on, were they hot enough at this time of year? In May? There was no doubt about it, it had to be absolutely sizzling.

I jumped out of bed and ran downstairs in my dressing gown to quiz Pippa on southern European meteorology. Big mistake. As I bustled into the kitchen, full of my newest plan, I caught her red-handed. She was standing with her back to me by the stove and as she heard my footsteps she turned quickly. I saw her eyes. Huge with guilt. She was clutching the evidence in her hands and damn nearly dropped it right there on the floor, but instead she panicked, and quickly rammed the whole thing into her mouth. The biggest, greasiest doorstep of a bacon sandwich you've ever seen in your life. Her eyes were still wide with fear as she chomped away frantically, butter oozing down her chin.

'Sorry,' she mumbled through half a pig, spraying me copiously with crumbs, 'thought you were still in bed!'

She grabbed an air freshener from the windowsill and began spraying furiously.

'No, don't!' I yelped, heaving on lavender and bacon grease. 'Just open the back door!'

She ran to push it open but it was too late. I was already running fast in the other direction, arriving just too late to deposit last night's dry biscuit and tonic water in the downstairs loo. I mopped up the floor and emerged a few minutes later looking very green around the gills.

'Thanks a bunch, Pippa,' I whispered.

'Sorry,' she muttered guiltily, taking my arm as I tottered back into the kitchen, clutching the furniture, 'thought I'd be able to get rid of the evidence before you came down.'

With a little help from my friend I gingerly lowered myself into a chair and rested my cheek on the kitchen table.

'Sorry about the pong in the loo,' I muttered.

'Couldn't matter less,' she assured me, ever the hostess.

She sat down opposite me and regarded my slumped form anxiously.

'You know, it's going to be bloody difficult to keep this pregnancy thing from everyone when you get back to Trewarren. You've got morning sickness written all over you. You'll be heaving in the post office and fainting in the dairy and it'll be round the village in no time, Nick's sure to hear.'

'I know,' I said, raising my head a couple of inches, 'which is precisely why I'm not going back yet.'

'Oh?' Pippa looked alarmed, perhaps not relishing the prospect of an enforced starvation diet continuing in her own home.

'Oh no, it's OK, I'm not staying here,' I assured her, 'I've got a cunning plan.'

'Oh really? What's that then?' Pippa looked even more nervous. She knew my plans of old.

I sat up and wrapped my dressing gown around me decisively.

'It's simple, I'm going to skip the country for a couple of weeks and go somewhere hot. I'll lie on a beach with a pile of books and come back refreshed, rejuvenated and with an incredible suntan. Then I'll go home and flaunt my suntanned body around the village and everyone will tell Nick how amazing I'm looking. I'll make sure all the eligible men in the village chase after me – I'll resist their advances, of course – but Nick will get wind of it and he'll be wild with jealousy. He'll come storming round to demand to know what's going on, see how gorgeously brown I am and how wonderfully blond and sunstreaked

my hair is, be absolutely mesmerized and forgive me unre-
servedly for having had a fling with Sam.'

'He will?' Pippa looked incredulous.

'Well.' I hesitated. 'OK, perhaps not, but it's worth a
try, isn't it?' I pleaded desperately.

'Well, I'm not sure. I can't help thinking there are some
socking great holes in your logic. For a start there are precisely no eligible men in your village, and secondly the
chances of Nick being mesmerized by a mere suntan are
pretty remote, aren't they?'

'Well, all right, you come up with something then!' I
snapped. 'I'm trying to be positive here. Sure, we both
know that the reality of the situation is I'll be holed up in
a council flat as a single parent with a baby to look after,
but, for God's sake, give me some positive vibes! I'm trying to look on the bright side.'

'Well, I'm all for looking on the bright side, Polly, but –'

'But in this case there isn't a bright side because I'm
married to a highly principled, uncompromising man who
is never in a million years going to overlook the fact that
his wife committed adultery with another man. Is that it?'
I demanded savagely, my jaw wobbling.

'Er, well –'

'Yes, Pippa, I know that, but if I kept that thought in
my mind every waking moment, first of all I'd go barking
mad and then I'd slit my wrists, wouldn't I?'

'Well, crikey, don't do that,' she muttered hastily.
'Heavens, Polly, I didn't mean to upset you, I mean – yes,
yes, have a holiday! I think it's a great idea, marvellous!
Wish I'd thought of it myself.'

'Good,' I said shakily, gaining control of my jaw, and

blinking back the tears. 'Right. That's settled then. Hand me the phone, would you? I'm going to ring the estate agents right now and ask them to book me a flight tomorrow. I want to go somewhere hot, cheap and absolutely sizzling with harmful ultraviolet rays.'

'Travel agents,' corrected Pippa, handing me the phone, 'and here, before you land me with a bill for directory enquiries, I've got Thomas Cook in my address book.'

I punched out the number she dictated and waited impatiently as it rang in my ear. Pippa frowned.

'Polly, I don't want to be a killjoy, but wouldn't it be better to get the baby business sorted out *before* you go away? Only I can't help thinking that when you come back you'll be really quite pregnant, and if you decide you don't want to go ahead with it it'll be a darned sight more difficult to do anything about –'

'Hello, Thomas Cook?' I shut my eyes and held up my hand to silence my critic on the opposite side of the table.

'Yes, I'd like a flight and a hotel please, preferably tomorrow and most certainly to somewhere radiating temperatures in excess of thirty degrees. D'you think Greece would fit the bill? . . . Twenty-five degrees? No, not hot enough, I'm afraid; I won't get third-degree burns in that. Where else have you got? . . . Where? Lanzarote?' I looked at Pippa. 'We've been there, haven't we?' I hissed, my hand over the mouthpiece.

She nodded and shoved two fingers in her mouth in a puke-making gesture.

I turned back to the girl. 'Bit grotty, isn't it? I seem to recall discos throbbing to "The Birdy Song" and heaving with bimbos in white high heels and ankle chains who

thought a banana daiquiri was the ultimate in sophistic . . .
Thirty-two degrees, eh?' I raised my eyebrows at Pippa.
'Well, that certainly meets the requirements in the burning-
flesh department, bugger the banana daiquiris, d'you have
any vacancies? . . . Would you? Terrific, thanks so much,
as soon as possible? . . . Brilliant, it's Polly Penhalligan and
I'm on eight, seven, two, five, nine, six, one. Speak to you
in a mo then, bye.'

I put the receiver down and grinned.

'Lanzarote, she's ringing me back in a sec to confirm
the booking, then I'll just pop round and sign the cheque.
I'm off! I'm off tomorrow, Pippa! Sun, sea, sand and –
well, no, none of that, of course, had quite enough of
that recently, but, God, I'm so excited! Something's actually going right for a change!' I clapped my hands together
gleefully.

Pippa screwed up her face in disgust.

'Hate to put you off but it's the pits, Polly, don't you
remember? It's not just the Sharons, it's the beaches. Black
volcanic sand that sticks to your suntan lotion whenever a
force eight gale blows, which I seem to remember is most
of the time – we couldn't work out why we were the only
idiots on the beach until we stood up and realized we'd
gone a shade darker than we intended. The only other
lunatic lying there was that drunk who was unconscious
most of the day until he lurched past us, pausing only to
throw up in my sunhat.'

'I know, I know, but all I need is the sun and hopefully
one of those comfortable lounger things by a hotel pool.
I won't even see the beach if I'm lucky, and I can wear
dark glasses to blot out the rest of the punters, and who

am I to complain about puke? I'll be puking with the best of them – oh no, nothing can stop me now. I'm really excited, it'll be brilliant, I'll relax, read some books – oh Pippa, why don't you come? Take some time off and get away from work and Josh for a bit, surely you could –'

The phone rang.

'That'll be for me!' I squeaked, grabbing it.

'Hello, is that Polly Penhalligan?' said a girl's voice.

'Yes, that's right, is it OK, is it booked?'

'Um, my name's Sally.'

'Oh, right, right, fine, Sally, you're my tour operator or something, are you? Sweet of you to introduce yourself but to be honest I'm not sure I want the whole package-deal bit – you know, camp fires on the beach and ging-gang-goolie, I'm just after a quiet –'

'My name's Sally Weston.'

'Marvellous, terrific, Sally but – oh! Sally Weston?'

I gazed at Pippa in terror. She clapped her hand dramatically over her mouth, eyes huge with horror, and backed away in the direction of the fridge. It occurred to me to simply drop the receiver and do likewise, perhaps climbing into it and shutting the door behind me, but by the time I'd got any sort of muscle co-ordination together Mrs Weston was already addressing my right ear.

'I hope it's not a bad time, not too early or anything?' she was saying hesitantly.

'Er, no, no, it's fine,' I gasped, 'fine!'

'I can quite understand that you don't want to get involved in all this, but I'd be so grateful . . . you see, Amanda told me she'd spoken to you but she wasn't sure if you'd really come and see me and – well, you're my only hope of finding out something concrete about m-my husband.'

She sounded shaky, uncertain. This wasn't the voice of a bitter, vengeful wife, but all the same . . .

'Look, I'm sorry,' I muttered, 'but I really don't think it's any of my –'

'Oh please don't say no, please, this is so important. I must talk to you! I know what happened between you and Sam, and I swear I don't hold it against you. I know – well, I know how persuasive he can be. Please, Polly, please just pop round for a moment, or maybe I could come to you?'

By now the palm of my hand was sweating up a treat and I had to hold the receiver in a vicelike grip to stop it slipping from my grasp. I rolled mad, expressive eyes at Pippa, who rolled mad, sympathetic ones back.

'Look, um, the thing is, Mrs Weston, if Amanda's told you about m-me and your husband, well, I'm not sure that there's an awful lot more I can add.'

'But I must talk to you about Serena. Amanda said you were convinced that she's the real – you know – protagonist in all this.'

'But it's all very much conjecture, nothing definite, and –'

'But you found a picture? In his Filofax, is that right?' she persisted.

'Well yes, but –'

'Please, I – I must have it, I must have some sort of proof to dangle in front of him, could I possibly have it? Could I? Could you bring it round? In the Filofax?'

She sounded really desperate, but blimey – not deliver the Filofax back to Sam? Take it round to the wife complete with photo of bird? Did I have that much of a death wish?

'I – I really don't think I'm in any position to –'

'Look, what d'you owe him?' Suddenly she was more assertive. 'If what Amanda told me is true, he took advantage of you when you were completely and utterly plastered, as I'm sure he's taken advantage of many other girls. Let's face it, he's taken advantage of me all our married life,' she said sadly.

I didn't say anything for a moment, but I could feel myself weakening. Perhaps she felt it too.

'OK,' she urged, 'don't bring the Filofax, I can see that puts you in a difficult position, just bring the photo. It doesn't have to be anything to do with you then. I'll just say I found it and took it out a few days ago, that way you can return the Filofax and you're in the clear, what d'you say?'

I bit my lip. She was right, what did I owe him? Thanks to him, my life was now one huge, comprehensive mess.

'OK . . .' I said slowly, 'I'll just bring the photo.'

'Oh, thank you so much!' she breathed quickly, before I had a chance to reconsider. 'I'm so grateful, really I am, and I know it's a dreadful thing to ask but I'm desperate, you see, really desperate!'

Yeah, so am I, I thought as I put the phone down, having promised to be there in about an hour, really desperate. I'm an abandoned wife too, you know, and I'm big with child, but no one rushes round to my house to offer to sort out my life for me, do they?

Nevertheless, half an hour later, Pippa duly trotted off to work, case in hand, complete with Filofax but minus the photograph.

'What if he notices?' she hissed in terror as I handed it to her at the front door. 'What if it's the first thing he checks for?'

'Well, he can hardly ask you, can he? He can hardly say "What's happened to that photo of my bird, the one I keep tucked behind the picture of my wife?"'

'I suppose not, but even so –'

'Bluff it out,' I said airily. 'Just say you haven't the faintest idea what he's talking about. Bye, Pipps, have a nice day.'

She still looked unconvinced so I gave her a little push and she set off hesitantly down the path, case in hand. Halfway down she turned back and walked towards me.

'What now?' I said, exasperated.

'I was just going to tell you that Lottie phoned last night,' she said huffily, 'when you were out. She was worried about you.'

'Oh, sorry, thanks, Pippa. I'll ring her later. Sorry.'

I shut the door and bit my lip. I hadn't spoken to Lottie since that night at Annabel's and I felt guilty about it, but I knew how deeply disappointed she'd be in me. Lottie was one of my dearest friends but she was incurably sensible and ran her life in a very orderly fashion. If she knew how comprehensively I was lousing mine up, she'd be horrified. I'd ring her when I got back from my holiday, when hopefully things had settled down a little bit. I'd ring my parents then too, I decided. I hadn't liked to worry them by telling them about Nick and me, and whenever I spoke to Mummy on the phone I just pretended everything was fine, but I'd come clean as soon as I got back from Lanzarote.

I sighed and picked up the photograph of Serena from the hall table. I stared at it for a moment. She really was jolly pretty. I popped it quickly in my bag, grabbed my car keys and slammed out of the house. Then I ran down the path, jumped into Rusty and set off for Chelsea.

Chapter Twenty-four

Oh, very nice, Sam, very nice indeed. I sat in the car, gazing up at the elegant white façade of a magnificent Chelsea town house. Five or six storeys of sartorial splendour in a quiet garden square just a stone's throw from the bustling King's Road, an estate agent would no doubt eulogize. Quite a lot to give up, one way and another, no wonder our Sam was clinging on by his fingernails. I sat there for a moment, biting my own and collecting my few remaining wits. I had a feeling I was going to need them. Except that the longer I sat there the more witless I felt, so in the end I told myself that if I stayed there for precisely one minute longer something unspecified but totally horrendous would happen to Nick or my parents. It always did the trick. I gazed at the second hand on my watch and, with ten seconds to spare, jumped out of the car, ran up the six or seven marble steps which led to the black front door and fell on the brass bell. It was shrill and feverish, which suited my mood.

Sally had clearly been sitting on the doormat waiting for me, because the door swung back before I could take my finger off the brass. She stood there, framed in the doorway, and I instinctively took a step backwards. Pippa had been right. The picture didn't do her justice at all: she really was extraordinarily pretty in a slightly sixties flower-child kind of way.

She was tiny, with bottom-length blonde hair, which was

rather tangled and a too-long fringe which fell into her eyes. She had a small, heart-shaped face and enormous slate-grey eyes that blinked nervously at me. Her pencil-slim figure was poured into a tight black Lycra dress which clung everywhere, emphasizing the fact that her hips and tummy were nonexistent. Her legs were long and brown and her feet were bare. I gulped. She looked rather like I look in my most outrageous fantasies. What the devil was Sam up to? Didn't he know that girls like this with rich daddies to match don't grow on trees?

She gave a hesitant smile. 'You must be Polly, come in.'

'Yes, that's right, thanks,' I muttered.

She wafted gracefully off down a bright-yellow hall smothered in prints and watercolours, a tiny black figure with a sheet of blonde hair shimmying in her wake, her bare feet padding silently in the deep blue carpet. Effort-lessly elegant. I lumbered clumsily after her in my clogs and the extraordinary attire of smocked blouse and long peasant skirt which for some reason I'd deemed fit for the occasion. I felt like The Thing from the Swamp. I must have been about six inches taller than her and twice as wide. I tried to sag at the knees and lower my bottom a bit to decrease my height but there was damn all I could do about my width.

At the end of the hall she turned a corner and led me into a large, white, predominantly marble kitchen. At the far end were two enormous french windows which were flung wide on to a walled garden absolutely bursting with white roses.

'Oh! What a beautiful garden!' I exclaimed, in spite of my nerves.

She smiled shyly. 'Roses are my passion. I spend most of the day out there, pruning them, feeding them and generally fussing over them. I practically go to bed with them!' She laughed and then gasped, pulling herself up short. It wasn't perhaps the most innocuous of opening gambits, bearing in mind the nature of my visit.

I flushed and she turned away, also blushing hotly, but somehow prettily pink as opposed to my own retired-general purple. She grabbed the kettle and hid her face in the sink as she filled it.

'Coffee?'

'Please, if you're having one.'

Damn. Why had I said that? Why hadn't I just slammed the photo down on the breakfast bar and taken to my heels? It would take a good three minutes for the kettle to boil, another five for the coffee to cool down and a good seven or so to drink it without scalding the roof of my mouth. Why couldn't I ever think before I spoke?

'We'll, um, sit down and chat when I've made the coffee, shall we?' she said nervously.

'Fine, fine!'

And thus she unwittingly condemned us to an embarrassing silence. We'd made a pact, you see, no talking till coffee time, and boy had she filled the kettle full. She twiddled her hair and gazed fixedly at it, willing it to boil. I cast around for an equally fascinating diversion, eventually plumping in desperation for the spice rack on the wall. I stared at it as if I'd never seen one before, gazing with rapt absorption at the rows of little labelled bottles. If roses were her passion, herbs and spices were clearly mine. Rosemary, sage, oregano – gosh, how I marvelled.

At last the bloody thing boiled and she shakily poured out two mugs of coffee and splashed some milk in. We sat down on either side of the breakfast bar and, out of relief, both spoke at once.

'You're not quite –'

'How long have you –'

We laughed. It broke the tension.

'Go on,' I said, 'what were you . . . ?'

'No, you first.'

'Oh, I was just going to ask you how long you'd lived here; it's such a beautiful house.'

'Three years. Since we got married.' She blushed again, perhaps thinking this wasn't quite the moment to shove her marriage down my throat. 'And – and I was just going to say,' she hurried on, 'that you weren't quite what I'd expected.'

'Oh! Really?' What on earth *had* she expected? I wondered. I abruptly brought the boiling coffee nervously to my mouth, predictably scalding myself.

'Um, what did you expect?' I asked, licking my sore lips.

'Oh, I don't know, someone . . . more obvious, I suppose, you know, short skirt, loads of make-up, that kind of thing.' She eyed me nervously.

I grinned. 'Tarty, you mean?'

She giggled. 'I suppose so.' Suddenly she looked anxious. 'Not that I thought you'd be a tart, of course, just the clothes, I – oh, I don't know . . .' She trailed off miserably.

'I put this lot on on purpose, actually,' I said, gazing down at the strange ethnic gear I'd raided from Pippa's wardrobe. 'I wanted to look – well, homely, I suppose, a bread-baker. Didn't want to seem like a threat. I think

I was trying to say – don't worry, I've got a husband of my own at home, I don't want yours.' I grinned.

Her eyes widened. 'No! D'you know, before you came round I was wearing almost exactly what you've got on now, but I changed into this spray-on number so you wouldn't think I was the down-trodden wife who couldn't keep a husband!'

'You're not serious! What, you like this kind of hippy gear?'

She nodded. 'I love it.'

'It's yours, pending my flatmate's permission of course. I can't wait to get out of it, but I'd die for your little black dress – not that I'd have a hope of getting into it!'

We giggled, laughed really, and it was such a release. All at once a cosier, more comradely atmosphere prevailed. We sipped our coffee and grinned across at each other. I'd been waiting for her to ask for the photograph but suddenly I reached into my bag and slipped it over the counter to her.

'Here. It's a very good photo, she's not that pretty,' I lied.

She smiled. 'Course she is, I've seen her in films, but thanks anyway.'

She picked it up and stared at it for a moment. 'This is good . . .' she said slowly, 'this is . . . sort of working.'

'What d'you mean?'

She looked up. 'I had a feeling if I saw some hard proof, some tangible evidence of his infidelity, I might be able to love him less, and d'you know, I was right. I can almost feel the last cloying traces of my love slipping away.' She gulped. 'I can almost begin to realize what a complete bastard he is.'

'Well, that's a start,' I mumbled uncertainly. I wasn't quite sure what sort of a line I should take on this; he was after all her husband and I wasn't convinced I should be too swift to denounce him as an out-and-out villain. 'I mean,' I stumbled on, 'he has – well, misbehaved rather, hasn't he?'

She reached up and shoved the photo between the pages of a cookery book on the shelf above her. She grinned.

'Just a bit. D'you know, I've fallen for his lies for two whole years now? That's how long I've known about his affairs. And for all I know he might well have started dabbling the moment he took his marriage vows.'

'Blimey.' I was silenced for a moment. 'So, there've been, um, quite a lot then, have there?' I asked tentatively. I wasn't exactly sure how deeply I should delve, but she had, after all, brought it up. 'I mean, not just one or two?'

She smiled ruefully. 'Hardly. There've been loads, hundreds probably. Let's put it this way, it hasn't just been you and Serena by a long shot.'

I rather baulked at being put in the same category as Serena, but I let it pass.

'Let me see.' She held up her elegant fingers and ticked them off one by one. 'First there was Samantha in accounts, a tacky little office affair, under the desk and behind the photocopier probably; then there was Rosy who lives round the corner, lots of frantic coupling in Battersea Park, according to one of my neighbours; then there was Charlotte, the wife of one of his best friends – I think they mostly got it together in the afternoons in a hotel in Westbourne Grove; oh, and let's not forget Trisha who works in the pub down the road – God knows where they did it, in the cellar with the beer barrels probably.' She shrugged. 'There've been plenty more – I've lost count actually – but those are the ones I've known about for certain.'

'Crikey, he must have been rushed off his feet!'

She gave a bitter little smile. 'Oh, our Sam likes a hectic social life.'

'But haven't you ever confronted him?' I was stunned. How could anyone live like this?

'Loads of times, but up until now I've never had any proof, and whenever I've accused him he's just categorically denied it. He's very careful, you see, never slips up. Oh, I've had lots of weird telephone calls late at night where the person at the other end just slams the phone down when they get me answering instead of him, but I've never actually seen him with anyone, never found any letters, any photos – until now, of course.'

She took the cookery book down from the shelf and studied the photo again.

'And he's always maintained that I'm just a bored, paranoid housewife, with nothing better to do than imagine him in a compromising clinch with a floozy.' I blanched again at this indirect allusion but obviously imperceptibly because she carried on. 'But it's funny,' she mused, 'I went on loving him all the same.'

She stared beyond my head out into the garden for a second, then turned back to me.

'Can you believe that? Throughout all the lies, the

deceit, I loved him and pretended to myself that it wasn't happening, forced it out of my mind.'

'And now?' I asked. I could tell she wanted to talk, get it all out of her system. 'D'you still love him now?'

She sighed and looked down at the photograph again. Her eyes narrowed thoughtfully and her lips compressed. She shrugged.

'I'm not sure,' she said softly. 'No . . . yes . . . a bit . . . nothing like as much as I did. I'm getting better anyway, I'm definitely on the mend. This helps.'

She took one last look, then tossed the photo defiantly into the book and slammed it shut.

'Thanks for bringing it, I know you didn't want to, but it might just give me the impetus I need to kick him out this time.'

'Well, in that case I'm glad I did.'

We smiled at each other. I drained my coffee and suddenly there didn't seem to be a lot more to say. I started to slip off my stool and reach for my bag on the floor.

'Well, I'll –'

'More coffee?' she asked abruptly, picking up both our mugs and raising her eyebrows, rather hopefully I thought. I hesitated. She wanted me to stay, wanted to talk. I put my bag down.

'Please,' I nodded, 'that would be nice.'

Why not? The worst was over and it was actually rather pleasant sitting here in her sunny kitchen bitching about her errant husband. She looked pleased and began spooning out the Nescafé with alacrity.

'So what about you?' she asked, pouring in the hot water. 'Have you ever been in love with a bastard? What about your husband, is he the reason you looked further afield? Were you getting your own back or something?'

'Oh no,' I said quickly, 'quite the opposite. He hates that sort of thing – you know, philandering, playing around.'

'Oh.'

Her face fell. I could tell she felt alone. The only betrayed wife in the world. I quickly rallied.

'But – but I've been involved with loads of other bastards in my time, oh gosh, yes, plenty, men who'd make Sam look like an absolute beginner, in fact.'

I wasn't lying either, I thought, shuddering as I recalled Harry Lloyd-Roberts, my boyfriend before Nick. He fitted the bill perfectly, and how.

'Oh yes!' I nodded vigorously, warming to my theme. 'I've been betrayed quite comprehensively in my time, *and* I refused to believe it was happening. My friends had to literally rub my nose in it to make me face facts. I only knew about one of his flings but he probably had countless others behind my back. God, I was such a fool.' I stared into space, remembering the bad old days.

'Not half as much of a fool as I've been, I bet,' she whispered.

I looked back at her quickly and was aghast to see a tear trickling down her face.

'Oh God, I'm so sorry,' I gasped, 'that was so tactless, thoughtless. I didn't mean you were a fool, I just meant –'

'It's OK.' She gave a watery smile and wiped away the tear. 'I know what you meant. But I am a fool, there's no two ways about it.'

'Oh, now come on, where's that fighting spirit of just a

second ago? That's all in the past! Like you said, you've got hard proof now; you can shove the photo under his nose, kick him where it hurts and then kick him out of the house. Tell him to bugger off and to conduct his sordid little affairs under someone else's roof!'

'Oh yes, I fully intend to do that, but that's not what I meant about being a fool. You see, I haven't just let him walk all over me, I've let him trample me. Body and soul.' She looked up, her eyes full of tears. 'I'm not actually sure I'll ever recover.' Her chin wobbled dangerously.

'Course you will!' I said staunchly. 'It's just a matter of time. You're bound to feel hurt and vulnerable at the moment, that's only natural, but you'll see, before long some gorgeous hunk will come along and sweep you off your –'

'No, Polly.' She frowned and shook her head. 'I'm not just talking about Sam being unfaithful, it's more than that. It's –' She gulped and bit her lip. Then she brushed another tear roughly off her cheek and looked at me defiantly.

'You see, I wanted children,' she said in a rather demanding tone.

I jumped. 'Well, yes, of course, who doesn't, me too, although funnily enough now that I am pre–' I nearly gagged on my tongue, 'preparing to ride at Badminton, I've rather gone off the idea!' I gabbled, my heart thumping madly.

I flushed. Christ, you idiot, Polly, what the hell d'you think you're doing? Luckily she didn't seem to have registered that I was either big with her husband's child or the next Lucinda Prior-Palmer. She was miles away with her own problems.

'As soon as we got married I wanted them. Thought I'd get pregnant straight away, and when nothing happened after a year or so I began to panic.'

'I know the feeling,' I muttered, 'been there, done that.'

'Sam said I was being ridiculous, said I was too impatient and it was bound to happen sooner or later if I just stopped worrying about it.'

'So did Nick,' I said quickly, pleased I could join her on at least one agony trip, 'that's exactly what he said.'

'Of course, Sam had two children from his first marriage, so he wasn't nearly as fussed as I was. I think he only said he wanted more because I did. And I really did. I got quite hysterical about it, in fact. I think I secretly knew that our marriage was a sham and I thought a baby would help, bring us closer together, or perhaps give me a focus for my love.' She shook her head. 'Crazy.'

'But understandable,' I ventured.

She shrugged. 'Maybe. Anyway, after a while I started to go for tests. Minor ones at first, blood tests, that kind of thing, then I started to take my temperature every morning to see if I was ovulating. It's supposed to rise, you know –'

I nodded. 'Only too well.'

She sighed. 'Well, then we got on to more serious things. I had an operation in hospital to check my tubes were open – they were. Then I had a scan to look at my womb – that was fine. Then the doctors started talking about IVF and I had to have all sorts of other tests and examinations to see if it would be possible, if I was suitable – and so it went on. There seemed to be no end to the different ways they could poke, prod and peer at my reproductive organs. I can't tell you how traumatic it was, Polly, physically and emotionally. I was a complete wreck.'

'God, I can imagine, and I only got to the thermometer stage.'

'And the worst of it was that every time they did a test they'd come back with the same reply – as far as we can tell there's absolutely nothing wrong with you, Mrs Weston, just keep trying.'

'But that's good, surely?'

'No, you see I *wanted* there to be something wrong. I wanted there to be a reason, I felt the doctors could do something about it then, put it right, make whatever it was that wasn't working *work*!' She slammed the palm of her hand down hard on the counter. 'You see, I just felt so bloody helpless. I was dying inside, there was this ghastly void, and there was nothing I could *do* about it, nothing I could do to *help* myself.'

'And Sam? Wasn't he supportive or anything?'

'Oh, Sam was wonderful. We talked endlessly, he reassured me, calmed me down – gave me hope, actually, because he was so thoroughly convinced everything would be fine. But you see, he wasn't the one going through the humiliating rigmarole and he'd already fathered two children, so he was completely in the clear.'

She paused and pulled a lock of hair out from behind her ear. She began twiddling it furiously around her finger.

'Then one day,' she said softly, 'I went to one of those Christmas charity fairs – you know the kind of thing, lots of worthy Sloanes selling you totally pointless but frightfully tasteful things like tartan bottle warmers and inedible game pies.'

I grinned. 'I know the ones.'

'Anyway, there I was, on the point of being talked into parting with the best part of fifty quid for a wooden box with a chicken on it to stash my loo rolls in, when suddenly I turned and bumped into someone I hadn't seen for years. She used to be quite a mate, actually, but she was also a great friend of Sam's first wife so we'd rather diplomatically lost touch.' She paused and sucked the end of her hair into a point, gazing avidly at the marble breakfast bar as she remembered. 'She had her baby with her, on her hip, a little girl with red tights and blonde curly hair. Divine. I was playing with her, cuddling her, totally enchanted. I must have murmured something about wishing I had one of my own, because I can see this girl's face now, full of pity, concern. Poor you, she said, isn't there anything they can do? I remember being surprised, because I'd kept my tests deadly secret, but I assumed she'd just guessed. "No," I said, "we've tried everything, but nothing seems to work." She stared at me. "But can't they just reverse it?" she asked. I stared back at her. "Reverse what?" I said. She looked away, embarrassed. I remember feeling the blood literally drain from my face, down my neck, through my body. I grabbed her arm. "Reverse what?" I said, "reverse *what*?" She licked her lips, trapped. "The – the snip," she said nervously, "I – I thought Sam had had a vasectomy, after his children with Veronica, but I must have got it wrong . . ."' Sally gulped, her eyes wide, staring past me now, her face ashen. 'I remember gazing at her with my mouth open. She was pink, flustered. Then she quickly leaned over and kissed me goodbye, saying she had to dash. She bustled away with her baby, covered in confusion.'

She bit her lip and looked down at her lap. 'I don't remember leaving that fair,' she whispered, 'don't know how I got home. All I remember is sitting here, on this stool, in this kitchen, waiting for him to come home. It was early afternoon and he wasn't due back till about six, but I sat here all that time, hour after hour as it got darker and darker, not putting any lights on, just waiting, waiting. When he finally opened the front door I flew at him. I ran down the hall and almost took off, landing on top of him, ranting, raving, pulling at his clothes, his hair, anything I could get at, screaming like a mad thing. Two years of agony and torment came out in a matter of seconds. I remember his face, white, trapped. He sank down on his knees right there on the doormat and covered his face so I couldn't see his shame. But I didn't have to, I could smell it, it was all over him. Then he cried. Hot tears, flowing down his cheeks, he broke down completely, told me everything.

'He said he'd wanted to marry me so much but thought I wouldn't have him if I'd known he couldn't give me children. Said he'd tried to have the vasectomy reversed and it had failed. That he hadn't been able to tell me, that it had killed him. Not as much as it had killed *me*, I remember shrieking, still pummelling him with my fists. He said he'd never imagined I'd want children so badly, that I'd go to the lengths I had. He said it had been horrific to watch me go through it all, to pick me up from the hospital each time I had an operation, knowing I was on a hiding to nothing. Said it had been a nightmare for him.'

She gave a twisted little smile. 'He clung on to me like a baby, and after a while I just let him. I gave up, effectively. One minute I was punching him, kicking him, screaming at him, and the next I threw in the towel. I just sort of went limp and let him cling to me. He sobbed into my hair and kissed my face, desperate, tortured kisses. We held on to each other, crying. He said he'd done it because he loved me so much, couldn't bear to lose me. Then finally he asked me to forgive him. He was on his knees, right there on the doormat.' Sally looked past me, her eyes full of pain. 'And I forgave him,' she whispered, 'because – because I still loved him, you see, and I wasn't strong enough not to. I'd forgiven him his infidelity by turning a blind eye and finally I forgave him his cowardice and his cruelty. Just like that.' Her face was blank, a mask. At last she found my eyes. 'So you see,' she whispered, 'that's how much of a bastard he is, and that's how much of a fool I am.'

There was a silence. I stared at her, wide-eyed, all sorts of conflicting emotions battling for supremacy within me. Pain at her pain – I couldn't remember when I'd been so moved by someone's anguish, but neither could I remember feeling quite so hysterically, madly, unbearably, deliriously happy. I breathed deeply, trying desperately to quell it, to keep it down, to control my overwhelming desire to shriek with joy. Sam had had the snip. Sam was incapable. Sam was firing blanks. Sam was not by any stretch of the imagination the father of my child, which by a deft process of elimination meant that Nick most definitely was. I clenched everything I possessed very hard – buttocks, teeth, knees – and shut my mouth very tightly, but it was no good. A strangled, joyous, whinny-like noise still escaped my lips.

'Hrmmmm!' I squealed, and then again, 'Hraaa! Hrm-mmm!'

Sally looked at me in horror.

'Sorry!' I gasped, but the moment I spoke I lost control of my mouth and it split my face into a mad, helpless grin.

'So sorry!' I yelped again, desperately wrestling with my facial muscles and trying hard to think about starving children in Ethiopia, multiple pile-ups on the motorway, anything horrendous. Didn't work.

'Can't help it!' I gasped, shaking my head helplessly, my face writhing with joy. 'Hrmmmm! Ye! Ha!' A succession of weird strangled yelps continued to escape me.

Sally looked first astonished, then desperately hurt. 'Wh-what's so –' she began in confusion.

I quickly reached over and seized her hand. 'Oh, I'm so sorry!' I gasped. 'I'm so sorry, what must you think of me? But please believe me, it's got nothing whatsoever to do with what you've just told me, I think that's the most horrific story I've ever heard, ghastly, barbaric, awful – but, oh God, I can't tell you what good news it is for me!'

She looked at me aghast. 'G-good news? But how can it – what on earth d'you mean?'

I had to tell her. There was no other way. I gripped her hand tight, eyes shining.

'I'm pregnant,' I breathed.

Her face twisted momentarily in envy and I winced at the pain I was giving her. Then she shrugged and looked confused. 'S-so . . . ?'

'So I slept with Sam.'

Suddenly her face cleared. 'Oh! So you mean you thought – oh!'

'Exactly!'

'You thought –'

'Thought! I was sodding convinced!' I yelped. I was desperate to do some full-blooded yelping now.

'Oh no, no way. No chance of that at all.'

'Because he's impotent!' I screeched. 'He's flaming well impotent, isn't he?'

She gave a wry smile. 'No chance of that either, unfortunately, but he's certainly infertile, if that's what you mean.'

'YE-HAA!' I screeched, loud and clear, punching the air with my fist. 'YE-HA, YE-HA, YE-HA! HE'S INFERTILE! YE-HA! AR-R-RIBA!'

It was no good, I couldn't help it, I simply couldn't keep it in any more.

'Oh, I'm so sorry,' I gasped when I'd finished, clapping my hand over my mouth, 'but I just can't help it, I'm afraid. I've been worried for so long, desperately worried. Nick and I have been trying for ages, I was convinced it couldn't be his, that it had to be Sam's, and now it's not! It's not, is it?'

She grinned. 'Most definitely not. Go on, go ahead, do a war dance or something.'

I breathed deeply, in and out, in and out, and shook my head furiously, gaining control. 'No, no, I'm fine now, honestly.'

My face, I knew, was wreathed in smiles, my eyes were shining uncontrollably, that was enough for her to cope with at the moment. I'd do my war dance later, out in the street perhaps, or, if I didn't make it that far, on the marble steps just outside the front door.

Suddenly she leaned across and patted my hand. She smiled. 'I'm pleased for you, really I am.' She looked surprised. 'Actually, I meant that too – I wasn't just saying it.'

'Course you weren't, you're far too nice.'

'Not that nice, I'm afraid. I'd still rather it was me. I still want what you've got, and I can't have.'

'But you can!' I said eagerly. 'You *can* have babies, you know you can, there's absolutely nothing wrong with you. Gosh, you've had a complete bloody overhaul! Everything's been flushed out and polished up till it's absolutely gleaming; you're probably as fertile as a gerbil now. And I just know that once you're shot of Sam you'll meet someone, someone totally divine, who's going to want to marry you and look after you and have babies with you and you'll only have to *look* at him and you'll be pregnant; you'll end up with loads! Hundreds! Too many! They'll all be running around this kitchen drawing on the immaculate walls before you can say bugger off up to your rooms!'

She laughed. 'We'll see,' she said.

Her laugh died away quickly, though, and her smile faded. She looked down at her wedding ring and twisted it. Suddenly I went cold. I knew she wasn't completely over him, wasn't completely cured. I wondered then if she'd ever really leave him.

A silence fell. We sat there, opposite each other, gripping our mugs of cold coffee, both preoccupied with our own thoughts. Me with my intoxicating joy – a baby, *our* baby, our first of *many* babies, he'd have to forgive me now, he'd just have to – and her with her pain. Suddenly it came billowing over the counter towards me like a thick, enveloping fog and I realized my own vibes must be doing the same. There didn't seem to be much point in sticking around rubbing in my happiness. I drained my freezing coffee in a quick gulp and slipped quietly off my stool.

'I'd better go.'

She looked up, and came back from a long way away. She nodded and gave a faint smile. 'Sure.'

I gathered my things together, still tingling with excitement, and followed her back down the yellow hall, trying hard not to skip, not to jig, not to leap in the air and punch it mightily.

As we went, we passed the open door to the drawing room and I caught a quick glimpse of a beautiful, high-ceilinged, pale-yellow room. The lemon walls were crowded with pictures, oil paintings mostly, all originals, and at ground level there were gorgeous, covetable, faded antiques scattered around on the Persian rugs. It was elegant yet comfortable and not too imposing. However hard I tried my house would never have that effortless grace.

'How beautifully you've done it,' I breathed. 'You really have got quite an eye.'

She looked surprised and followed my gaze. 'The drawing room? Oh, that's not me at all – I'm much more interested in the garden. No, this is all Sam's idea.'

I frowned, and stepped forward to take a closer look. 'Really? But this is all old stuff, isn't it? Antiques? I thought he wasn't interested in that sort of thing; he told me he was only into the really modern look, state-of-the-art and all that.'

Sally threw back her head and hooted. 'Sam? He told you that? God, you must be joking. He lives for all this antiquated rubbish, can't get enough of it. He's always off at some auction house or another buying more junk to clutter up the place with. He's obsessed by it, if he was here now he'd tell you precisely where each piece came from, when it was made and whether it's true to its period or not. That's his pride and joy over there – he spends hours with his head in that,' she said, pointing to an elegant Queen Anne corner cupboard.

'What – that cupboard?'

'Oh no, not the cupboard, what's inside it. I'll show you.' She walked over and took a key from a china box on the shelf above it. Then she bent down and fitted it into the lock. I followed her, my heart pounding. The door swung back.

'There,' she said with a slight sneer, 'his precious collection. Sometimes I think I'm only here to finance his obsession.'

I gazed inside. All four shelves were crammed fit to bursting with the most exquisite collection of porcelain figurines I'd ever seen outside of Trewarren.

'Meissen!' I breathed.

Chapter Twenty-five

'That's right, how did you know?' asked Sally in surprise.

'Oh, um, Nick likes it,' I muttered, my mind racing. 'We used to have one or two pieces.'

'Oh really? Oh well, Sam's a complete fanatic. You should see him sitting here on the floor every Saturday morning with all these figures spread out around him, polishing every piece lovingly with his little yellow duster.'

'But . . . is it all his?' I asked, picking up an artisan figure and turning it around in my hand. 'Did he collect all this?'

'Oh no, I only call it his collection because he's the one who takes an interest, but in actual fact it's all mine. My grandfather left it to me – he was mad about porcelain. All this furniture was his too, in fact,' she said, looking around. 'We've added very little. Just a couple of chairs over there, oh – and that mirror. You see, it sounds ridiculous but we've never really had much money. We were given the house but it's so expensive to run and Sam doesn't make very much. I suppose we look as if we're loaded because of all these antiques and things, but it all belongs to my family.'

'I see . . .' I said slowly, as she locked the cupboard. My heart was still pounding. 'But Sam knows a lot about antiques, does he? I mean, porcelain in particular?'

'Oh yes, he's a bit of an expert in his own quiet way. He's always up at the V & A, nosing around, and whenever we go abroad we always have to trudge around a few dreary museums and peer at their bits and pieces. It's more than a hobby really, it's an all-consuming passion. His *other* all-consuming passion,' she added caustically, popping the key back in the china box.

'Gosh,' I said, following her out to the hall again and trying hard not to sound too interested. 'I had no idea he was such a – a whassicalled, aficionado.'

'Well, why should you? He keeps it very much to himself, doesn't really talk about it, can't think why.'

I can! I thought tremulously.

'Perhaps he thinks nosing around stuffy old museums doesn't quite go with the trendy-film-director image,' she went on, opening the front door for me.

Perhaps, I thought, but perhaps not.

Sally smiled shyly as we stood on the step together, blinking in the sunlight.

'Thanks for coming round, Polly. It can't have been easy, but I really appreciate it and, honestly, I'm really happy about your news.'

I smiled back. 'I'm glad I came.' *So* glad, I thought privately.

We kissed each other on the cheek and I ran across the road. I waved as I got into my car. She stood on the steps, a tiny blonde figure in her little black dress, watching as I pulled off.

I drove sedately down the road, keeping an eye on her in my rear-view mirror, but as soon as I knew I was out of sight I gave a great whoop of delight. I hit the gas, and shot off down the road. Bloody hell! What a morning! What an unbelievably riveting morning! I took my hands off the steering wheel for a second and gazed at them in wonder. They were trembling! They were actually trembling with excitement, and why not? I mean, God, first of all – and here I threw back my head and gave another great shout of joy into the roof of the car – Sam was not the father of my child, that much was wonderfully, beautifully, blissfully clear! He might strut around like a highly sexed tom cat, like a walking, talking sperm bank, but his missiles were all doing U-turns the moment they'd been fired. Hoo-bleeding-ray!

I looked down at my tummy and took a hand off the steering wheel for a second, stroking it gently, gazing with wonder, with awe almost. I was pregnant. By my husband. No one else. A radiant smile spread dreamily across my face. What a wonderfully warm feel – Oh Christ! I hastily dropped the radiant smile and put my hand back on the wheel as I narrowly missed colliding with a double-decker bus. Horns blared and obscenities were mouthed but I was much too excited to care.

Because what about that other revelation? What about that, eh? So much for Sam the modernist man. What an equally intriguing discovery that had been. Our Sam was no more a trendy minimalist than the entire *Antiques Roadshow* team put together: he was a history man, a heavily-into-antiques-and-porcelain man, a *Meissen* man no less!

I turned for Pippa's house, feverish with excitement now, all thoughts of rushing off to Thomas Cook to book my holiday in Lanzagrotty totally forgotten. Oh no, I couldn't lie on a beach getting sand in my eyes; I had to lie quietly in a darkened room and think, think, think!

But what did it all mean, though? So what if Sam was a Meissen expert, could it just be one huge coincidence? I shook my head. No, it was much too huge for my liking, much too staggeringly colossal. I set my mouth in a grim line as I drove fast and furiously through the back streets of Chelsea, my mind whirring. Oh yes, make no mistake about it, Sam was up to his neck in the nicking of our precious porcelain, and I was the super sleuth who was going to nail him!

I careered up to some red lights, just managing to stop in time, and gripped the steering wheel hard as I tried desperately to think of some more incriminating evidence. I was pretty sure I had to have a bit more than just the fact that he was a Meissen enthusiast to go to the police. I mentally ticked off a few starters in my head.

Right, first of all, Sam had no money. He was stony broke, that much was clear, so he needed the loot. Secondly, he'd know how to get rid of the stuff. He obviously had his finger on the pulse of the porcelain market so he'd know when and where to pass it on without arousing suspicion – probably knew every collector in the country. Thirdly . . . I bit my lip and frowned. Thirdly, on the night of the burglary he'd been two hundred miles away, holed up in a hotel room with yours truly, much too drunk to drive and much too late to catch the last train to Cornwall, which would have gone hours ago. Damn! I punched the steering wheel hard. How the hell had he done it then?

I stared out of the window at the row of shops I'd pulled up in front of. Unless . . . unless he hadn't actually done it himself. The lights went green, I shunted into first gear and shot off. Yes, of course, brilliant! Sam wouldn't actually want to get his own hands dirty, would he? No, he'd have an accomplice, a lackey, someone who'd do the job for him. But who could that be? Did Sam know someone in Cornwall, perhaps? Someone who'd run the risk? I sighed. The list could be endless; he might know every light-fingered crook in the West Country for all I knew. He probably knew a hell of a lot of antique dealers, and if Lovejoy was anything to go by they were all a pretty dodgy lot.

I roared up the road to Pippa's house in a state of high excitement, parked – well, screeched to a halt – and ran up the garden path. I found the spare key under the pot, bustled importantly into the sitting room and grabbed a piece of paper and a pencil to take notes. I sat down purposefully on the sofa, all ready to think.

I chewed the end of my pencil. Now think, Polly, think. I gazed into space. Nothing much seemed to be happening. I pursed my lips. What would be the most thought-provoking position? I wondered. I swung my legs up and lay down with my head on the arm of the sofa. Then I shut my eyes. Huge mistake, I began to feel a bit sleepy. I quickly got up and sat with my head between my knees so that lots of blood could flow into my brain and help things along. I frowned at the carpet. Now come on, Polly, think. *Think!*

I bashed my head with my fist. Why was I so slow? Where the hell had I been when God had been handing out the little grey cells? Round the back of the bike sheds, probably, having a quick fag and touching up my lipstick. I groaned in frustration. Why couldn't I be one of those people who only had to look at a puzzle and it snapped into place? Like those eggheads on *Countdown* who did conundrums in under twenty seconds, or people who did *The Times* crossword while they were waiting for the toast to pop up. Why couldn't I be more like . . . Nick! Yes, of course, Nick! He'd know. I'd ring him. He'd know *exactly* what to do.

I leaped up with a little squeak of joy and ran to the phone, delighted to have such a good excuse to speak to him. I was halfway through punching out Tim and Sarah's number, however, when I hesitated and lowered the receiver. Should I be doing this? How would he react to hearing from me? As far as I was concerned he was my darling husband, father of my unborn child, no less, but as far as he was concerned I was still public enemy number one, the unfaithful hussy of a wife.

All the same, I thought, slowly bringing the receiver back up to my ear, this was surely something Nick should know about, wasn't it? We were talking about his precious porcelain collection here; it might even lead to him getting it back – he'd thank me for that, wouldn't he? It would help to – you know, ingratiate me, wouldn't it?

I finished dialling and listened with some trepidation as it rang at the other end. I cleared my throat nervously, but after a while trepidation turned to frustration as no one answered. I tried Trewarren but it just rang and rang there too. Oh, come on, Nick, where are you, how come you're never *there*? Finally the answering machine clicked into action.

'Hello, this is Nicholas Penhalligan, I'm sorry we're not . . .' and so on. I listened dreamily. It was a pleasure to hear his voice. Suddenly I realized I was beyond the beep.

'Oh, er, Nick?' I began clumsily. Oh help, why hadn't I thought out what I was going to say? 'Um, it's Polly here, your wife – obviously enough!' I giggled nervously, then cleared my throat and struggled to sound sensible. 'Um, look, the thing is I've got this idea, well, more of a suspicion really. I think it's possible – well, I'm almost certain actually – that Sam's somehow connected with our burglary, because I've found out that he's got loads of Meissen in his house – don't you think that's weird? And he obviously really knows his stuff – his porcelain stuff, I mean,' I added quickly. 'Er, so that's it really. I'm going to do some more investigating but I really need to speak to you, for – well, for advice really. Um, bye then.'

I put the receiver down. Terrible, Polly, really terrible. Totally convoluted and inarticulate. I sighed. Oh well, what did he expect from a pregnant woman? I looked at my watch. Ten past one. He'd surely come back for some lunch soon, I'd just nip to the shops and get some food, then I'd sit by the phone for the rest of the day and wait for him to ring.

I raced up to the high street, bought some provisions, then ran back to the house. I set up camp by the phone in the hall and nibbled a piece of raw broccoli, quite disgusting, but full of folic acid, apparently, good for a baby's brain, or back, or something. Now that I knew about this baby's illustrious parentage I'd decided it had to be on the receiving end of something slightly more nutritious than dry biscuits.

I nibbled away and stared at the phone. Eventually my bottom got sore from sitting on the hard chair so I commandeered the portable phone and lay down on the sofa with it by my nose. I watched it closely. I rang the operator once or twice just to check it was still working. I carried it around with me. It had lunch with me. It watched a lot of television with me. It even had a bath with me.

By the time Pippa's key turned in the door at six thirty I'd clocked up almost five hours of solid telephone watching without so much as a tinkle from Nick, and I was almost going berserk. I fell on her as she came through the front door, relieved that at last *somebody* in the world would be forced to listen to my story.

'Oh, Pippa, thank goodness you're back, I've got so much to tell you – you won't believe what sort of a day I've had, you just won't believe what's happened!'

Pippa dumped her bag and jacket on the hall chair and gazed at me rather dreamily. Her cheeks were pink and her eyes were shining.

'Really?' she said in a distracted manner. 'I've got some news too . . .'

She smoothed her hair in the hall mirror, gazing abstractedly at her reflection. She looked radiant. Suddenly she turned and grabbed my hand. She beamed.

'Oh, Polly, something most extraordinary has happened, something so unbelievably wonderful I still can't really believe it's true! Come on, let's go and get a glass of wine and you can tell me your news, then I'll tell you mine!'

She dragged me into the kitchen, fairly skipping with excitement, and reached for a bottle of wine in the fridge.

'You first!' she trilled. 'I want to save mine till last!' She shoved the corkscrew in and screwed furiously.

'Well, first of all,' I said, perching on the edge of the

table, 'Sam's not the father of this baby, Nick is.' I grinned. 'Sam's had a vasectomy.'

'What!' She popped the cork out and almost dropped the bottle. 'Are you sure? Did Sally say so? Oh, Polly, that's terrific!' She put the bottle down and hugged me. 'I'm so pleased! You must be delighted.'

'I am, ecstatic, and I can't wait to tell Nick about the baby. I think he might see things differently now, don't you?' I asked anxiously.

'Of course he will!' she said staunchly. 'Once he knows he's going to be a father he'll forgive you anything.'

'Well, hopefully,' I said nervously, twiddling my hair round my finger. 'But listen, Pippa' – I slipped off the table and sat down in a chair – 'there's something else, something really quite serious.'

'What?' She poured out a couple of glasses and sat down opposite me. 'You look all sort of strict and head-mistressy, what is it?'

'Sam collects Meissen china – I saw his collection at his house.'

Pippa frowned. 'So?'

'Meissen, Pippa, the same porcelain that was stolen from Trewarren, don't you see?'

'See what?'

'Well, he has to be involved somehow, doesn't he? I mean, it's much too much of a coincidence. D'you think I should ring the police or something?'

She stared at me. 'And say what? That Sam collects the same china as you, so therefore he nicked yours? Don't be ridiculous, Polly, Sam's not a thief, and anyway he was with you on the night of the burglary, wasn't he?'

'Well yes, but that doesn't stop him from being involved, does it? He probably got someone else to do it.'

'What, you think he masterminded the whole operation from the dance floor of Annabel's while some Cornish tea leaf was doing his dirty work? Don't be absurd, it's just a coincidence, and anyway what about Bruce, what about the bit he gave to his mother? Or d'you think that was really Sam in disguise? Mincing around the hospital in a pair of tight jeans and a blond wig, hoping Bruce's mum wouldn't suss him?'

'Now don't be flippant, Pippa, this is serious –'

'Well tell me then, tell me how you think he did it.'

'Well . . .' I scratched my head. I'd been so sure, so convinced. I struggled to get back to my train of thought.

'Yes?' she demanded.

'Now hang on a minute, Pippa, you're confusing me. I had some good ideas earlier, just let me think a minute –'

'Oh, for goodness' sake, Polly, forget it, will you? It's absurd. Totally crazy. And anyway,' she seized my hand across the table, 'what about my news – just listen to this! Guess what?'

'What?'

'Josh is leaving his wife!'

'Oh! Oh, that's . . . wonderful, Pippa.'

'Isn't it fantastic? When he got home last night she confessed that she'd been unhappy for ages and was having an affair with some guy at work – Josh had no idea! She wants her man to move in with her, so Josh is going to come and live here.'

'Really? What, here with you?'

'Yes, of course, why not? And guess what, Polly, he

hinted – only hinted, mind – that when the divorce comes through, we might even get married. Married!' She leaped up and danced around the kitchen, clutching the bottle of wine to her chest. 'Aren't I just the luckiest girl in the world? Aren't I? God, I can't believe it! There's only one thing, though.' She sat down again and looked anxious. 'D'you think we can still get married in a church? Because Josh has been married before? D'you think I can still have the whole ivory-silk-and-orange-blossom bit? Do you? Only I really want all that.'

'Well, I –'

'Actually I have a feeling it's OK so long as the vicar jumbles the vows up a bit. My cousin married a divorcee and she had the works, but I seem to remember the words were a bit different, which is fine by me. I don't mind what Josh says so long as "I do" is tucked in somewhere – oh, and all his worldly goods, of course!' She giggled. 'Oh, and, Polly, you can be my bridesmaid, or – no, you're married – my matron of honour! My *pregnant* matron of honour. Gosh, you'll probably be about nine months by then – you can waddle up the aisle after me, what a scream! Oh, isn't it brilliant, isn't it just fantastic?' She leaped up and did a few pirouettes round the kitchen.

'It's great news, Pippa, really it is.' I forced a smile. I couldn't help thinking that Josh wasn't exactly leaving his wife – she was kicking him out. But it wasn't just that, there was something else, something about Josh, something nagging . . .

'Listen,' I said, 'sorry to harp on, but about Sam, d'you really think I shouldn't just mention it to the police? I mean, that he's a collector?'

Pippa stopped in mid-twirl. 'No, I don't think you should.' She stared at me. 'You know what you're doing, Polly? You're trying to get back at him. You're trying to pin something on him because he got you drunk and then went to bed with you. You're just pissed off with him, aren't you? You haven't got the slightest bit of proof, for heaven's sake, you just know he collects the same china as you! And anyway, what about my news? What about my life, for a change, did you hear what I said? Josh and I might be getting married. Isn't that marvellous, or doesn't my life matter?'

'Of course it does and I'm thrilled for you if . . . well, if that's what you want.'

She stared at me. 'Of course it's what I want, it's what I've always wanted – you know that. What's the matter, don't you like him or something?'

'Of course I do, it's just – oh, I don't know, forget it.'

'What? It's just what?'

'Well . . . it's nothing really, it's just – well, you know how he doesn't get on with Bruce?'

'Yes, so what?'

'Well, I just thought –' I licked my lips, I was getting into really deep water here. 'Forget it, Pippa, it's nothing.'

Pippa sat down and narrowed her eyes. 'No, come on, Polly, what? I'd really like to know. So what if he doesn't get on with Bruce?'

I squirmed around on my chair. 'Well, I just wondered . . . whether he had anything to do with it – but forget it, Pippa, I'm way out of line here, I –'

'No, no, I will *not* forget it! Hang on a minute now, you think Josh had something to do with the burglary? You think he framed Bruce, is that it?'

'Well, I –'

'Because his sister got AIDS from a blood transfusion and as a result he can't bear homosexuals? You think that because of that he and Sam framed Bruce and nicked your china, is that it?' She gazed at me for a moment, then sat back in her chair, her eyes widening with comprehension. She nodded slowly.

'Ah yes, of course, I've got it now! You think that when he stormed out of the restaurant that night he went down to Cornwall to steal your porcelain. Then he passed it on to Sam and together they framed Bruce, that's it, isn't it?'

'Look, I know it sounds far-fetched, but –'

'Far-fetched? Polly, it's obscene! For your information Josh was very upset that night because his sister had taken a turn for the worse. When he left the restaurant he went straight to the hospital. He spent the whole night sitting by her bed, holding her hand, comforting her and mopping her up as she threw up all night. If you need an alibi,' she said, looking cold and furious now, 'I'm quite sure the nurses at the hospital will verify his story. Why don't you go and ask them? St Stephen's, Fulham Road, go on, ask them!' She was white now and her lips had all but disappeared.

I put my head in my hands and groaned. 'Oh God, Pippa, I'm sorry, I'm so sorry!' I wailed. 'I had no idea. What must you think of me? I just – oh, I don't know, I've obviously got this whole thing completely wrapped round my neck.'

'You certainly have,' said Pippa, her voice trembling a bit. 'I can't think what's got into you. These are my *friends* you're talking about. Josh is my *boy*friend, for God's sake, and Sam is an extremely good mate, added to which they've both got responsible jobs in the film industry – they're not petty thieves! Christ, you'll be accusing me next. Perhaps you think Josh popped into the hospital for ten minutes then he and I *both* charged down to Cornwall and robbed you blind, is that it?'

'No, of *course* not, Pippa, of course not, and I'm so sorry, really I am –'

'And what about Bruce? I mean, I know you like him, but take it from me, he is one hell of a mixed-up kid, and if you want my *very* candid opinion – which up until now I wouldn't have voiced, but seeing as how you've forced me into it – I wouldn't put it past him at all. Not at all!'

She lit a cigarette, puffing the smoke out fast and furiously and shaking the match out vigorously. She was clearly upset. She waggled her finger at me.

'You know what you're doing here, Polly? You're trying to clear the people you *do* like and pin it on the people you *don't* like, don't you realize that? It's crazy!'

I stared at her. She was right, of course. I was behaving like a loony, like some sort of amateur Sherlock Holmes. Whatever was I thinking of? I shook my head.

'Oh God, I'm sorry,' I said miserably. 'I don't know what's the matter with me, I seem to be seeing the worst in everyone at the moment. It must be this pregnancy lark. I think Josh is great, really I do, and I'm desperately sorry about his sister. Pippa, I'm so sorry, just call me hormonal, OK?' I gazed at her beseechingly.

She glared at me fiercely, then looked away. After a minute she looked back. She grinned abruptly. 'OK, forget it.' She pushed the wine bottle over the table. 'Life's

445

too short. Here, have another glass of wine, it might relax those hormones.'

'I think I'd better,' I muttered, sloshing some into my glass. 'I certainly need something.' I shook my head. 'I just can't think what got into me.'

'Forget it, I said. Oh, and listen – Josh is taking me out to dinner tonight, can I borrow your pink skirt?'

'My short one? I thought you said it was passé. What happened to all your flowing robes?'

She went pink. 'Oh yes, well actually Josh says he likes me best in minis.' She grinned ruefully. 'And, let's face it, who am I really trying to please here?'

I grinned back. 'Who indeed?'

She looked at her watch and jumped up. 'Must go and have a bath, he'll be here in a minute, will you dig it out for me then?'

'Sure.'

She disappeared upstairs.

I sighed heavily and traced my finger around a knot of wood in the pine table. What did I want to get involved in all this detective malarkey for anyway? What business was it of mine who stole the china – it was for the police to sort out, wasn't it? I had my baby to think of now, our baby. I couldn't rush around the country exposing villains. I sipped my wine thoughtfully. I'd go home tomorrow, go and face Nick. Tell him about the baby. Ask him to forgive me. Sort my life out. Go to antenatal classes, decorate the nursery, be normal for a change. I began to feel excited. The little yellow room next to ours would make a great nursery, lots of light. I'd make it beautiful, have a border, ducks and rabbits – no, teddies, pink and blue, just to hedge my bets. Oh, and a mobile, lots of mobiles, and Winnie the Pooh pictures all over the walls.

Just then the phone rang.

'I'll get it!' I screeched upstairs to Pippa, who was running her bath. Nick, it had to be Nick. I'd tell him I was coming home. No, *ask* him if I could come home. I ran to the hall.

'Hello?' I said breathlessly.

'Hello, Polly? It's Lottie.'

'Oh! Hi, Lottie.' I tried to keep the severe disappointment from my voice.

'Where the hell have you been? I've been trying to track you down for ages. Nick was most elusive when I spoke to him last night, said he hadn't a clue what you were up to. What's going on, have you had a row or something?'

'Er, well, yes, a bit. Something like that – sorry, Lotts, I've been meaning to ring you but –'

'And how are you feeling? Gosh, I've only just heard, you don't still feel ghastly, do you?'

I frowned. How the devil did she know?

'Er, not too bad, still feel pretty sick in the mornings actually, but how did you know?'

'In the mornings? What, every morning? How *awful*! Polly, you must see a doctor. I told Nick and he agreed.'

'Nick?' I breathed. 'You told Nick?'

'Well, of course, I thought you would have told him already actually, but he had no idea. Polly, you *must* go and see someone – it's not right to feel sick every morning.'

'Isn't it? I thought it was fairly normal, but – but hang on a minute, Lottie, who told you?' I stammered.

'Peggy, I ran into her in the street the other day.'

'PEGGY!' I screeched. 'How the hell does *she* know?'

'Well, she saw you leave. She asked me how you were, said she'd never seen anyone in such a terrible state.'

'L-leave where?' I babbled helplessly, totally at a loss.

'The club, of course, Annabel's – remember? Tom and I left before you but Peggy said she saw you go.'

'Ah yes.' I was beginning – slowly – to see the light. 'Yes, I was pretty drunk that night.'

'Pretty drunk? Peggy said you were unconscious!'

Well, she would, wouldn't she, I thought savagely, she probably only drank orange juice, and now she was running around telling tales out of school about me, filtering them back to Nick, no less.

'Well, all right,' I conceded, 'paralytic actually.'

'No, Polly, she said you were actually unconscious.'

I frowned. 'What?'

'Yes, she said you had to be carried out, literally lifted out of the club, by that guy you were with, that film director chappie. Peggy went over to ask if she could help and he said something about you being prone to fainting from tiredness and that you had jet lag or something. She didn't think anything of it because she doesn't know you very well, but when she told me I couldn't believe it! I've never known you faint and as for jet lag – where the hell had you been to get that?'

I sat down heavily on the chair in the hall, trying hard to accommodate all this.

'Are you sure, Lottie?' I whispered.

'Positive! Peggy said the doorman at Annabel's helped carry you to a taxi, said he'd seen some pretty plastered people in his time but you really took the biscuit.'

Christ! I made a mental note not to frequent that particular joint for a while.

'And you're still feeling sick? Every morning? That's terrible! You must go for a check-up, really.'

'Oh! Oh er, no – no, that's something else.'

'What?'

'Oh, um, nothing really, nothing at all. It's almost gone now anyway, a bug sort of thing. Tummy bug. Listen, Lottie, I've really got to dash now, thanks so much for ringing.'

'Why have you got to dash?'

'Well, I've got this – this person coming round, odd-job man – oops – there's the doorbell now, must be him. Thanks for ringing, Lottie, bye.'

'But –'

'Bye!'

I put the phone down. I stared at the floor. Unconscious. Jesus! Not just a little the worse for wear, a bit tiddly-tight, a trifle woozy, but out for the count. The bastard. The complete and utter bastard. Sally had been right, he was totally unscrupulous, unspeakably vile. What sort of a man would get a girl so disastrously drunk that she couldn't even speak, let alone stand, then carry her to the nearest hotel and proceed to have his wicked way? I felt physically sick, and this time it was nothing to do with the hormones. This was rape then, wasn't it? This wasn't just a drunken one-night stand, this was a ghastly – I sat up straight, my eyes bulged – yes, it was a date rape! God, I'd been date raped!

I gasped. I clutched my mouth, horror and revulsion rising within me. I managed to stagger to my feet but my legs were like jelly.

'Rape!' I whispered, gasping for breath and clutching the banisters. All at once I found some air.

'RAPE! R-A-P-E!' I screeched at the top of my voice.

There was a great sploosh of water from the landing above me. The bathroom door flew open, hit the wall with a resounding crash and Pippa came hurtling down the stairs, stark naked and streaming with water.

'Where? Where is he? What happened?' she shrieked, grabbing an umbrella from the stand in the hall and brandishing it wildly.

'Rape!' I squeaked again, collapsing into the chair and clutching my head. 'Ooh, Pippa, I've been raped!'

She seized my shoulders. 'Oh, Polly! Oh my poor darling! Where is he, has he gone?' She looked around wild-eyed. 'Which way did he go?' She flung open the front door and brandished the brolly, clearly ready to pursue him down the street stark naked.

'Oh – no,' I gasped, 'not just now, ages ago. It was Sam but I've only just found out!'

Pippa stared at me. She slowly lowered the umbrella. Then she shut the front door. Her jaw slackened.

'Sam?

'Yes, I've only just found out, that night in the hotel, he raped me!'

Pippa put the umbrella back in the stand. She sighed heavily and folded her bare arms against her bare chest. 'Oh God, Polly, not that again. Is that what you got me out of the bath for? You think Sam raped you now, do you?'

'Yes, yes! Because listen, Pippa,' I babbled, 'Lottie's

friend Peggy was in Annabel's that night, she saw me leave with him, she said I was unconscious!'

'Really?' Pippa looked grim. 'Well, you probably were, does that really come as a complete surprise? I mean, let's face it, you do tend to shift the liquor and it's not unheard of for you to lose it in the leg department as a result. For God's sake, Polly, that Peggy girl's as straight as they come. She probably saw you reeling around a bit and couldn't believe her puritanical eyes.' She raised her eyebrows. 'All right if I go back to my bath now? I mean, there's no one you actually want me to clobber over the head, is there? No one's brains you want me to beat to a pulp? Only I'm freezing to death here. As you might have noticed, I've got nothing on.' She shivered violently.

'But, Pippa –'

'Listen.' She looked at me sternly. 'Sam is undoubtedly a bit of a lad and I'm quite sure he got you plastered and then coerced you into bed, but that's not quite the same thing as rape, is it?'

'But it explains why I don't remember anything,' I wailed, wringing my hands hysterically. 'It explains every-thing!'

Pippa grabbed a coat from the coat stand and wrapped it around herself. Her teeth were chattering now. She knelt down beside me.

'It explains nothing,' she said gently. 'OK, maybe you did pass out momentarily and then perhaps you came round in the taxi or something, who knows? But honestly, Polly, I wouldn't make a big thing of it, because, believe me, it won't sound good. I mean, think about it, it's a classic, isn't it? A girl feels guilty about an extramarital bunk-up, she broods on it for a while, feels bitter and resentful and then eventually, ages after the event, accuses the guy of raping her.'

I stared at her.

'Well, that's about the size of it, isn't it? And, believe me, that's certainly how it's going to look. And, anyway,' she said with a quizzical smile, 'I thought he was a thief? Two minutes ago you were convinced he was a burglar, now he's a rapist.' She cocked her head to one side. 'I mean, which is it, Polly? Know what I mean?'

I gulped and stared at the floor.

She grinned, gave my hand a quick squeeze and then with chattering teeth turned and leaped back up the stairs two at a time to the bathroom.

'Look, I'll talk to you about it in a minute when I'm out of my bath, OK?' she yelled. 'But I'm freezing to *death* here!'

I watched her go. The bathroom door slammed. I heard the radio go on. I sat dumbly, staring at my reflection in the hall mirror opposite. A rapist or a thief. A thief or a rapist. My eyes stared back at me. Yes, I wondered, which indeed? I set my mouth in a grim line. And why not both? Far-fetched? We'll soon see about that. Forget about it? No way. I'd had a feeling all along there'd been something very fishy about that night, and now I was going to prove it.

I waited until I heard Pippa splashing away happily in the bath again, then I stood up and quietly plucked my car keys from the hall table. I silently opened the front door, tiptoed around it and shut it softly behind me. Then, with my heart thumping wildly, I ran down the garden path to my car.

Chapter Twenty-six

I closed the car door softly behind me and glanced anxiously up at the house to see if Pippa was looking out of the window. I didn't want to have to explain myself; she thought I was mad enough as it was and she'd think I'd gone completely doolally if I told her where I was going, but I'd had an idea. I was going to go to the hotel. I was going to go and find out if anyone remembered me from that Friday night, find out what sort of condition I'd been in. The only trouble was, apart from the fact that it was a reasonably classy joint in Mayfair, I was a little vague as to its exact location. There was going to be a certain amount of trial and error involved here. Duke Street? I wondered. Stratton Street, perhaps? I started the car. Somewhere like that anyway. Maybe if I meandered around the vicinity it would all come flooding back.

I roared off to Mayfair, trying hard not to think about Sam in case I was sick all over the steering wheel, and instead concentrated like mad on trying to remember which particular road the taxi had picked me up from on that fateful morning-after-the-night-before. I drove slowly round and round Berkeley Square, peering anxiously down side streets and feeling more and more unsure and confused. Suddenly, on a gut impulse, I hung a left. I parked the car on a yellow line and dashed up Mount Street.

I ran towards Grosvenor Square, glancing up at the tall, elegant buildings which towered on either side of me. It hadn't been a large hotel, that much I remembered, and it was just a hunch, but I had a feeling it was somewhere around . . . here! I skidded to a halt and gazed up at the ancient redbrick building I'd stopped in front of. It was definitely a hotel – albeit a discreet one, just a tiny gold plaque on the outside to let its punters in on the secret – but was it the right one?

I pushed through the smoked-glass doors and peered dubiously around the reception area. It didn't actually look terribly familiar and I was just about to go when – oh yes! Hang on a minute. I stared down at the carpet. It was royal blue with a tiny gold fleur-de-lis pattern on it. That pattern, surely I remembered it from the towels in the bathroom? I crouched down and took a closer look, peering at it.

'Yes, brilliant, Polly, right first time, this is it!' I exclaimed, much to the astonishment of a group of jabbering Japanese tourists who were clustered at the reception desk.

They instantly broke off from their animated discussion and bustled over to have a look. Had they overlooked some fascinating ancient carpet? A first-class tourist attraction in front of their very noses, right here in the hotel? I smiled and nodded.

'Seventeenth century,' I whispered, 'genuine Aubusson.'

They instantly erupted into an excited babble and thousands of yen's worth of camera equipment whirred into action. I left them to snap and flash furiously as I hurried over to the now empty reception desk.

There didn't appear to be anyone about so I banged the little gold bell and shouted 'Hello! Hello!' once or twice.

After a minute a pale, rather bored-looking young man appeared from a back office. I had the feeling he hadn't liked the urgent way I'd rung his bell because he took his time to arrive at the desk and peered down his nose superciliously at me.

'Hello,' I said rather breathlessly, 'um, d'you remember me?'

He raised a laconic eyebrow. 'Should I, modom?' he enquired in an unnaturally plummy voice.

'Well, hopefully, yes, you see I was in here – well, I think I was in here – about four weeks ago with – with a friend of mine. It was a Friday night and I believe I was rather, you know, out of it. Ring any bells?'

He regarded me coolly. 'I'm afraid not. An awful lot of people stay in this 'otel, modom, as I'm sure you'll appreciate. Just the one night was it? You and your, er, friend?' he said with a sneer.

One of these days, I decided, I'd tell one of these snotty-nosed receptionists or shop assistants who worked in smart London joints and looked at you as if you were a pile of poo when you walked in that they weren't fooling anyone, because that's exactly what they were, *receptionists*, for God's sake, *shop* assistants. They could be as superior as they damn well liked while they were in Mayfair but I was pretty sure at the end of the day they went home to their bedsits in Kilburn, dropped their h's, crucified their vowels and ate Vesta curries on their laps in front of *Brookside*.

However, I pretended I hadn't understood the implication and smiled sweetly. 'That's it, just the one night.'

'Name of?' he said wearily, flicking through a large diary on the counter.

'Penhalligan and, er, Weston. Or possibly just Weston – yes, Mr and Mrs Weston.'

He pursed his lips to hide another sneer.

'Yes . . .' He ran a finger down the entry for Friday 8th. 'Here it is, Mr Weston and Mrs Penhalligan.' He snapped the book shut.

'Oh! Really? Did I sign it then?'

He sighed and opened the book again. 'You tell me, modom,' he muttered, swivelling the book around for me to see.

I shook my head. 'No, that's not my writing.'

'Must be your friend's then,' he purred.

'Yes, must be. Good, so we were definitely here, that's a start. Were you on the desk that night, by any chance?'

'I was, as it happens.'

'But you don't remember me?'

'As I said, modom, an awful lot of people pass through these –'

'Here, what about this then?'

I ruffled up my hair, smudged my lipstick across my face and pulled my T-shirt off one shoulder. He looked alarmed. I slumped forward on his desk, rolled my eyes and stuck my tongue out of the corner of my mouth, frothing a bit. He started to back away in horror, but then abruptly stopped. He peered, stepped forward and took a closer look. His face cleared.

'Oh blimey! Yeah, yeah, hang on a minute, it's all coming back!' Suddenly we were in Kilburn. 'Yeah, I've got it!' he said cheerfully, waggling his finger at me. 'I didn't recognize you at first wiv your clothes on an' that, but you were the bird wot was carried in wiv her undies hanging out!'

'Er, yes, yes, quite possibly, was I actually carried in?'

'More or less, yeah. I mean 'e had 'is arm around you and was sort of draggin' you along, but you couldn't stand up. An' then while 'e signed the register 'e propped you up on that sofa over there but you kept toppling over, like. You was in a terrible state, terrible!'

'Really,' I breathed, 'go on.'

'Well, I asked your bloke wevver I should call a doctor, like, but he said no, you often got like that an' you just needed a good night's sleep. Said it was a mixture of jet lag and booze but, I tell you, I've seen some pretty godawful drunks in my time and you looked more than half cut to me: your eyes were rollin' round your 'ead somefing terrible. It was 'orrible! Maria said we shouldn't 'ave let you in in that state, but he'd paid the bill and was up them stairs before we could say 'ang on a minute, mate!'

'I knew it!' I cried, slapping the counter with my hand. 'I knew I had to be a hospital case to let him bring me here, the bastard – and did you see him leave too? In the morning?'

'Nah, my shift finished about ten minutes after you arrived. Maria took over. She shut the place up for the night then manned the desk till I came back on at about nine the next morning. You can ask her if you like.'

'Is she around?'

''Ang on.' He poked his nose into the back office. 'Maria!'

A moment later a Spanish girl popped her head round. '*Si?*'

'You know that flash git wot carried that bird in 'ere a few Fridays ago, the one that was right out of 'er tree, well this is 'er. She wants to know if you saw the bloke leave the next morning.'

She sidled up to the desk and nodded nervously. '*Si*, I see heem go.'

'At about seven, was it?' I asked.

'Ah, no no, the same night, at about half the twelve.'

I frowned. 'That night? Are you sure?'

'*Si, si*, I was just locking up all ze windows and he come queekly down ze back stairs. I don't zink he was even seeing me; it was very dark because all ze lights were off zen. He didn't leave by ze front door zough, he went out of ze back, zrough ze fire escape. I started to go after heem, to tell heem he no get back in again, all locky up, but he ran off to a car.'

'Yes?' I breathed.

'Well, he get in. He get into ze car and zey drive off really fast, all screechy tyres, so I no get a chance to tell him he no get back in ze hotel again.'

'They? There was someone else?'

'*Si, si*, driving the car.'

'What did he look like, did you see? Blond, dark, a beard, anything?'

'Ah, no no, not a man, a girl, I recognize her!'

'You did!'

'*Si!* I see her in fcclms of course, the feelm star lady!'

'Serena Montgomery?' I breathed.

'*Si*, that's it!' Maria nodded and grinned. 'Beeg surprise for me, I can tell you!'

I leaned heavily on the desk, suddenly needing some support. Serena. I gazed at the mahogany. Serena, blimey.

'Big surprise for me too, Maria,' I muttered.

Mr Kilburn peered at me nervously. ''Ere, you all right, luv? D'you wanna glass of water or somefing, not gonna collapse on us again or anyfing, are you?'

I slowly raised myself up from his desk. 'What? Oh, no. No, I'm fine . . . fine . . .'

Suddenly I swung round to Maria and grabbed her arm. 'Listen,' I said urgently, 'would you swear to that in court? You know, what you've just told me, would you swear to it?'

Maria backed away, her eyes huge with fear.

Mr Kilburn stepped in protectively. ''Ere, don't you freaten her, she ain't done nuffing wrong.'

'No, no, of course she hasn't, it's just – oh, never mind, it probably won't be necessary. Thank you, though, thank you so much!' I seized Maria's hand and shook it warmly. 'You've been a great help!'

On a sudden impulse I grabbed Mr Kilburn's hand too and pumped that up and down, beaming widely. 'Thank you, thank you very much!'

They both looked at me in astonishment and retreated towards their office, their eyes wide with wonder. I turned on my heel and, skirting round the group of fascinated Japanese tourists, who were still on their hands and knees peering at the carpet, legged it out of the hotel.

I leaped the front steps in one, fell over, picked myself up and raced down Mount Street back to my car. I could hardly do my seat belt up my hands were shaking so much, and it took quite a few stabs to get the key in the ignition, but once in I crashed the gears with a vengeance and roared off in a state of high excitement. My mind was absolutely fizzing.

Of course! It all made perfect sense. Sam had obviously slipped me something totally lethal in Annabel's, something quite a lot stronger than a double gin and tonic, thank you very much. Oh yes, we were talking drugs here, heavy duty ones too, because whatever it was had clearly knocked me senseless. Then he'd carted my limp body off to the hotel and booked us both in, making damn sure I was registered under Penhalligan and also making absolutely sure that we were well and truly noticed.

Oh, I could see it all now, the amorous drunken couple returning from the nightclub, out of their minds with booze, hanging on to each other, reeling around the reception area making a hell of a racket. Me, already half undressed and practically comatose on the sofa, and Sam, ringing the bell, roaring his head off and acting the drunken Lothario whose sole intention appeared to be to get his plastered bird up those stairs as quickly as possible and bonk the living daylights out of her.

Once upstairs he'd obviously taken my clothes off – I gripped the steering wheel hard and bit back the bile: please God that had been the extent of his lechery, please God he hadn't raped me just for the hell of it – and scribbled the note which purported to have been written at seven the next morning.

Then, when he thought the coast was clear, he'd slipped down the back stairs to Serena, who was revving up the car at the back of the hotel. Together they'd whizzed off down to Cornwall – which at that time of night in a fast car would only have taken about four hours – arriving at Trewarren in plenty of time to relieve us of our precious porcelain.

And of course, I thought bitterly, cutting straight across the traffic into Piccadilly and leaving a blare of angry horns in my wake, Serena was the perfect accomplice, wasn't she? Oh yes, she knew the house inside out – she knew every inch of it from her days with Nick – and was bound to know where the key to the porcelain cupboard was kept. All she had to do was reach up to the top of the dresser, slip her long, elegant fingers into the jug, produce the key with a triumphant little smirk and swing it in Sam's admiring face on one of her sharp red nails. I ground my teeth.

Badger, of course, would have been an absolute pushover, not that he was much of a guard dog anyway, but he probably gave her a rapturous welcome. So how had they got into the house? I wondered. I shook my head. No matter, that was a minor detail, I had most of the jigsaw in place and it all fitted perfectly. I thumped my forehead with the palm of my hand and groaned. Oh, you moron, Polly, why didn't you think of all this before?

I swung right at Scotch Corner, frantically imagining the scenario. I saw them running down Trewarren's staircase together, swag bag in hand. I saw them darting quickly across the drive to their car, stashing the bag safely in the boot and jumping into the front seat. Then I saw them roaring back to London amidst gales of triumphant laughter, stealing the occasional kiss on the motorway, stroking each other's thighs perhaps, ruffling each other's hair, oh so incredibly pleased with themselves. Finally I saw Sam arriving back home that morning at about ten o'clock, looking suitably shamefaced and sheepish, leading poor Sally to imagine he'd had another of his frequent nights out on the tiles.

And of course, if the shit did happen to hit the fan, if someone did bother to ask Sam where the devil he'd been that Friday night, he had the perfect alibi. How could he possibly have had anything to do with the burglary at Trewarren when he'd been holed up with the lady of the very same house in a smart hotel in Mayfair? Oh yes, if Serena had been the perfect accomplice then I'd been the perfect alibi. God, how they must have laughed. I clenched my teeth and shook my head. Very clever, my little love birds, very clever indeed!

I roared up to Pippa's house and due to lack of space parked at a ludicrous angle with the front wheels practically in her garden. Yep, there was no doubt about it, I thought, slamming the car door behind me, it had been an absolutely brilliant plan. Fiendish even, and if it hadn't been for Maria – and me, of course – they might just have got away with it. Thank goodness for Maria! Thank goodness for me! I hurried up the garden path.

So what were they planning to do now? I wondered. Lie low for a bit and then sneak the stuff on to the market gradually? Go abroad, perhaps, and live off their ill-gotten gains? Not so fast, my little darlings, I thought grimly as I rooted around under the flowerpot for the key, not so blinking fast!

The first thing I'd do, I decided, as I let myself in, was ring the police. Not the crappy old Cornish police but Scotland Yard or MI5 or something. I mean, heavens, we were in London now; there was nothing parochial about this inquiry any more. This was of national importance – the press would be on to it in a moment. I could see the headlines now – 'Missing Meissen Mystery – Film Star and Director Charged'. Oh yes, the tabloids would have a field day, and of course they'd want to speak to me, interview me, take a few pictures, that kind of thing. Naturally I'd be frightfully modest, pepper my story with lots of 'Oh, it was nothing's, and – oh gosh, wouldn't Nick be proud? He'd be beside himself!

I shut the door behind me. The house was in darkness. It was well past ten o'clock now and Pippa had obviously gone out for dinner with Josh and forgotten to leave any lights on. Poor Pippa, how awful of me to accuse Josh like that, especially just as she'd got the happy ending she'd dreamed of. I was so pleased it wasn't him. I could get excited with her now, work out possible wedding plans, go shopping for a dress, perhaps, choose her flowers, organize the bridesmaids, that kind of thing. I felt along the wall for the light switch but when I flicked it down, nothing happened. The bulb had obviously blown.

Muttering darkly, I felt my way round to the sitting room and bent down to turn on the little lamp on the table just inside the door. As I fumbled for the switch halfway down the flex, my hand brushed against something warm, something – moving. I pulled back sharply – God, a hand! I clutched my throat with a scream. In an instant the lamp came on by itself. I screamed again, louder this time, and my hands flew up to my mouth. I stared in horror. Because there, sitting in the armchair with his hand on the light switch, was Sam.

Chapter Twenty-seven

His amber eyes looked almost yellow in the sudden bright light, his face pale and twisted with loathing. I backed away.

'Sam!' I gasped.

'Hello, Polly,' he said softly, 'how nice to see you.'

The words were slightly slurred and his mouth only just managed to articulate them. I saw at a glance that he was extremely drunk.

'H-how did you get in?' I stammered.

'Same way as you, I expect, first geranium pot on the left. Very careless of Pippa, especially in these dangerous times. Anyone could get in. Anyone.'

There was something deeply menacing about this statement. He licked his front teeth, unsticking them from his bloated, dehydrated lips, then he swayed a bit to one side and steadied himself with his hand on the arm of the chair. God, he was out of his head.

I gulped and scuttled to the far end of the room where I perched on the arm of the sofa. I didn't want to sink too deeply into a chair in case I needed to get up and do some fast running. I quickly leaned across and flicked on another table lamp, noticing as I did so that all the curtains were drawn. Pippa never bothered.

'Oh yes, the spare key,' I twittered nervously, 'yes of course, very silly, I – I must tell her about it, you're right.

Um – did you want to see her? Only I think she's gone out with Josh.'

'She has. Won't be back till late. No, it's you I want to see, Polly.' He was breathing heavily now and sweating profusely, his skin looked damp and waxy. 'Just you. You little bitch.'

The venom in these few short words made me flinch. A cold hand gripped my heart. He'd come to get me, to silence me. He'd found out that I'd been nosing around and he'd come to rip out my tongue.

'Now, now, Sam,' I said nervously, 'there's no need to be like that. Let's try and discuss this in a civilized fashion, shall we?'

'Civilized!' he spat. 'Don't talk to me about civilized, you with your dirty, scummy little tricks. You went to see my wife this morning, didn't you?'

Oh that! Gosh, I almost breathed a sigh of relief. I'd forgotten about that, he surely wasn't going to kill me because I'd been to see Sally, was he?

'Showed her a photograph, didn't you? Stolen, incidentally, from my private diary. That was pretty bloody civilized of you, wasn't it?'

On second thoughts, perhaps he was going to kill me, his eyes were twitching maniacally and he was grinding his teeth in an alarming manner. Thanks, Sally, I thought, inching back up the arm of the sofa, thanks a bunch, really terrific of you to drop me in it. I tried a lie.

'Well actually, Sam, that's not quite the way it was. You see –'

'Oh, don't give me that cock-and-bull story she tried about finding it weeks ago!' he hissed. 'I know damn well it was in my Filofax when I left my case in that taxi. You just rifled through it and thought – Gosh, a photo, I wonder if Sam's wife has seen this – and then you clasped it in your hot little hand and toddled off to show it to her, didn't you? You conniving little bitch, you just couldn't wait to get even. Just because your marriage was shot to bits you thought you'd pop round and blast a few holes in mine!'

'Sam, it wasn't like that, really it wasn't. She asked me to take it round, rang me up and begged me to, and I didn't tell her anything she didn't already know. I promise I –'

'You're a fucking LIAR!' he bellowed, and thumped the wall with his fist.

There was a terrifying silence. I watched as a tiny hairline crack appeared in the paintwork. How long would it be before one of those appeared in my head? He started to lever himself out of his chair. Quite soon, obviously, I thought with a gulp, really quite soon. I felt cold with fear.

'Now look, Sam,' I whispered, 'let's not get this thing out of proportion, shall we? I mean, it would be silly to fall out over –'

'You're just an interfering little busybody,' he hissed, struggling to his feet, 'with nothing better to do than –' Suddenly he stopped. He sank back into his chair again. His shoulders sagged and his head dropped like a stone into his hands. He tugged savagely at his hair, pulling at the roots.

'She's leaving me, you know,' he muttered, 'or should I say' – he gave a hollow laugh – 'she's throwing me out. Not that it matters,' he went on almost to himself, 'I was going anyway, little cow. But not yet . . . not quite yet . . . fouls things up a bit, you see . . . all a bit . . . sudden.'

There was a silence; he seemed scarcely aware of my presence. I gazed at him in wonder. Was this really the same Sam? The glamorous, fun-loving guy I'd met in Cornwall, oozing charm and bonhomie? The mighty film director? My, how he'd fallen. He looked up abruptly. I could see the veins pumping away in his forehead. He stared at me.

'You see, I like to be in control, Polly,' he said quietly. 'I don't like other people taking the initiative – it upsets me, d'you know what I mean? It's for me to decide when I want to go, when I want to leave my own house. I don't like it when little bitches like you take it upon themselves to decide for me, I take it very personally, d'you understand?'

'Yes, but –'

'DO YOU UNDERSTAND?'

'Yes, yes!' I yelped. 'I understand!'

Christ, he wasn't just drunk, he was stark staring mad. I gripped my knees to stop them from shaking; my heart was pounding furiously.

His head dropped back into his hands and he began massaging his temples. He started mumbling to himself; it was as if he'd forgotten about me again. I breathed deeply and licked my lips, plucking up the courage to speak steadily, to calm him down. I was pretty sure that was the received wisdom with maniacs.

'I do see, Sam, really I do,' I began tremulously, 'but honestly, Sally wasn't even particularly upset. She knew about Serena, she knew about all the others – God, she'd even heard about you and me, can you believe it?' I laughed nervously. 'So soon!'

He looked up abruptly. His top lip curled. 'About you? Don't make me laugh. Don't flatter yourself, Polly. I wouldn't touch you if you were the last woman on earth.'

A great tidal wave of relief washed through me but I tried my best to be outraged.

'How dare you!'

'Oh, it's quite true,' he sneered. 'If you must know, you make me want to vomit, have done since I met you. I knew what you were the moment I saw you, a bored, frustrated little housewife, spoiled rotten by your husband and bored to tears with your big house in the country and all your money. You just loved playing lady bountiful with the film crew, didn't you? Got such a cheap little thrill out of it all, being so gracious and magnanimous, having us all up to dinner at the big house, wearing a skirt that didn't even cover your pants and then flirting outrageously with me in front of your husband – you got yourself worked up into a right little lather, didn't you? Trying to prove you still had some go in you, trying your damnedest to get me into bed – you were desperate to commit adultery with the first attractive man who came your way. It was pathetic; you made me feel quite ill, if you must know.'

'How dare you!' I stormed. I glared at him. 'Christ, you've got a nerve to talk about adultery, you with your string of women, your sordid little flings – if anyone's pathetic around here it's you! Oh yes, I admit I flirted with you, and maybe I was a bit bored, but it was all totally harmless, there was no way I was contemplating an affair, no way! And as for blasting holes in your perfect marriage, you did that yourself the moment you left the altar! You've been seeing other women since you put a ring on

Sally's finger and now you're knocking off that jumped-up two-bit floozy who couldn't act her way out of a paper bag! And I make you quite ill now, do I? Not exactly what you said in Daphne's, if you remember, you said you were crazy about me.'

'Oh, that was so perfect,' he sneered. 'There I was thinking I was going to have to get rid of you subtly, and before I could get a word in edgeways you handed it to me on a plate! "Oh, Sam,"' he mimicked, ' "I'm so sorry but this simply can't go on!" All I had to do was pretend to be heartbroken and off you trotted. Serena and I had quite a chuckle about it that night, I can tell you.'

'I bet you did, but don't be too sure she isn't laughing at you too, Sam.'

'What d'you mean?' he said quickly.

'Oh come on, d'you really think she's in love with you? She's an opportunist – you must know that by now; she's out for what she can get. True love doesn't come into it.'

He stared at me for a second, then looked away.

'You don't know what you're talking about,' he muttered.

I was startled. Had I hit a nerve? Had things started to go wrong between the little love birds already? I pounced.

'Oh, don't I? I know her extremely well actually, in fact I could write a book about her nasty, conniving, calculating little ways. She's totally manipulative, Sam. She uses people – men especially – and when she's finished with them she just flushes them straight down the loo without a second thought. I bet she's done that to you, hasn't she? I bet you're somewhere in the S-bend even now and you haven't the faintest idea how you got there, am I right?'

I cocked my head sideways to see his face. It crumpled briefly, then he resumed his grim contemplation of the carpet. I straightened up.

'Well, I wouldn't be too hard on yourself if I were you,' I said softly. 'That's always the way it is with Serena. Most people don't find out they've been shafted until it's too late. Bad luck, Sam.'

Call me foolhardy but suddenly he didn't frighten me any more. I saw him for what he really was. A coward. A weak, pathetic man who didn't have the guts to say no, who let the tide wash him this way and that as he floated aimlessly through life. Only this time the tide hadn't just washed him round the corner to Rosy, or through the next office to Samantha in accounts, it had taken him to Serena. Serena, the wrecker, who with her lantern of bright blonde hair had beckoned him on, luring him towards her, tempting him with her beauty and her fame, but who was ultimately poised to dash him on the rocks and smash him to smithereens when she'd finished with him. I looked at him now, savagely massaging his brow, sweat gushing from every pore. God, he was a wreck already.

Had he really meant to lose Sally, I wondered, or had he just let his affair with Serena get out of hand? Had he really meant to jettison his film career and become a petty thief, or had he just been too weak and too greedy to say no when Serena had shown him a way to pay off his crippling debts at the same time as relieving the only man who'd ever dumped her of his family heirlooms? Oh yes, I detected Serena's hand at the back of all this, no doubt about it. And for how long would she be sticking around with the failed film director? Just long enough for him to serve his purpose and leak the porcelain on to the market, I suspected. And, looking at him now, I knew he suspected it too.

'You're talking crap, Polly,' he muttered eventually.

'Am I?' I folded my arms. 'Oh, well in that case I hope you'll be very happy together. You and Miss Montgomery.'

He didn't answer me.

'I suppose you'll get married then, will you? I mean as soon as Sally gives you a divorce?' He didn't look up, but the circles he was rubbing on his forehead were becoming frenetic. 'I don't suppose Sally will want to hang around, will she?' I went on. 'I dare say she'll want to get every-thing sorted out as quickly as possible, get her life back together again, sell the house perhaps, make a new start, that kind of –'

'Shut up!' he hissed suddenly, shooting me a glare. 'Just shut up, will you!' He looked down again but not before I'd seen the despair in his eyes. He shook his head.

'Such a mess . . .' he whispered, 'such a godawful . . . terrible . . . mess . . . got to think . . .'

I sat quietly and let him think, let him stew in his rancid juices. After a while he muttered something inaudible. I leaned forward.

'What?'

'I said I need a cigarette.'

'Actually I don't smoke any more,' I said nonchalantly, crossing my legs and rearranging my skirt. Gosh, I felt almost in control here. Soon it would be time to ask him to leave.

'GET ME A FUCKING CIGARETTE!' he bellowed.

Did I mention control? I leaped up like a cat who's been sat on and scampered out to the hall. I looked around wildly. Pippa's briefcase was still sitting on the chair where she'd left it. I ran to it, snapped it open, rummaged around furiously and found a half-empty packet of Silk Cut at the bottom. As I took them out, I noticed her Dictaphone. I stared at it for a moment. Suddenly the house seemed awfully quiet and still, just the hall clock ticking away behind me. I felt ridiculously brave. I took the Dictaphone out and with a trembling hand pressed the record button, then I carefully lodged it behind the case, out of sight.

I went back into the sitting room, handed Sam the cigarettes and a lighter and walked, rather shakily, back to the far end of the room, where I perched on the arm of the sofa again. Sam lit a cigarette and pocketed the rest. I cleared my throat.

'So you didn't sleep with me after all that night at the hotel?' I said clearly.

'No I bloody —' Suddenly he halted. He narrowed his eyes and blew the smoke out thoughtfully in a thin stream. The full implications of admitting to how revolting he found me gathered in his eyes.

'No I didn't,' he said shortly. 'You were far too drunk. I put you to bed and, er, tried to sort of get you interested, but you were totally out of it. I just went to sleep next to you in the end.' He took another deep drag on his cigarette and exhaled through his nostrils, watching me carefully.

'Not what you said in the restaurant the other day.'

'No.' He licked his lips. 'No, I – well, I suppose I wanted to shake you up a bit, give you something to think about.'

'And you stayed with me all night? Left early the next morning?'

'That's right,' he said slowly, 'at about seven. You got the note, didn't you?'

'Yes, I got the note.'

There was a tense silence. The room felt oddly still. He watched me warily, the veins throbbing away in his wet forehead. I summoned up what little courage I possessed.

'You were seen, Sam,' I said hoarsely.

'What?'

'You were seen leaving the hotel at about twelve thirty that night. You ran down the back stairs and went out of the fire exit at the back. Maria, one of the maids at the hotel, saw you go.'

The few remaining traces of colour in his face drained clear away. He stared at me. I'd got him. The satisfaction was immense but short-lived, like me probably. What did I have, a death wish or something?

He got unsteadily to his feet and advanced towards me. I quickly got up and backed away towards the french windows.

'Her word against mine,' he breathed, advancing slowly. 'Who d'you think cuts the most ice, a maid who can hardly speak the lingo, or an eminent film director, who, it transpires, was simply nipping into the garden for a quick cigarette before going back to his room five minutes later? The mere fact that she didn't see me return is neither here nor there, is it?'

474

'No, no, you're right,' I said quickly, slipping round the side of the sofa, 'neither here nor there. Absolutely right, couldn't agree with you more.'

The fact that she saw him get into a car and drive off at top speed with Serena was not to be mentioned under any circumstances, not unless I wanted to be bludgeoned to death on the carpet with one of Pippa's Conran candlesticks.

I crept round the sofa as he stalked me, our eyes locked in combat. I felt my way around with my hands, not daring to lose his gaze for an instant.

'Y-you know you're absolutely right, Sam,' I whispered. 'The maid was probably very tired and she obviously got it all wrong. After all, it was very late; she was probably daydreaming or – or hallucinating or something. I'm sure there's a perfectly rational explanation, nothing to worry about at all. I mean, as you say, she's just a maid who can't even speak English, there's no way they're going to get you just on her say-so, is there?'

He stopped and stared at me from the other end of the sofa, his yellow eyes burning into mine.

'Get me for what?'

I swallowed hard. Christ! Why couldn't I just keep my mouth shut?

'Get me for what?' he repeated evenly.

'F-for . . . for nothing really, Sam, nothing. I meant, um, for not paying your bill, perhaps, or – or –'

'I paid my bill,' he hissed, circling the sofa. 'What are you blabbing about, Polly, what do you know?' He was gaining on me now. 'You interfering little cow, what the hell d'you think you're –'

Suddenly the doorbell rang, interrupting his stream of abuse. We both froze in mid-creep and stared at one another. Sam looked alarmed.

'I – I must get that,' I whispered, taking one very brave but futile step towards the door.

'Don't even think about it,' he breathed, instantly welding me to the spot.

'B-but I must, it might be Pippa, she might have forgotten her key or something, or it might be –'

It rang again, long, loud and shrill, cutting short my nervous babble. We gazed at one another, transfixed, like a couple of statues. Then there was silence. Oh God, please don't go away, I thought desperately, digging my nails into the palm of my clammy hand. Whoever you are, please don't go away!

We listened. The silence continued. Sam's mouth began to twitch triumphantly. He took a step towards me, when abruptly – the bell rang again. This time a series of short, sharp, urgent blasts.

We both stared at the door. The whole house seemed to reverberate to the shrill, persistent summons. Then silence again. I bit my lip. Please don't go, please don't *go*. There was a rustle, then – footsteps. Retreating footsteps, going back up the garden path. I felt my heart sink through the floor. Sam's face lifted with relief.

'Oh what a shame,' he said, smiling nastily. 'They've gone. Bad luck, Polly, looks like you're on your own.'

He swayed slightly and grabbed the back of the sofa to steady himself. 'Now,' he said quietly, 'you were saying?'

'W-was I?'

'Yes.' He moved towards me. 'Oh yes, you were, about

how "they" were going to get me, remember? Get me for what?'

He was close now and I could see hundreds of tiny beads of sweat glistening on his forehead and upper lip. His tawny hair was streaked with dark and stuck to his temples.

'Oh, er, nothing,' I gasped. 'Nothing at all, it was just a – a figure of speech, really, an expression, can't think what I meant at all!'

He gazed at me intently. 'You know something, don't you?'

He was almost upon me now. I kept going back, but ultimately I was going to hit the wall. Like now. I flattened my hands against it and slid sideways towards the front door.

'What the hell do you know?' he breathed into my face.

'Nothing!' I yelped. 'Don't know anything!'

'You think I stole your precious porcelain, don't you?' he hissed.

'No, no, of course not,' I whimpered.

He stared at me for a moment, then his top lip curled.

'Oh, what does it matter?' he spat scornfully. 'Say what you like, no one will ever believe you. We were too clever, and you were too stupid and drugged up to the eyeballs with the little beverage I slipped you to know what the hell was going on. Do your worst, Polly. It won't get you anywhere – we outsmarted the lot of you.'

I slid slowly along the wall towards the door again, feeling my way with my hands. He crept after me, shadowing me all the time, sneering contemptuously into my face.

'You and your stupid, trusting husband who leaves his

477

keys lying around where anyone can find them, the dopey police in that backward village of yours, Brucey the Botty with his convenient passion for porcelain and his big homosexual secret that he wanted kept from Mummy at all costs, making him ripe for a spot of blackmailing. Oh yes, it all dovetailed together very nicely indeed, thank you very much, and there's not a damn thing you can do about it now.'

He rested his hands on the wall on either side of my head, stopping me in my slide towards the door and, ultimately, the free world. Then he brought his head down level with mine. Our noses were practically touching. His was wet with sweat and his eyes had a touch of madness in them. I felt sick with fear.

'And don't think it bothers me one iota if Serena sticks around or not,' he hissed into my face. 'Silly bitch – I've got no illusions about her, never have had. I used her as much as she used me. She got the Meissen out but at the end of the day I'll be the one selling it on, and when I do, *I'll* be the one holding the purse strings and she can come crawling to *me* for a change.'

He thumped his chest for emphasis, swayed and gripped my shoulders to steady himself. I cringed at his touch and felt myself begin to shake under his hands. He tightened his grip and leaned forward. His yellow eyes were huge and staring, his teeth bared like a dog's. I retched as a mixture of sweat and gin-soaked breath shot up my nose.

'And don't think anyone's going to believe your little fairy story either, Polly,' he breathed. 'You squeak about being drugged and they'll think you're just an adulteress who's trying to save her marriage. Too many people saw you with your undies hanging out that night, too many people saw you being carried upstairs, they all knew what a rollicking good time I was going to give you. You mention drugs and the police will smell a guilty conscience a mile off.' He shook my shoulders. 'But then you won't be mentioning anything to the police, will you, Polly?'

I stared at him, I couldn't speak.

'Will you?' he repeated, shaking me a bit harder. 'Come on, Polly, speak up. I can't hear you.' He inclined his ear to my lips.

I shut my eyes and let out a strangled sob, but still I couldn't utter. My voice seemed to be wedged in my throat somewhere, along with my heart. I was dumb with fear.

'I said, will you, Polly?' He shook me roughly this time, and my head bashed against the wall.

I covered my face with my hands, whimpering. I was shaking violently now. He grabbed my hands and yanked them away from my face.

'You won't be mentioning anything, WILL YOU, POLLY!' he bellowed into my face, shoving me backwards.

I gasped with pain as my head struck the wall again. I stared up into his bulging yellow eyes, his gritted teeth and his white face, dripping with sweat. He was terrifying, but he was desperate too. Suddenly I knew I had one chance and one chance only. I dug deep for courage, opened my mouth and summoned up all the breath in my body.

'H-E-E-L-P!' I shrieked at the top of my voice.

Sam stared at me in fury. He raised his hand, I ducked, and suddenly there was a resounding smash. A brick came hurtling through the front window, sending glass flying everywhere.

'Christ Al–' I ducked as pieces of glass sprayed around the room and the brick landed with a crash in the fireplace.

'What the –' Sam stepped back in alarm.

I gazed in astonishment as the yellow chintz curtain at the front window was ripped roughly from its brass rail. There was a jagged hole where the glass had been smashed. Through the hole, from the dark night beyond, a hand appeared. A man's hand. It swiftly unfastened the broken window and flung it open. Two hands then gripped the top of the frame, and a pair of very familiar blue-jeaned legs dropped deftly into the room, crunching glass underfoot. They were followed by an even more familiar torso and head. I gave a strangled sob, wrenched myself free from Sam's grasp and flew across the room.

'Nick!' I shrieked, as I ran into his arms.

Chapter Twenty-eight

I buried my face in his shoulder and sobbed into his jumper. He held me close for a moment then pulled away and lunged towards Sam, who was making a desperate dash for the door. He fell on his legs and rugby-tackled him to the ground. They wrestled for a moment, but it wasn't much of a contest. Nick was stronger and fitter and Sam was too drunk to put up much of a fight. Before he knew what had hit him, Sam was flat on his face on the floor, his nose pressed hard into the Axminster, his arms pinned behind him full-nelson style with Nick sitting firmly astride his back.

'Get out of that, you bastard!' gasped Nick, wrenching one of Sam's arms a bit further towards his head.

'Aarh! You're breaking my arm!' screeched Sam.

'I'd like to break your bloody neck!' Nick gave the arm another jerk. 'You creep!'

Just then a little blond head popped through the window. 'Safe to come in yet?' said a nervous voice.

'Get in here, Bruce,' yelled Nick. 'You could give me a hand!'

Bruce climbed tentatively through the broken window. 'I'm not too sure I'd be much help, actually. I do hope you've got him firmly. I was never much of a one for wrestling.'

'Just be ready to help if I shout, OK?'

I, meanwhile, had rushed to the dresser and picked up a large Chinese vase which I held high, poised over Sam's head.

'Shall I? Shall I?' I shrieked excitedly.

'Don't be silly, Polly,' panted Nick, 'we don't want to kill him, just immobilize him. Go and phone the police, for God's sake.'

'Oh! Right.' I put the vase down with a twinge of disappointment, but at the mention of the police Sam gave one last desperate heave. Nick struggled to keep him down.

'Quick, sit on his legs, both of you!' he ordered.

Bruce and I scampered round and sat, with great pleasure, and as hard as we possibly could, on the backs of his shins. Sam struggled, but I for one was no lightweight. We'd got him.

'You bastards!' he screamed. 'You've got nothing on me, you've no right to do this!'

'Oh, haven't we?' I retorted. 'He stole our porcelain, Nick, he just admitted the whole thing. He wasn't with me at all on that Friday night; it was him and Serena – they did it together!'

'I suspected as much,' said Nick through gritted teeth. 'The police in Helston were beginning to put two and two together, said it was just a matter of time before they had enough evidence to pull him in.'

'You mean,' spluttered Bruce incredulously, 'he – he tried to frame me?'

'That's about the size of it, Bruce,' agreed Nick.

'You bastard!' screeched Bruce, bouncing up and down hard on Sam's shins. 'You pretended you were so concerned and all the time you were trying to get me put away. How dare you!'

'Crap,' spluttered Sam into the carpet, 'it's all hearsay, won't stand up in court. You've got nothing on me, nothing!'

'Tell that to the police when they get here,' said Nick grimly. 'OK, Polly, I've got him now, run and phone.'

I leaped up and ran to the hall, but as I picked up the receiver a police siren came wailing round the corner and up the road. Through the stained-glass window in the front door I could see a blue flashing light. It stopped right outside the house. A car door slammed and then another – heavens, were they here already? I flung open the front door to see two burly policemen legging it up the path towards me.

'You all right, luv?' one of them panted. 'Your neighbour rang to say she'd heard smashing glass, thought it might be an intruder, a burglar.'

'Yes! Yes, you're right, in there, quick!' I squeaked.

They pushed past me into the sitting room. I scurried after them.

'All right, sir,' said the larger policeman to Nick, kneeling down and grabbing Sam's hands, 'you can let go now, I've got him.'

Nick got up and Bruce leaped off Sam's legs, scurrying quickly back behind Nick, out of harm's way. The two policemen heaved Sam to his feet. They clamped his hands behind his back and snapped a pair of handcuffs on him.

'Right, mate, I'm arresting you on suspicion of burglary at Fifty-two Stanbridge Villas, Kensington –'

'Don't be bloody ridiculous!' screeched Sam.

' —You are not obliged to say anything, but anything you do say will be taken down and used in —'

'Er, excuse me,' cut in Nick, 'you're absolutely right, he is a burglar, but he hasn't actually burgled this house.'

'Course I bloody haven't!' exploded Sam. 'Haven't burgled any bloody house! I'll have you for false arrest! I'll sue you, I'll sue the lot of you!'

The policeman frowned. 'But . . . he came through the window?'

'Well, no, actually I did,' said Nick. 'You see —'

'You see, it's a set-up!' screeched Sam. 'I was simply sitting here minding my own business, talking to Polly, when these two idiots came crashing through the window like the bloody SAS! Talk to them about breaking and entering, not me! I want my solicitor here right now. I'm not saying another word until he gets here! Treating me like some sort of petty thief — it's outrageous — get these handcuffs off me right now!'

The policeman looked bewildered. 'So this bloke isn't a burglar?'

'Oh yes,' I assured them, 'he's a burglar all right, but not a petty thief. He didn't break in here to steal the video or anything, he's wanted in connection with a haul of Meissen porcelain that went missing from our house in Cornwall recently, about two hundred thousand pounds' worth, in fact. If you check with the police in Helston, they'll fill you in on all the details. This is most definitely your man, Sergeant, he's just admitted to it. His accomplice, by the way, is a Miss Serena Montgomery. Shall I write that down for you?'

The policeman looked dumbfounded. 'The actress?'

He took off his cap and scratched his head. 'With all due respect, madam, I'm not sure we can arrest this man just on your say-so, let alone a famous actress, especially on suspicion of a crime committed all the way down in Cornwall. We're going to need a bit more evidence, a bit more proof, like.'

'Hang on a minute, you've got it!' I squealed, suddenly running to the hall. I grabbed the Dictaphone and dashed back.

'Here,' I cried breathlessly, 'it's all here! I got every word of it! At least I hope I did.'

I pressed the rewind button. Five men stared at me open-mouthed; the police in astonishment, Nick in wonder, Bruce in joy and Sam in absolute horror. I snapped the play button at random. Please God, let it work.

'. . . Say what you like, no one will ever believe you,' sang Sam's dulcet tones. 'We were too clever, and you were too stupid and drugged up to the eyeballs with –'

'Yes! Yes!' yelped Bruce, jumping up and down and clapping his hands with glee. 'Got him!'

'Give me that!' screeched Sam, making a lunge for the tape recorder.

'Oh no you don't, mate,' said the policeman, roughly yanking him back. He took the Dictaphone from me. 'Thanks, luv, I'll take this for the time being.'

'I think you'll find there's everything you need there, Officer,' I beamed, bouncing around a bit. 'Let me know if you need any more information, won't you; if the recording gets a bit faint I'm sure I can fill in the gaps. Oh, and, incidentally, he used quite a lot of threatening behaviour, violence even, that might not come over too clearly on the

485

tape, but I can certainly tell you all about it. I might even have some bruises to show you.' I pulled my T-shirt off my shoulder to have a look where Sam had shaken me, but rather disappointingly there didn't seem to be much of a mark.

'You bitch,' breathed Sam between clenched teeth, 'I'll get you for this. I'll, I'll –'

'Yeah, yeah, all right, all right, save it for your court appearance, mate,' said the policeman. 'Come on, you're nicked.' He shoved Sam over to his younger colleague. 'Take him to the car, Bob, and wait for me there. I just want to listen to the rest of this tape in case this lady needs to explain any of it.'

'Right you are, sir.'

The other policeman gave Sam a gratuitous shove in the back and pushed him towards the door. Sam turned and gave me one last contemptuous glare before he was propelled through the front door and led away into the night. Bruce and I watched through the broken window.

'Good riddance to you, you bastard!' yelled Bruce as Sam was hustled up the garden path.

'Right then, let's see what we've got here, shall we?' The policeman sat down on the sofa and wound back the tape. I came away from the window and waited anxiously. Nick stood behind me and put his hand on my shoulder as the recording began.

I needn't have worried, it was all there. From Sam bragging about blackmailing Bruce, to drugging me in the nightclub, stealing the porcelain with Serena, and finally my piercing scream as he threatened me. When the tape finished there was a silence. Nick squeezed my shoulder hard. Suddenly I realized I was shivering. The policeman opened the recorder and took out the cassette.

'Thank you, madam, I think that's all pretty self-explanatory. I'll look after this, if you don't mind.' He pocketed the cassette and stood up. He grinned. 'How very neat, a taped confession. I wish all our arrests were as easy as this.' He patted his breast pocket with satisfaction. 'Helston, you say?' he asked Nick as he made for the door.

'That's right, speak to an Inspector Carter at the station there – he'll fill you in on all the details.'

'Right you are, sir, will do. Goodnight to you all.' He touched his cap briefly and made for the door.

When he'd gone Bruce turned to me, his eyes shining with tears. He grabbed my hand. 'Polly, I – I don't know how to thank you. If it hadn't been for you, I don't know what would have happened. I might have gone to jail!'

I patted his hand. 'Think nothing of it, Bruce,' I gave a wry smile, 'all part of the Polly Penhalligan super-sleuth service. But I must say I can't quite believe I did that, I mean, I can't quite believe I had the nerve to tape him.'

'Neither can I,' admitted Nick admiringly. 'You took a hell of a risk. What if he'd popped into the hall and seen that thing recording? I hate to think what he'd have done to you.'

'So do I. Thank God you arrived when you did. But how come you were both out there anyway?'

'Well, I came up from Cornwall to find out what the hell was going on here – I'd had an extraordinary conversation with Lottie and a weird message from you on the answering machine – and when I arrived I found Bruce sitting outside in his car.'

'I'd just come round to talk to you, Polly,' said Bruce. 'I'd had a really bad day and I needed a shoulder to cry on, and you were the only person I could think of who wouldn't mind the fact that it was so late. I rang the bell loads of times but nobody answered.'

'Oh, so that was you ringing the bell?'

'Yes, and when I got no reply I thought I'd just sit in the car and wait for you to come back from wherever you were, then Nick showed up.'

'Bruce was just telling me there was no one in when we heard the most almighty scream. That's when we came crashing through.'

'Well,' grinned Bruce, 'Nick came crashing through. I was what you might call the rear party.'

'Crucial,' smiled Nick, 'couldn't have done it without you, Bruce.'

'Well, thank heavens you did come in then – I think I was about to have my brains bashed in.'

'Don't.' Nick grabbed me and held me close. I buried my face in his neck. He smelt of fresh air and hay lofts. We stayed like that for a minute, clutching each other, holding on. Then we remembered Bruce. We pulled apart sheepishly.

'Oh, don't mind me,' said Bruce with a grin, 'go for the full-blooded reunion. I was just off anyway.'

'Just off? Where?' I asked.

'To see my mother. I'm going to drive down there now.'

'Now? In the middle of the night?'

'Why not?' he said defiantly. 'She hasn't got much longer to – well. Let's just say I want to make sure I make

488

it in time. If I leave it till tomorrow morning, it might be too late.'

'But – what about your bail?' asked Nick. 'Are you allowed to do that?'

'Probably not, but since it was so obviously Sam who stole the porcelain, and not me, what does it matter? The whole story will be out by tomorrow and presumably the police will drop the charges so there won't be any bail, will there? They can hardly accuse me of concocting false evidence with my mother if there's nothing to concoct, can they?'

Nick grinned. 'No, I suppose not. But – will you get into the nursing home at this time of night?'

'Well, it'll be about five or six in the morning by the time I get there, and I guess it'll all be locked up, but the windows are usually open. I'll climb in and sit by her bed. I want to be there when she wakes up.' He looked calm and determined.

Nick smiled. 'Good for you, Bruce. I'm so glad it's turned out like this.'

'So am I,' said Bruce with a heartfelt smile. 'Never been so relieved in my life!' He held out his hand rather shyly to Nick. 'Well, goodbye then, and thanks for everything.'

Nick shook it heartily. 'Goodbye, and good luck.'

He turned to me and gave me a great big hug. 'Thanks again, Polly,' he whispered.

'Bye, Bruce.' I squeezed him hard. 'Give my love to your mother, won't you?'

'Will do.'

He gave us one last triumphant wave and then turned

and left. We heard him run, or maybe even skip down the path to his car. The engine turned over and he roared off.

When he'd gone the room seemed strangely silent. Nick took my hand.

'Polly, I'm so sorry,' he whispered.

I turned in surprise. 'But why should you be –'

'Shh . . .' He lifted my chin gently and his lips found mine. We kissed. A long, tremulous kiss, full of the sense of being apart for too long, of nearly losing each other. The great boulder of distrust and unhappiness that had kept us apart had finally been rolled away, but not before we'd both caught a glimpse of what life would have been like without each other. We'd had a near miss. Tears of joy and relief sprang to my eyes as we drew apart. They flowed down my face.

'Sorry,' I sniffed, wiping them away. 'I'm just crying because I'm so pleased to see you, ridiculous, I know.'

Nick hugged me back to him again. 'I know,' he muttered into my ear, 'and so much of this has been my fault. Can you ever forgive me?'

I pulled away in surprise and wiped my eyes. 'What for?' I sniffed.

'For not believing you. When I heard on that tape how that creep had drugged you and dumped you in that hotel room – Christ, you could have gone into a coma or something; you could have died!'

'Could I?' I gasped in alarm, my eyes wide with horror. 'Could I really? What – swallowed my tongue, gagged on my vomit or something?'

'Well, it's possible, but let's not dwell on it; it didn't happen, thank God.'

'No. Thank God,' I muttered, feeling a bit shaky. It hadn't occurred to me that I might have had a bit of a close shave. I shuddered. 'But – what I still don't really understand is why you came up here in the first place. Why didn't you ring?'

He sat down on the sofa and dragged me down next to him. 'I was worried, Poll. I came up to see what on earth was going on. First of all I had this weird telephone call from Lottie, last night, in fact. She kept asking me if you were all right because a friend of hers had seen you being carried out of Annabel's by some film director, said you were actually unconscious. Well, that really made me think, I can tell you. Then I got your garbled message on the answering machine about how you were beetling off to investigate Sam, and that worried the hell out of me. The Helston police had already said they thought he and Serena might be involved in some way and I had visions of you waltzing round to his house and confronting him, only to be boffed on the head and dumped in the Thames in a black bin liner. I wasn't far wrong as it happened, was I? I hate to think what he might have done if I hadn't been outside – you don't half jump in feet first, Polly. I rang at lunchtime to tell you to back off and stay away from him, but there was no answer.'

I groaned. 'Oh God, I popped to the shops for literally two minutes.'

'Well anyway, by that stage I was so hyped up and worried I couldn't just sit around in Cornwall waiting for you to get to the phone, so I jumped in the car and drove up here. Bruce was sitting outside when I arrived. We were just saying we thought we recognized Sam's Range Rover in the road and how odd it was that your car was here too – parked, incidentally, at a most artistic angle in the front garden – when we heard a scream. That's when I came through the window.'

'Thank God you did – he was about to rearrange my face.'

'Was he?' Nick sat up and looked alarmed. 'He didn't really hurt you, did he?' he asked anxiously.

I grinned. 'Nah, you know me, tough as old boots. He just shoved me around a bit and scared me half to death, that's all, nothing serious. I was jolly glad to see you when I did, though; things were certainly getting a bit hectic. He's an absolute nutter, you know, Nick. I really thought he was going to kill me.'

'Don't.' Nick held me close. 'I wish I'd punched his lights out instead of just twisting his arm.'

'Should have let me brain him with that vase.'

'Couldn't be sure you wouldn't miss and get me instead. You never could aim, Polly.'

I grinned and snuggled up to him. Suddenly I pulled back and frowned.

'What did you mean about the police in Helston getting on to him? How did they know?'

'Oh, old Mrs Bradshaw started to cough.'

'Mrs Bradshaw!' I sat up. 'What did she have to do with it?'

'Quite a lot, actually. Serena and Sam popped round to her house that Saturday night and collected the keys from her prior to lifting the Meissen.'

'What! She gave them the keys? To our house? But why?'

Nick grinned. 'Because she hates your guts, darling, or so I was reliably and eagerly informed by the entire village. Furious with you for firing her, apparently. It also turns out that she stayed pretty thick with Serena, two of a kind I suppose, and of course she'd never really forgiven me for marrying you instead of her.'

'Don't I know it?' I said grimly. 'She never could get used to charring for an erstwhile secretary instead of a Hollywood movie star.'

'More Pinewood than Hollywood, but I know what you mean. So, anyway, when Serena asked her for the key she was pleased and flattered to be asked to do a favour, I imagine.'

'But did she know they were going to rob us blind?'

'Apparently not. Serena just told her she needed to collect a few things from the house, stuff that belonged to her that I'd been too mean to give back – or some such spurious excuse. Anyway, she handed the key over without a murmur, and then, rather cleverly, Serena got her involved even deeper, making it hard for her to extricate herself and say she knew nothing about the burglary.'

'Why, what did Serena do?'

'She asked her to go to the nursing home where Bruce's mother was and put a package on her bedside table. Old Ma Bradshaw didn't know what it was all about or what was in the package, but again I reckon she was flattered to be asked and much too much in awe of Serena to say no. Anyway, off she toddled with this piece of porcelain in her bag, and of course no one turned a hair when she wandered into the hospice. There are so many old dears wandering around visiting each other she just blended into the scenery. Just another geriatric in a plastic mac clutching a Co-op bag. All she had to do was pass by Bruce's mother's bed when she was asleep, slip it on the bedside table, and waddle away again.'

'So that's how they did it,' I breathed. 'The sneaky bastards, and they blackmailed Bruce to make it look as if he was really desperate for money.'

'Exactly. But when Bruce was arrested, old Mrs B began to put two and two together. She realized what she'd done and began to wobble a bit. Apparently she got hold of Serena, who put the fear of God into her by saying she was in much too deep to get out and would definitely go to prison for her part in it if she so much as breathed a word.'

'God, poor old Mrs B. I almost feel sorry for her.'

'Well, quite, it was a pretty dirty trick, and of course Mrs Bradshaw was so terrified she kept quiet. Then the other day old Ted Simpson popped over to her place with a bottle of cherry brandy which the two of them sank together, and that's when she started to blab. She burst into tears and told Ted all about it. Of course, Ted promptly told Mrs Stanley at the post office, Mrs Stanley told her daughter, her daughter told her husband and her husband went to the police.'

'My God! The Helford mafia!'

'Quite, never underestimate the power of the village gossips. Anyway, the police went round and questioned her and she got herself into a complete paddy, cried like a baby but resolutely refused to say a word. But she didn't have to really – it was pretty obvious there was something going on. Even so, the police still didn't have enough evidence to arrest Sam and Serena, so they were just biding their time and waiting for the pair of them to slip up, to start shifting the gear on to the market.'

'Typical,' I said bitterly. 'All those boneheads in Helston ever do is bide their time. No killer instinct.'

'Well, anyway, that's why I shot up here so quickly. Last night Inspector Carter tipped me off that Sam might be involved and I had ghastly visions of him getting completely desperate and finishing you off. Black bin liners, as I said.'

'You're not kidding, he's an absolute maniac, and completely unscrupulous too. My God, when I think of how he nearly ruined Bruce. He pretended to be so sympathetic – paying his bail, getting him a barrister –'

'Who, incidentally, turns out to be Sam's best man, so he's hardly likely to shaft his best mate, is he?'

'Really? Gosh, and I bet Bruce had a perfectly decent barrister all along.' I shook my head. 'God, I don't know what I ever –' I broke off abruptly.

Nick grinned. 'Saw in him?'

'No, no, of course not, I wasn't going to say that,' I said quickly, desperately trying to fight the raging blush which was doing its best to liven up my features. I bit my lip. 'Well, all right, perhaps I was, but the only reason I liked him was – well, I respected him, for his work, his films. Yes, I must admit I admired him and I –'

'Fantasized about him?' Nick was still grinning.

'No! No, of *course* not!' I was purple now.

Nick laughed. 'It's OK, Polly, it's not a crime. It would be a pretty stoic husband or wife who never thought about anyone of the opposite sex apart from their spouse.'

I gasped. 'Nick!'

He roared with laughter. 'I said think, not do! Thinking doesn't constitute adultery, does it? Which is why ostensibly there was nothing wrong with you wearing that obscene pink skirt, dousing yourself in Chanel, lounging provocatively all over the dining table and generally flirting outrageously with that creep, because of course you never intended the flirting to go any further, did you?' He raised his eyebrows quizzically at me.

'No!' I gasped. 'No, of course not, not in a million years!'

'Good. Just checking.' His mouth twitched.

I flushed to my toes and stared at the carpet. 'Sorry,' I mumbled. 'Gosh, was I that obvious? I'm really sorry, Nick.'

'Don't be. It's over now and I'm just winding you up. Anyway, I'm the one who should be apologising.'

'Why?'

'For not believing you when you said you couldn't remember what had happened that night in London. Trouble was, Poll' – he frowned and scratched his head – 'it sounded like such an incredibly lame excuse. Like one of your typically terrible, extraordinarily bad lies.'

I grinned. 'Brilliant. The one and only time I tell the truth, it sounds like a lie. Terrific, isn't it? I might just as well stick to lying. I'm obviously better at it.'

'Speaking of which,' he said, reaching into his pocket, 'perhaps you could do some fast talking about this one?' He handed me a piece of paper.

'What is it?' I asked, unfolding it.

'It's a bill from Harrods car park, where your BMW has

apparently been residing in splendour for over three weeks now. What d'you suggest, Polly, a remortgage on the house, perhaps? Sell all the Meissen that we're hopefully about to recover?'

'Oh my God!' My hand flew to my mouth. 'Nick, I can explain. I just completely forgot – well, no not forgot exactly, I knew it was there but – yes, I know! I thought – I thought Pippa was going to pick it up! Yes, that's it. I seem to remember asking Pippa to get it out for me while I was away; she must have –'

'Polly, don't even *think* about wheedling your way out of this one!' laughed Nick, squeezing me hard.

'Ouch!' I gasped. 'Careful!' I pulled his arm away.

He sat back in surprise. 'What? Did I hurt you?'

'Oh no, it's just that –' I stared at him. Was this a good time? I'd been so terrified about breaking the news in case he thought the baby was Sam's, but now that Sam was well out of the frame, now that Nick knew that nothing could possibly have happened . . .

I smiled. 'I'm pregnant.'

He stared at me. 'You're what?'

'I'm pregnant,' I repeated, somewhat shyly. God, I was starting to blush again. 'You know, having a baby.'

He dropped his hands from my waist and his jaw dropped too.

'You are?' His eyes were wide with wonder. 'Really?'

'Yes, really!' I laughed. 'Don't look so astonished, Nick. It was bound to happen one day, you kept telling me so, remember?'

He smiled, slowly and broadly. The smile became a beam, stretching right across his face. 'You're pregnant!'

he breathed. He kissed me hard on the mouth but the beam didn't waver for a moment. I grinned back. We held hands, gazing at each other like a couple of teenagers. Suddenly his eyes narrowed. He looked at me carefully.

'You're sure about this, are you, Polly? I mean, you've been to see the doctor? Only I can just see you with some makeshift chemistry set, sending litmus paper blue and test tubes pink and getting thoroughly convinced you're up the duff when in actual fact you're just a bit late or –'

'Of course I'm sure, and the word is gynaecologist, actually. I saw him a couple of days ago, I'm four or five weeks pregnant now,' I said proudly.

Nick peered at my tummy in wonder. 'Wow. A month old. Hello, little chap.'

'Or chap-ess,' I corrected him.

'Oh absolutely, or chap-ess. So – what's that then, a February baby?'

'Something like that,' I grinned.

'Try to get it all over with before I start lambing, would you?'

'Nick!' I bashed him with a cushion.

He laughed and held me close. 'Oh, Poll, I'm so pleased!' Suddenly he drew back. 'And you feel all right?' he asked, looking concerned. 'Not sick or anything?'

'Oh no, that's more or less passed now. I was as sick as a dog for a while, though, but – oooh, d'you know, now you come to mention it' – I put my hand to my throat and looked a bit pained – 'it seems to have come back. I do feel a bit queasy.'

'Really? Glass of water?' he asked, getting up anxiously.

'Mmmm, please, might help – oh, and while you're

there, maybe a small piece of toast, with a smidgen of honey. Oh, and a chocolate biscuit if it's not too much trouble.'

Nick hastened to the kitchen.

'Oh, and, Nick?'

He hurried back, a glass of water in his hand.

'Before you make the toast, d'you think you could just move that stool so I can put my feet up on it? Perfect – oh, and that cushion for my head . . . right a bit, down a bit . . . lovely . . . and perhaps you could find a rug or something for my knees? Super. Oh, is that my water? Thanks very – hey, what are you – hey, not on my face! Oh God, Nick, not down my – aaarh! All down my neck! Ugh, you bastard, I'll get you for that, I'll get you!'

Catching up with Catherine

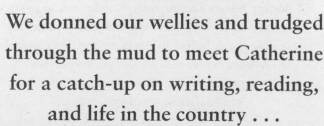

We donned our wellies and trudged
through the mud to meet Catherine
for a catch-up on writing, reading,
and life in the country . . .

Catching up with Catherine

How and where do you write?

In the garden in the summer, and on a sofa by the fire
in the winter, literally with the nearest pen,
which as a result often runs out.

Any tips for alleviating writer's block?

I'd probably go for a long walk with the dogs but also
never call it writer's block. It's just a day to do
something else; tomorrow will be different.
With luck and everything crossed, the muse
might perch on one's shoulder again.

You live in the countryside in a village not too dissimilar from those you write about. How does country life in your books compare to real life?

There are some remarkable similarities, but obviously
names have been changed to protect the innocent . . .

What do you like to do when you're not writing?

I ride my horses and, recently, wander round poultry
farms. I'm trying to decide which ducks to get for
my new pond: Indian Runners are terribly comical,
Aylesburys would be more geographically
appropriate, yet I'm strangely drawn to good
old Mallards, too. Decisions . . .

If you had to live the life within a classic novel and star as a literary heroine, who would you be and why?

Possibly Jane Austen's Emma Woodhouse,
who lived something of a charmed life,
even if she didn't realize until
it was almost too late.

What's your favourite place to escape to?

Over the hills and far away. The valley behind my
house is actually not very far at all and the Downs
start there so it's very peaceful. Devon is,
of course, heaven, but a little further.

**What's the best way to survive a day in the
British countryside?**

In an ideal world I probably wouldn't take my
own very badly behaved dogs; I would take
someone else's – that way I wouldn't be chasing
them all day shrieking unattractively.

Catherine's top tips
for the perfect countryside break

The same rules apply for children as for dogs (see before),
depending on age and reliability of your children –
husbands, too.

Never picnic (as in the romantic ideal of rug,
hamper, chicken drumsticks à la Delia). Pubs tend to be
far more successful, although I am nostalgically drawn
to beach picnics. Sand in sandwiches is surely part of any
child's education and there's nothing funnier than the
man of the family getting to grips with a windbreak in
a force-eight gale. Particularly if his own childhood
holidays were spent in Tuscany.

Don't be deceived by the English countryside.
It looks pretty but can turn on you in an instant.

Leave the horses to the professionals – that doesn't
include me. A horse that decides to nap (go home) in the
middle of a village which also happens to be something
of a tourist magnet is embarrassing for all concerned,
particularly the red-faced, middle-aged woman on top.

Again on the subject of horses, 'not a novice ride'
means bucks like fury, while 'a fun ride' means carts you
into the next county. Male horse-dealers are fond of both
expressions, but never forget they are stronger
than we are. The men and the horses.

When you answer the door in your coat in winter to a surprised friend who asks if you're just going out, don't be afraid to let them stay an hour or two until they put their coats on too.

If invited to a dinner party in London in January, don't forget there will be women in little dresses who have proper central heating. In the car en route, turn the heater up full blast and try to shed at least three of your layers. Don't forget the Ugg boots. If you stay in the vest and the cashmere roll-neck, you will be in a critical state by pudding, particularly if you're approaching fifty.

If anyone offers you the use of a flat in town in winter, bite their hand off.

Catherine's top ten countryside reads:

The Pursuit of Love
Nancy Mitford

Untold Stories
Alan Bennett

The Irish R. M.
Somerville and Ross

High Fidelity
Nick Hornby

Persuasion
Jane Austen

Pomp and Circumstance
Noël Coward

84 Charing Cross Road
Helene Hanff

The Woman in White
Wilkie Collins

Franny and Zooey
J. D. Salinger

Atonement
Ian McEwan

'Supremely readable, witty and moving. I adored this' *Daily Mail*

'If I'm being totally honest I had fantasized about Phil dying.'

When Poppy Shilling's bike-besotted, Lycra-clad husband is killed in a freak accident, she can't help feeling a guilty sense of relief. For at long last she's released from a controlling and loveless marriage.

Throwing herself wholeheartedly into village life, she's determined to start over. And sure enough, everyone from Luke the sexy church-organist to Bob the resident oddball, is taking note. Yet the one man Poppy can't take her eyes off seems tantalizingly out of reach – why won't he let go of his glamorous ex-wife?

But just as she's ready to dip her toes in the water, the discovery of a dark secret about her late husband shatters Poppy's confidence. Does she really have the courage to risk her heart again? Because Poppy wants a lot more than just a rural affair . . .

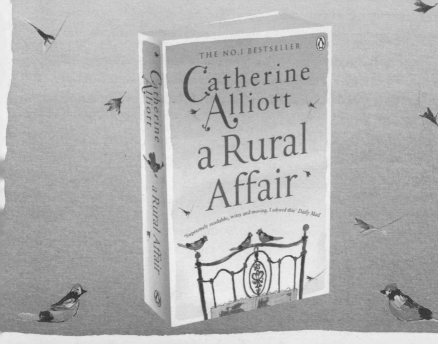

THE NO.1 BESTSELLER

Catherine Alliott

a Rural Affair

'Supremely readable, witty and moving. I adored this' *Daily Mail*

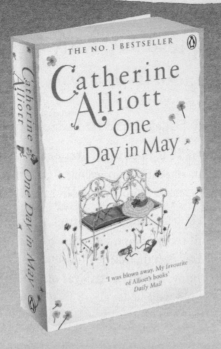

Catherine
Alliott
One
Day in May

'I was blown away. My favourite
of Alliott's books'
Daily Mail

May is the month for falling in love . . .

Hattie Carrington's first love was as unusual as it was out of reach –
Dominic Forbes was a married MP, and she was his assistant.
She has never told anyone about it. And never really got over it.

But years later with a flourishing antiques business
and enjoying a fling with a sexy, younger man, she thinks her
past is finally well and truly behind her.

Until work takes her to Little Crandon, home of Dominic's widow
and his gorgeous younger brother, Hal. There, Hattie's world is turned
upside down. She learns that if she's to truly fall in love again she
needs to stop hiding from the truth. Can she ever admit what
really happened back then?

And, if so, is she ready
for the consequences?

'A fun, fast-paced page-turner' *OK!*

**Evie Hamilton has a secret –
one she doesn't even know about. Yet . . .**

Evie's an Oxfordshire wife and mum whose biggest worry in life is
whether or not she can fit in a manicure on her way to fetch her
daughter from clarinet lessons. But she's blissfully unaware that her
charmed and happy life is about to be turned upside down.

For one sunny morning a letter lands on Evie's immaculate doormat.
It's a bombshell, knocking her carefully arranged world
completely askew and threatening to sabotage all she holds dear.

What will be left and what will change for ever?
Is Evie strong enough to fight for what she loves?
Can her entire world really be as fragile as her best china?

'We defy you not to get caught up in
Alliott's life-changing tale' *Heat*

THE NO.1 BESTSELLER

Catherine Alliott

A Crowded Marriage

'Another gem from the pen of Ms Alliott'
Closer

'Another gem from the pen of Ms Alliott' *Closer*

There isn't room in a marriage for three . . .

Painter Imogen is happily married to Alex, and together they have a son. But when their finances hit rock bottom, they're forced to accept Eleanor Latimer's offer of a rent-free cottage on her large country estate. If it was anyone else, Imogen would be beaming with gratitude. Unfortunately, Eleanor just happens to be Alex's beautiful, rich and flirtatious ex.

From the moment she steps inside Shepherd's Cottage, Imogen's life is in chaos. In between coping with rude locals, murderous chickens, a maddening (if handsome) headmaster, mountains of manure and visits from the infuriating vet, she has to face Eleanor, now a fixture at Alex's side.

Is Imogen losing Alex? Will her precious family be torn apart? And whose fault is it really – Eleanor's, Alex's or Imogen's?

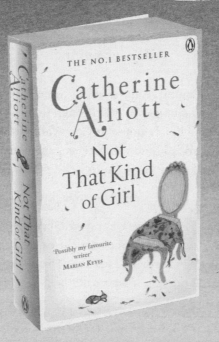

THE NO.1 BESTSELLER

Catherine Alliott

Not That Kind of Girl

'Possibly my favourite writer'
MARIAN KEYES

**A girl can get into all kinds of trouble
just by going back to work . . .**

Henrietta Tate gave up everything for her husband Marcus and their kids.
But now that the children are away at school and she's rattling around
their large country house all day she's feeling more than a little lost.

So when a friend puts her in touch with Laurie, a historian in need of a PA,
Henrietta heads for London. Quickly, she throws herself into the job.
Marcus is – of course – jealous of her spending so much time with
her charming new boss. And soon enough her absence causes cracks
in their marriage that just can't be papered over.

Then Rupert, a very old flame, reappears and Henrietta suddenly finds
herself torn between three men. How did this happen?
She's not that kind of girl . . . is she?

'Compulsively readable' *Daily Mail*

Annie O'Harran is getting married . . . all over again.

A divorced, single mum, Annie is about to tie the knot with David.
But there's a long summer to get through first. A summer where
she's retreating to a lonely house in Cornwall, where she's going to
finish her book, spend time with her teenage daughter Flora and
make any last-minute wedding plans.

She should be so lucky.

For almost as soon as Annie arrives her competitive sister and her wild
brood fetch up. Meanwhile Annie's louche ex-husband and his latest
squeeze are holidaying nearby and insist on dropping in. Plus there's the
surprise American houseguest who can't help sharing his heartbreak.

Suddenly Annie's big day seems a long, long way off –
and if she's not careful it might never happen . . .

'Alliott at her best' *Daily Telegraph*

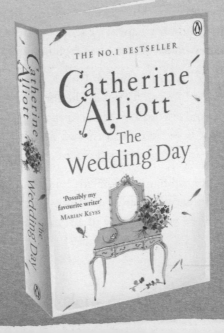

'What could be nicer than living in the country?'

Lucy Fellowes is in a bind. She's a widow living in a pokey London flat with two small boys and an erratic income. But, when her mother-in-law offers her a converted barn on the family's estate, she knows it's a brilliant opportunity for her and the kids.

But there's a problem.

The estate is a shrine to Lucy's dead husband, Ned. The whole family has been unable to get over his death. If she's honest, the whole family is far from normal. And if Lucy is to accept this offer she'll be putting herself completely in their incapable hands.

Which leads to Lucy's other problem. Charlie – the only man since Ned who she's had any feelings for – lives nearby. The problem? He's already married . . .

'Hilarious and full of surprises' *Daily Telegraph*

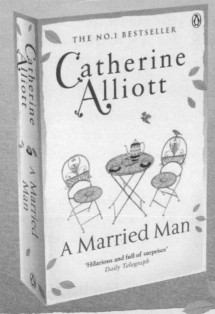

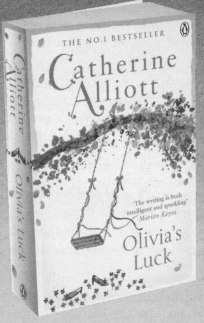

'I don't care what colour you paint the sodding hall. I'm leaving.'

When her husband Johnny suddenly walks out on ten years of marriage, their ten-year-old daughter and the crumbling house they're up to their eyeballs renovating, Olivia is, at first, totally devastated. How could he? How could she not have noticed his unhappiness?

But she's not one to weep for long.

Not when she's got three builders camped in her back garden, a neighbour with a never-ending supply of cast-off men she thinks Olivia would be drawn to and a daughter with her own firm views on . . . well, just about everything.

Will Johnny ever come back? And if he doesn't, will Olivia's luck ever change for the better?

'The writing is both intelligent and sparkling'
Marian Keyes

'Tell me, Alice,
how does a girl go about
getting a divorce these days?'

Three years ago Rosie walked blindly into marriage with Harry.
They have precisely nothing in common except perhaps their little boy, Ivo.
Not that Harry pays him much attention, preferring to spend his time
with his braying upper-class friends.

But the night that Harry drunkenly does something unspeakable,
Rosie decides he's got to go. In between fantasizing how she might
bump him off, she takes the much more practical step of divorcing
this blight on her and Ivo's lives.

However, when reality catches up with her darkest fantasies,
Rosie realizes, at long last, that it is time she took charge of her life.
There'll be no more regrets – and time, perhaps, for a little love.

**Every girl's got one – that old boyfriend
they never quite fell out of love with . . .**

Tessa Hamilton's thirty, with a lovely husband and home, two adorable
kids, and not a care in the world. Sure her husband ogles the nanny more
than she should allow. And keeping up with the Joneses is a full-time
occupation. But she's settled and happy. No seven-year itch for Tessa.

Except at the back of her mind is Patrick Cameron. Gorgeous, moody,
rebellious, he's the boy she met when she was seventeen. The boy her
vicar-father told her she couldn't see and who left to go to Italy to paint.
The boy she's not heard from in twelve long years.

And now he's back.

Questioning every choice, every decision she's made since Patrick left,
Tessa is about to risk her family and everything she has become to find
out whether she did the right thing first time round . . .

'You're in for a treat' *Daily Express*

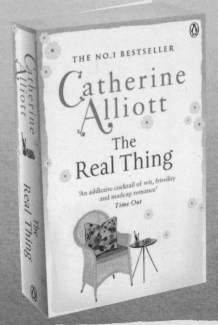

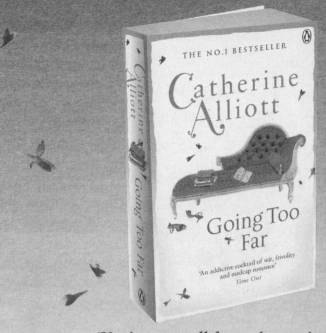

'You've gone all fat and complacent
because you've got your man, haven't you?'

Polly Penhalligan is outraged at the suggestion that, since getting married
to Nick and settling into their beautiful manor farmhouse in Cornwall,
she has let herself go. But watching a lot of telly, gorging on biscuits, not
getting dressed until lunchtime and waiting for pregnancy to strike are not
the signs of someone living an active and fulfilled life.

So Polly does something rash.

She allows her home to be used as a location for a TV advert. Having a
glamorous film crew around will certainly put a bomb under the idyllic,
rural life. Only perhaps she should have consulted Nick first.

Because before the cameras have even started to roll – and complete
chaos descends on the farm – Polly's marriage has been
turned upside down. This time she
really has gone too far . . .

'An addictive cocktail of wit, frivolity
and madcap romance' *Time Out*

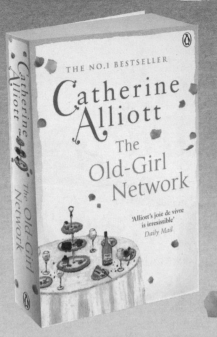

THE NO.1 BESTSELLER

Catherine Alliott

The Old-Girl Network

'Alliott's joie de vivre
is irresistible'
Daily Mail

**Finding true love's a piece of cake – as long as
you're looking for someone else's true love . . .**

Polly McLaren is young, scatty and impossibly romantic. She works for
an arrogant and demanding boss, and has a gorgeous-if-never-there-when-
you-need-him boyfriend. But, the day a handsome stranger recognizes her
old school scarf, her life is knocked completely off kilter.

Adam is American, new to the country and begs Polly's help in finding
his missing fiancé. Over dinner at the Savoy she agrees – the girls of
St Gertrude's look out for one another. However, the old-girl network
turns out to be a spider's web of complications and deceit in which
everyone and everything Polly cares about is soon hopelessly entangled.

The course of true love never did run smooth.
But no one said anything about ruining your life over it.
And it's not even Polly's true love . . .

'Possibly my favourite writer' Marian Keyes

Step into *Alliott Country*

at www.catherinealliott.com

WIN wonderful WELLIES
by joules

WE'RE GIVING AWAY

10 PAIRS of JOULES WELLIES
MADE TO MAKE A SPLASH WHATEVER THE WEATHER!

To be in with a chance of winning this welly good prize visit www.catherinealliott.com/winwellies

Joules are also giving readers **15% OFF** *plus* **FREE P&P.**

Simply visit www.joules.com and enter offer code **WELLY12** at the checkout.

Competition closing date **31ST AUGUST 2012**

For full terms and conditions and details of how to enter visit www.catherinealliott.com/winwellies